Dylan needed to stop this marriage before his dad woke up one day and realized he'd made a monumental mistake.

Breaking them up would be hard, but with Ella's help, it might be possible. She couldn't be happy about her mom getting married, could she?

"So you see," he said, "you and I are in the same boat."

Ella stared at him for a good fifteen seconds before striding across the room and leaning on the chair back. "I can see that you actually believe that. But, you know, aside from being asked to plan the engagement party together, we don't have anything much in common."

"No?" He switched tactics. "I'm opposed to this wedding. I don't want anything to do with planning this party."

"Fine. I'll do it myself. It will be so much easier without you." She captured his gaze. Something about the flush in her cheeks made his heart skip a beat.

"Don't count on it being easier," he said, meeting her angry stare with his own determination.

"And why is that?"

"Because I'm going to do everything I can to break them up."

PRAISE FOR HOPE RAMSAY

The Moonlight Bay series

"Ramsay paints a quaint portrait of Magnolia Harbor and its earnest, salt-of-the-earth denizens, but she doesn't shy from drama and drops in a few deliciously hateable villains to liven up the tale. This cozy small-town romance will please Ramsay's fans and should attract new ones."

—*Publishers Weekly* on *Return to Magnolia Harbor*

"*An Officer and a Gentleman* meets Nicholas Sparks's *Dear John* in the second captivating installment of the Moonlight Bay series."

—*Woman's World* on *Summer on Moonlight Bay*

"An endearing and strong second contemporary."

—*Publishers Weekly* on *Summer on Moonlight Bay*

"Ramsay mixes a tasty cocktail of sweet and sexy in this heartfelt launch of the Moonlight Bay series. Ramsay's expert characterization (particularly with the multilayered hero and heroine), entertaining cast of secondary characters, and well-tuned plot will make readers long for a return trip to Magnolia Harbor."

—*Publishers Weekly* on *The Cottage on Rose Lane*

The Chapel of Love series

"[A] laugh-out-loud, play-on-words dramathon...It won't take long for fans to be sucked in while Ramsay weaves her latest tale of falling in love."

—RTBookReviews.com on *The Bride Next Door*

"Getting hitched was never funnier."

—FreshFiction.com on *Here Comes the Bride*

"Ramsey charms in her second Chapel of Love contemporary... [and] wins readers' hearts with likable characters, an engaging plot (and a hilarious subplot), and a well-deserved happy ending."

—*Publishers Weekly* on *A Small-Town Bride*

"Happiness is a new Hope Ramsay series."

—FreshFiction.com on *A Christmas Bride*

The Last Chance series

"I love visiting Last Chance and getting to revisit old friends, funny situations, the magic and the mystery that always seems to find their way into these wonderful stories."

—HarlequinJunkie.com on *Last Chance Hero*

"4 stars! Ramsay uses a light-toned plot and sweet characters to illustrate some important truths in this entry in the series."

—*RT Book Reviews* on *Last Chance Family*

"5 stars! I really enjoyed this book. I love a little mystery with my romance, and that is exactly what I got with *Inn at Last Chance*."
—HarlequinJunkie.com on *Inn at Last Chance*

"Ramsay writes with heart and humor. Truly a book to be treasured and a heartwarming foray into a great series."
—NightOwlReviews.com on *Last Chance Knit and Stitch*

"Last Chance is a place we've come to know as well as we know our own hometowns. It's become real, filled with people who could be our aunts, uncles, cousins, friends, or the crazy cat lady down the street. It's familiar, comfortable, welcoming."
—RubySlipperedSisterhood.com on *Last Chance Book Club*

"Amazing...This story spoke to me on so many levels about faith, strength, courage, and choices. If you're looking for a good Christmas story with a few angels, then *Last Chance Christmas* is a must-read."
—TheSeasonforRomance.com on *Last Chance Christmas*

"A little Bridget Jones meets *Sweet Home Alabama*."
—GrafWV.com on *Last Chance Beauty Queen*

"Full of small-town charm and Southern hospitality...You will want to grab a copy."
—TopRomanceNovels.com on *Home at Last Chance*

"Ramsay's delicious contemporary debut introduces the town of Last Chance, SC, and its warmhearted inhabitants...[she] strikes an excellent balance between tension and humor as she spins a fine yarn."
—*Publishers Weekly* (starred review) on *Welcome to Last Chance*

A WEDDING ON LILAC LANE

Also by Hope Ramsay

The Last Chance series
Welcome to Last Chance
Home at Last Chance
Small Town Christmas (anthology)
Last Chance Beauty Queen
"Last Chance Bride" (short story)
Last Chance Christmas
Last Chance Book Club
"Last Chance Summer" (short story)
Last Chance Knit & Stitch
Inn at Last Chance
A Christmas to Remember (anthology)
Last Chance Family
Last Chance Hero
"A Midnight Clear" (short story)

The Chapel of Love series
"A Fairytale Bride" (short story)
A Christmas Bride
A Small-Town Bride
Here Comes the Bride
The Bride Next Door

The Moonlight Bay series
The Cottage on Rose Lane
Summer on Moonlight Bay
Return to Magnolia Harbor

A WEDDING ON LILAC LANE

A Moonlight Bay novel

HOPE RAMSAY

FOREVER
New York   Boston

Copyright © 2021 by Robin Lanier
Cover design by Daniela Medina. Cover images © Shutterstock.
Cover © 2021 by Hachette Book Group, Inc.

Forever
Hachette Book Group
1290 Avenue of the Americas, New York, NY 10104
read-forever.com
twitter.com/readforeverpub

First mass market edition: April 2021

Forever is an imprint of Grand Central Publishing. The Forever name and logo are trademarks of Hachette Book Group, Inc.

The publisher is not responsible for websites (or their content) that are not owned by the publisher.

The Hachette Speakers Bureau provides a wide range of authors for speaking events. To find out more, go to www.hachettespeakersbureau.com or call (866) 376-6591.

ISBNs: 978-1-5387-5328-6 (mass market); 978-1-5387-5329-3 (ebook)

Printed in the United States of America

CW

10 9 8 7 6 5 4 3 2 1

*For all the doctors and nurses who provide
health care in rural places.
You are heroes.*

Acknowledgments

I started writing *A Wedding on Lilac Lane* just about the same time that the governor of Virginia imposed a stay-at-home order to halt the spread of COVID-19. Writing a book is always a lonely affair, and you might think that writing a lighthearted book in the middle of a pandemic would be harder than normal. But it turned out not to be. In fact, all that social distancing made it hard to goof off. There just wasn't much else to do but write. So here's to silver linings.

Many thanks to Cathy Corman Hill for directing my local Christmas Chorale and showing me how a disciplined choral director can get the most out of a group of amateur singers. Cathy gave me many ideas that found their way into Brenda McMillan's character, not only in this novel, but in the prequel Christmas story, "Joy to the World," included in the anthology *A Little Country Christmas*.

Rev. St. Pierre's Palm Sunday sermon included in this novel was heavily influenced by Fr. Michael K. Marsh. His wonderful sermon "Returning the Colt—A Palm Sunday Sermon, March 26, 2018" is readily available online.

I'd also like to thank the writers of the Ruby Slippered Sisterhood's morning writing group, who showed up in the chat room every weekday like clockwork. Not only did we get a lot of writing done during the early days of the pandemic, we also shared recipes for stress-baking our way through it. Thank you, Nancy, Heather, Susan, and Cristina, for being such great friends.

Finally, as always, many thanks to my longtime editor, Alex Logan, who never fails to give me exactly the right advice to fix the problem I thought was unfixable. She makes every book so much better.

A WEDDING ON LILAC LANE

Chapter One————————————

Dylan Killough couldn't decide what to make of Ella McMillan. She stood on the stage with a fiddle tucked under her chin as she played a mournful accompaniment to "Molly Malone." A crown of green carnations encircled her brow, and her feather earrings floated on the air as she played. With each stroke of her bow, another lock of unruly auburn hair tumbled out of the messy knot at the top of her head.

She looked as if she'd stepped out of an Irish fairy tale. But the boho dress and feathered earrings suggested that she reliably voted the Democrat line, if she voted at all.

"I do love listening to your daughter play the fiddle," Dad said, beaming at Brenda McMillan, Ella's mother and Dad's current girlfriend.

The whole Dad-Brenda thing unsettled Dylan even though it shouldn't have. Dad had been a widower for decades. He should have a girlfriend, even if he was in his fifties. But maybe not Brenda. Dylan didn't like Brenda much.

Or her daughter, who had arrived around the holidays, moved into Brenda's beach house out at Paradise Beach, and evidently had no plans to actually work for a living or leave anytime soon. Since Dylan and his father shared a house, Dad had recently resorted to sneaking away in the afternoons or taking long weekends with Brenda on the mainland.

Dad had never brought her home for an overnight. Thank goodness. The mornings after in the kitchen they shared might get really awkward.

His father was acting like a sex-crazed teenager, which embarrassed Dylan. The geriatric set in Magnolia Harbor, many of whom were patients in Dylan's family practice, seemed to regard Brenda and Dad's romance as the juiciest topic du jour. And they thought nothing about asking Dylan for details, which he forthrightly refused to supply.

Dylan took a sip of his Guinness and glanced at his cell phone, checking the score for the NCAA First Four game being played in Dayton. Clemson, his alma mater, was down by two points.

He would much rather be home lounging on the sofa watching the ball game. But no, Dad had made his presence at this dinner mandatory because Ella was subbing for Connor O'Neal at the yacht club's annual St. Patrick's Day bash. Connor, one of Dylan's patients, was down with a late-season case of the flu, which had been bad timing for a guy who made a living playing Irish music.

"Well, that wraps up our first set of the night," Jason Tighe said in his broad South Carolina drawl. "Y'all drink up now. We'll be back in fifteen."

"I miss Connor's Irish accent," Dylan said.

Brenda and Dad turned toward him with twin frowns, although Brenda's was way more intimidating.

"What?" Dylan cast his gaze from Brenda to his father. "I

love the way Jason sings, but he sounds like a good ole boy from Georgia when he talks."

Brenda gave Dad one of those glances, where she rolled her eyes. Brenda didn't like Dylan much either. They didn't have a mutual admiration society going. He also resented the way Brenda made him feel whenever the three of them were together: Exactly like a fifth wheel, or a party pooper, or something like that. Maybe he should excuse himself now that Ella had finished her first set. The club was playing the game on the TV above the bar, which was across the room.

But before he could make an escape, Ella arrived at the table and took the empty chair to his right. If he got up the minute she sat down, he'd never hear the end of it. So he hunkered down, glanced at the score on his phone, and took a deep, calming breath.

Which was filled with Ella's scent. Damn. The woman even smelled like a hippie. What was that aroma? Sandalwood? Patchouli?

She probably burned incense when no one was looking. Or used essential oils or some such thing. The aroma tickled his nose and not entirely in an I'm-about-to-sneeze way either. With her hair all tumbling down, and wearing that green velvet dress, which belonged on the set of *Game of Thrones*, she was attractive. If you had a thing for free-spirited musicians.

"You're a better fiddler than Connor," Dad said, sucking up to Brenda's daughter. Who, in truth, was a pretty good fiddler, but Dylan didn't want to admit it.

"Thanks," Ella said in a high, piping voice, as she glanced at her mother. Something passed between them in that glance. A family in-joke he would probably never get.

The conversation stalled for a moment as Dad turned toward Brenda. The two of them appeared a little nervous now that Dylan thought about it. And right then, just before Brenda opened her mouth, an overwhelming sense of dread seized him.

It was as if a freight train were speeding right at him, the headlight cutting through the fog, but he couldn't move himself out of its path.

"I guess it's now or never," Brenda said under her breath, then reached for Dad's hand. She gave Ella and Dylan a forthright look out of her dark gray eyes.

"Jim and I have been talking things through, and we've decided to get married. We want both of you to plan the engagement party."

* * *

Ella struggled to draw breath. She wasn't surprised that Jim and Mom were tying the knot, but she was incredibly disappointed that Mom had chosen this moment to announce the happy news.

Typical behavior for Mom. Not that Ella wanted to be the center of attention, but hell, she'd been learning songs like mad, practicing until her fingers hurt for this fill-in gig with Sackweed, Connor O'Neal's Irish band. It was supposed to be her night to shine. Her night to prove to Mom that she'd mastered her craft, even if she wasn't playing a violin concerto or sonata written by some long-dead composer.

She'd been excited that Jim and his son would be coming to hear her play, but now it turned out that this gig had been a convenient excuse to get the "family" together. Not that the four of them felt like a family.

Ella snatched up a glass of water and took a big gulp. She never drank alcohol when she was performing because only a tiny bit of booze buzzed her head. But right now, sitting here with Jim's uptight son beside her, she could have used a bracing shot of Jack. She put her water glass down and glanced at Dylan.

He'd certainly dressed for a yacht club party in khakis, white shirt, navy jacket, and bow tie. Come to think of it, she'd never seen Dylan wear any other kind of tie. To say he dressed conservatively was to understate the point by a mile.

He clearly wasn't happy about Mom's announcement. A muscle pulsed in his jaw, and his fingers closed into a white-knuckled fist.

What was his problem? Did the medical doctor resent being asked to plan a party? Or was it more sinister than that? She watched him watch her mother.

Oh, yeah. More sinister. Dylan didn't like Mom.

Ella's irritation with her mother evaporated, replaced with a strong need to defend her. How dare Dylan give her mother a judgmental look like that?

"So?" Jim asked, his bright blue eyes hopeful as he captured her gaze.

Damn. She didn't want to disappoint Jim. She liked him. A lot. He was kind and generous, and he made Mom laugh. He was, in fact, the best thing that had ever happened to Mom.

"I think it's great," Ella said. "Congratulations, you guys."

"You're okay with this?" Mom asked.

"Of course I am. I'm so happy for you. Jim's terrific."

This earned her a smile. She'd actually made Mom happy. Wonder of wonders. Sometimes figuring out how to make Mom happy was a challenge.

Jim turned toward his son, who was staring down at his cell phone, more interested in the Clemson basketball game than anything else. The guy had been glued to his iPhone all night.

"What about you?" Jim asked.

Dylan looked up but didn't make eye contact with anyone. "Are you guys sure about this?"

Wow. Nothing like blurting out your feelings without regard for anyone's emotions. Was Dylan always like that? If so, he and Mom were going to have a rough relationship. Mom believed in the old saying that, if you didn't have something nice to say, you said nothing at all. Of course, Mom had never applied that rule of comportment to herself when it came to critiquing Ella's violin performances.

Jim laughed, pulling Ella from her sour thoughts. "We're sure. I know you don't have much party planning experience, but we're confident you can handle this." Jim was a master at defusing conflict. But it didn't quite work this time.

"Dad." Dylan invested that word with a boatload of irritation. Her soon-to-be stepbrother was not a happy camper, but he was going to learn that speaking out loud about his negative feelings would not endear him to Mom. Mom was giving him the frown-of-death, which suggested that the scene was about to get ugly if Ella didn't head Dylan off at the pass.

"What kind of party do you want? Where were you thinking of getting married? How many people? Sit-down dinner or buffet? Music? Mom, I need details," she said in a rush.

Mom's frown evaporated like dew on a summer's day. Whew. "We talked to Ashley Scott about getting married in her garden in May."

"We actually booked a date," Jim added. "May twenty-second."

"And we wanted to keep the wedding to the family only, but since Jim is such a prominent member of the community—"

"We thought maybe an engagement party would be in order," Jim said, finishing Mom's sentence.

It was cute. And she was warming to the idea, sort of. But one glance in Dylan's direction told her she was the only one. Her soon-to-be stepbrother was not down with the program.

Whoa. That was a thought. Did she want a brother?

Not really.

"You know," Dylan finally said, "it might be best if you kept things small. I mean it's not as if…" His voice faded out the minute Jim turned his intense blue eyes in his son's direction. Wow. Who knew Jim could silence Dylan with a mere look. Jim's cred went up by a factor of ten.

Ella jumped in, continuing in her gung ho tone. "So, um, did you have an idea of how big you wanted your party to be?"

"We need to put together a guest list," Jim said. "Maybe a hundred people."

"Wow. I guess with a big guest list like that, we'll have some trouble finding a venue," she said.

Dylan slumped back in his chair and might have rolled his somewhat attractive blue eyes. Oh boy, it was her lucky day. She could just see the fun times ahead planning this party with him.

"We were thinking maybe the reception hall at Grace Church," Jim said.

"We were?" Mom's tone suggested that Jim had been thinking about the church and had failed to communicate with his bride-to-be. Not good.

"It's a big room, Brenda," Jim said.

"Right. But that's its main attraction. It's big and empty and kind of boring."

"Well, maybe we could rent out Rafferty's for an evening."

Dylan sat up in his chair. "Dad, have you any idea how much that would cost?"

"Some. But, you know, you only get married twice." Jim lifted a half-full glass of green beer.

Dylan glowered.

Just then, Jason waved in Ella's direction, signaling the start of the second set. She'd never been so happy for the end of a break. "Look, I gotta go to work. Can we talk about this tomorrow?"

"Of course. We wanted to tell you two tonight since we're all together," Mom said. "And, honey, the violin sounds wonderful."

Something warm spilled into Ella's core. Mom hadn't failed to notice all the hard work she'd done over the last few weeks. She might even have enjoyed the unusual praise were it not for the grumpy stare Dylan Killough aimed in her direction.

Chapter Two

Magnolia Harbor Primary Care Physicians were located on Palmetto Street in a squat brick building. The bottom floor housed the Jonquil Island free clinic, and the family practice was located in the suite above.

Ella opted not to wait for the slow elevator and climbed the stairs, her heart pounding more from trepidation than exertion. Last night, Dylan Killough had made it clear that he wasn't thrilled by Mom and Jim's engagement. This morning, he'd surprised her by leaving a message on her phone at 8:30 a.m. suggesting that they meet today at 2:00.

She hadn't expected that. She'd expected him to duck the responsibility. So she was willing to give him the benefit of the doubt. Maybe he was okay after all.

She pushed through the office doors on the second floor and walked up to the reception desk. "Oh, hey, Ella," the lady said as if she'd known Ella all her life. Ella had no idea who this woman was. Probably one of the ladies Mom knew from A Stitch in Time, the yarn store where Ella's mother worked.

"Hi," she said, forcing a smile.

"I'll let Doctor D know that you're here. He was asking about you five minutes ago." The woman glanced at the clock.

It was officially five minutes after two in the afternoon. Ella was late. She would have been on time, but the traffic on the beach road had been horrible. Some idiot college kid, here for spring break, had crossed the center line and hit a car coming in the opposite direction. Based on the wreckage, people had gotten hurt.

But obviously any injured folks hadn't been brought here to the local family practice. She clamped down on the urge to say the words "I'm sorry." Instead, she waited without another word until the receptionist picked up her telephone handset and paged the good doctor.

A minute later, she was ushered down a long hallway with exam rooms on either side. Dylan's office was at the end, and it wasn't large but it did have a window with a view down Palmetto Street.

"You're late," Dylan grumbled. His eyes were a dark shade of blue flecked with amber that should have made them warmer than his father's. But the cool distance in his regard set her on edge. What did he want from her?

Had he called her here so he could foist the party planning off on her? Which would be fine because Dylan didn't look like a guy who had a clue about anything fun or joyous. His button-down was buttoned up, and his bow tie—a red one this time— was perfectly knotted at his throat.

She sat down, folded her hands in her lap, and gave him the mildest look she could manage. Years of living with Cody had taught her how to hide her emotions and put on a blank look. Having a poker face had been a hard, but useful, skill to learn.

"So," he said, leaning back in his swivel chair, "what do you think about this whole wedding idea?"

What did she think about the wedding? Hadn't she been clear

last night? She was happy for Mom. She opted not to say a word because this guy might be playing some kind of game with her. Cody had been so good at playing games. Trapping her with her own words. Better not to say anything that could be used against her later.

"You don't know?" Dylan asked into her silence, his voice inching up a little.

She stared at him mildly but remained silent.

He stared back, almost unblinking. "You don't have any thoughts on this at all?"

She studied him before answering. He was so corporate. Curly hair cut short, broad brow, probing stare, square jaw. A lot of women would find him attractive, but he was most definitely not her type. But he didn't look brotherly either.

Maybe she should have never prayed for a sibling back when she was eight years old. This had to be a case of God laughing at her.

"Look," she finally said, "I think I made it clear last night that I'm happy for my mother. And happy that Jim loves her. I gather you don't feel that way. If that's the case, then—"

"No, it's not the case. I mean, yes." He stopped and took a big breath. "If Dad wants to have a lady friend, that's fine. But to get married. At his age—" He bit off the last words but needn't have bothered.

Ella straightened her shoulders, irritation firing her synapses. "So what is it? Don't you think my mother is good enough for your father to marry?"

He blinked. "Well, no, actually."

OMG. Did Mom know he felt this way? Probably not. And Ella was not about to tell her that Dylan didn't think she was good enough. His opinion of Mom didn't matter. And she, for one, didn't really want him helping to plan this party.

She stood up. "Okay, we're done. I'm happy to plan the

party without you. I'm sure that's what you want me to do." She turned toward the door.

"Wait."

She kept walking.

"Did you know that Dad plans to move into Cloud Nine?" Cloud Nine was the name Mom had given her beach house out on Paradise Beach. "I think they want you to move out." Dylan hurled the words at her like sharp, pointy arrows.

Ella froze in front of the door. Mom wouldn't do that? Would she?

* * *

The minute the words left Dylan's mouth he knew they'd hit their mark. Ella stood still, her back to him, shoulders stiffening. A tiny mote of remorse trickled through him, and for an instant he thought about a beautiful butterfly being ruthlessly pinned to a display board.

Was he that cruel? Evidently so. But he needed an ally, and who better than Brenda's daughter, who had abandoned her own mother for years? Surely she would understand his misgivings, if he could get her to understand all the implications. But he had to play this carefully.

"Look, I'm sorry if that hurt you, but my father is definitely moving into your mother's house. He told me so."

Ella turned, her blue-gray eyes a little brighter than they had been before. She was good at hiding her emotions, but not perfect. "So that part about them wanting me to move out..." Her voice trailed off in a question mark.

"Conjecture. But I'm sure it's true. Dad hasn't brought your mother over for a sleepover. We share a house, you know, and he's never been comfortable about that sort of thing with me there. So..."

She nodded. She was listening to him now.

"And besides, we both know the beach house has only one bathroom and paper-thin walls," he continued, pressing his point. "Even if they don't ask you to move out, are you prepared to stay?"

"I don't know." Her voice was so small and soft.

"You know what? You shouldn't feel especially aggrieved, because when Dad moves out, he's probably going to sell the house I grew up in. So I'm going to have to find new living arrangements too."

Her shoulders slumped a fraction. "I'm so sorry about that," she said.

"I suppose I should have moved out a long time ago," he admitted. He'd moved in after his residency when he'd decided to join his father's medical practice. Until then he'd been living on his own, so he ought to be okay with the idea of his father selling the house. But he wasn't.

His feelings about the house were not the main reason he was so opposed to Dad's engagement to Brenda McMillan. Dylan was sure Brenda would break Dad's heart, and Dad had suffered one too many broken hearts over the years. Mom's death had destroyed him for a few years, and then Tammy Hansen swooped in and knocked him off his feet...until she dumped him four years later.

Tammy had been super needy, but nothing like Brenda. Even worse, since getting involved with Brenda, Dad's personality had changed. He'd lost some of his drive. He was ignoring parts of the practice. He was giving up items on his bucket list.

In short, Dad was changing into someone Dylan hardly recognized.

He needed to stop this marriage before Dad woke up one day and realized he'd made a monumental mistake he couldn't get himself out of easily. Breaking them up would be hard, but with

Ella's help, it might be possible. She couldn't be happy about what was going on, could she?

"So, you see," he said, following up on his advantage, "you and I are in the same boat."

Ella stared at him for a good fifteen seconds before striding across the room and leaning on the chair back. "I can see that you actually believe that. But you know, aside from being asked to plan a party together, we don't have anything much in common."

"No? We're both going to be homeless. And beyond that..." He paused a moment before continuing. "I know you don't want to talk about it. And I don't want to pry. But even though you went through the motions of being happy for them last night, I got the feeling that their announcement annoyed you."

She blinked. Had he scored a point, or had he surprised her? "What I was feeling last night is none of your business."

"No? Are you happy with your mother?"

"Am I happy *with* my mother, or *for* my mother? I'm not sure what you're asking."

"You know what I mean."

She stood up straight, squaring her shoulders and giving him a look that could turn anyone to stone. "My relationship with my mother is none of your damn business."

"Look. I don't mean to offend. But we're going to be part of the same family. So your relationship with your mother *is* my business. Everyone knows you and your mother had a falling-out. Didn't you stay away for years? There had to be a reason for that, right? And now here you are finally reconnecting with her, and she's pushing you away."

"That's not what she's doing. She asked me to plan her party. And if Jim wants to move into the beach house, that's fine with me. So don't try to tell me what I think or feel, okay?" She jutted out her chin, the picture of a devoted daughter. Wow, he hadn't expected that.

He switched tactics, throwing more ammunition at her. "Don't you think they're a little old to get married?"

"Is there an age limit?" Her brows rose.

"No. I'm just saying that they're too old to have kids, and if you're okay with them living together, then why should they get married?"

"Because they're in love?"

"Yeah, but when they break up, it would be so much easier without a bunch of lawyers and prenups and whatever."

"Wow. You're a real pessimist, aren't you?"

"No, I'm not a pessimist. I'm a realist. And I'm opposed to this wedding."

"You've made that abundantly clear."

"I don't want anything to do with planning this engagement party."

"Fine. I'll do it myself. It will be so much easier without you." She captured his gaze. Something about the angry flush in her cheeks made his heart skip a beat.

"Don't count on it being easier," he said, meeting her angry stare with his own determination.

"And why is that?"

"Because I'm going to do everything I can to break them up."

Chapter Three

Ella had to fight to keep her mouth from dropping open. "You're insane. I'm going now." She turned on her heel and rushed through the door. When she reached the sidewalk outside the doctor's office, she stopped to get her bearings.

Now what? She jammed her hands into her jeans and stared up at the pale haze of spring green on the trees lining the street. She wanted to murder someone.

Starting with Doctor D.

But she had a bone to pick with Mom too. Why hadn't she said one word about her plans? And did Jim really want her to move out of the beach house? She didn't think so, but it would be a mistake to make assumptions either way.

She swallowed back the swelling lump in her throat. She was not going to cry right here on the sidewalk outside Doctor Dreadful's office. Oh no. She was going to stay cool and calm and get to the bottom of this.

Although if Jim did want to move in with Mom, she wasn't sure she'd be entirely comfortable living in the same place, sharing a bathroom with her new stepfather. She may have lied about that to Dylan, but hell if she was going to give him the lowdown on her feelings.

She started down Palmetto Street, walking with no purpose until her feet carried her toward Granny's house. Just like that, the knot in her stomach eased.

Granny was sensible. Granny would know what to do.

Her pace quickened, and it occurred to her that, if Jim wanted to move in with Mom, Ella could always move in with Granny. There was a spare bedroom in Granny's house, and now that her grandmother was getting older, it might be a good thing if Ella claimed it. She could keep an eye on her grandmother, and Mom could have some privacy. It was the perfect solution.

Take that, Doctor D.

She arrived at her grandmother's house and stood on the sidewalk for a moment. Granny's house wasn't big or fancy but said "home" to Ella. Granny had recently fixed it up using the insurance money she'd gotten when a tree had crashed through her roof last December during a freak snowstorm. She'd painted it a pretty shade of yellow with cream-colored trim and forest-green shutters. A bright American flag fluttered on a pole attached to one of the porch columns, and Granny had already hung baskets of petunias that made a splash of deep purple against the yellow paint.

It reminded Ella of a vintage photograph or an old-time postcard. Ella had a weakness for postcards, especially since they were becoming obsolete. As a fiddler in a country-and-western band, she had spent months at a time on the road, eating in diners and gassing up at truck stops. At every stop along the road, she perused the postcard rack looking for the special ones.

For years, Ella's only communication with Mom had been postcards sent from various places where the band had stopped to play. Mom had kept every single one of them, pinned to a corkboard in her kitchen. Mom loved her, and she loved Mom, no matter how rocky their relationship had been when she was a teenager.

Now Ella was trying her best to rebuild that relationship, and the last thing she needed was Dylan Killough butting his head into it and analyzing it or judging it or trying to use it. No, she was not going to let Jim's son do that.

With that affirming thought, she hurried to Granny's front door, which was never locked. "Hi," she called as she stepped into the front parlor. "It's me. Are you in the kitchen?"

"No, I'm here," Granny said, coming down the stairs.

Granny was a pretty woman for someone in her seventies. She had stark white hair cut in a short spiky style and wore cool tortoiseshell glasses. Today her ensemble included a pair of designer jeans, nicely creased, and a blue and white boatneck T-shirt accessorized by a chunky red bead necklace, matching earrings, and red canvas shoes. Granny had a style all her own.

"Hey, darlin'," Granny said, coming across the parlor with her arms outstretched. "What brings you here?" Granny enveloped her in a big hug.

Ella let herself savor the contact for a long moment—the loving touch across her back and the scent of Yardley's lavender that followed Granny everywhere.

"I assume you've heard the news?" Ella stepped back.

"About Brenda and Jim?"

Ella nodded.

"I have. And I'm surprised."

"Surprised? Why?"

Granny shrugged. "To be honest, I've always worried that your mother is too much like me. I never thought she'd allow another man into her life." Granny turned toward the kitchen. "Want some sweet tea?"

"Sure."

Ella followed her grandmother into the brand new kitchen at the back of the house, with its shiny white cabinets and a quartz countertop. Ella sat in one of the kitchen stools while Granny pulled down a couple of glasses and poured tea from a pitcher in the fridge.

A bright marketing brochure featuring pictures of older people playing golf and tennis lay on the counter. Ella picked it up. THE BEST IN SOUTH CAROLINA ACTIVE LIVING was printed across the top of the brochure in a fancy script typeface.

Ella studied the marketing spiel all about lifestyle amenities at the Bayview Vistas development, which ran the gamut from art classes to Zumba lessons. She turned the page and found herself staring at glossy photos of various condo floor plans, each featuring a sizable "lanai."

Did people have lanais in South Carolina? It seemed such a Pacific Coast concept. Down here, people had screened porches and verandas.

"Granny, what's this?" Ella asked, just as her grandmother settled on the kitchen stool beside her.

"I've put down a deposit on one of those condos."

"What?" Ella's stomach flipped over as a horrible sense of loss slipped through her.

"I've decided to sell the house," Granny said.

"But why?" Ella's voice cracked with emotion. How could Granny sell this house?

"Oh, hon, I should have sold this place years ago. I've been living here with my sad memories of your granddaddy for way too long. I don't know, maybe seeing Brenda and Jim get together made me think I needed to move on with my life, quit using grief as an excuse, and get on with living what's left of the years I've got. When that tree fell on the roof last December, it shook my foundations.

"Look here," Granny continued, pulling the brochure toward

her and flipping pages. "This is the model I bought. It has an open floor plan and a big master bedroom with an en suite bath and a walk-in closet. I've never had an en suite bath or a walk-in closet ever."

Ella blinked down at the floor plan for the one-bedroom condo as her plan for moving into Granny's spare room went up in smoke. "So, when is this happening?"

"They have one ready for me to move into right away. I was just fixing to call your mother to let her know the news. I'm going to need some help packing. But I reckon it's a good thing I did a lot of downsizing before the contractors came in here last January.

"Once I move into my new place, I'm putting the house up for sale. I've already talked to Bobby Don down at Berkshire Hathaway. He seems to think I'm going to make enough from the sale of this old place so that I won't have to worry about money for the rest of my life."

"That's great, Granny," Ella said, trying to sound enthusiastic. This development was like a gigantic fly in the ointment of her life. She wouldn't be able to move in with Granny, but that was a minor point. She couldn't stand the idea of some stranger living in this house. If she had the money, she'd buy Granny's house right now. Unfortunately, she didn't have a job and wasn't creditworthy, thanks to Cody and her own foolishness.

Homelessness loomed large in her future unless she was willing to make good on what she'd just told Dylan—that she was fine with Jim living in the same house. And really, what was the problem with that, anyway? Hadn't she shared space in the tiny RV with the boys in the band all those years on the road?

She didn't care about the lack of privacy, but she hated the idea of Jim getting in between her and Mom. After all the years apart, Ella had come to enjoy sharing the house with Mom these last few months. Jim would be like an interloper or something.

Which was an ugly thought she immediately repressed. She loved Jim. He was a great guy. His son, not so much.

"Maybe I should call your mom right now," Granny said, pulling Ella from her thoughts. "I figure she's at the store. Maybe she can come on over for dinner, and we could talk about her engagement party and my moving plans. What do you say?"

Ella nodded. "Sure. I need to consult with her about the party anyway because Dylan's made it clear he doesn't want to help."

* * *

Granny's surprise move took up a lot of discussion time once Mom got off work and joined Ella and her grandmother for dinner. Mom wasn't all that happy about this surprise news, mostly because she was stressing out about the wedding and needed Granny's lifestyle change like a hole in the head.

Ella kept her head down for most of dinner. She didn't think letting Mom know that Dylan had begged off the party planning would be a good idea. But Granny outed her.

"So," her grandmother said after they'd shared some of Granny's pound cake, "Ella told me that Dylan doesn't want to help with the engagement party."

Mom turned in her direction, the frown-of-death riding her brow. This was not a good sign. "What's this?"

"We talked this afternoon."

"And he flat-out refused?"

Great. As much as she wanted to tattle on Dylan, she decided it would be a bad idea. Mom was already pretty stressed, so she decided to keep his final words this afternoon to herself. Who wanted to find out that their fiancée's son was determined to break up the romance? No one.

On the other hand, this was a perfect time to get to the bottom of the living arrangements. "Well, I guess Dylan is kind of busy. But, um, I do have a question. Is Jim going to move into the beach house?"

Mom's forehead now resembled deep-plowed furrows. "Did Dylan tell you that?"

Ella nodded. "He called me over to his office today. I thought it was to talk about the engagement party, but he had a bunch of things on his mind. He said Jim wanted to move into the beach house."

"Oh, honey, I'm so sorry he did that," Mom said.

"Is he...moving in?"

The frown-of-death disappeared, and Mom reached out to take Ella's hand. "The truth is, Jim and I have talked about where we want to live after the wedding. I love living at Paradise Beach."

"I know."

"Would you mind terribly if he did move in?"

Boy, nothing like getting asked an impossible question. She did mind. And she didn't fully understand why, except that she felt as if Mom was pushing her away. Which wasn't exactly the truth. Besides, Mom shouldn't have to give up the home she loved just because she was getting married. That would be grossly unfair.

"I'm okay," Ella said. "I just wanted to know because Dylan made it sound like you and Jim wanted me to move out."

"Oh my goodness. No!" Mom seemed pretty upset.

"Well, maybe I misunderstood. Maybe—"

"No. I'm sure you didn't. Jim's son can be a pain in the neck. Honey, you are always welcome at Cloud Nine. I know the house is tiny, but no one had any intention of asking you to leave. Jim isn't going to be moving in right away. I mean, the wedding isn't until May, and then we're planning to go to Italy for a month. Who knows, by then maybe you'll find a job and an apartment."

"You're going to Italy? How wonderful," Granny said, clearly trying to defuse the conversation the way she always did. "You've always wanted to go there."

Mom's cheeks flushed. "We had this disagreement about it, actually."

"Oh?" Granny seemed a little worried. Wait, Mom and Jim disagreed about something? That was new. They never even fussed at each other.

"Well, it's expensive," Mom said, "and I figured if Jim was going to spend his money on a big trip like that, we should go to Ireland. Jim told me once that Ireland tops his bucket list. But he insisted on taking me to Italy because Italy tops mine."

"That's because he loves you and wants to make you happy," Granny said, a grin on her face.

Mom turned toward Granny. "I made a big mistake, y'all. I didn't tell Ella about Jim's plans because I wanted to talk to you about the possibility of Ella moving in with you." Mom glanced toward Ella. "Not because we don't want you at Cloud Nine but because there's more space here, you know. And a guest bath. We were thinking you might feel more comfortable here. And living in town would be more convenient for you since you don't have a car. But..."

"Oh, poop," Granny said. "I would have loved to have Ella come stay with me." Now Granny sounded upset.

Dammit, maybe Ella should have kept her mouth shut about what Dylan had said. She didn't want Granny or Mom to feel guilty. Both of them deserved happiness.

Granny let go of a big breath. "Ella, sugar, I know it's not much, but you are welcome to stay here until the house is sold. Who knows. It might take a while."

Never mind that Granny had just been talking about how the

real estate broker was sure the house would sell in a few weeks' time at most.

"Only if she wants to move," Mom said, turning toward Ella.

"If I want to? I love this house. I would love to live here. I'd love to live here forever after, if you want to know the truth. But it's okay, Granny. I understand why you want to downsize."

"Thanks, sugar. I'm glad you understand." But Granny looked troubled, despite her words to the contrary.

* * *

On Saturday night, Brenda slid into the booth at Annie's Kitchen and faced the love of her life. She and Jim had been together for the last three months, and they were still going out for dates on Saturday night. She hoped that never ended.

She had certainly hit the jackpot with him. He was fifty, fit, and handsome as the devil with a slightly-too-long mop of salt-and-pepper hair, a pair of twinkly blue eyes, and a heroic chin.

He made her feel special without doing anything at all. She loved him more than she'd ever loved anyone, but tonight she needed to broach an unpleasant topic.

This was the sort of thing that had always touched off a fight with Keith, her ex-husband, so she was nervous, her heart rocking oddly in her chest. She didn't want to argue with Jim.

But she couldn't let the Dylan situation fester, or the problem would only get bigger. And Lord only knew, she didn't want to give Ella reasons to go back to Cody Callaghan. Brenda was pretty sure the man had gone out of his way to discourage Ella from coming home. All those years that Ella had toured with Cody, her daughter had barely stayed in contact, sending only the occasional postcard from the road.

Now that her child had come home, Brenda would move heaven and earth to keep her here in Magnolia Harbor. But

Momma had made things a bit more difficult by deciding to downsize.

This was a disaster, and she didn't know how to solve it. She took a couple of deep breaths, but her heart continued to run amok inside her rib cage as she met Jim's twinkly gaze.

"I need to talk to you about something difficult."

As usual, Jim gave her his undivided attention. Jim was a good listener as she filled him in on her mother's fateful decision to sell the house in town and move into a one-bedroom condo. "And to make matters worse, Dylan told Ella all about our post-wedding plan for you to come live at the beach. And I feel as if he may have purposefully tried to make Ella feel unwanted."

"What?" Jim's casual posture evaporated. Dylan was an emotional hot button for him. But Brenda could hardly expect otherwise. Jim loved his son as fiercely as Brenda loved her daughter.

"Jim, honey, I hate to say it, but right now Dylan is behaving like a spoiled brat. In addition to making Ella feel unwanted, he refused to help her with the engagement party. So our plans to help them get to know each other through planning this party have failed. And now I'm afraid that his behavior might drive her away."

"We never intended to make Ella feel unwanted."

"I know, honey. But that didn't stop Dylan from doing so. I think it's because she heard about our plans from him instead of from me. Why on earth did you tell him you were planning on moving to Cloud Nine?"

"It seemed like the honest thing to do. I didn't make a big deal about it. I just—"

"Oh, Jim. Dylan is probably hurt by that too." She shook her head.

"You think?"

"Yes. Did you tell him you planned to give him the house?"

"Uh, well, maybe not. It was just something said in passing."

"Okay. It's coming clear to me. You need to tell him you're not selling the house out from under him, okay?"

"Fine. But what do we do about Ella? Maybe, since your mother is moving into the condo, we should reconsider. There's plenty of room at my house. You could move in with me. Dylan can still have his space, and Ella could have Cloud Nine."

Brenda reached across the table and interlaced her fingers with Jim's. "Do you think Dylan would be okay with me moving into his mother's domain?"

"I don't know. But to be honest, I don't really care."

"Well, you should care, Jim. I mean, that house is where he grew up. He doesn't need me intruding. The situation with Ella is different. We never owned a house in Indiana. I never could quite afford one. We moved around a lot. Cloud Nine isn't Ella's childhood home, so you moving in doesn't feel like such a violation. It's just a bit cramped is all."

"I guess so. But you said she feels pushed away."

Brenda nodded. "I don't know for certain. But I'm afraid of that. No matter what we do, even moving into your house, isn't going to make her feel better. And it doesn't help that Dylan flat-out refused to help her with the party. So she's going to feel dumped on from every corner."

"God, what a mess. Maybe we shouldn't have asked them to work together in the first place." Jim's support encouraged Brenda. He wasn't minimizing her worries. He was actually trying to understand them. This was why she loved him so much.

"Maybe we shouldn't have. But I was hoping..."

"Me too. It would be so much easier if they were friends."

She nodded. "Well, I guess we can't force them to like each other, can we?"

"No."

"I'm so glad you understand my concerns. I was afraid you'd be angry about this."

"Angry? At what? You're raising an important family dynamic that we've got to negotiate."

Brenda shrugged. "Bear with me. I'm new at this thing we're doing. My ex wasn't all that sensitive to things like this."

He squeezed her hand. "We'll get through this. But...you know we could cut through a lot of drama by running away together." His earnest gaze warmed her heart. His suggestion not so much.

She let go of his hand and stared across the dining room, filled tonight with locals who were avoiding the crowded tourist spots in town.

"Why can't my family be happy?" she asked, her eyes suddenly filling.

"Aww, sweetie, it's not your family. It's mine. Dylan is the problem."

She brushed a tear away. "It shouldn't matter that much, but I want a wedding where I've got my family with me. All of us. And I want this party so that Ella and Dylan can get to know each other. I want your son and my daughter to get with the program. Is that selfish?"

"No."

"What are we going to do?"

"I'm going to talk to Dylan and read him the riot act."

"No, I don't think that's a good plan." She paused a moment, getting a grip on her emotions. "Maybe it *would* be best if we eloped."

"No!" Jim's chin firmed.

"But—"

"I said no. We're going to have a wedding. A real one. I want you and Ella to go off to Charleston or Atlanta or wherever to shop for a super-expensive wedding dress. I want flowers and champagne because it's what you want."

"I don't need—"

"Of course you don't. But you want a wedding, and you should have it. And I'll be damned if my overprotective son stops that from happening. There is no excuse for him trying to make Ella feel as if we wanted to push her out of the beach house. No excuse at all. And he was raised better than that."

"Please don't tell Dylan this is because of something Ella said. Or that I tattled. It will only make matters worse."

"No, I think the time has come for a father-son conversation."

"Please don't be too hard on him or he'll blame me. Or worse, he'll blame Ella. And that won't be good."

His mouth quirked to one side, and he nodded. "I'll make sure that doesn't happen. And don't worry. He'll come around eventually. Dylan is a good kid with a big heart. The problem is that I've spoiled him, and after his mom died, he nominated himself as my keeper. It was cute when he was little, but not so much now. He needs to stop trying to protect me and get on with living his own life."

"He's trying to protect you? From who? Me?"

Jim rolled his bright blue eyes. "I think he's worried you'll break my heart."

"I would never do that."

"I know you won't, but Dylan doesn't."

Chapter Four———————————

On Monday morning, Dylan rode his motorcycle into the office early. His helmet sat on the corner of his desk while he kicked back, drinking his second cup of coffee and reviewing a stack of lab reports.

"Hey." Dad peeked around the edge of his office door.

Dylan clamped down on the urge to ask his father where the hell he'd been the last few days. Dad had been MIA most of Saturday, and Dylan had spent his Sunday fly-fishing. Dad had also not come home last night.

"Hey," he said, trying hard not to sound as annoyed as he felt.

Dad strolled into the office carrying a bunch of files under his arm. "You got a minute?"

"Sure." Dylan's stomach roiled. Here it came, the inevitable woodshed talk. Ella had probably told Brenda everything about their meeting last week.

Dad sat down in the side chair, but he didn't speak for a long moment. Instead, his gaze wandered around the small office, never lighting on anything for long. What the hell? Was Dad nervous?

"Whatever you have to say, just say it." Dylan's chest tightened as if someone had put a rope with a slipknot around it.

Dad finally met his gaze. "Is it true that you told Ella that I was moving into Brenda's beach house?"

"I did, but I assumed she already knew about it."

Dad's shoulders sagged. "No, she didn't know because Brenda wanted to tell her in her own way, and you screwed that up. You made Ella feel terrible. And I won't have you doing that again. Understand?"

"Why didn't she tell Ella about your plans? I mean, you told me a couple of weeks ago."

"And now I regret it because you used the information to make Ella feel bad. And don't deny it, Dylan. You've made your feelings about my relationship with Brenda clear. And I'm here to tell you that I don't care if you're happy about my plans to get married."

"What?" Dammit, Brenda was twisting Dad's mind around on itself. Of course Dad cared about his feelings. Didn't he?

"You heard me. I'm getting married to Brenda McMillan, and I'm not going to stand by and let you upset Brenda and her daughter. Frankly, I'm surprised you don't even realize that you're driving a wedge between Ella and her mother. For god's sake, Brenda has waited years for this chance to reconnect with her daughter. You will not screw that up, understand?"

Wow. Dad was furious. He hadn't seen his father this angry ever. Not even that time in high school when he'd totaled the Explorer. Dad had yelled that night, but mostly because he'd been worried that Dylan had gotten hurt. Luckily, the Ford was built like a brick house and took a beating pretty well.

"Are you listening?" Dad asked into Dylan's silence.

"I'm listening."

"Good. I don't want to be angry or fight with you, but I do expect better of you. Brenda and I are getting married. We're having a party whether you have anything to do with it or not, although I would expect you to at least show up for it. And Ella is going to be your stepsister, so be nice to her."

A strange feeling of jealousy bubbled through him. Everyone was so worried about Ella. What about *him*? He felt pushed out too. Although he damn sure didn't want to admit that to his dad.

"I'm sorry," he said, looking down at his desk. He didn't like his father being so angry with him.

"I'm not the one you need to apologize to," Dad said.

Dylan looked up. "You want me to apologize to Ella or Brenda?"

"You have to ask me that, really? Where did I go wrong raising you?" Dad gave him his intense, blue-eyed, I'm-the-dad-and-you-better-get-with-the-program look.

"Okay. I'll give Ella a call."

"No. You will take her out for a nice meal, and you will grovel. And I would be most pleased if you would also change your mind and help her with the party, although I'm not insisting on that unless you can show some enthusiasm for the task. Am I clear?"

"Eminently."

"And you should probably apologize to Brenda too. But a simple phone call is all that's required."

"Okay."

"Thank you. Now, I need to talk to you about something else." What now?

Dad placed the folders he'd carried into the office onto the desk. "These are some of my patient files. Most of these folks have been coming here for a long time. I want you to take them over."

Dylan glanced down at the stack of files. On top was a particularly thick one. He opened the folder and read the name: Virginia Whittle.

"You're giving me Ginny Whittle?" he asked. Mrs. Whittle was forty-five and in seemingly good health. But that didn't stop her from coming to visit on a regular basis, complaining of one thing or another. She suffered from somatic symptom disorder, which was a fancy way of saying she was a hypochondriac.

"I know. She can be difficult."

"Who else?" Dylan flipped through the files. First up was Milo Parker, a sixty-seven-year-old male with type II diabetes and hypertension who was also morbidly obese. Milo was one of those patients who simply would not, or could not, make lifestyle changes.

Then came Coreen Martel, eighty-eight and suffering from heart failure for the last two years. She'd been on the usual meds for the condition, but the structural damage to her heart was too great. She was in end-stage failure, and there wasn't much more he could do for her. Her heart was wearing out.

In truth, there wasn't much Dylan could do for any of these patients.

"Why?" He looked up from the files.

"Because you're going to be the man in charge around here sooner or later. Sooner if I have my way."

"What?"

Dad leaned forward. "I've been working my tail off here and at the clinic for almost thirty years. While I plan to keep seeing patients, I also want to step back a little and enjoy life. After your mother died, I buried myself in work and the job of raising you. When you left for college, I doubled down on the work just to keep loneliness at bay.

"It's time for me to kick back and do some traveling. Brenda and I want to go to Italy for our honeymoon. We're thinking about taking a whole month off. Which is why I need you to start looking after some of these patients."

"You're taking a month off?"

"Yeah. We're making the plans now. And that's another thing. Our practice has gotten larger over the years, what with the new developments up the coast. I think we need to consider adding a nurse practitioner."

Dylan was so surprised he could hardly wrap his brain around what Dad was saying. Was Dad abandoning him in every way?

"I know," Dad said. "No one will believe it until we leave for the airport. But trust me, the reservations have been made, so it's time for you to start planning for my vacation."

"I always thought you wanted to go to Ireland."

"I do, but Italy is on Brenda's bucket list."

Damn that woman. What was she doing to his father?

* * *

Ashley Scott, the owner of Howland House, Magnolia Harbor's five-star bed-and-breakfast, laid her grandmother's cake plates on the quartz countertop. She'd placed the squares of Mississippi mud cake she'd made this morning on the serving platter Grandmother had always used for sheet cakes. Then she laid out dessert forks and cloth napkins.

The Piece Makers, Grandmother's quilting group, which Ashley had inherited along with Howland House after her grandmother's death, would be arriving any minute. And the ladies had been served scratch-made cake for literally decades.

Grandmother had started the quilting group back in 1942, not long after Pearl Harbor. Many of the original quilters had passed on, but their daughters, all of whom were senior citizens now, had continued on. Ashley was a third-generation quilter—the only third-generation quilter, although Jenna St. Pierre joined them every once in a while.

And sometimes, like right this minute, she wished she hadn't inherited the group. The ladies gossiped the way some people breathed. And to a woman, they all expected her to bake a cake every week. Just like her grandmother had.

Maybe she was being hard on them. When Ashley had first come to live with her grandmother, right after her husband, Adam, had been killed in action in Afghanistan, baking those cakes had been a distraction from her grief.

But things had changed. After Grandmother passed, she'd been forced to turn Howland House into a B&B just to make ends meet. Now that she'd become a successful businesswoman, with guests coming and going, the weekly Tuesday-evening meetings had become one more thing she had to manage.

And sadly, she was still missing Adam as if he had died just weeks and not years ago. That grief had settled into her and showed no sign of ever leaving. She hated to think about how many nights she still cried herself to sleep.

She turned away from the cake and dashed up the stairs to the third floor. "Homework done?" she asked her nine-year-old son, Jackie, who was propped up in his bed reading a graphic novel about Blackbeard, the pirate.

"Yup." He looked up from the page and gave her a metal grin. It seemed ridiculous that he needed braces at the tender age of nine. They made him look older. Her boy was growing up.

Although, judging by his reading material, he'd not yet grown out of his fascination with pirates. At least he wasn't reading about the infamous William Teal, who had lost his life during the 1713 hurricane as he was trying to return to Rose Howland, his lady love.

Rose, Ashley's six-times-great-grandmother or some such thing, was widely regarded as the town's founding mother. According to local legend, she'd mourned Captain Teal so profoundly that she'd planted daffodils all over the island in his memory. The wild daffodils still bloomed every year in late

February, giving Jonquil Island—the sea island where Magnolia Harbor was located—its name.

"There's Mississippi mud cake downstairs. You can come on down after the ladies arrive and help yourself to a piece," she said to her son.

"Thanks," Jackie said before turning his attention back to his picture book. He read more than graphic novels these days. In fact, he was turning into a bookworm. She supposed there were worse things, but she wondered what Adam might think about his bookish son. Jackie was not a chip off the old block, even though he reminded Ashley of Adam sometimes when he cocked his head just so.

Ashley left her son and returned downstairs just as the first quilters began to arrive. For the next twenty minutes, she served cake and coffee and listened to the local gossip.

Barbara Blackwood grumped about her granddaughter Jessica, who was insisting on a small October wedding instead of the June extravaganza Barbara wanted. But what else was new? Barbara lived to complain.

Barbara's sister, Donna Cuthbert, didn't complain as much as Barbara. She gossiped instead. She had juicy news about Bobby Don Ayers, who was apparently seeing Lessie Snow, Dr. Killough's receptionist, on the down low.

"And what about you?" Donna asked, placing her cake plate on the kitchen counter and turning toward Nancy, whose eyes grew round behind her glasses.

"I'm not seeing anyone on the down low," Nancy said in a voice that was slightly louder than her usual near whisper.

"Of course you aren't," Donna said, waving her hand in dismissal. "But I did hear from Cathy Conseca down at the post office that you filed a change of address. Nancy, did you buy one of those new condos down on Redbud Street?"

The members of the group turned toward Nancy almost

as one. Piece Makers never made life decisions without fully discussing them over the quilting frame.

Nancy met the collective stare. "I got my house fixed up, and it seemed like a good time to sell."

"Did Bobby Don talk you into this?" Karen asked.

"No. I just wanted to downsize."

"And you didn't tell us this last week?"

"I hadn't decided last week. I decided on Wednesday."

"But you must have been thinking about it on Tuesday," Donna said.

"I was, but I didn't feel that I needed to talk to anyone. Although..." Her voice faded out.

"What?" asked Patsy Bauman, who fancied herself the leader of the pack because her husband was a member of the town council. "Are you regretting the decision?"

"No. But..."

"But what, for goodness' sake?" Barbara said in her grumpiest tone.

"Well, y'all know that Doc Killough proposed to my daughter."

"That was last week's news," Patsy said, glancing Ashley's way.

Ashley had been the source of that bit of gossip, even though she hadn't intended to blab anything secret to the ladies. She'd naturally assumed that Nancy knew about her own daughter's engagement. Evidently, the starry-eyed lovers had neglected to inform Brenda's mother that they intended to marry.

Nancy shook her head. She looked deeply troubled. "Y'all, I think maybe I should have had a conversation with someone before I signed those condo papers. Because with Brenda getting married and Jim deciding to move into her beach house, there isn't a spot for Ella. And I neglected to think about Ella when I was getting excited about the idea of downsizing."

"They're kicking Ella out of the beach house?" Karen asked.

"No. They've told her she can stay, but the girl is uncomfortable about that. It's a small house with only one bathroom. I gather that Brenda simply assumed Ella would move into my house, but now Bobby Don says the old house should sell in no time at all." She sighed heavily.

"Y'all, this is a classic example of what happens when people make bad assumptions. What a disaster," said Patsy. "Girls, we need to find Ella a place to stay. We can't have her leaving again, even if Brenda is getting married. It took so long to get her back here in the first place." Patsy tapped her upper lip for a moment before her eyes sparked, and she turned toward Ashley.

Ashley braced for Patsy's words. The woman could be so bossy. "You've been looking for a kitchen assistant ever since Judy decided to move to Colorado, right?" Patsy asked.

Ashley nodded, her gut clenching. The Piece Makers did this to her all the time.

"That's perfect," Nancy said.

"Exactly," said Patsy. "Ashley can give Ella that job and let her stay in that extra bedroom she has on the third floor." Patsy spoke as if Ashley weren't even standing there.

The ladies turned toward her as one.

Cornered again. "Sure," she said.

Chapter Five —————————————

Ella moved her things into Granny's spare bedroom on Saturday afternoon even though Mom insisted that it wasn't necessary until after the wedding. But by the time Mom got married, Granny's house would probably be sold, and Ella wanted to live in the old place for a few weeks before that happened. Besides, Mom and Jim deserved some privacy.

And Granny's house had been the scene of many happy childhood memories from Thanksgiving and summer visits. She would savor this last visit to the house she loved so much.

In the meantime, she had nothing but time on her hands, so she could help Granny pack up and get the house ready for the market. She dived in, spending several days up in the attic poking through Granny's memories, boxing up china and books, and driving stuff to the Salvation Army in Granny's car.

It kept her busy, but by Tuesday afternoon, all that frantic activity gave way to the mother of all pity parties. She sat up in her mother's old bedroom, feeling lonely and unsettled. What was she going to do after Granny moved? Where was she going to live for the rest of her life? She couldn't continue to let time pass her by without a plan.

She got out a piece of paper and started making a to-do list. She'd done this many times before. Her wastebasket at the beach house had overflowed with to-do lists that hadn't gotten done. Not this time. This time she had to pick herself up and move on. Like Mom and Granny were doing.

The summer season was just starting. Maybe she could get a job waiting on tables, or maybe there were gigs to be had in the town's many tourist traps. She was studying the Help Wanted listings on Indeed when her phone rang.

It was probably Cody...again. He'd been calling her two or three times a day recently. And she'd been hiding from him because she knew what he wanted. Urban Armadillo, his outlaw country band, usually started their summer tour in March, and Ella was sure he hadn't been able to find a fiddler.

In truth, she needed that job, but she had been resisting because Cody was toxic to her mental health. But in a moment of weakness, she glanced at the caller ID.

Glory. It wasn't Cody. The number was local but unknown. Intrigued, she pressed the connect button. "Hello."

"Hey." The voice on the other end was low and masculine and familiar, although she couldn't quite place it. "I was wondering if you had time this evening. You know, to grab a bite at Rafferty's."

"Who is this?"

"Oh. Uh. It's Dylan."

She made a mental note to put Doctor D's number into her contact list. He was about to become her stepbrother, after all. Even if he did have a crazy-ass plan to break up Mom and Jim's romance. That being the case, she was less than enthusiastic about having dinner with him.

"I'm kind of busy and—"

"Look, I thought we should get to know each other better," he said.

She wasn't sure she wanted to know him better, although that would certainly please her mother. And he was offering her a free meal, which was ten times better than staying home making a to-do list filled with things she wouldn't actually do.

"Okay," she said. "Rafferty's is fine. What time?"

"You mean you'll actually have dinner with me?" He sounded truly surprised that she'd accepted his offer. Probably because he'd been so unpleasant last week.

Which was the point, wasn't it? Having dinner with her wasn't his idea. Someone—probably Jim—had put him up to it. And Jim had done that because Mom had complained about him. She couldn't let him off the hook, could she? He needed to do penance.

"Of course I want to have dinner with you. I mean you're going to be my stepbrother, right?" She had to work hard to sound all happy and bubbly about this prospect.

"Yeah, I guess. So, um, I'll meet you at Rafferty's in half an hour?" He didn't sound happy or bubbly.

"Sure."

An hour later, after a shower and a change of clothes, Ella strolled into Rafferty's Raw Bar, the biggest restaurant on Harbor Drive. The bar area and patio were completely overrun with college kids celebrating spring break, but the back dining room wasn't nearly as crowded.

Dylan sat at a corner table, looking like a card-carrying member of the Young Republicans Club. Did the guy own anything other than a white shirt and bow tie? Maybe she should start calling him Doctor Dull. Although the smile he sent in her direction was pretty nice. He was handsome and clean-cut, and his teeth were really white against his tan. He looked as if he spent time outside. Living in Magnolia Harbor, he probably loved sailing or fishing. Now that she thought about it, he looked exactly like a member of the yacht club.

He lifted his gaze. Was he judging her faded jeans and favorite peasant shirt? Or was he annoyed because she'd kept him waiting? Did he realize she was late on purpose?

His eyes were blue, but not nearly as brilliant as his father's. And he didn't wear his emotions on his face the way Jim did, so he was hard to read.

"Hi," she said, slipping into the chair facing him.

"You're late."

She shrugged. "Sorry. I was all dusty from packing stuff in Granny's attic. I needed a shower."

"You want a beer or something?" he asked. His half-empty glass suggested he'd been waiting a while. Good.

"I could go for some wine."

He waved at a passing waitress, who immediately stopped in her tracks. Doctor D gave the impression that he ate at Rafferty's a lot and was a fave among the female waitstaff. And why not? He was all buttoned up and smoothed down, except for a little curl of dark hair that fell over his forehead Superman style. It suggested that his Clark Kent identity was a flimsy disguise for something else altogether.

But what?

She ordered a glass of rosé and one of Rafferty's Caesar salads. Dylan ordered the biggest steak on the menu, which surprised her since he looked fit and trim and was also a doctor. But then, who said doctors couldn't eat red meat?

"So," he said, when the waitress left them, "I want to apologize." His words sounded totally rehearsed.

"What exactly are you apologizing for?" she asked, lobbing the conversational ball back into his court.

He pressed his lips together for a moment, telegraphing

surprise. He must not have expected that she would challenge his apology.

After a too-long moment, he finally said, "The other day, when we met to discuss the engagement party, I shouldn't have said what I did about Dad moving into your mother's beach house."

"You only told me the truth. There's no need to apologize for that."

"Maybe it was the truth, but it wasn't my place to tell it. And besides, I was being..." His voice trailed off.

"What?" she asked. He seemed almost contrite. Did he get it? Really?

"I'm sure I left you with the impression that I'm unkind."

So typical. Instead of talking about her feelings, he was talking about himself. She was so tired of guys who did that. Cody was a master of this particular game. He never really apologized for anything.

"Look," she said, leaning forward. "I can deal with the truth. And being nice to me now isn't going to convince me to help you break up Mom and Jim. So save your breath, okay?"

Their gazes locked, and his eyes turned midnight blue, but without any stars in them.

"I understood you the first time you told me that," he said.

"Good. Now, just so we're clear, I know why you asked me here for dinner. It's because I told Mom what you said last week, and she told Jim, and then your father demanded that you come apologize. So let's just drop it, shall we?"

He had the temerity to give her another smile, this one without flashing his beautiful teeth. She liked this one better. It was kind of sexy, which was a little startling since he was going to be her stepbrother.

"You've read the situation accurately," he said.

"Of course I did. I know how Mom's mind works."

* * *

Dylan snatched his beer from the table and took a couple of big gulps while he regrouped. Ella was not the sensitive little thing Dad thought she was. She was, in fact, kind of incredible.

And just like that, he realized he'd been looking at this situation from the wrong end of the telescope. He'd misstepped with his opening gambit. Trying to make her angry about the living situation had only stiffened her resolve to support her mother.

He should have worked to win her trust first because if she trusted him, she might divulge important clues to her mother's personality and give him exactly what he needed to expose Brenda as the absolutely wrong woman for his father.

He put his glass down, suddenly enthused by this new idea. He didn't have to be Ella's enemy.

"So, can we start again?" he asked.

"Start how?" she asked in a suspicious tone. Gaining her trust was going to be hard.

"We could start with the engagement party," he said. "Dad made it clear that he really wants me to help."

"I'm sure he did. But you've made it clear that you don't want—"

"I've changed my mind."

"Oh." She blinked.

"I want to make him happy. He's ticked off at me right now."

Her gaze widened a little. What was going on in that head of hers? She was hard to read. Maybe because her face was so adorable—like some anime character with a turned-up nose and eyes that were just a bit too big and too deep for her face. That big-eyed look could melt anyone.

"I don't know . . ." Her voice trailed off as the waitress arrived with the food.

He tucked into his steak while she nibbled at her salad. No

wonder she was so skinny. The salad had no protein, not even an anchovy.

"Are you a vegetarian?" he asked.

Her shoulders moved a little. "Not really, but I avoid meat when I can." She eyed his steak. "You know . . . cows and carbon emissions."

He swallowed a bite of pure grade-A, Angus beef. "Carbon emissions?"

She rolled her eyes. "Not to be indelicate, but methane from beef flatulence. It's a big contributor to climate change. If everyone in the world ate one vegetarian meal a week, it would cut down on carbon emissions by a lot." She eyed his steak again, but this time she licked her lips.

Maybe he should offer her a bite.

"So, about the engagement party," he said.

She studied him, fork poised. The sober look in her big eyes and the tension in her shoulders told him that she wasn't buying his BS. He would have to do a lot more work to earn her trust. He braced himself, ready to argue his case.

But instead of telling him to take a long walk off a short pier, she laid her fork down and nodded. "Okay. You can help plan the party."

Whoa, wait. She just gave in? Without a fight. What was she up to?

He covered his surprise by popping a hunk of steak in his mouth and chewing. By the time he swallowed, he'd decided to play along with this charade. But he wasn't going to underestimate Ella McMillan a second time.

"Have you found a venue?" he asked.

"No."

"No? Well, we better get on that right away. We don't have much time."

She cocked her head, a little blush rising to her cheeks. "Sorry. I got sidetracked because Granny is moving into one of those new condos on Redbud Street and she has a lot of stuff to pack up."

Why was she apologizing? "So what have you done so far?"

She looked down at her salad. "I've made a couple of to-do lists?" she said, but he couldn't miss the uncertainty in her tone.

Maybe he should let her plan the party on her own so she could be the one to face Brenda's ire when it turned into a disaster.

Wait... *That* was a pretty good idea.

But he'd have to help her steer the whole thing off the cliff. A nudge here and a suggestion there would be all he needed. And then, when Brenda had her bridezilla moment, Dad would realize exactly what he was getting into.

It was a delicious idea. Even better than the steak.

"I suggest that we get working on this party right away," he said.

"Okay."

"So, we need a guest list and a venue. I'll talk to Dad about his must-invites. You talk to your mother, and you can call me tomorrow with a rough count. That will give us a start. And as for the venue, I'll see what's available at the yacht club on short notice."

"The yacht club?"

"Yeah."

"Uh, I don't think so." Ella shook her head.

"Why not?"

"I don't think Mom would like the yacht club."

"Oh, really? Why?" Here it came. Ella was about to unconsciously dish the dirt on her mother, and he was ready to take mental notes.

"I don't know why. I just know she hates the yacht club. That's the last place on earth she'd want to have her party."

Perfect. He knew exactly what he had to do—make sure the party happened at the yacht club.

Chapter Six————————————————

On Wednesday morning, Ella got up with the chickens and spent the morning helping Granny pack and sort her stuff. By eleven o'clock, she was dusty and tired, so she took an iced tea break on the porch while a mockingbird serenaded her with spring birdsong. That bird's song lifted her heart a tiny bit, which was a good thing because Doctor Domineering had left her feeling slightly useless.

Why had she allowed him to take over the party planning?

Simple answer: he'd made her feel incompetent or something. He was just like Cody: a big bully who was skilled at undermining her confidence. And besides, he had a point. She should have done more than make a few lists. She should have worked on Mom's party instead of allowing Granny's move to sidetrack her.

Besides, Mom hadn't been pushing her the way she usually did. She seemed preoccupied with planning her Italian honeymoon.

She leaned her head back on the rocking chair and reviewed last night's conversation with Dylan. He was going to be difficult to work with. Every idea she offered up had been rejected. Instead, he was hell-bent on having the party at the yacht club.

But every instinct told Ella that the best party for Mom would be something informal and stress free. Maybe a nice get-together on the beach, with lots of yummy Carolina barbecue and some beer and wine. But clearly Jim and Dylan wanted something swankier.

And what the heck. Mom wanted to make Jim happy, so maybe it would be better to let Dylan take the lead. He'd know exactly what Jim wanted. And with Dylan doing the heavy lifting on the party planning, she could give Granny the attention she needed.

Her phone vibrated. It was most likely Cody. He'd left five messages yesterday—an all-time high. He was evidently desperate for a fiddler. She pulled out the phone and glanced at it.

Yup. Cody. She pushed the ignore button.

The sound of Granny moving boxes around the living room reached her through the open windows. She needed to make Granny sit down. And Ella needed to get up, stop the poor-pitiful-me party, and go do something useful.

But instead, her finger hovered over the call button. Cody's increasingly frantic messages were so seductive. He wanted her. He needed her. Maybe for the wrong reasons, but being wanted and needed was seductive.

She might have called him back, but Ashley Scott strolled down the path. "Hey," she said. "You're just the person I came to see."

"Uh, if you've come to pitch me on the idea of hosting Mom's engagement party at Howland House, I'm afraid Jim is leaning toward the yacht club, perish the thought."

Ashley's wide smile put Ella at ease. According to Granny, the innkeeper had her crap together. She was a single mom running an important business and, as a direct descendant of the town's founding mother, was nothing short of Magnolia Harbor royalty.

Ella would love to have a life like that. She wouldn't even mind single motherhood. Having kids had been another thing she and Cody had argued about. No home, no ring, no children. Just the road and her fiddle. As much as she loved playing music, the road was an empty life.

"I'm not here about your mother's engagement party," Ashley's said.

"Oh?"

Ashley gestured toward the jostling board on Granny's porch. "I haven't jostled in years. May I?"

"Of course."

Ashley sat down on the long wooden bench beside Ella's rocking chair. The jostling board was ten feet long, made of Carolina yellow pine, and was designed to bounce when you sat on it. Ashley put it to use, bouncing on it for a few moments as a tiny giggle left her lips.

The idea of Ashley Scott giggling kind of blew Ella's mind. But then the jostling board had a way of transporting people back to their childhood. Ella had grown up in Indiana and had visited her grandmother infrequently. But she'd almost lived on the jostling board as an eight-year-old. And the board was one of many reasons she held Magnolia Harbor deep in her heart.

Granny's wonderful old house was like the jostling board. Letting them go was going to be hard.

"Is your grandmother taking her jostling board to the condo?" Ashley asked.

"I don't know. I don't think her new lanai is big enough."

"Well, if she's not, I might be interested in buying it. When I was a kid, my grandmother took me to visit Patsy Bauman one time. She has one of these on her porch, and I spent the whole afternoon bouncing while Grandmother and Patsy were back in the kitchen drinking sweet tea and gossiping."

Ashley closed her eyes as if she were savoring the moment. "I didn't get to visit here often as a child," she said after a long silence. "Dad was in the army, and we moved around all the time."

"I was the same way," Ella said. "Mom and I came to visit for Thanksgiving and sometimes in the summer for a couple of weeks."

"I could jostle all day, but I came on a more important errand." Ashley stood up and moved to the second rocking chair. "I wanted to talk to you about a job."

"What?" Ella stopped rocking.

"I'm sure you know how the Piece Makers gossip. Your grandmother is not really one of the worst offenders, but it was only a matter of time before we heard about your situation. And I think I've got a solution."

Her situation? Damn. Was all of Magnolia Harbor pitying her because of her precarious living situation? "What kind of solution?" she asked cautiously.

"I'm in need of an assistant. Someone to help with the breakfast service in the morning, and also take care of stocking the kitchen, handling reservations, and doing webpage updates. My helper, Judy, just moved away, and I'm desperate. I've interviewed a few people, but I haven't found the right person yet, and in the meantime, I've got a few part-time high school kids helping out, but the kids are not always dependable."

"Okay. But, um, I don't have a lot of experience. Except, you know, playing fiddle in a country band."

Ashley nodded. "I know. But this is entry level. And the best part is that I have a room at the inn that you can have rent-free."

Ella got the picture. Granny's friends had joined together to help her out. Was it charity? Not quite, but maybe.

Ella wanted nothing more than to take charge of her own life, but refusing this offer would be supremely stupid, and maybe even ungrateful. Ashley had a job and a room, which were the two things Ella needed most in order to start rebuilding her life.

Emotion hit her like a rogue wave. The lump that had been sitting in her throat all morning suddenly dissolved into tears that flooded her eyes and trickled down her cheeks. "Oh my goodness," she said on a puff of air. "Thank you. Yes, I'll take the job."

She wiped the tears away just as Granny came through the front door and said, "Oh, thank the Lord. I was afraid you'd turn out to be stubborn and proud like your momma." Then Granny turned toward the innkeeper. "Ashley, if you want to make me an offer on the jostling board, it's definitely for sale."

* * *

Dylan knocked on the exam room door and walked in when Mrs. Whittle gave him the all clear. His patient was in her midforties with sharp features and prominent cheekbones. She was painfully thin, as if she might be suffering from a wasting disease.

Mrs. Whittle was a teacher at the elementary school, so he'd met her a time or two around town, but this was his first time treating her as a patient. She'd been in his father's care for the last few years, but before that, according to her file, she'd been hither and yon, consulting one expert after another, none of whom could find anything wrong with her.

"Hello, Mrs. Whittle," he said in his best bedside voice. "What seems to be the problem today?"

"Where's Doctor Jim?" she asked, nervously gazing at the door and then back toward Dylan.

She was the third or fourth patient so far who hadn't been happy to find themselves shifted into his care. Dad's patients loved him, and with good reason. Dad was so lovable.

Him, not so much.

He was determined to earn their trust. But Ginny Whittle was going to be a hard one, precisely because she'd been on a medical odyssey, searching for relief and never finding it. He sized her up and jettisoned the notion that her symptoms were somatic. She had lost weight since her last visit, and that wasn't in her head.

He continued to make eye contact. "I know it's stressful to be shifted off to the new guy in town, but my dad is cutting back on his hours because he's getting married. So he asked me to take over your case."

"How old are you?"

People asked him this question all the time, even though he was thirty-one and had graduated from med school with honors. He'd given some thought to growing a beard, but people didn't like bearded doctors. And they certainly didn't like doctors who showed their annoyance. Med school had insisted on hours of doctor-patient training, so he'd mastered the art of the impassive stare even though he was weary of having his competency endlessly questioned.

"I'm old enough to be board certified," he replied. It wasn't the funny comeback Dad might have used to defuse the situation, but Dylan sucked at that sort of thing.

Mrs. Whittle sniffed and crossed her arms over her chest. "I see you didn't get your father's charm."

"What can I do for you today?" he asked again.

She leaned back in the chair and begrudgingly described symptoms that might have been a urinary tract infection or possible signs of diabetes. She complained of thirst and also of frequent trips to the restroom.

He glanced down at her paper records, irritated that Dad had yet to digitize his practice. Maybe now was the time. If Dad was going off with Brenda for a month, Dylan could install a new data system for the practice. Ginny Whittle's file was a mess, filled with pages and pages of symptoms and tests. They'd done a blood sugar test within the last six months. It had come back normal, so the thirst was probably not diabetes.

But what else could it be? He was stumped.

He chatted with her for a few more minutes, maintaining eye contact and using language that wasn't filled with medical jargon. At every turn, Ginny Whittle questioned his wisdom and the competency of every doctor she'd seen in the last few years. She was angry and unpleasant, but then again, his intuition said that she had a right to be.

"I'm going to do my best to figure out what's going on."

Her shoulders slumped as he explained the tests he was going to order for her. He decided that he would move heaven and earth to find a diagnosis for her. But telling her that wouldn't win her over.

Words were cheap. Mrs. Whittle needed action.

He didn't blame her for leaving the office in a grumpy mood. She'd probably tell all her friends that young Doc Killough wasn't nearly as good as his old man. But it didn't matter. He was on her side.

Toward the end of the day, as he was sitting in his office rereading Mrs. Whittle's voluminous case file, Dad strolled into his office and took a seat. "So I heard you ordered a bunch of tests for Ginny Whittle."

Great. Dad wanted him to take over the case, but here he was second-guessing him. "You think I shouldn't have?"

"It's a pretty big expense for her."

Dad was right. But dammit, if Dad wanted him to take over this case, he needed to let him take over.

"She wasn't happy to see me instead of you."

"So you ordered these tests to get on her good side?"

So much for that lame excuse. Maybe he should challenge his father's assumptions about Mrs. Whittle. "Something is wrong with her," Dylan said, capturing his father's gaze. In the year Dylan had been sharing a practice with his father, Dad had never once called a diagnosis into question.

"She's had all these tests before."

"I know, but—"

"Well, let's hope her insurance company doesn't balk."

"Yeah, let's hope," he said, covering his annoyance. Dad had this way of knowing all the details about his patients, even their financial situation. Dylan didn't understand how or why Dad let himself get so involved with the people he cared for. Getting involved could be emotionally draining.

And in this case, maybe Dad had missed the truth because of his emotional involvement. But Dylan didn't want to pick a fight, so he let it slide and changed the topic of conversation.

"By the way," he said, "I had dinner with Ella last night."

"Oh, good. So you apologized?"

"Yeah. We're all good. We're working together on the party, which I know will make you happy. Speaking of which, I need an estimate of the number of guests you plan to invite. We were thinking about scheduling it at the yacht club."

"The yacht club would be perfect. You think they still have space on such short notice?"

"I checked. There are a couple of evenings available. We aren't going to get a Friday or Saturday."

"That's fine. Let me talk to Brenda, and I'll get you the list tomorrow."

"So you don't think Brenda will have a problem with the yacht club?" he asked.

Dad shook his head. "No. Why?"

"No reason. Just trying to make your bride-to-be happy."

Dad leaned forward a little. "I'm sure she'll be very happy when I let her know that you and Ella are working together on this. That's really the most important thing, you know. And I'm sure that one day the two of you will look back fondly on this time. You're lucky to be getting a sister like her."

"I never wanted a sister." Dylan blurted the words without thinking. Damn.

Dad laughed out loud, as if he'd misread Dylan's words. "No, I guess you never did want a sister. I recall you asking Santa for a little brother before you figured out that I had to find a wife for that to happen."

Dylan's face heated. Dammit, Dad needed to stop reminding him of the stupid stuff he'd done as a kid. How was anyone, least of all the practice's patients, going to take him seriously if Dad kept telling embarrassing stories about him?

* * *

On Wednesday afternoon, Ella moved out of Granny's house and into a third-floor room at Howland House. She might have stayed at her grandmother's place, but the real estate agent insisted that it would be easier to sell the house if she wasn't living there.

And Granny needed to sell the house.

Besides, staying there made her sad. And moving from place to place was something Ella had been doing for years. She'd mastered the art of traveling light.

This new room was in a beautiful historic house and looked like something from out of the pages of *Southern Living*. Her own space had a shiplap feature wall, flowered wallpaper, and wide-plank pine floors. The antique iron bedstead wore a hand-made quilt in shades of blue that picked up the forget-me-not motif of the wallpaper. And even though it was an attic bed-room, with oddly angled walls, the dormer window let in plenty of daylight and provided an elevated view of Magnolia Harbor's central business district.

She put down her fiddle case and started to unpack, hanging her clothes in a small closet and folding T-shirts and undies into the old oak bureau with a silvered glass mirror.

Tomorrow she'd have to get up with the chickens to start her new job. But having a job was a good thing, even if the old ladies in Granny's club had arranged it for her. When she got settled, she would run down to the yarn shop where Mom worked to discuss the engagement party guest list with her mother.

"Hey."

She turned with a jump to find Ashley Scott's son leaning in the bedroom doorway. The little brat had opened the door with-out knocking. Ella judged him to be about ten or eleven, and she made a mental note to make sure her door was locked from this time forward. Ashley had already warned her that Jackie had boundary issues, and the kid's room was evidently just down the hallway. Howland House's third floor was the private space where Ashley lived as well.

"Hi," she said on a puff of air, choosing not to bawl out her boss's only child. "I'm Ella, and I'm going to be staying up here for a while."

He nodded and glanced at her violin case. "You play the fiddle?"

"I do."

"The captain says he likes jigs, reels, and hornpipes. You know any of those?"

"The captain?"

The kid rolled his eyes. "Come on, don't tell me you haven't heard about the captain."

"I'm not from around here."

"Captain William Teal. He was a fierce pirate who went down with his ship during the hurricane of 1713."

"Okay," she said. Magnolia Harbor's main business district was awash in touristy gift shops that sold pirate crap. Black Beard, among others, had sailed the waters of Moonlight Bay, back in the day. But this was the first time someone had professed personal knowledge of a pirate's musical preferences.

She stared the kid down. "If the captain went down with his ship, how do you know he likes jigs and reels?"

The kid pushed away from the doorframe and sat on her bed. He was a pest. "Because he haunts the inn," he said in a thoroughly matter-of-fact tone.

"Really?"

"Yup. And I'm the only one who can see him."

Wiseass. The kid was trying to scare her or something. Not that she believed in ghosts or was about to play this game. "I'm not afraid of ghosts, so don't try that on me. And yes, I do know how to play jigs and reels. And please get off the bed."

The kid stood up. "Oh, sorry," he said. Then he continued in a rush. "You should play for the captain."

"I wouldn't want to disturb anyone." Especially her new employer, who would probably take a dim eye to her encouraging her son's rude behavior.

Unless, of course, Ashley was using the pirate as a marketing ploy. The Travel Channel was awash in ridiculous shows about haunted inns. Cody used to watch that mind-numbing crap all the time. Now that she thought about it, haunted inns could probably charge a premium just because gullible people were willing to pay extra for ghosts.

"The captain says that his first mate used to have a whistle he played all the time. His first mate was Henri St. Pierre," the kid said like a historic tour guide to the supernatural.

"St. Pierre, like the minister's name?"

The kid nodded. "Henri St. Pierre was the only survivor of the shipwreck. All the St. Pierres are related to him."

"Really," she said in a neutral tone. The kid certainly knew his local history. She turned back to the bureau, putting the last of her meager wardrobe into the top drawer.

"The captain says his crew used to get drunk, and Henri would play his whistle, and they would all dance. Pirates drank a lot of rum."

"I guess they did."

"But anyway, the captain says he hasn't heard a reel or a jig in hundreds of years, and he misses it."

Something in the boy's tone wormed its way past Ella's skepticism. She closed the bureau drawer and turned to face the kid. Was he teasing her? Goading her? Or did he just want some attention? "If you want me to play my fiddle, all you have to do is ask."

The kid beamed a big smile. "That's great. But, um, could you play the fiddle out by the tree?"

"The tree?"

"Out in the yard. It's where the captain hangs out. I'm not sure he could hear you if you played up here."

"Right now?"

The kid's eyes got bright with excitement. "Yes, please."

There was something so earnest in the way the boy said "please." He was good at this game, but she wasn't about to play games today. She had things to do.

She checked her watch. "I'm sorry, I can't right now. But I'll check with your mom when I get back from my errands to see if she'd like me to do some music in the evenings."

The boy's shoulders sagged a little. "Great." He seemed oddly crestfallen.

"So you don't think your mother would be interested in live music for the guests?"

He shook his head. "The minute she finds out the captain likes jigs and reels, she'll say no." He turned away, leaving Ella alone and adrift, as if she'd misread the kid from the beginning.

Did he believe in ghosts? He seemed a little old for that somehow. Either way, she wasn't about to screw up her new situation. She needed this job. She needed the structure of work to figure out what she wanted to do with the rest of her life.

Besides, she wasn't about to embarrass her grandmother, who had called in help from her friends. So no music until Ashley signed off on the idea. And in the meantime, she had an engagement party to plan.

Twenty minutes later, she stepped inside the cozy confines of A Stitch in Time. The place had a homey vibe, with comfy chairs in the front, where an endless stream of knitters and crocheters visited on a daily basis. The store was filled with color, from the bright cubbies of yarn to the bolts of quilting cotton. Underfoot, the wide-plank pine floors had seen so much traffic they were worn down to softness.

Mom was at the checkout helping a silver-haired lady purchase a bunch of self-striping sock yarn. It struck Ella as odd that anyone would spend time knitting socks when they could buy them at the Value Mart for a fraction of the price. Somehow she'd never been bitten by the knitting bug, but she could remember the endless parade of hand-knit sweaters Mom had made for her over the years. When she'd been little, Mom's sweaters had been special, but then, when she'd gotten into middle school, the kids had teased her about them. After that, Mom's sweaters got pushed to the back of the bureau drawer.

Mom hadn't knitted her anything in years. Why had she run

away from that? She had no answer except supreme stupidity. Both of them were responsible for the relationship running off the rails, which was why Ella was determined to make Mom's party the best ever.

"Hey," Mom said when the customer left the counter. "I thought you were moving into Howland House today."

"I didn't have much to move." She leaned into the counter. "I'm all settled, and I've met Ashley's son, who is a piece of work. He gave me a whole spiel about how the inn is haunted and the ghost wants to hear jigs and reels so he can remember the days when he used to sail the ocean, drink rum, get drunk, and dance like a fool."

Mom snorted a laugh. "That sounds like Jackie Scott, all right. Granny says Ashley is determined not to advertise that the inn is haunted."

"You think it is?"

"Probably not."

"Well, that's good to know. Because I was thinking about approaching Ashley about maybe playing some music for the guests."

"I would avoid any mention of Jackie's ghost."

"Thanks. I'll keep that in mind."

"So what brings you down here?" Mom asked.

"I need to get your invite list for the engagement party. Dylan and I are trying to put together a master list."

"So you're working together, then?" Mom's eyebrows rose a little, which meant she was either surprised or pleased. It was a good sign.

"Yeah, we're working together...sort of."

Mom's eyebrows lowered a tiny bit. "Sort of?"

"He pretty much wants to be in charge. So I'm sort of letting him for now."

"Oh?" Mom sounded wary.

"There's a problem with that?"

"Well, I guess not." Mom didn't sound sure.

What the hell? Did Mom want her to run the show? She could have sworn Mom wanted her to be nice and make friends with Dylan. Sometimes Mom was hard to figure out.

"Mom, he has some good ideas about the party and—"

"What ideas?" Mom pressed a hand to her throat as if she was dealing with a sudden attack of heartburn, which was apt now that Ella thought about it. Dylan could give anyone heartburn.

"He thinks we should do the party at the yacht club. He had some good arguments. I mean, it's a nice place, and it would be easy to arrange catering. So...easy-peasy."

Mom's eyebrows lowered into the frown-of-death, which could kill anyone's optimism at twenty paces.

"You don't like the idea of the yacht club, do you?"

Mom's mouth twitched. "Not really. I'm not a yacht club kind of person. They're so stuffy up there."

She'd been afraid of this. "Okay, I'll let him know that you've nixed the idea. I tried to tell him that you probably wouldn't be wild about having the party there, but he's..." She stopped speaking. Maybe she shouldn't call him a bully in front of Mom.

"Oh, well, don't tell him that. I mean, let me talk to Jim first and make sure he isn't committed to the yacht club."

Ella wanted to let go of a deep, long, primal scream and grab her mother by the shoulders and give her a shake.

"Mom, you should just tell everyone what you want, and we'll make it happen."

Mom shook her head. "It's not that easy. I don't want Jim or Dylan to feel left out or whatever. I just want everyone to be happy."

Right. Somehow Ella didn't think that was possible. And then Mom wouldn't get what she wanted, and she'd let the world know all about her dissatisfaction. Ella could see the disaster looming ahead on the horizon.

Wait one sec... What if Dylan was pushing the yacht club *because* he knew Mom would hate the idea? Oh, the insufferable jerk. He'd *played* her. And she'd let him do it. That was not going to happen again if she had anything to say about it.

"Mom, it's your engagement party too," she said.

"I know, but I want Jim to be happy. So if Dylan thinks the yacht club is the right choice, we should maybe go along with that idea."

Great. Now what?

Chapter Seven

A deluge hit the island on Thursday morning, so Dylan decided to take the Honda instead of the Harley. He pulled the car into the Howland House parking lot at about seven o'clock for his regular monthly breakfast meeting with Rev. Micah St. Pierre.

They'd been having breakfast together since last November, ever since Dylan had assumed the role of secretary on the Jonquil Island Museum Foundation's board of directors. Micah was its president, taking the position because his sister-in-law, Jenna, who had endowed the project, had nagged him until he'd given in. Jenna's husband, Jude, had twisted Dylan's arm and he'd also reluctantly agreed. But Dylan had never expected to become the board's recording secretary. That had happened when Simon Paredes suffered a stroke last November, and Dylan had been goaded into taking the position.

Today's breakfast provided a face-to-face opportunity to review and tweak the agenda for this week's meeting before Dylan sent it out to the rest of the board. Since Micah lived across Lilac Lane from the inn and had a standing invitation to take his breakfast at Ashley Scott's table, these breakfast get-togethers were always at Howland House.

Micah and Dylan took their usual places at the end of the inn's communal dining table, which was almost full this morning because of the influx of spring break tourists. Ashley's guests weren't college kids, of course. They were young marrieds and a family with school-age kids. But all of them seemed unusually grumpy this morning.

"Where the hell is my coffee?" one Izod-shirt-wearing customer muttered as he twisted in his chair to glare at the kitchen door.

"Uh-oh," Micah said, leaning in. "Things have been a bit chaotic since Judy left for Colorado. Maybe I should—" He started to get up, but the door into the kitchen swung outward, and Ella McMillan appeared, her auburn hair more awry than usual. She wore a blue striped apron over her jeans and T-shirt, and judging by the scowls aimed in her direction, the guests were not pleased with her.

"Sorry," she said on a huff of air. "I'm new, and I have yet to reach an understanding with the industrial coffee maker." She leaned awkwardly and placed plates of eggs and bacon in front of the most impatient guest and his wife. And then started refilling coffee cups.

The coffee ran out before she reached Micah and Dylan. "Be right back," she said in a tense voice and raced into the kitchen.

Dylan turned toward Micah. "Ashley hired Ella? Really? That was a mistake."

Micah turned a pair of dark brown eyes on him, and Dylan had to stifle the urge to slink under the table in shame. Hadn't he been irritated with Dad's patients who had judged him harshly over the last few days? He'd just done the same thing to Ella. He was a better man than that. Maybe he didn't want Dad to marry Brenda, but that didn't mean he had to take his frustrations out on Ella.

"Sorry. That was unkind," he said to the minister, who nodded.

"She just started today, and I'm sure she had issues with that coffee maker. I've had my own run-in with that machine."

"You've made coffee for Ashley?" Dylan asked.

"Last Friday, when the temp Ashley hired failed to show up."

"You're a good man, Micah."

Just then, Ella came flying out of the kitchen again, her tray heaped with plates of food and glasses of orange juice. She rushed to the man sitting beside Micah and placed his plate in front of him. Then she turned and headed the other direction, to where the man's wife was sitting. But as Ella came flying around the end of the table, she must have lost her balance or stubbed her toe on something. Whatever the reason, she tripped, and her tray went flying off like an errant Frisbee.

It connected with the side of Dylan's head, where its forward momentum came to an abrupt halt, dumping four plates of eggs and bacon and two glasses of OJ onto Dylan's shoulders.

Dylan was momentarily stunned by the blow to his head and the twin sensations of hot eggs and bacon and icy-cold OJ inching down his back and landing in his lap. He reached up to touch the spot where the tray had connected with his head. A bump was already forming.

Damn. That hurt.

He blinked a couple of times, trying to process what had just happened, and then he heard Ella's cries of pain.

"Ow, ow, ow," she said from the vicinity of the Persian rug, where she'd apparently done a face-plant. Dylan would have normally gotten up to render aid, but time seemed to be moving in slow motion for him.

Not so for the minister, who got up and helped Ella up from the floor.

"Are you okay?" Micah asked.

She studied her palms. "Uh, um, yeah. I think just rug burns."

"You didn't break a wrist?"

"Uh..." She looked up, her gaze landing on Dylan like another blow. "Oh my god, Doctor D. I'm so sorry. Are you okay?"

She grabbed a napkin and started ineffectually beating his soaked shoulders, but when she leaned over and started scooping eggs and bacon out of his lap, he finally pulled himself together and grabbed her hands.

"Stop," he said. "I think you've done quite enough for one morning."

* * *

Dylan's hands were warm and rougher than Ella expected. They paralyzed her for a moment as she shifted her gaze to his face. A strange hum sounded in the back of her head, but it soon became an urgent siren when a bright gush of blood welled up from a cut on Dylan's temple and trickled down his face.

"Oh my god, you're bleeding." Ella's heart went into a full gallop as she let go of his hands and grabbed another napkin from the table. As she pressed it to Doctor D's temple, panic began to swell inside her.

Oh, crap, crap, crap. She was a disaster. She couldn't make coffee. She couldn't deliver food. And now look what she'd done. She'd given her future stepbrother a concussion and a head wound that probably needed stitches.

She glanced at his eyes, which was what you were supposed to do when checking for concussions, right? They seemed normal...beautiful even. Dark blue with little amber flecks in them.

She pressed the napkin tighter against his head. Doctor D's beautiful eyes turned up toward her. Woah. Was it weird to find them beautiful? Or worse yet, icky?

"Someone should call a doctor," one of the guests said in a voice that carried a world of censure.

"I *am* a doctor." Dylan pressed the napkin even tighter against his head, his hand covering hers. "Harder," he said, applying pressure that reignited the weird awareness that had seized her a second ago.

"Right, I knew that."

"Scalp wounds bleed a lot. It's scary but not serious." Kindness rang in his voice.

"I'm so sorry. I'm such a klutz."

"It's okay. Accidents happen."

Who was this man? Had the knock to his head unleashed a kinder, gentler Dylan, or had he morphed into Doctor Dazed?

"Here, I've got it," he said a moment later, taking control of the napkin.

Oh good, he was back in control. Maybe she hadn't concussed him, but he was certainly a mess. Globules of egg had adhered to his suit jacket and pants, and blood had dripped down his face to stain the pristine collar of his shirt and yellow polka-dotted bow tie.

She took a step back, a remorseful lump forming in her throat and tears filling her eyes. She'd really screwed things up. Mom was going to kill her.

But then Ashley materialized beside her like a guardian angel or something. "It's okay, Ella. You go into the kitchen, wash your hands, and make another pot of coffee, okay?"

"I'm so sorry. I—"

"It's fine. Everyone spills something sooner or later," Ashley said.

Ella turned to look into the innkeeper's big brown eyes and found only compassion and forgiveness.

"Go. Calm down. Make some coffee and then bring the bucket of cleaning stuff from the closet."

She turned, giving Dylan, who was being tended by the minister and one of the guests, one last look. Maybe he wouldn't be scarred for life, which was a good thing, because Mom wouldn't be happy if she'd damaged Jim's son.

She hyperventilated as she started another pot of coffee, barely keeping her tears in check. Then she found the bucket in the closet, which contained some foam carpet spray, a sponge, a roll of paper towels, and everything needed for cleaning up a mess.

Spills in the dining room must be an everyday occurrence.

When she returned to the dining room, Dylan was gone, and Ashley was chatting with the few remaining guests. A lot of them had left.

Oh no. This was so bad. Ella's mistakes this morning had probably earned Howland House a few bad Yelp reviews, or maybe even lost Ashley some repeat customers. Granny would be so disappointed in her, especially since her grandmother had used her connections with the Piece Makers to help Ella find this job.

The thought goaded her into action. Maybe she was a disaster with the stupid coffee maker, but she knew how to clean up messes. Cody had been a champion mess-maker, and she'd been the only one in the band who'd followed behind him, tidying up.

She rounded the table and got down on her knees in order to pick up the egg and bacon scattered all over the floor. She scooped up the bits and pieces, putting them in a garbage bag she'd brought from the kitchen. Down under the table on her knees, her humiliation and embarrassment redoubled. She was fighting tears when Jackie arrived on the scene, poking his head under the table with a metal-mouth grin. "You screwed up big-time, didn't you?" he said.

"Yeah, I did. I'm so sorry." Her voice wobbled.

The kid cocked his head and paused as if he'd expected some other response from her. "Hey, it's okay. You should have seen the time Mom tripped and dropped the Piece Maker's cake all over the kitchen floor. She had to feed the ladies store-bought doughnuts. She's never heard the end of that one."

He slipped under the table and started picking up clumps of egg and bacon that were beyond her reach. "Please don't cry."

She stared at the kid. "I'm not crying."

"Okay, that's good. The guests don't want to see you crying. The guests just want breakfast."

She blinked at his wisdom. Obviously, he'd been living at the inn for much of his young life. She might do well to listen to him.

She scooped up the last bit of egg and tossed it in the garbage, but the carpet still smelled of orange juice, so she reached for the can of carpet cleaner and gave the area a big spray, rubbed it in with the sponge, then blotted up the wet spot until the paper towels ran out.

"I think that's good enough," Ashley said when the last towel went into the garbage bag. "And thank you for helping, Jackie."

"No problem. You want me to get coffee for the guests?" Jackie asked.

"If you would, please."

The kid scampered away to the kitchen, and Ella changed her opinion of him. He wasn't a wiseass at all. He was merely a little different.

"Come on," Ashley said, "the biscuits are warm in the oven, and we still have a few hungry guests to feed. Next time don't put so many plates on the tray. And don't run."

"Right."

She went back to work, inwardly cringing every time she thought about that horrible moment when she lost control of the tray and knew she was going down. She could see that stupid tray in her mind's eye, sliding out of her control and heading right at Dylan's head.

She would never live that moment down. For the rest of her life, when Mom and Jim and the blended family got together for any occasion or holiday, Dylan would inevitably tell the story of the morning when his soon-to-be stepsister tried to take his head off with a breakfast tray.

* * *

The scalp wound was still oozing as Dylan drove himself back home to change his clothes. He hoped to hell he didn't need any sutures for the damn thing. Scalp wounds were notorious for bleeding like crazy.

He was also a little concerned about the bump forming right above the gash, where one of the plates had nailed him. Thank goodness the china hadn't broken. Otherwise he might have been injured more seriously, and Ella might be apologizing for the rest of her life.

Why was she so apologetic for what had been an accident? She must have said "I'm sorry" a dozen times. On the other hand, her concern for him had been touching.

No, maybe a better word might be stunning. The unshed tears in her anime eyes had undone him, even though she was different from the women he usually found attractive. Most of the women in his life had been well-put-together Southern girls who never stepped out of the house unless their hair and makeup were perfect. Lauren had been like that.

Born in Charleston and educated at Wellesley and the University of Virginia Law School, Lauren was on her way to becoming a high-powered corporate attorney. And they could have become a power couple if Dylan had remained in Charleston and joined a practice there.

But when he'd told Lauren his plans to return home and practice medicine in an underserved community, she'd dumped him. That had been a year ago. He'd been living like a monk since then, probably because the single women at the club were a lot like Lauren.

Wait a sec. Was he comparing Ella to Lauren? That was just wrong. The blow to his head must have been worse than he thought. He was not allowed to notice Ella. Ever.

He pulled his car into the garage only to discover Dad's Jeep parked in what had been its usual space for the last year. What the heck? Why wasn't Dad at the office?

He climbed out of the car and hurried through the back door, finding Dad in the kitchen, surrounded by packing boxes. The smart speaker blared some classical piano piece, and the music beat at his head like the hammers on a Steinway. He came to a sudden, jarring stop as Dad tucked Mom's favorite casserole dish into one of the boxes.

"What the hell?" he said aloud, screaming above the music. A sudden, ominous vertigo had him reaching for the wall to steady himself.

Dad turned down the music and gave him an assessing stare.

"What are you doing with that casserole dish? That's Mom's," Dylan said.

"What happened to you? You're bleeding all over the place." Dad took a step forward.

"And why aren't you seeing patients?" Dylan asked, his tone

accusatory. What the hell? Was Dad planning to move all of Mom's stuff to *Brenda's* house?

"I took the day off," Dad said, taking another step forward, his voice calm as ever. "Brenda and I have decided to move in together now that Ella has moved out of Cloud Nine. I came over here to pack up a few things. But you don't have to worry. I'm not cleaning out the kitchen. We've got more pots and pans than either of us have used in years."

"But that's Mom's casserole."

Dad frowned. "It's not Mom's. It's...well, whatever. If you want it, I'll leave it here for you," he said, then closed the distance between them. "Let me see that cut. What happened?"

"I was having breakfast at Howland House with Reverend St. Pierre to talk about the museum foundation, and I got nailed by a plate of eggs."

Dad gently took one of his arms. "Let's get you into the living room and take a look. You sit. I'm going to go get my bag from the car."

Dylan's anger ebbed away, and he allowed Dad guide to him into the living room and down into the comfortable wing chair. He closed his eyes, rested his head on the high back, and waited. Dad returned a moment later, carrying an old-fashioned medical bag. His father was a total throwback who had been known to make the occasional house call even though it made no economic sense. But that was Dad. That was why Dylan loved him so fiercely.

He relaxed and let his dad take care of him.

"That's going to need a couple of sutures," Dad said. "And you'll probably have a scar."

A wave of nausea slammed into Dylan. The room took a wild spin, and he had to focus on the designer wall clock to keep things steady. "I think I may have a concussion. I'm having vertigo."

Dad shined a light in his eyes to check his pupil reaction. "Maybe a mild one. I need to take you to the office in order to stitch you up. Hang tight for a moment."

Dad left and then returned in a blur with a glass of water and a couple of acetaminophen. "Here, take these for the headache."

Dylan followed orders like a little boy, and then his father drove him to the clinic, using the Honda instead of the Jeep because the Honda had a smoother ride. His father stitched up the wound, but after an hour or so with Dylan's headache no better, Dad called the imaging center in Georgetown and scheduled a CT scan for later that afternoon.

The scan found no skull fracture or bleeding into the brain. But he had an edema and maybe a slight concussion. The prognosis was good though. He would live.

Chapter Eight ──────────────

Ella was bone tired when she finally made it up the stairs to her small room under the eaves. In addition to the tray disaster, she'd been through a difficult training session trying to grasp the inn's reservation system and webpage. She wasn't a Luddite exactly, but she'd never been great with technology.

This might be an entry-level job, but that didn't make it an easy one.

She just wanted to go back to sleep even if the clock said noon. She wasn't cut out for getting up so early. For most of her life, she'd stayed up late performing and slept into the afternoon. This early riser thing was for the birds. Literally.

She collapsed onto the bed and buried her head under the pillow. She had almost drifted off when her phone jolted her back to consciousness. Groggy and disoriented, she pressed the connect button before checking the caller ID.

"Finally." Cody's voice came over the line. "What the hell, Ella? You walk out and then you refuse to talk to me. What kind of way is that to act?"

She should disconnect the line, but for some pathetic reason, the sound of Cody's voice trickled into the deep well of loneliness at her core. He'd never really filled that well, but he could give her a taste of something good from time to time.

His need was seductive. Who else needed her the way Cody did?

"Are you not going to talk to me?" Cody asked.

She thought about his question for a moment, and then, finding courage from some inner source, she said, "I'll talk to you. But I already know what you want. You want me to come back because you can't find another decent fiddler."

"Look, babe, that's not it, and you know it. I love you."

Wow. Like she hadn't heard this before. Cody loved her because she could play the fiddle. That was the beginning and end of his love. But hearing the words out loud still left an unmistakable warm, fuzzy feeling in their wake.

"Please come back," he said in a wheedling tone that made the fuzzy feeling evaporate.

"No."

"C'mon, babe. I'm sorry for whatever it is I did that got you riled up."

What? Did he think she would accept an apology like that? The list of his shortcomings was so long it would take days to enumerate them all.

"I mean it," Cody said. "I want you to come back home."

So this was just about what *he* wanted. What else was new? She took a deep breath and spoke her mind. "Where is home exactly, Cody? An RV filled with a bunch of band boys always on the road?"

"I guess I could work on the house in El Paso."

He guessed? Boy, she had heard these promises before.

"I'm sorry. I've got a job here and—"

"You got a gig?" For the first time, he sounded worried.

"Not a gig. A job."

"Doing what? *Waitressing?*" He said the word with such scorn that hot anger boiled through her.

"I *am* a waitress." Her voice sounded hard and brittle.

"No, you're not. You're a musician. The same as me. Come on, we need you in the band. It's not the same without you."

He could go screw himself.

"Stop calling me, Cody," she said, then pressed the disconnect button. As she took a couple of deep breaths, her anger ebbed away, leaving a certain clarity in its wake. Cody was right. She *could* be more than a waitress. But that didn't mean she had to go back to being a fiddler for an unremarkable warm-up band. Once, a long time ago, she'd been ambitious. What had happened to that Ella?

She didn't know much about her future, except that music needed to be a part of it. And she'd been neglecting her fiddle recently. She needed to practice.

So she grabbed her fiddle case and headed down the stairs and out the back door. Howland House had a long, broad lawn with Adirondack chairs scattered around, a fire pit, and a small swimming beach with access to Moonlight Bay. At one end of this expanse stood an ancient live oak that had to be three hundred years old at least. Its trunk was massive, and its low-hanging branches made it easy to climb.

Ella had no intention of climbing. But she settled herself on a low branch, took out her fiddle, rosined up her bow, and started playing the "Sailors Hornpipe," in order to appease any restless nautical spirits. She didn't truly believe in Jackie's ghost, but she had promised the boy to come out here and play a few jigs. And after his help this morning, it seemed like the right thing to do.

Besides, playing the fiddle always altered her mental state. The music was her drug of choice, and it never failed to adjust her attitude.

After performing the well-known sailor's dance, she moved on, playing one reel and jig after the other, most of them Irish. She'd loved playing these tunes from the time she'd first learned them as a young violinist in grade school. Jigs and reels were the student pieces that had helped her master the fiddle.

Mom had always regarded these pieces as trivial learning songs. From the time Ella could remember, Mom had pushed her toward classical music, always hoping that Ella would one day gain a place at one of the nation's premier music colleges and maybe become a concert master with a big-city orchestra.

But that had been Mom's dream.

Ella had rejected that dream by the time she turned fourteen. She could still remember the day she'd seen Martie Maguire play fiddle on the country music video channel. It made a huge impression on her to see a woman with chops like that. And Martie was beautiful too. She wanted to become Martie Maguire.

So while Mom was watching, she practiced her classical music, but on the sly, she played along with the country music station every minute she could spare.

By the time she was seventeen, she had learned a lot by listening and playing along with the likes of Maguire, Natalie MacMaster, and Alison Krauss. She'd also discovered Irish fiddlers like the incomparable Mairéad Ní Mhaonaigh.

The first time Cody ever heard her play, he'd told her she'd one day make it to the Grand Ole Opry. It hadn't been a promise, of course, although she'd taken it that way. She'd been so young and foolish.

Cody's praise was all it had taken to get her to run away from home. But that had changed last December when she'd started running *toward* home. Wherever that might be. Could she be a musician and support herself in Magnolia Harbor? She didn't know.

But maybe she needed to figure it out.

* * *

Ashley had been about to climb the stairs to the third floor when the sound of the fiddle reached her through the open window in the kitchen. The music floated in on the sea breeze, haunting in a way, as if coming from a great distance.

It sent a shiver up her spine at first and turned her around and brought her out the back door. She walked down the path past her rose garden and the cottage, all the way to the lawn on the north side of the property.

At first, she couldn't see the source of the music, and that sent more shivers cascading up and down her back. Was Jackie's ghost a fiddler? Then she spied Ella sitting on the lowest branch of the live oak, which, according to Jackie, was exactly where Captain Teal had been spending eternity. Or at least, the last few hundred years since his demise in 1713.

What was she doing up there? Serenading him?

Or maybe she was serenading the guests. A surprising number of them were out on the lawn this afternoon, lounging in the Adirondack chairs, drawn there by the beautiful weather that this morning's rain had ushered in, as well as Ella's music.

One of them, Mr. Levine, who'd been coming to Howland House for several years, hurried down the path to meet Ashley. He smiled. "Now I see why you hired that girl. The music is a really nice touch," he said with a big smile. "You should have her play in the library during your Saturday-afternoon teas."

Now, there was an idea. "You know, Mr. Levine, I think I might just do that," she said.

Mr. Levine nodded and headed off in the direction of one of the Adirondack chairs. Ashley continued across the lawn, approaching the live oak as Ella finished the haunting piece she'd been playing.

"What was that music?" Ashley asked.

"It's an old ballad called 'The Streets of Derry,'" Ella said, taking the fiddle down from her chin.

"It sounded so sad."

"All Irish ballads sound sad, but this one has a happy ending. The Irishman is saved from the hangman at the last moment when his lady love gets a pardon from the king." Ella's eyes sparkled with mirth. She sat up in the tree like a wood sprite, her red hair wind-tossed and her large eyes catching the blue of the spring sky.

"It was beautiful, but..."

"But you don't want me disturbing the guests? Sorry."

"Oh no, not at all." Ashley studied the young woman. "You should stop apologizing."

"What?"

"You apologize all the time. Did you know that?"

"I'm sor— Uh, what were you about to say?" A blush rose to the young woman's cheeks.

"I was going to ask why you're sitting up there in the tree. Did Jackie put you up to this?"

"Not exactly." Her blush deepened.

"No? I'll bet he asked you to play for the ghost."

Ella's shoulders stiffened a little. She seemed suddenly nervous. "I'm sorry. I don't believe in his ghost. But I needed to practice. So I came out here to play. I didn't want to annoy anyone in the house, you know, who might be trying to get an afternoon nap or something."

Did this young woman not realize how talented she was? Obviously not, if she was going out of her way to hide her light under a bushel basket. Ashley had to do something about Ella. And not because she was related to one of the Piece Makers, but because she deserved it.

"It's fine if you want to come out here and play. In fact, it's more than fine. The guests seem to like it. And now that we're talking about it, what would you charge to play during our Saturday-afternoon teas?"

"Uh, well..." Ella's eyes grew even bigger.

"What's the matter? I know you've booked gigs before."

"I have. I used to manage Urban Armadillo's tours, but—"

"Urban Armadillo?"

Ella rolled her eyes. "That was the name of the band I was in. Cody thought it was a fabulous name. And who knows? Maybe aficionados of outlaw music thought it was fab. I always thought it was a bit ridiculous, but I'm not from Texas."

"Outlaw music?"

"It's a branch of country music, which is about as far from what I was just playing as you can get and still be in the traditional music genre."

"Ah, I see. You've always been in a band and never a solo act."

Ella shook her head.

"Well, maybe now's the time to make a change. I'd like to book you for next Saturday's tea. How much do you charge?"

Ella looked off toward the bay for a moment before naming a fee that was far too low, but Ashley wasn't going to argue with her. Ella needed to figure that out for herself.

"I'll book you as a trial on Saturday from three-thirty to five," she said, without renegotiating the price. If it worked out, she would increase the fee by at least fifty percent.

"Thanks," Ella said. "I appreciate it, especially after the mess I made this morning."

Ashley shook her finger. "No more apologies. Now, I have another request. My babysitter just crapped out on me. Were you planning to be out this evening?"

"No."

"If you don't mind, could you keep an eye on Jackie?"

"No problem."

"Thanks."

Ashley turned, checking her watch. She was now running late. She scooted into the house, picked up her purse, and headed off to the parking lot where Rev. St. Pierre was waiting for her.

Since the Rev lived right across Lilac Lane from the inn, it seemed foolish for them to drive separately to this evening's museum board meeting. So they had arranged to carpool.

"Sorry I'm late," she said as she unlocked the car and slid into the driver's seat. The Rev had to fold himself into the tiny front seat of her old Toyota. He was maybe six foot three and filled up almost any space he entered. He had a presence about him, and her car's cabin was too small to contain it.

His body heat invaded her space, and the scent of his after-shave tickled her nose in a pleasant way. A minister shouldn't smell as good as he did.

"A penny for your thoughts?" Micah asked in his deep baritone. She jumped at the sound of his voice, surprised to discover that she'd managed to start the car and drive halfway down Harbor Drive to City Hall on autopilot. Where had her mind been?

Thinking about Rev. St. Pierre's aftershave, evidently.

She wasn't about to admit that, so she said the first thing that came to her mind. "I was thinking about what cake to make on Tuesday. I haven't made German chocolate cake in a while, but not everyone likes that one."

"Ashley, why do you keep baking cakes for the Piece Makers?"

She glanced at him and then back to the road as she turned into the parking lot near City Hall. "Because I like to bake."

"BS."

Hearing the preacher of Heavenly Rest Church use the initials for manure was a bit of a shock. But then he'd been a chaplain in the US Navy for many years, so he'd probably heard and said worse. He'd just called her on her little white lie, and she hated it.

It invaded her privacy or something. If she wanted to bake cakes for the Piece Makers, then it was none of his business. And the fact that she found his aftershave pleasant was certainly none of his business either.

She pulled into a parking spot and stopped the car with a noticeable jerk.

"Whoa," he said, grabbing the handle above the passenger door even though he was strapped in.

She clamped her jaw tight as she set the parking brake. "I like to bake," she said, hoping to end this conversation.

She killed the engine, but before she could open the door, he said, "I know you do. You bake every day for customers, but you've as much as told me that baking for the Piece Makers has become a chore."

He wasn't going to let this go, was he? She shifted in her seat and met his stare. He had deep, soulful brown eyes that demanded confession. Lying to Micah was impossible, but telling the truth wasn't an option either.

Besides, Micah was the last person on earth she wanted rummaging around in her feelings and thoughts. He might do serious damage if she let him in.

She squared her shoulders and pushed back. "I just told you that I like baking, so can we—"

"I know what you said. But that's not how you feel."

What the heck? Was he picking a fight? The Rev was the last person she wanted to argue with, but she wasn't about to let him run roughshod over her either. She needed to end this conversation.

She yanked the car door open and got out. He followed suit, and even with her battered Toyota as a barrier between them, Micah was able to unsettle her with his stare. What was wrong with him? What did he want from her? She was afraid to ask, and she wasn't going to volunteer anything.

"You can get the heck out of my feelings, okay?" She locked the car door and stalked off in the direction of City Hall. It didn't take him long to catch up to her. His legs were incredibly long.

"I'm not trying to pry, you know. Have you ever considered that you bake for the Piece Makers because you're trying to honor your grandmother's traditions? Maybe it's time to give up some of those traditions. Maybe it's time to recognize that knocking yourself out for the Piece Makers won't ever bring your grandmother back."

She stopped halfway up the stairs to City Hall's front doors and crossed her arms over her chest. "Micah, what in the Sam Hill are you driving at? Because right now you're ticking me off."

"Ashley, have you ever considered seeing a grief counselor?"

"What? I'm fine. I'm more than fine."

He nodded. "Yes. I can see that you're managing. And I'm sure that you've fooled a lot of people into thinking that you're okay. I mean, your business is thriving. But I remember how things were when I first moved back here. You were struggling to make ends meet. You were ready to give up. And then Jenna showed up and gave you a helping hand. You needed a helping hand then. Maybe you do with other things in your life.

"I'm not asking you to stop caring about Adam or your grandmother. But you can't keep them alive in this world anymore. And trying to do that is keeping you from finding joy in your life. I hate to see you so sad all the time."

Whoa, she thought they'd been talking about Grandmother and the Piece Makers. How the hell had they segued into a conversation about her late husband? Adam was the last thing she wanted to discuss with Micah, precisely because she sometimes noticed the scent of the minister's aftershave.

And that seemed disloyal. And scary. And inappropriate.

"I'm never going to get over Adam, Micah. That's just the way it is."

"Of course not. But you're hiding your heart behind your grief. You're letting the grief close doors that you could open."

"Just…leave me alone," she said, her voice cracking with emotion. Then she turned away from him, hurrying up the stairs so he wouldn't see her tears.

So what if she still loved her husband. So what if she still mourned what she'd lost. She'd lost everything: her best friend, her lover, the father of her child, and all the things they'd planned to do together. She'd lost her life. And she could never go back to the way things had been. She had to be happy with the way things were now. She didn't need anything else to make her life complete.

She was fine. She'd built a business. She had a place in this town. Of course she'd been carrying on Grandmother's traditions, baking cakes for the Piece Makers every week. She'd made a good life, even if she missed her old life with Adam. Micah had a hell of a lot of nerve suggesting that her life needed improvement.

What? Did he think she should go out looking for another husband?

Nothing irritated her more than people who thought she needed another husband to complete her life. Maybe those people were well meaning, but to Ashley just thinking about dating again required her to jettison the man she loved more than life itself. Adam would always be important. His loss was still like a burning hole in the middle of her chest. And you know what? She almost liked that pain. It reminded her of how much she'd loved Adam in life. If she hadn't loved him so fiercely, she wouldn't grieve his loss so deeply.

No. She didn't need a new husband, or even a boyfriend. Surely the minister understood that? Didn't he?

Chapter Nine————————————

Ella left Howland House directly after breakfast service on Saturday morning and walked all the way to Bayview Vistas, the new condos on Redbud Street. March was in full bloom this morning, the azaleas in Lavender Lane Park putting on a show of rich magenta and deep purple. It struck her how much she'd missed this verdant landscape all those years she'd called El Paso her home base.

Not that Cody had a real home in Texas. He'd inherited a run-down ranch house from his grandparents, but he'd never lifted one finger to keep the place up. Over the years, it had deteriorated, and half the time the boys in the band squatted on the land, living in a couple of run-down RVs out back.

The house in El Paso was like a metaphor for her life. It needed some serious renovation. And yet she felt a little better about herself this morning. She hadn't made any mistakes in the dining room this morning, and she was anticipating her gig this afternoon. She'd already made her set list, which consisted of a wide variety of genres, from pop and country to traditional and classic.

After Ashley's pep talk out by the live oak, she was also starting to think about the upcoming wedding season. Maybe she could score a few gigs at wedding ceremonies and receptions. Heck, maybe she could play for Mom and Jim's wedding, although that might be risky.

Mom always had something to say about her violin performances. Unfortunately, Mom had always been a better violinist than Ella, so her opinion counted more than anyone else's.

She was a little sweaty by the time she made it to Granny's new place, but then, she'd probably be grimy before too much longer. Her grandmother was moving into Bayview Vistas today. The movers had been out to the old house yesterday and moved whatever furniture Granny was planning to keep. The rest was going to be sold at a gigantic yard sale next Saturday. Today Granny needed help arranging the furniture and hanging pictures and unpacking boxes.

The new condo building was three stories high, with an antique brick facade broken by large windows and balconies with wrought-iron railings. Large palms and colorful flowers graced the walkways. Granny's apartment was on the second floor, so Ella took the stairs and turned left to the end of the hallway.

When she arrived, the door was propped open, and a couple of delivery men were angling a large refrigerator through the narrow portal.

"Hey, Granny," Ella hollered past the appliance dudes, "I'm here. Finally. It's a longer walk than I thought."

The men got the fridge through the door, and Ella followed them into Granny's open-concept kitchen, which had cabinets in a cherry finish and midtone granite countertops. It had state-of-the-art appliances, except for a refrigerator. Granny had evidently spared no expense on the new one being hauled through the door.

"Hey, sugar," Granny said, reaching out to give her a warm,

lavender-scented hug. Ella's grandmother seemed more happy than stressed over this move, which seemed strange to Ella because she couldn't imagine letting go of her beautiful old house to move into a cookie-cutter place like this.

"You're really okay with moving out of the old house?" Ella asked.

"Oh, honey, I am so glad to be rid of it. I should have moved out years ago. I don't know why I thought living in that house was the only way to keep memories of your grandfather alive." She shook her head and grabbed Ella by the arm. "Come on, you can help organize the bedroom until these guys are finished installing the fridge and the washer and dryer."

Granny pulled her through a generously sized living room with windows which provided a distant view of the bay that fell a bit short of a vista.

"The master bedroom's over here," Granny said, gesturing to the right. Ella stepped into the room, which already had one too many people in it.

Jim was up on a ladder hanging Bahama shutters. Mom was unpacking stuff into the bureau and had her back turned toward Ella, and Dylan wasn't doing anything, except sitting on the bed with a huge-ass bandage on the side of his head.

Oh, crap. She'd really injured him.

Instead of a button-down shirt and a bow tie, he wore a pair of faded jeans and an ancient Clemson University T-shirt that had a hole in the neck. He hadn't shaved in a couple of days either, suggesting that he hadn't been to work for a while. Or maybe he was just one of those guys with a heavy beard.

She froze like some nocturnal animal suddenly caught in a flash of light. He was altogether too handsome. Too male. And too focused on her right at the moment. She wanted to run, but she couldn't make her legs move.

She hadn't expected Dylan to help unpack her grandmother.

And really, now that she thought about it, having Jim here was a bit of a surprise too. Her extended family had always consisted of three women, and that had seemed compact enough to manage. But now her family numbered five people, one of whom she'd seriously injured with a breakfast tray.

Were they judging her for her mistake? Probably. Anxiety made her feel hot and sweaty. She wanted Jim and Dylan (mostly Dylan) to disappear so things could go back to the way they'd always been.

Mom looked up from the bureau. "Oh, there you are," she said. Was that a judging tone, or was Ella letting her angst run away with her emotions?

"Hey," Ella managed to say in a neutral tone. She didn't want to make eye contact with anyone in that room. Unfortunately, the room was so jam-packed that the only safe place to look was down at her feet.

This wasn't going to work. She needed to escape her own embarrassment, so she turned to her grandmother and said, "Maybe I can help somewhere else. You seem to have the bedroom covered."

"Hmm, you know, maybe you could get started on the bookshelves in the living room."

"Great," Ella said, turning around and running like a fox, hoping the hounds didn't give chase.

The living room had a gas fireplace and built-in shelves on either side that were perfect for Granny's voluminous collection of mysteries. Ella got busy opening boxes of books and arranging them by author. She'd made it through half a box when Mom came into the room.

"I need to talk to you," she said in that judgmental voice that Ella had grown to hate as a child. Every time she had failed to perform flawlessly at an audition, Mom always began the conversation with these words.

She didn't respond to them now but kept putting books on the shelf.

"Honey. Look at me."

She shelved the P. D. James mystery in her hand next to a collection of Dashiell Hammett stories, then turned toward her mother. Mom wasn't frowning, which was a good sign.

But it didn't matter because she'd seen the size of the bandage on Dylan's head, and that was sufficient to make her feel inadequate and guilty even without Mom's frown-of-death to contend with.

Mom leaned in and spoke in a near whisper. "Honey, I know you and Dylan got off on the wrong foot. But I hope you didn't throw that tray at him on purpose. I mean, my goodness, he had to have several stitches, and Jim says he's got a mild concussion."

Ella's remorse morphed into defensiveness. She stepped back, turned, and picked up another handful of books. They served as a nice barrier between herself and her mother, and they gave her something to do while she tried to process what Mom had just said.

Mom thought she'd hurt Dylan on purpose?

Damn. The anger hit her so hard that she felt dizzy for a moment, right before she let loose in a voice loud enough for even the nearly deaf residents of Bayview Vistas to hear.

"Of course I didn't hit him on purpose!"

Mom made hushing motions with her hands, which only fanned the flames of Ella's sudden need to defend herself. And what better way than to deflect the blame. "Honey, I didn't say you—"

"You know, Mom. I'm not the troublemaker. Dylan is. Do you know that he told me right to my face that he wants to break you and Jim up?"

"Isabella Louise," Mom said, using *that* tone—the one Ella

hated most of all. "You know better than to say something ugly like that. Why would you say such a thing?"

"Because it's true." Her voice hardened. "And if he told you I hit him on purpose, that's just a lie."

"I didn't say that he said—"

"You know, y'all, your voices are kind of loud," Jim said, strolling into the living room and standing with his hands on his hips. Until this moment, Ella could have sworn that Jim never lost his temper. But he looked pissed off right now.

"Honestly, Ella, why do you always have to make trouble?" Mom said, then turned and stalked toward the bedroom door. As she passed Jim, she said in a loud whisper, "Maybe you can talk sense into her."

Great. She'd always wanted a real family with a mom and a dad and a sibling or two. But maybe she should have had her head examined. She met Jim's stare. The man had incredibly bright blue eyes, but for once they didn't twinkle like Santa's.

"Your mother is under a lot of stress," he said.

"She's not the only one."

His jaw flexed. Was he grinding his teeth? Because of her? Boy, he needed to open his eyes and see the truth.

Jim took a step forward. "Ella, just calm down, okay? You know your mother loves you, and we can—"

"No. I won't calm down," Ella interrupted as her self-restraint collapsed under the weight of her anger. "I'm trying hard to make Mom happy, okay? But your son doesn't seem at all concerned about her happiness. And I'm trying to get my life together at the same time. Has anyone ever thought about that? No. I'm weary to death of having to tiptoe around angry, demanding people. When do I get to be angry and demanding and difficult?"

She slammed the books in her hand onto the shelf, turned,

and stomped past the delivery guys, who were now manhandling a ginormous washing machine. She strode into the hallway and kept going all the way down the stairs and out onto the street.

* * *

Dylan stood in the doorway to Nancy Jacobs's bedroom, his head throbbing, as Ella finally stopped apologizing and just let fly with the truth. Why on earth hadn't she told her mother or Dad about his plans for breaking them up before this?

Dylan hadn't asked Ella to keep it a secret, and when she'd refused to join him in the plan, he'd fully expected her to go off and tattle to her mom. But she hadn't. Why?

And why on earth would Brenda ever think that her daughter had *purposefully* clocked him with that breakfast tray?

In a cogent instant, he understood. With a mother like that, Ella had probably spent her whole life being careful about the things she said out loud.

"I give up," Dad said under his breath, as if to confirm Dylan's worst fear. He hated the idea of his father having to run interference between Ella and Brenda all the time.

But someone had to do it, because blaming Ella for the breakfast tray mishap was unfair. He stood there for a moment to see if anyone would follow Ella, but Dad just shook his head and wandered back into the bedroom.

Well, hell. Someone needed to go after her, so he headed toward the condo's front door. He wasn't able to easily slip between the appliance guys, like Ella had done. She was small and agile and had moves like a star running back.

He had to wait a minute before he could slip past the delivery guys. By then Dad and Brenda were fussing at each other in the bedroom. He was glad to get away from that scene. All this drama was making his bruised head ache.

Luckily, Ella hadn't gone far. He found her not more than half a block away, leaning up against Bayview Vistas' front facade, sobbing.

Dammit. Tears undid him. They made him itchy and uncomfortable.

He fought against the burn in his throat. "Hey," he said, taking a tentative step forward.

"Oh my god," she replied when she turned toward him. She straightened, her shoulders going rigid. "You."

Her red nose and puffy eyes made him want to head for the hills. He didn't want to get emotionally involved, but then again, he'd still followed after her to make sure she was okay.

He needed to man up and face the fact that he bore some responsibility for the devastation written on her face. The woman needed a brotherly hug.

"Come on," he said gently, reaching out to take her shoulders.

She whirled away from him. "What the hell, Dylan. Did you tell them I hit you on purpose?"

"Of course not. I told you on Thursday when you apologized for the fifteenth time that I didn't blame you."

"Great, then you could do me a favor and go tell your dad the truth. The whole truth. Because he seems to think I injured you on purpose, and no one believes you really want to break them up." Her voice got thin, and water streamed out of her eyes. "And, by the way, I didn't know I gave you a concussion. I feel so bad about that. I . . . crap." She hid her face in her hands.

He was seriously allergic to crying people, so the urge to hug her came as a total surprise. This time when he moved in to provide comfort, she didn't pull away. "I accept your apology. I accept all of them. It was an accident, and I'm fine." He pulled her into his arms.

She leaned against him, hiccuping and getting snot all over his old T-shirt. He stood there being her human snot rag while half a dozen Bayview Vista residents passed by. Most of them scowled at him, and he accepted their censure with equanimity.

On the other hand, he didn't quite know what to make of the people who beamed at him. What was up with *that*?

Ella finally stopped bawling and pulled away, dashing tears from her red cheeks. "Thanks," she muttered, staring at her feet.

"It wasn't anything."

She looked up. "No?"

He jammed his hands into his pockets. He should go now, but he didn't want to go. He wanted to solve the problem that was Ella McMillan. "Why do you take all the world's troubles on your shoulders?" he asked.

"What are you talking about?"

He didn't exactly know how to explain the thought that had wormed its way into his slightly shaken brain. "You apologize for stuff that's not your fault."

"But dropping the tray was my fault. I mean, I shouldn't have put that many plates on it, and I shouldn't have let that jerk at the table rattle me and make me walk too fast, and I—"

"I'm not talking about the tray. I'm talking about everything. I heard what you just said about tiptoeing around. That's what you do. You didn't tell your mother about my plans to break them up because you didn't want to rock the boat. You didn't want to make her angry. You didn't want—"

"Stop, okay? Look, thanks for the shoulder, but I'm not going to dish dirt on my mother, even if she ticked me off a minute ago. And just because I got angry with her doesn't mean you should use my anger to your advantage. I'm not going to help you break them up. Mom loves your father. And I'm kind of ashamed that I yelled at him. I should apologize."

"For what? Speaking the truth?"

"No, for getting so angry. It wasn't his fault." She sighed and glanced back toward the condo's entrance. "I just don't feel like facing them right now."

"Then don't."

"I don't need your approval."

"I wasn't giving approval. I was validating your feelings."

She cocked her head. They might as well have been speaking two different languages.

"Look, can you do me two favors?" she asked.

"I'm at your service," he said, trying not to show any amusement. A few days ago, she wouldn't have asked anything of him. Maybe they did have a future as stepsiblings.

"First, you can tell them that I didn't hurt you on purpose. They will believe you. And second, you can give my apologies to Granny. I'm going back to the inn, and I'm taking a long bath and maybe a short nap. And then I've got a gig."

"You have a gig?"

"Yeah. At the inn. I'm playing at the afternoon tea service. I booked it at the last minute. It might turn into a regular thing though. So tell Granny I'm sorry I lost my temper and I'll see her at church tomorrow. Also, I'll be back to help her unpack her books on Sunday afternoon."

She turned and headed down the street.

"Do you need a lift?" he asked to her back.

She turned, backpedaling. "No. I just told you what I needed."

He nodded. "Okay, I'm on it. But, um, we need to get together to work on the engagement party."

She stopped, her hands fisting on her hips. "Are you still determined to break them up? Because if you are, I'm not going to help, even if you did come out here to validate my feelings."

He cracked a smile in spite of his determination not to. "I promise that I won't use the engagement party as a means to break them up," he said.

She gave him a probing stare. "You know, that was a non-denial denial. You could still work like mad trying to bust up the romance, outside of the party planning."

"I guess I could." He wiped the smile from his lips and aimed his best poker face in her direction. It wouldn't do for her to know how much he was starting to like her.

"I'm going to be watching you." She pointed at him. "And I suspect Mom and Jim will be too. So in my opinion, you should stop this little game you're playing. You might have a lot of regrets if you keep this up."

Maybe. But he might have more regrets if he didn't try to get Dad to see reason. And Ella was the best argument in his favor. He hated to think about his father spending the rest of his life tiptoeing around Brenda's anger the way Ella did.

He wanted to save Dad from that. And weirdly, he wanted to save Ella too. But he had no idea how he was supposed to do that.

* * *

Brenda stared at herself in the bathroom mirror. She was an idiot. After all these years of hoping that Ella would come back home so Brenda could make amends and start over, she'd just fallen back into the same behavior that had driven Ella away in the first place.

When would she learn? She turned around, unable to look herself in the eye, and leaned her back against the bathroom vanity. Tears filled her eyes.

What on earth had possessed her to think that Ella might have hit Dylan on purpose? Her daughter wasn't the same rebellious teen who had once challenged her at every turn.

Ella was a grown woman now. She wouldn't have purposefully hit Dylan, although now that she thought about it, Jim's son probably deserved it if what Ella had said was true.

Instead of fussing at Ella, maybe she should have applauded her daughter's actions.

No. No. No. She pressed her face into her hands as the room started to close in. This would not be a good time to have an anxiety attack, and yet her heart rocked precipitously in her chest and charged off in a full-out gallop.

She groped her way to the commode, lowered the lid, and sat down, dropping her head to her knees as a wave of dizziness struck.

"Brenda?" Jim was outside the bathroom door. And the dear man was so respectful of her privacy that he hadn't blundered into the room even though the door was unlocked.

She took in a big breath, counting out four beats as she inhaled, held it for seven beats, and then exhaled slowly for eight more. She'd learned this technique years ago as a single mother, running from her abusive husband, trying to make ends meet and restart her life and education.

She repeated the deep-breathing pattern one more time.

"Brenda, are you okay?" Jim's voice was kind and concerned, and he drawled a little like a Southerner even though he'd been born in New York. A lifetime of living in South Carolina had slowed him down.

Just like her heartbeat was starting to slow. Funny how the sound of Jim's voice worked better than the breathing technique she'd learned from the social worker in the women's shelter all those years ago.

That winter, after she'd run from Keith's abuse, had been the longest of her life. She'd promised herself during that dark time that Ella would never go through the same thing.

And she'd failed. Cody might not be the complete screw-up Keith had been, but that man hadn't been good for her daughter. It broke Brenda's heart to see Ella alone and struggling to figure out what came next. Brenda had been through that. She'd had to look reality in the eye and give up on a lot of dreams. But it had been worth it. She'd poured everything into Ella.

But Ella didn't have a child. Ella was alone.

"Honey?"

Brenda's new life was just beyond the door.

"I'm okay," she said, speaking the truth. The dizziness had started to fade. Weary beyond measure, she wiped away the tears that had leaked from her eyes, then opened the door.

Her heart swelled with the sight of him. He was her anchor. He'd pulled her from her depths of her misery. And now she was afraid to rock the boat too much. Maybe she should shut up about Dylan. Dylan was the one she should be furious with, not Ella.

"I'm sorry," she said, because it seemed like the right thing to say.

"I'm not the one you need to apologize to."

"No, I *do* need to apologize because I just ruined a chance for our kids and us to behave as a family. And I'm torn up about it."

"Well, maybe so. But if you want my opinion, I think Dylan is the one who bears the most responsibility for what happened today."

She blinked. "But—"

He moved in and took her into his arms. "Dylan is a problem. He resents you. He might be thirty-one years old, but he's clinging to the memory of his mother. Just the other day, he got upset because I was packing away a casserole dish that I've had since I was a college student. He insisted that it was his mother's favorite pot. It's not. Julianne was not much of a cook, but that's not the way Dylan remembers things.

"I'm afraid he's behaving like a child. And pushing your daughter around is his way of acting out. And poor Ella is only trying to please you. And me. And we both failed her today."

Brenda's eyes welled up again. "I know. When she was little, she always tried to please me. We used to play music together all the time. When she became a teen, things went south. I need to remember she's not that out-of-control girl she once was."

"No, she's not. And in my opinion, she's treading very carefully and trying a little too hard to make everyone happy. And you know what? Dylan has always been more concerned about my happiness than his own. I wish he'd stop, to tell you the truth. But it's hard not to love him despite his misguided concerns."

Brenda gave Jim a skeptical look.

"I'm sorry," Jim said. "It's got to be hard when my son is so determined to break us up. I'm going to talk to him again. I think we'll have to give it some time. I'm sure he's going to come around. I know you can't see it right now, but he's a sensitive kid."

She rested her head against Jim's shoulder and refrained from telling him that his son was the antithesis of sensitive. Jim already understood how she felt. Complaining about Dylan wouldn't get her what she wanted, but she gave voice to that dream, anyway. "I so wanted us to become one happy family. And bad on me for taking my frustrations and stress out on Ella. Do you think I'll ever learn?"

"Yes."

She looked up at him. He seemed so sure.

"You're always so even-keeled. But you know, the thing is…" She hesitated.

"What? Spit it out. You can't hurt me by telling me what's on your mind." He gave her a sober look out of those bright eyes of his.

"Well, I guess I'm not even-keeled. And when Ella told me a few days ago that you and Dylan were insisting on having the engagement party at the yacht club, it stressed me out. That and Dylan's behavior has made me a little crazy. That's not an excuse, of course. Maybe an explanation. And I know this sounds stupid and immature or something, but…" She hesitated again.

"What? You don't want it at the yacht club?"

"Mom never was a member there, you know? And..."

"Oh, I see."

"Do you?"

"Brenda, I've lived in this town for a long time. I get it. You think the members are snobs." His mouth twitched.

"Not you. I overlook your club membership."

He laughed out loud. "Well, that's settled. We aren't having the party at the yacht club."

"No, that's not necessary. I mean, I'm the one who's—"

He pressed his fingers across her lips. "I don't give a damn where we have this party, or if we have it at all. But you want to have a celebration, and I agree with the idea that we should have the kids plan it. Besides, throwing the kids a curve might induce them to work together to find a solution."

"But I don't want to be—"

"Difficult?" His eyebrow arched.

She nodded.

"Honey, you can't please everyone all the time. That's what Ella has been trying to do, and I think she demonstrated to both of us how stressful that can be. You're the bride. You should get what you want. That's the way it works, you know. And I don't think you're difficult at all."

"I love you," she said, and rested her head on his shoulder, her heart rate finally dropping into a normal rhythm.

"I love you too. And I'm going to have a word with Dylan about the things Ella said."

"And I'm going to apologize to Ella and make it clear she doesn't have to please everyone to be loved for herself."

He gave her a kiss, and they smooched for a long time, until Momma came into the bathroom and said, "Are y'all going to help me unpack or what?"

Chapter Ten

By the time Ella settled into the back corner of the Howland House library and started to play her fiddle, her eyes had lost the I've-been-crying puffiness. She stuck with a medley of lively jigs and reels as Ashley's customers arrived for tea service, which was set out in the dining room, buffet style.

Howland House had been built in the early 1800s, and Ashley Scott had recently restored the place, filling it with period-appropriate antiques, wallpapers, and window treatments. Her collection of antique china teacups was probably not quite as old as the house, but they certainly set the mood for her formal tea service.

The mismatched collection from various floral patterns gave the tea service a garden-party feel. Each teacup was festooned with flowers: yellow daffodils, pink and red roses, purple violets, and blue irises and forget-me-nots. A wide selection of cakes, muffins, scones, cookies, and dainty sandwiches had been put out in the dining room, where guests could load up their plates and grab tea, then circulate through the inn's historic public rooms.

In addition to a fainting couch and a couple of armchairs covered in deep blue velvet, a handful of wooden folding chairs—the kind used for outdoor weddings—had been placed in the library to accommodate additional guests who wanted to listen to the music up close.

The spring day had turned warm, with temperatures in the low eighties, so many of the guests chose the solarium and the patio, but Ella's music drew a few of them into the library. Maybe next week she should set up outside, although to do that effectively she'd need a sound system, which would cost a lot of money she didn't have.

Ashley strictly limited the number of guests at her Saturday teas, which became an embarrassing problem when Doctor D arrived shortly after 4:15 p.m. From her station in the library, Ella had a great view of the front door through the room's cased opening. So the moment he walked through the door, she knew about it.

He'd lost the jeans and ratty T-shirt he'd been wearing earlier and had shaved and donned his daily uniform of blue blazer, gray slacks, white shirt, and bow tie. Today the tie was red, which seemed daring for him somehow. He'd also lost the big bandage on his head in lieu of a smaller Band-Aid.

Even though he'd reverted to type, Ella was never going to see Dylan the same way again, not after she'd cried all over his Clemson T-shirt. Not after he'd shown a remarkable ability to see right through her.

He wasn't Doctor Dull. Not with a bright bow tie like that. In fact, he was a lot more like Doctor Dreamy, standing there conversing with Candace Gladwin, the high school senior Ashley hired on Saturdays to check reservations at the door.

Ella's finger slipped, and the note she'd been bowing went

a tiny bit flat. Thank God Mom wasn't in the room; she would have noticed.

She couldn't hear what Dylan was saying to Candi, but he appeared to be arguing with her, no doubt trying to talk his way into the tea party without a reservation. Having taken the brunt of Dylan's persistence, Ella sympathized with the young woman trying to play bouncer at the door.

Ella finished "Loch Lavan Castle" and was about to start playing "Rocky Road to Dublin," when Candi left her post by the door and crossed the library. She leaned in. "I'm sorry, Ella, but Doctor D says he's your brother and is only here to listen to you play. I didn't know you were Doctor D's sister."

"Well, not exactly. His father is about to marry my mother."

Candi's gaze widened. "So you *are* his sister. Cool. He's adorbs. But he doesn't have a reservation. Do you think I should ask Ms. Scott if I can let him in?" Candi seemed uncertain.

"Let him in. But tell him he has to sit in the library and can't have any tea," Ella said.

"You don't mind?"

Ella shook her head. "No. He's my brother." She had trouble keeping a straight face. What was Dylan up to? Was he here to get on her good side? Or was this another apology moment Jim had demanded from him? Either way, his penance would be to sit quietly and listen for the next hour and a half. And if he took out his cell phone one time, she'd never let him forget it.

Wasn't that the sort of teasing siblings engaged in? Yeah. But even if she'd claimed him as a brother, she was so over the desire to have a father and a sibling. Besides, he was too...handsome?

To be her brother anyway.

Oh boy. She studied her set list and started to play, trying with all her might to push Doctor D from her mind. It proved impossible, since he sat there handsome as the devil with his leg cocked over his knee, taking up man space and never taking his gaze from her.

That look made her uncomfortable. It almost reminded her of those days when Mom would sit in the audience judging her performances. But Dylan wasn't a musician. He wasn't counting her mistakes. Or at least she hoped he wasn't. So why did the intensity of his gaze make her skin tingle and itch?

She played straight through until five thirty, ending on the classic "Danny Boy." When the last note rang and she dropped the fiddle from her chin, Dylan stood up and clapped. A moment later, Ashley, Candi, and the helpers from the kitchen came to the library door and applauded too. By then most of the guests had departed.

"That was wonderful," Ashley said, sweeping into the room, her classic polka-dotted dress floating around her legs. Ashley and Dylan had each dressed for a garden party, while Ella wore one of her stage dresses—a bargain she'd found at a Value Mart a few years ago, made of paisley polyester in shades of peach and turquoise. That dress would have looked fine in So Ho. But it didn't fit here.

And maybe it had never fit. Cody had always complained about the high waist, long pleated sleeves, and short flowing skirt. He'd always wanted her in something tight that showed too much skin. But Ella liked loose dresses. They were comfortable. And instead of wearing heels, she'd always opted for a pair of sturdy Doc Martens. A girl's feet could get tired standing for hours on end.

Of course, her boots posed a sharp contrast to Ashley's conservative navy-blue heels. Ella had only worn pumps like that back in high school, when she'd played in the school orchestra or participated in musical competitions. And only because Mom made her wear them.

"I would like to hire you for the rest of the summer," Ashley said, pulling her away from her thoughts. "And we'll need to adjust the fee."

"Oh, um—"

"You're worth double what I paid you," Ashley interrupted. "And don't argue with me. I just loved all that traditional music. Is that what your band played?"

"Uh, no. Like I told you the other day, we played mostly country music. You know, like Willie Nelson and Johnny Cash."

"Oh, well, I think we should keep the music traditional for the teas. And at least one of the guests told me he enjoyed it when you played the medley of Strauss waltzes. So if you wanted to include a smattering of classical pieces, that would be great."

"Sure," she said, suddenly trapped by her limited success. She could play classical music, but she'd never truly liked doing it because it required a kind of perfection she hated. Classical music had to be played the way the composer wanted it played. Improvisation was frowned upon.

She remembered that summer in tenth grade when she'd gotten a spot at Interlochen Music Camp in Michigan. It had been the worst summer of her life. She'd been judged by her ability to play the notes on the page. No one cared much about her ability to play really fast jigs and reels. Instead of boosting her confidence, that summer had destroyed it.

Candi and the kitchen help got busy with the dining room cleanup, while Ashley turned toward Dylan. "I'm so sorry you ended up sitting here. I require reservations, but I'll let Candi know that you are welcome to tea any time when Ella is playing."

The innkeeper turned back toward Ella. "Are you planning to play for your mother's wedding?"

"Uh, well, um..."

"You should." Ashley tapped her mouth as if in thought. "You know, we do our share of weddings out in the garden when June rolls around. And weddings often disrupt our Saturday-afternoon teas, so keep that in mind. But I'm wondering... Brides are always asking me to recommend musicians. I've got a harpist and a flutist I recommend, but I'd like to add you to the list, if that's okay."

"Yes, thanks. That would be great." Wow, Ashley was such a kind person. Ella had never met anyone so interested in giving her a break.

"Wonderful job, Ella, really. I'm so glad you've joined our community in Magnolia Harbor." With that praise, Ashley breezed out of the room, leaving Ella alone with Doctor D.

For the second time that day, Ella wanted him to disappear into thin air. But this time was different. Earlier he'd been destroying the family dynamic. But now he was charging the atmosphere, setting up a strange, almost electric hum in her brain that threatened to spark lightning.

"So," he said. "I have reservations for two at Cibo Dell'anima. It's a new Italian restaurant that just opened on Harbor Drive. It's supposed to have a party room. Want to go check it out?"

"I thought you and Jim wanted the engagement party at the yacht club," she said, turning away and putting her fiddle in its case.

"Change of plans. Your mother has nixed that idea."

"Oh?" She turned. "When did she do that?"

"Right after you stormed off in a snit."

A blush crawled up her face as she remembered the feel of his hard shoulder against her face as she'd cried. He'd been so sturdy and patient in that moment. He hadn't told her to shut up or that she was stupid for crying. He'd just stood there and held her up. It had been... nice.

But now? Now she worried that he was judging her again. "Is that why you came this afternoon? To deliver that message?"

"No. Although for the record, I concede that you were right about your mom's reaction to the yacht club."

"Thanks. I think."

The corner of his mouth curled into a little comma. Like the Amazon smile. "But I didn't come for that reason. I came because I wanted to listen to you play this time, instead of surreptitiously watching the basketball game. And also, I came to, well..." He shrugged.

"Your father asked you to apologize again?" She snapped the fiddle case closed.

"No. He didn't think I needed to apologize to you. He's furious that I'm not down with this idea of him getting married. But that's between him and me."

"So...why are you here?"

"Like I said, I have dinner reservations. For two."

She studied him for a long moment. He wasn't handing her some BS line this time. He was being honest. And actually, he'd always been honest. From the start. He'd never tried to hide his feelings about Mom and Jim's relationship.

"Okay, thanks for being honest."

"Honest?" He seemed surprised.

"For telling me exactly what you think of my mother, even though I'm sure you knew I didn't want to hear it. I almost admire that. It flies in the face of what we were always taught. You know, about not saying anything unless you had something nice to say."

"Ella, I don't think your mother follows that advice."

He was right about that. Mom had always told her exactly what she thought of her violin performances. So maybe Mom had been honest from the start, and Ella's biggest problem was that she didn't like to hear the truth.

On the other hand, Cody's BS had worn thin after a while.

"Well," she said, "I guess there is something to be said about not wasting your time trying to make everyone happy." *The way I do.* She didn't say the last part out loud.

"I'm interested in my dad's happiness," he said. "We simply have different ideas about what that might look like."

"Shouldn't he be the one who chooses?"

"I'm sure he feels that way."

"And you don't?"

He shrugged. "I care about him. But I'm going to get with the program for the time being. And help with the party. So...dinner?"

He obviously expected her to drop everything and go off to dinner with him. It seemed a bit high-handed. But she didn't have anything else going on in her life. And if they weren't going to have the party at the yacht club, they needed to figure something else out quick.

And there was a free meal at a nice restaurant involved...

"Sure. Why not?" she said, giving him a smile. "But I'm going to hold you to your promise."

"What promise?"

"The one you made on the sidewalk today. No sneaky attempts to sabotage the party planning, okay?"

"I promise." He crossed his chest with his finger and held up his hand. The gesture was kind of adorable.

Dylan looked honest, and he sounded honest, and he was adorable with that curl falling over his forehead. She ought to trust him. But she didn't. Even mild-mannered Clark Kent told lies and kept secrets from Lois, and she'd given her trust away one too many times.

* * *

Ella was a funny woman. Not ha-ha funny, but like a mystery or a puzzle that needed solving. When Dylan had applauded her stunning solo performance, she'd blushed right up to her hairline, almost as if she wasn't used to being praised. But certainly, someone with her musical skills had gotten praise all her life.

There had been moments during her performance when her violin seemed to weep. Then in a flash, she'd segue to a tune that made him want to get up and dance, which was nothing short of astonishing because he was deathly afraid of dancing in public. She was that good.

He needed to change his assessment of Ella, and he needed to stop judging people so quickly. Maybe he'd spent too much time in Lauren's company. His ex-girlfriend was exactly the kind of person who always wanted to know which clubs someone belonged to, whether they came from a wealthy or well-connected family, and how much they earned in annual income.

Ella was nothing like that. She had hidden depths that allowed her to channel deep emotion into her music. She wasn't mean-spirited like Lauren. And she was every bit as beautiful, even though she wore army boots. In fact, Dylan was enjoying the hell out of the way the sea breeze floated her skirt, exposing the curve of her leg.

Whoa. Back off, boy. She's your *sister.*

Almost. Sort of.

The reality of the situation should have stopped him cold, but the moment she climbed into the car, her scent—a heady mix of something exotic like sandalwood—tickled his nose and every one of the synapses in his brain.

By the time he pulled into the parking lot at Cibo Dell'anima, he was ready to put some distance between them. The woman made his head go fuzzy. Or maybe he was merely allergic to her perfume.

The new restaurant occupied an old brick storehouse at the corner of Ash Street and Harbor Drive, directly across from the commercial pier where local shrimpers sold their catches every day. The place billed itself as a new-age fusion restaurant blending classic Italian with traditional Southern soul food. Dylan regarded that as an impossibility, but one of his patients had recommended the place, and since it occupied an old warehouse, it had a party room upstairs.

It had been far too easy to get a reservation this Saturday evening on short notice though. And when he entered the dining room, he knew why. The place wasn't exactly thriving, and the decor wasn't new age anything. With its red-checked tablecloths and exposed-brick walls, Cibo Dell'anima could have been any of a thousand other Italian restaurants around the world. The only things Southern about the place were the vintage sepia-tone photographs of Jonquil Island covering the walls.

They sat down at a table near the front window, and Dylan got his first look at the menu. Everything from the antipasto to the desserts was overpriced, which explained why the college kids who had flooded Magnolia Harbor for spring break were conspicuously absent in the nearly empty dining room.

Ella picked up the menu, her brows knitting as she read, and the resemblance between mother and daughter hit him like a two-by-four. Or maybe his headache had returned with a vengeance. The concussion had been mild, but the come-and-go headaches were annoying.

"So, you're unhappy with the menu?" he asked.

She shifted her gaze, the frown melting away.

"No," she said, cocking her head. "What makes you think that?"

"You were frowning."

"Oh, jeez, I'm sorry. I hope it wasn't the frown-of-death."

"What?"

She shook her head. "Sorry. It's an in-joke. You know, Cody used to say that I frowned when I was thinking."

Would she ever stop saying sorry? What was up with that? "Cody?" he asked.

She turned and studied the traffic. "He was the leader of Urban Armadillo."

"The outlaw band..." He drew out the words.

"Yeah. And you can go ahead and say it. The band's name is awful."

"I wasn't thinking that."

"No? What were you thinking?"

He couldn't exactly tell her that he'd been studying her amazing eyes or that he liked the way the fire of the afternoon sun had gotten tangled up in her hair, or that Cody, whoever he was, was an idiot for letting her get away. "So was Cody just a guy in the band, or is he your ex?" he asked, and then regretted the question even though he wanted to know the details.

"He's my ex," she said, and then hid behind her menu. Served him right. He had no business prying into her private life. She wasn't a real sister. And besides, his main mission was to dig up dirt on her mother. Not that this afternoon's blowup hadn't provided plenty of ammunition. But he couldn't be overtly obvious.

"So, one of my patients recommended the greens and spicy meatballs."

"Not a fan of greens, particularly," she said.

"No?"

She looked up from her menu. "Salty and bitter. Not my thing." She paused a moment. "You know, I'm not seeing a lot of fusion here. It's like you can get pulled pork or you can get pasta."

"Yeah. And I'll bet the pulled pork isn't as good as at Annie's Kitchen."

"Now, there's an idea. What if we have a party and get Annie to cater it?"

"Okay, but where?"

"I don't know. I'm not a native. You are."

"Well, there's always the big room at Grace Church," he offered.

"There's a big room there?"

He nodded.

"Okay, maybe we should check it out. And I can talk to Annie about her catering menu."

"So we've nixed this place?" he asked.

She examined the uninspiring decor. "It's kind of pricy, don't you think?"

"Maybe a little. But I'm glad we agree. So I'll call and see about setting up a time to look at Grace Church's event space."

"Great."

"Now, how about we try the wine? We can celebrate your amazing performance today at Howland House."

She responded to his suggestion with a smile as bright as a klieg light. It illuminated the dark interior of the restaurant. His praise had pleased her. He made a note to compliment her whenever possible. She needed to have her confidence boosted for some reason he couldn't fathom.

"Thanks, but my performance wasn't *that* amazing," she said.

"I was impressed. And besides, based on what Ashley said, your gig is going to lead to more opportunities, and that's a good thing. So, red or white?"

Chapter Eleven

Ella yanked her gaze away from the man sitting across the table from her. What had happened to the infuriating Doctor D? In the blink of an eye, he'd morphed into a sweet, kind man filled with compliments for her violin playing.

They chatted about not much at all until the waiter returned and made a big show of pouring the wine. Dylan played along with the ritual like a man skilled in the selection of fine vintages. She tried to imagine Cody doing the same, but it was impossible. When the wine was poured, she chose one of the shrimp pasta dishes while Dylan chose the greens and meatballs, which sounded totally unappetizing.

When the waiter departed, Dylan lifted his glass. "To your performance," he said, giving her the slightest smile. It crinkled up the corners of his eyes in a really sexy way.

Wait. What? Noticing the sexiness of his manly laugh lines was not allowed. Was it? No, it was not. And she needed to stop comparing him to Cody.

She raised her glass and took a big gulp to steady her nerves.

"It's pretty good wine," she said. Boy, as a conversation starter that was pretty lame, but her tongue had suddenly tied itself into knots.

"You might want to slow down there," he said when she took another gulp of the vino. His tone sounded judgmental, but then again, maybe he was simply settling into the role of the bigger, wiser brother, even though they were almost the same age.

"So, tell me about your mother," he said.

She wasn't entirely sure, but she got the feeling he'd been waiting to spring this question on her. He wasn't nice. She needed to remember that. He was trying to break up Mom's romance with his father. She had to be careful not to let him charm her into revealing too much or giving him ammunition.

She stared him down. "You're relentless."

"Yeah. I've been accused of that before. But, you know, I need to know the lay of the land. She's going to become my stepmother."

He gave the word a twist, as if he were talking about Cinderella's wicked stepmom. Good grief, did that make her a wicked stepsister? Thank you, Disney, for forever making the whole step thing complicated and fraught with emotional overtones.

"What do you want me to say?" she said, taking yet another swig of wine. The alcohol infused her nervous system, calming her down.

"Whatever I need to know."

She drummed her fingers on the checked tablecloth. "For what? To use against her?"

"Of course not."

The corner of his mouth twitched. He was not being honest. And she was so disappointed.

"I don't trust you."

The little twitch turned into a smile. "Probably a wise move on your part," he said.

Whoa. Wait. He was admitting everything. She honestly didn't know what to think about him.

"But…" he said with a charming gleam in his deep blue eyes. "I am going to become her stepson. So, you know, information would be good to have."

"That's true," she said. And he did have a good point. When Mom and Jim got married, Dylan would have to negotiate his way around Mom. Otherwise there would be family drama more or less continuously. She didn't have to divulge deep family secrets to give him a few pointers on dealing with Mom.

She took another sip of wine and considered her words carefully. "Well, if there is one important thing to know about Mom, it's that she can sometimes be very hard to please."

"Well, that's a problem, isn't it?"

She cocked her head. "I'm not going to let you probe my relationship with my mother, Dylan."

He leaned back a fraction. "Oh, of course not. But, you know, we've got a party to plan, and if she's hard to please, that means we are up a creek without a paddle. She's nixed the yacht club already. Are we going to have nothing but headaches?"

Well, he did have a point there, but Ella wasn't going to cede it. Instead, she drained her wineglass and nudged it across the table. "More, please. The wine's good."

He gave her another look, which she filed under the heading of big-brothers-can-be-annoying, but he did refill the glass.

"So," he said, "has she told you what she wants? Aside from not wanting the yacht club, that is. Which she told Dad instead of us."

"Well, I hate to say I told you so, but I did. I told you she would hate the yacht club."

"So what would she like?"

Ella shrugged. "I have no clue. Something informal though. But that's just a gut feeling. She wants us to figure it out."

"So she can find fault with what we do? Seems a bit passive-aggressive, actually."

Ella blew out a breath that stirred her too-long bangs. "Your words, not mine."

"Which means they're true. She *is* passive-aggressive."

Ella took another sip of wine, letting the buzz fill her head. She was drinking too much too fast, especially since she had a sordid relationship with booze of any kind. But getting buzzed seemed a lot easier than trying to deal with Doctor Determined-to-Diss-Her-Mother. In fact, the buzz was calming after a day filled with too many highs and lows. Where the hell was her middle ground, anyway? She was tired of living on a roller coaster.

"Are they?" he asked again, prodding her.

Okay, he'd asked for it. She stared him straight in the eye. "It's not that she's passive-aggressive. It's more that she's a perfectionist. And it's hard to meet her expectations. She doesn't mince words. When she's not happy with your performance, she tells you straight-up."

"Performance? Is that how you feel around her, like you have to perform?"

Ella's face heated. Had she just exposed another crack in her brittle armor? "No," she said. "That's not what I meant. You simply don't understand."

"Try me. I'm listening."

He was, but to what effect? So she said nothing and took another swig of wine.

"I get it. You still don't trust me."

"Of course I don't. Why should I? But you know what? My issues with Mom are unique because we both play the violin. And she's a brilliant musician. She should have gone to Juilliard, but she got knocked up and had me instead. So, when I turned out to have a talent for the fiddle, I was expected to become a vehicle for her lost ambitions. I was supposed to live out the dream she screwed up. Only problem was, I wasn't down with her plans.

"So yeah, my life for a long time growing up was graded by the quality of my performances. It wasn't easy, and I resented it. So I ran away to join the Grand Ole Opry because I knew it would drive Mom crazy. In retrospect, it was a dumb move on my part because Cody was never going to get me to the Grand Ole Opry, and I failed to realize that for way too long. Bottom line: I should have listened to my mother. It's a lesson I'm not likely to ever forget."

She paused for a moment to drain her glass a second time. She held it out for him to refill, and he obliged.

* * *

Dylan should have cut Ella off after her first glass of wine. The woman didn't know how to hold her booze and obviously hadn't learned that wine was to be sipped, not gulped.

On the other hand, once the alcohol had kicked in, she had opened up. Although he wasn't exactly happy about the secrets she'd shared. She certainly hadn't painted a flattering picture of her mother. Was Dad going to end up in a relationship where he was criticized and judged every minute? It unsettled Dylan.

And now he had to deal with a slightly wasted future stepsister. If Dad ever learned about this, Dylan would be subjected to yet another woodshed talk. That would be three in almost as many days.

The McMillan women were wreaking havoc on the Killough men. Dylan was in deep trouble with Dad, and Dad was blinded by sexual attraction, an affliction Dylan could entirely understand because Ella resembled her mother, and she was adorably sexy now that she was toasted. Feeling this way about an inebriated woman who was about to become his stepsister wasn't exactly one of his finer moments though.

He guided her out to the parking lot, intent on driving her home and seeing her safely to bed with a glass of water and a couple of acetaminophen. But she had other ideas.

"Ooooh, lookit, the sunset." She'd gotten halfway across the parking lot before veering away from his car and heading toward Harbor Drive. "We should take a walk on the boardwalk."

She put her head down and raced off in the direction of the crosswalk without paying attention to the traffic lights. He sprinted after her and caught her right before she darted into the street.

He took her by the hand, intent on pulling her back to the car. But she tugged him in the opposite direction. "Come on. Don't be so dull. Let's walk."

"When the light changes," he said, giving her a ruthless yank as a car whizzed by.

She let go of a girlie gasp and turned toward him, weaving a little. "You just saved my life," she said in a boozy whisper. "Thanks."

"It was nothing."

She turned away just as the light changed and then dragged him out into the street. He could have stopped her, but maybe a walk down the boardwalk would clear her head. He checked his watch: Only eight o'clock and the sun was just sinking toward the horizon.

The evening was warm, and the sun painted the sky with pink and magenta, while the lights along the boardwalk came on, one by one. They strolled northwest toward the public pier, where Rafferty's Raw Bar presided over a lively spring break crowd. A band had set up on the patio and started to play as they approached. He didn't recognize the loud music, but then, he'd never been musical.

"Cover band," she said, stopping and leaning on the railing as she listened.

"Are they any good?"

She cocked her head. "You don't know?"

"I've got a tin ear," he said.

She blinked. "So that means your opinion of my fiddling has to be taken with a grain of salt."

He was an idiot. He'd just undone all his earlier compliments, which had been completely sincere. "I liked *your* music."

"And them?" She pointed over her shoulder with her thumb.

"Uh, not so much. They're too loud. They're likely to damage your hearing."

She nodded and turned. "Yup. The drummer's pretty good. The rest of them are ordinary." Then she giggled. "Listen to me passing judgment like Mom." She turned again and leaned back against the rail. "They're doing okay, aren't they? They got a gig, right? That's all that counts. I mean, the grunge bands of Seattle weren't paragons of musicianship, but they made a lot of money in their day."

She slurred the words "paragon of musicianship." But he was impressed by her ability to even attempt a three-dollar phrase like that. He was willing to bet that her lips were numb.

"Now *you're* frowning," she said.

"Am I?"

"Most definitely. Are you looking down on me because I listened to grunge music?"

"No. I'm looking down at you because I'm six foot three."

She rolled her eyes in an adorable fashion, and a wave of lust crashed over him. What the hell was wrong with him? He needed to pull her away from this place and get her back to the inn, where she belonged.

But she eluded him again, turning and jogging down the boardwalk. "Come on, let's see if the gelato place is open," she said over her shoulder.

She was a danger moving that fast and unsteadily. He charged

after her. "Slow down," he said, taking her hand just as they
rounded the corner by the public pier. Sure enough, Cherry on
Top, the ice cream place, was mobbed. At least twenty people
were standing in line.

"Oh, goodie, let's get some. I love the mint chocolate chip,"
she said, hurrying to the end of the line.

"How can you be hungry?" he asked.

"Are you going to give me a lecture about pasta and carbs?"

"No, but we should really—"

"You know, Doctor Disdainful," she said, poking him in the
chest with her index finger, "you should learn the golden rule."

"What?" Her finger was as sharp as an arrow. His chest
burned where it pressed against his sternum.

"You spend a lot of time telling folks not to be grumpy.
You're pretty grumpy yourself. Honestly, you could give Mom
a run for the money when it comes to your frown-of-death
technique." She rose on tiptoes, the action bringing her breasts
perilously close to his chest. He flinched away but not before
she managed to snag his tie.

"Hold still, silly. I'm setting you free."

"What? Stop."

"Stand still. You look like a jerk walking down the boardwalk
all buttoned up like that."

She might be tipsy, but the woman sure knew how to undo
a bow tie, not to mention the collar button. But when she went
after the button below that one, he put his hands on her shoulders
and gently pushed her away.

"That's enough," he said, letting go. The bones in her
shoulders were tiny and fragile under his palms. Why hadn't he
stopped her after the second glass of wine?

She was never going to forgive him for this. Tomorrow, he
was going to get an earful about how he should have stopped refilling her glass over and over again. But right now Ella leaned

forward, putting her palms against his chest. "No," she said, shaking her head. "It isn't nearly enough."

And then she threw her arms around his neck and kissed him.

He took a step back, and she followed. He tried not to return the kiss, but he was a human male and she tasted exactly like the Sangiovese, all berries and plums and fruit, overlaid with her sandalwood scent and something darker and more complicated. For the first time in his life he understood the lyrics from that old country song about kisses sweeter than wine.

He stopped moving and let the kiss unfold, losing himself in it for a moment as he tangled his hand in her wild, untamed hair.

Oh yeah, he could enjoy this for a while.

Or not.

Damn.

He took her by the shoulders again and pushed her away. "That's it," he said in his most stern voice. "I'm taking you home."

"Really?" Her unsteady gaze was full of promise. Dammit. She'd gotten the wrong idea when he'd said "home."

"Yes, I am taking you home to the *inn*. Where I'm going to make sure you go to bed with a couple of acetaminophen for the headache you're going to have tomorrow morning."

Chapter Twelve

Some vengeful god, maybe Thor with his hammer, was using Ella's head as an anvil when she awakened at 5:30 a.m. on Sunday morning. She cracked her eyes in the predawn gloom only to see the empty glass of water and the bottle of Tylenol on the bedstand.

And then the memories flooded in.

What had she been thinking?

Had she been thinking at all?

She rolled over, and her skull threatened to split open and spill her brains all over the pillow. She took a bunch of deep breaths as nausea roiled in her stomach.

What an idiot.

Beyond her closed door, Jackie thumped down the hall and into the bathroom. Boy, he was up early. Oh, wait. Today was Sunday.

Palm Sunday. A day of obligation. And Howland House still served breakfast on Sundays, even if the service consisted of a simple help-yourself buffet that would end by 9:30 a.m.

Out in the hallway, Ashley quietly knocked on the bathroom door. "Jackie, don't take too long. Ella needs to use the room."

Right. She dragged herself up, but the room was still spinning fifteen minutes later when she stepped out of the shower, making her stomach uneasy. The scent of biscuits and bacon didn't help when she finally made it to the kitchen.

But before Ella could say one word, Ashley turned away from the stove and said, "Here, eat this." She pushed a bowl of oatmeal across the island's sleek quartz countertop.

"I don't—"

"Eat it. There's no way you'll make it to fellowship hour without something in your stomach."

Ella took a seat on one of the counter stools and stared down at the oatmeal. "I'm sorry," she said.

"Honey, you have nothing to be sorry about."

"But I..." An unwanted memory of Dylan's warm lips against hers invaded her thoughts, and she flushed hot. Was this lust, embarrassment, or some manifestation of dehydration brought on by binge drinking?

"He's cute. And a doctor. So enough said."

"What? No. He's going to be my—"

"Well, yes, he is going to become a member of your family," Ashley said, pulling a sheet of biscuits from the oven. "That's going to make things complicated, I suppose. That could get awkward, although he doesn't strike me as the kind of guy who does affairs or summer flings. You know?"

"No, wait. You don't understand. It's not like that. I mean we don't like each other. I was just...celebrating my success or something, and I had too much to drink. And he brought me home like a good big brother would."

"Uh-huh." Ashley nodded and pointed at the oatmeal. "Eat. Then you can put out the orange juice and the big self-serve coffeepot."

Oh boy. This wasn't good. If Ashley talked, then Granny would find out, and if Granny found out...Her goose was cooked. Mom would be furious.

Her deep unease hadn't diminished later in the day when she took a seat in the pew next to Granny. But at least she wasn't dizzy and nauseated anymore, and her headache had settled into a dull roar.

Which was a good thing because, it being Palm Sunday, there was a big processional this morning with Myrna Solomons playing away on the newly restored pipe organ and Mom leading the newly formed Heavenly Rest choir singing Hymn 154 in their loudest and most joyous voices.

All glory, laud and honor to thee, Redeemer, King!
To whom the lips of children made sweet hosannas ring.

By the time the last blast of organ music faded away, Ella was doubly glad for the Tylenol she'd gulped down right after breakfast.

She settled in for the Palm Sunday service, complete with its retelling of how Jesus borrowed a colt and entered Jerusalem while the crowd waved palm branches in celebration. But Ella wasn't quite prepared for Rev. St. Pierre's sermon on the Gospel reading, because, as usual, he managed to turn the familiar story into some kind of new age, self-help message.

"Now, in our reading today," the minister said in his deep baritone, "we're told that Jesus came into the city and went to the temple, but He left because it was getting late. Did that mean it was late in the day? Or was Jesus running behind schedule for something? He was a celebrity that day, so it's fair to wonder if He had parties to attend."

Ella and several other parishioners stirred in their pews. The idea of Jesus attending a party wasn't an image many of them had ever thought about.

"You know what?" the preacher continued. "I have a theory

about why He left. I think it's because He promised to return the colt He'd borrowed. Which is kind of interesting because, you know, everyone who'd celebrated His arrival would have forgiven Him for failing to return the colt. But that wouldn't have been Him. Jesus let go of that celebrity in order to be true to Himself and to keep His promise to the colt's owner.

"So what can we learn from this? Maybe it's as simple as to be closer to God, we have to be true to our best selves, even on days that get busy or stressful. Even when there are roadblocks that keep us from being true to ourselves.

"Jesus gave up His celebrity because it was a false face of who He truly was. What do you need to give up? Guilt? Perfectionism? A grudge? Grief? The need for approval? Envy? We all carry around a lot of baggage that delays us, and the time is getting late."

The preacher spoke for several more minutes, but Ella hardly heard another word he said because his sermon had penetrated to a place deep inside her. She stared up at the beautiful old stained-glass window behind the altar, and tears filled her eyes.

She'd been so utterly selfish over the last few days, while Mom was trying her best to stitch together a family. First, she'd wanted Dylan and Jim to disappear, then she'd picked a fight over a simple misunderstanding, and then...

Good god. She'd gotten drunk and kissed her soon-to-be brother. The guilt was enough to swallow her whole. But she couldn't just jettison the guilt. To get rid of this burden, she would have to apologize.

* * *

Brenda stood in the church vestry, hanging her choir robes in the closet and trying not to chat about Rev. St. Pierre's sermon. His talk today had evoked a lot of emotion that still sat heavy on her chest. Even now, her heart seemed to be jumping around in there.

No question about it, she needed to make some changes. Otherwise, she'd never become her best self or live the life she'd always wanted. And there was no time like the present to start.

She left the vestry and headed to the fellowship hall, where the ladies of the altar guild had coffee and snacks already laid out. She spied Momma and Ella standing together by one of the windows, and she made a beeline to them, bypassing Ashley Scott's delicious coffee cake.

"Hey," she said, coming to a stop before her daughter.

"Hi, Mom." Ella met her gaze. "About yester—"

"I wanted to—"

They spoke at the same moment.

"You go first," Ella said.

"Oh honey, I am so sorry about what I said yesterday. I don't know what came over me. I could say it was stress, but..." She paused, letting her gaze drift to the windows. Outside, a heavy mist clung to the live oaks in the churchyard and left jewel-like beads of dew on the Spanish moss.

"Well, the thing is," Brenda finally continued, "I know I've been hard on you sometimes. I mean..." She paused and shifted her gaze back to her daughter. "Well, I'm sorry about trying to force you to live the dream I screwed up years ago. Judging you because you refused to practice violin every moment of the day was just wrongheaded on my part, and I'm sorry. I'm going to try to be better, okay?"

Brenda didn't know what to expect from Ella. But the smile that opened on her daughter's face made the pressure in her chest ease a fraction. "You know," Ella said, "I played for Ashley's tea yesterday, and now I have a regular gig there. I played a lot of traditional Irish music, but the people really enjoyed the medley of Strauss waltzes I included in my set. I'd like to add a few more classical pieces to my repertoire. I was wondering if you could help me choose a few."

"Really?"

She nodded. "I've decided to give up being afraid of making mistakes. Which is hilarious considering all the mistakes I've made in my life. I have no idea why I'm so afraid of a few wrong notes here and there."

"Because of me," Brenda said. "And I don't want you to feel that way anymore."

She opened her arms, and Ella stepped into them, giving her a fierce hug that opened her heart and made a different kind of future possible, if only for a moment.

"I accept your apology," Ella said. "And I offer one of my own. I'm so sorry I made a scene yesterday. I don't know what came over me."

"I do. It was me blaming you, when in fact the problem is Dylan. I forgive you, sweetie."

Ella smiled. "There's one more thing."

"What's that?"

"I was wondering if I could play for your engagement party."

"I've got a better idea," Momma said, grinning.

Mother and daughter turned in her direction. "What?" they asked in near-unison.

"I think y'all should play something together, the way you sometimes did when you came to visit," Momma said.

Brenda turned toward Ella to gauge her daughter's reaction to this suggestion. She was relieved and delighted to find Ella smiling. "I think that would be great," Ella said.

"So at least that's one detail of the party we've nailed down," Brenda said.

"Mom, I know this is stressful for you, but I'm trying my best."

"Oh, honey, I know you are." Brenda gave her daughter another hug. "And when it's over, we'll all be one happy family."

"It's just that I'm not sure what you want when it comes to the party."

"Well, to be honest, I'm not sure what I want either. I guess I know what I *don't* want. I'm sorry."

"It's okay. So, besides the yacht club, anything else I should be aware of?"

"Nothing that comes immediately to mind." She paused a moment, thinking about the preacher's words this morning. "I guess that puts you in a bad place, huh? I mean, you are working hard and coming up with ideas and I'm being difficult."

"Yes, honey, you are," Momma said. "But you're the bride. So it comes with the territory. I'm sure Ella will figure something out."

"I'm working on it. Dylan and I had dinner at that new Italian restaurant on the East Side, but we jettisoned that. Too expensive, and the food isn't all that good." Brenda could have sworn that Ella was blushing. What was *that* all about?

"When did you have dinner there?"

"Last night. Dylan came to tea at the inn."

"He did?"

"Mom, stop frowning."

Brenda relaxed her facial muscles. She had been frowning. "I'm sorry. I guess I'm not sure I trust Dylan after what you said about him yesterday."

"I don't really trust him either. But you know, you have to give him points for being honest about his feelings. I made him promise me that he wouldn't screw up the party planning. That's progress, right?"

"I guess. Thank you for trying to work things out with him."

"Sure." Ella tossed off that word in a weird way that sent up warning flares. Had Ella worked things out with Dylan, or was Jim's son bullying her? Dylan could be so unpleasant at times.

"So anyway," Ella rushed on. "We talked about some other places."

"Good, because time's a-wasting," Momma said.

Ella turned toward her grandmother. "I know, Granny. I'm doing the best I can."

"Momma, you don't think Dylan is trying to delay things, do you?" Brenda asked.

"I have no idea. I'm just stating the obvious. But if y'all want my opinion, I think you should invite some friends over and grill out on the beach. Don't you remember how much your daddy loved that sort of thing?"

Momma's wistful tone carried Brenda back to her childhood memories of Daddy grilling shrimp out on the beach. Those had been such happy times. Maybe Momma was right. "It would be nice to have a small, informal thing on the beach at sunset," Brenda said.

"I like that idea. I'll put that on the list," Ella said. "But if it rains, it could be a disaster."

"True," Momma said. "But that's why God invented tents."

"Good point, Granny."

Momma nodded. "Y'all really need to get on it and decide one way or another."

"By Easter if possible," Brenda said. "Actually, that brings up another thing. Momma has invited all of us to Easter dinner at her condo."

"Great," Ella said with false enthusiasm.

And Brenda's heart wrenched one more time. Was it ever going to be possible to make a family out of Jim's son and her daughter?

Increasingly it seemed like an impossible task.

* * *

Ashley was on call to supervise the fellowship-hour this week. She'd organized most of the refreshments before services began, but she'd still ducked out of the back of the church before the recessional, using her responsibilities as an excuse to avoid the usual after-services meet and greet.

She wasn't in a mood for socializing with anyone, least of all Micah St. Pierre. She checked the coffee, straightened the paper napkins and plastic forks, and tried not to cry. What had he done? Used her as some kind of inspiration for that sermon?

That whole bit at the end where he'd started talking about letting things go, like grief. She didn't have to be a genius to know that he was sending messages.

She just wanted things to go back to the way they had been. She didn't want him prying into her feelings. She didn't want him using her as some sort of inspiration for sermons. Who did?

But she didn't mind feeding him every morning. In fact, she liked feeding him. His preference for oatmeal had changed her menu offerings. But he hadn't been to the inn for breakfast since Thursday. And he rarely missed the continental breakfasts on Sunday morning.

And here she'd made oatmeal for him every day and no one had eaten any of it, except for Ella, who had been forced to eat it. So her efforts hadn't been entirely wasted. If only oatmeal could set Ella back on course. But it couldn't, and she was skating on some seriously thin ice with Dylan.

The congregation was finally making its way to the fellowship hall. She poured herself a cup of coffee and chatted with Sandra and Karen about the sermon and the quality of the choir's performance. The atmosphere changed the moment Micah entered the room, divested of his priestly robes and back in his workaday suit and Roman collar.

A lot of people had liked his sermon today, so it took him a while to make it across the room. But at least one thing hadn't changed. Micah had a sweet tooth. He might give her grief about baking for the Piece Makers, but he'd never turned down leftover cake.

And she'd made his favorite coffee cake today as a peace offering.

"Coffee cake," he said when he finally reached the refreshment table. "Did you make this for me?" He seemed so pleased.

And for some unfathomable reason, his enthusiasm for the cake didn't please her at all. Maybe because she had to face the truth: she'd baked this coffee cake *for him*. And that seemed...wrong or selfish or something. Because the cake was supposed to be for everyone. But she had to face the fact that cooking for Micah had become a guilty pleasure.

So what now? Should she give up the guilt or the pleasure in order to become her best self? The doubt left a sour taste in her mouth. She needed to stop overthinking and get things back to their normal place. "No, I didn't make this just for you, Reverend St. Pierre. I made the cake for fellowship hour."

"Oh." He took a bite. A little smile danced at the corner of his mouth.

Which gave her a lot of pleasure. Too much, really. She needed to put the minister back in his place with the rest of her community. She cooked for everyone.

"Look, I did want to apologize for last Thursday," she said. "I'm sorry I got upset with you, and I hope that's not the reason you've skipped breakfast the last few days."

"No. I've been busy the last few days."

"Oh, good."

"And Ashley, there isn't any reason for you to apologize," he said between mouthfuls of her cake.

"But I was kind of...I don't know...emotional."

"Everyone gets emotional."

She blew out a breath, suddenly annoyed at him. "Okay, I'm going to quit beating around the bush. Was today's sermon inspired by our argument on Thursday? Was it all about me and the things I need to give up in order to find a more fulfilling life?"

He glanced down at the cake and then back at her. "No. It was about everyone here. We all have something we need to let go of. No one is perfect."

"And you think, what? That I need to give up Adam? Or the Piece Makers? Or what, exactly?"

"Ashley, you need to figure that out for yourself. That's for you to decide."

"Oh, well, last Thursday I got the feeling you were telling me that I needed to let go of Adam. But I'm never going to do that, you know. I'm never going to stop loving him." There, she'd spoken the words out loud. "And I don't mean to be argumentative. I just need you to understand."

He nodded. "I get it, Ashley. Now, if you don't mind, I see Edith Carr over there waving at me. I need to go visit with her for a bit." He walked away, leaving his unfinished cake behind.

Chapter Thirteen

On Monday morning, Dylan sat at his desk, studying Ginny Whittle's lab report. He pulled at a lock of his hair as he mulled over the results, which confirmed that Ginny didn't have type II diabetes.

He'd been all set to send her off to see an endocrinologist on the mainland, but now he hesitated. Maybe Dad was right. Maybe she *was* suffering from somatic illness. And yet...

No. He'd stake his career on the fact that Ginny Whittle wasn't faking this illness. Besides, he hated the "it's all in your head" diagnosis the way most patients did. No one wanted to be told that their symptoms weren't real. He picked up his tablet and started searching medical journals for some new avenue to explore.

Dad interrupted him a few minutes later. His father was actually working today, dressed in his familiar white lab coat. His presence had become increasingly rare these days. After years of working ten- and twelve-hour days, suddenly Dad had become a nine-to-five kind of guy, but only on Monday, Wednesday, and Friday.

The rest of the time, he'd been painting Cloud Nine, Brenda's beach house. It was pitiful the way the man had lost his bearings. But then, a woman could do that to a man. Hadn't Brenda's daughter wormed her way into *his* brain? Thirty-six hours after that kiss, and he still hadn't managed to excise the memory or assuage his guilt for kissing her back. Or, for that matter, cutting her off before the kiss had even happened.

"You got a minute?" Dad asked.

"Sure. In fact, maybe you can help me brainstorm what to do about Mrs. Whittle."

Dad came into the room and sat in the side chair. "What's there to do? You hold her hand and tell her she's fine."

"She's not fine."

"Oh? Did you get her labs?"

"I did."

"And?"

"They're normal. It's not type II diabetes. But there's something going on. She's complaining of burning thirst."

"Son, we've talked about this. Sometimes there just isn't an answer, and it's more about compassion than medicine."

"So you think it's compassionate to tell her it's all in her head?"

Dad shifted in his chair. "That's not exactly fair. That's not—"

Dylan waved away Dad's comment. "I've been doing some sleuthing. Her symptoms could be diabetes insipidus."

Dad gave him a fatherly look. "Are you trying to be Marcus Welby?"

"Who the hell is Marcus Welby?"

Dad shook his head. "I am definitely getting old. Marcus Welby was a TV doctor back in the day. He was a GP, but every week, some patient would present with mysterious symptoms, and he'd figure it out. It became a disease-of-the-week show."

"Oh, you mean like *House*?"

Dad chuckled. "A whole lot more PG than *House*. Son, diabetes insipidus is exceptionally rare."

"I know. But her symptoms fit. I'm going to send her to an endocrinologist."

"Have you thought about what all those tests are going to do to her finances? She doesn't have good insurance."

"Oh. I didn't know that."

"Of course you didn't, because you leave all the billing to Lessie. But you should pay attention. Not everyone can afford every test. And the truth is, Ginny has been coming here every three months like clockwork. For five solid years, she's complained about everything from headaches to muscle pain. I know about her finances because she often shows up downstairs at the free clinic. And I've tested her for all sorts of things, and they all come back normal. What's ailing her is loneliness. She lost her husband in a car accident seven years ago, and she's never gotten over it."

"I'm sure you're right about her loneliness. But that doesn't mean she isn't sick this time. She doesn't look well."

"Do not send her to an endocrinologist. It's going to be a dead end, and she can't afford it."

Dylan ground his teeth in frustration. Dad meant well. He was always concerned about the whole patient, not just their symptoms but their finances and their job status and whatnot. He had a knack for knowing everything that was going on in a patient's life.

Dylan not so much.

But this time Dad's compassion was blinding him to the truth. Besides, Dad had handed him this patient presumably to teach him a lesson. He didn't have the right to second-guess him now, did he? He tried to tamp down on the anger that flared, but he failed, lashing out at his father.

"You know, Dad," he said in a hard voice, "maybe if you

weren't spending your time painting Brenda's beach house, you'd realize that Mrs. Whittle has been losing weight rather precipitously. I'd suspect cancer were it not for her reported symptoms. So maybe, if you were paying more attention to the patients you are forever telling me to get chummy with, you'd recognize an illness when you see one."

Dad stood up and leaned on Dylan's desk. "That was a low blow."

"Was it? Dad, you need to get your head on straight. I'm sure you came in here to read me the riot act about something Brenda is unhappy about. But now that's morphed into you second-guessing my opinion about Mrs. Whittle."

"One thing has nothing to do with the other," Dad said, straightening and folding his arms over his chest. Wow, he and Dad were having a rare fight. But then, maybe this was exactly what Dad needed in order to come to grips with reality.

"Have you ever considered the fact that you might be stressed out?" Dylan asked. "Maybe you've been burning the candle at both ends trying to please that woman. You should hear the stuff Ella has to say about her."

"Oh really, and what does Ella have to say?"

"Evidently Brenda is never happy. Ever. And Ella had to bear the brunt of that growing up. It's messed with her mind."

"So it's true, then. You two had dinner at Cibo Dell'anima."

Who had told him that? Did Dad know the rest of what happened on Saturday? Crap.

"We did. We were checking the place out for the party. It's a no go. Too dark. Too expensive. Too East End."

"And she spilled all this stuff about Brenda at dinner? Or did you pry it out of her?"

Oh boy. Dad was ticked off. "I didn't pry anything," Dylan said. But he had willingly refilled her wineglass. Did that count as prying? Maybe.

"I've had it with you, okay?" Dad's voice got low and soft, which was a surefire indication that Dad wasn't just annoyed, he was furious. "First, you will not send Ginny Whittle to an endocrinologist for tests she doesn't need and can't afford," he continued, counting points on his fingers. "And second, you will stop trying to mess with Brenda by bullying her daughter. So step away."

"Bullying? I haven't bullied her. I've paid attention to her. Maybe Brenda should do the same thing."

"Dylan, the whole idea is for us to make one big, happy family. So stop trying to screw things up and get with the damn program. Is that clear?"

Dylan said nothing as Dad turned and strode from his office. But the moment the door shut behind his father, Dylan picked up the phone and called Ginny Whittle. He told her about her lab work, as well as his long-shot hunch, and then he advised her to make an appointment with the endocrinology practice affiliated with the hospital in Georgetown. He was honest with her about the costs and the rarity of the condition known as diabetes insipidus.

Dad wasn't in his right mind if he thought Dylan would keep something from one of his patients. In fact, he was going to follow his instincts from now on. He respected Dad's opinion, but he had to stop living by it as if it were the holy word of God. Doctors often disagreed about things. This was why people got second opinions. Science could be cut-and-dry, but patient care was a whole different thing entirely.

So he defied his father for the first time in his life. He did it even though some of what Dad had to say came perilously close to the truth. Dylan hadn't bullied Ella on Saturday night, but he had manipulated her in order to get dirt on Brenda. And that wasn't right.

But then Ella had turned the tables on him, hadn't she? He'd certainly kissed her back when she'd thrown her arms around his neck. Even worse, he'd thoroughly enjoyed every moment.

* * *

On Wednesday afternoon, Ella strolled up the curving path to Grace Methodist Church under a canopy of live oaks, which filtered the surprisingly warm March sunlight. The rain earlier in the week had departed, leaving behind enough humidity to wilt her cotton dress.

Sweat was beginning to dampen her back between her shoulder blades. She should have worn a tank top or something cooler than the dark-blue India-print dress that sucked up the sun's heat. But the dress seemed more appropriate for a meeting at a church than shorts and a tank top.

She was here to take a tour of the reception hall with Dylan. Over the last few days, they had eliminated at least five possible venues for the engagement party, including a couple on the mainland, mostly because of availability. Grace Church was available.

She headed toward the church's front doors as the sweat poured down her skin. In truth, she couldn't blame the perspiration entirely on the sun. Some of this heat came from her insides, driven by embarrassment, or worse yet, desire.

She remembered far too much about last Saturday night and that moment when she'd thrown her arms around Dylan's shoulders. If only she'd been just a little more buzzed, maybe she could have excised the memory. But no. She remembered it all.

So far, in their brief phone conversations, Dylan hadn't mentioned the kiss at all. Would he continue to pretend it hadn't happened? If only her conscience (or maybe her somewhat starved libido) could do the same.

Ella pushed through the doors that led into the church's

vestibule. The sanctuary was to the left, and the meeting rooms, Sunday school, and day care center were to the right. Grace Methodist was by far the biggest church in town. Its facilities dwarfed Heavenly Rest.

The air-conditioned foyer made her damp dress feel clammy against her skin. She paced and tried to stay warm while she considered several rehearsed apologies. She had to apologize, right? The kiss had been totally out of bounds. And she needed to let it go in order to become her best self. She paced and fretted until she could almost hear the blood rushing through her veins.

But all the rehearsed words left her brain when Dylan came striding up the walkway five minutes later. And when their gazes locked, her runaway pulse also settled back into her chest as if he'd reached out and told her heart to calm down. And it struck her: apologizing to him wouldn't be that hard at all.

"Sorry I'm late," he said. "I had to make a phone call to a patient that took longer than I thought it would."

"No worries," she said, then lost her nerve. Maybe she didn't need to apologize at all. Maybe she should wait for him to bring up Saturday night.

But he didn't, which was disappointing on some level even though it provided her an escape hatch from her own bad behavior.

"So, let's go talk to the church secretary," he said, turning and striding down the hallway like a man with a purpose. He'd probably been attending services here since he was a little kid, so he knew his way around. Heck, he'd probably been an altar boy here. She could imagine a younger version of him, maybe with freckles across his nose and a wayward curl falling over his forehead, wearing robes and lighting altar candles. He'd probably been a model child, a Boy Scout who helped little old ladies across the street. And now he was Doctor Dependable.

He might have been five minutes late, but he'd had an excellent excuse. He'd been taking care of someone.

Damn. When had her opinion of him altered so dramatically? She couldn't quite say for sure, but maybe it had been that moment last Saturday when he'd come after her and let her cry on his shoulder.

Cody would never have done a thing like that.

The unwanted comparison startled her. She pushed it away firmly and followed him into the church office, which was empty.

"Mrs. Walsh?" Dylan called out.

A second later, Rev. Pasidena came through the door. "Hey, Dylan. I'm afraid Mrs. Walsh had a family emergency. Her momma is in the hospital, so I'm covering for her. Hope you don't mind."

"Not at all. You know Ella McMillan?"

"No, but I certainly know your mom," the minister said, offering his hand.

Rev. Pasidena had a strong grip, a ready smile, and a shiny bald head. He winked at her as he let go of her hand. "In fact," he said, "I'm trying to woo your momma away from Heavenly Rest."

Something about the way he said the words annoyed Ella. Was Jim trying to convince Mom to switch churches? Probably.

"Come on, I'll give y'all a tour of the reception facilities." The minister led them down the hall to a room big enough to accommodate a wedding reception or an engagement party. The room had no windows, a utilitarian floor, and dark paneling. Even worse, the place reeked of scorched coffee and old doughnuts. No doubt about it, this was where the Methodists held their fellowship hours.

"Y'all should know that it's our busy season coming up," Rev. Pasidena said. "Lots of May and June weddings. Dylan, I mentioned this to your daddy on Sunday. Jim went ahead and booked the room for April sixteenth, which is a Friday. It was the only time we had available."

"April sixteenth?" Ella said. "That's less than three weeks away, and—" She stopped speaking before she said something unkind about Jim or the minister. If she made the wrong move, Jim would hear about it from Dylan, and then Mom would hear about it from Jim. And then…

"Well, I'm glad he jumped on the date," Dylan said.

Forget everything nice she'd been thinking about Dylan Killough. He and his father were ganging up on her and Mom in a subtle power play.

"Great," Rev. Pasidena said. "Y'all can give Mrs. Walsh a call to work out the details. Have you picked a caterer? If you haven't, we have a list."

"We're thinking about having Annie Robinson do it," Dylan said.

The minister nodded. "A good choice. She's done a lot of receptions and parties here."

As they left the room and strolled down the hallway, the minister cleared his throat and said, "You know, Ella, we would love to make a home for you and your mother here."

Ella clamped her mouth shut on a bunch of words that didn't need to be said out loud. After last Sunday, she wasn't going to leave Heavenly Rest. She liked Rev. St. Pierre's sermons because they made a person think and provided a road map for self-improvement—something she needed in her life right at the moment. Rev. Pasidena was undoubtedly a good clergyman, but Granny would never go over to the Methodists, and Mom would never walk away from the choir she'd just formed.

"And you know," the minister continued, oblivious to Ella's unspoken annoyance, "our choir director, Simon Paredes, has had to retire. He had a stroke a few months back, and while he's made a good recovery, he doesn't need the stress of the choir. We have thirty members in our choir, you know. And many of them have recommended your mother as a replacement for Simon. They know her from last Christmas, when she stepped up to direct the Christmas Chorale when Simon couldn't do it."

Ella couldn't let this pass without some pushback. She didn't want to be unpleasant though. "Have you asked my mother directly?" she asked, hoping that this question didn't open a big, nasty can of worms.

"Well, no. But Jim and I talked about it on Sunday."

"When Jim reserved the room?"

"As a matter of fact, yes."

She nodded. "Well, I'll certainly mention it to her," Ella said in her most polite voice. Wow. Jim and the pastor were getting ready to blindside Mom, in a low-down and dirty maneuver, in Ella's opinion. Who needed Dylan messing things up when Jim was doing a fine job of it all by himself?

The minister said goodbye, and Ella stalked out of the church, ready to stand in the yard and let go of a primal scream. But that was impossible. Not only would the minister hear it, but Dylan was right there and she wasn't going to give him any ammunition. Even if she kind of liked him and had shared a memorable kiss with him.

"I want you to know that I had nothing to do with what just happened," Dylan said before Ella could even formulate a coherent sentence.

She blew out a long breath, but it failed to cool her anger. "I'm going now before I say something nasty." She headed down the path to the sidewalk.

He followed, keeping pace with her. "No. Don't go. Stay. Talk to me."

She stopped and turned. "I don't want my mother to abandon the choir at Heavenly Rest just to make your dad happy."

"Fair enough. And Dad shouldn't have booked the room without consulting us. I'm annoyed at that."

"You are?"

"Yeah. He's been doing stuff like that recently. He'll put me in charge of something, and then he goes off and does it for himself anyway. It's really ticking me off." He paused a moment, glancing at the big shade trees on the church's grounds as if he was carefully choosing his words. "I had a fight with him this morning about this exact thing. I accused him of trying to please your mother."

She blinked. "And I'm angry because Mom might do something dumb, like leave the Episcopalians, just to please your father."

He nodded. "I guess maybe they're trying to make each other happy."

"Yeah. And even though I'm annoyed at the little game Jim is playing, I'm not about to launch a program to break them up. Just sayin'."

He nodded and jammed his hands into his pockets. "I know. But I'm worried about him."

"And I'm worried about her. But you know, I think it's all going to work out," she said.

"Is it?"

"Actually, I have no idea, but I'm hoping." She paused, glancing at the church with its brick facade and pristine spire. Grace Church was like something on an old-time postcard. A perfect picture of small-town American faith.

"Do you want to have the party at Grace Church?" she asked.

He shook his head. "I don't know. It's not as nice as the yacht club, but it might be the only room available. Maybe Dad was onto something when he made the reservation."

"Maybe," she said on a long sigh.

"Why don't we run Grace Church past them this coming

Sunday? Since the room is booked. It could be our fallback position."

She nodded. "Okay," Ella said. Suddenly she had no words, except the ones she'd rehearsed. It was now or never. No more putting it off. "About Saturday, I—"

"Don't apologize," he interrupted.

"But I—"

"No apologies. You'd had a rough day, and I should have cut you off."

"It wasn't your responsibility to cut me off."

His lips broadened into that smile—the one that lit up his face and everything around him. "Wasn't it?"

"No. You're not *responsible* for me. I'm actually responsible for myself."

"Maybe, but since I'm a few months older than you, I have a responsibility to look after you. Cutting off little sisters before they get toasted is part of big-brother territory."

He wanted to be her brother? After he'd kissed her back? No way. He didn't want her as his sister. And she didn't want him as her brother. Which was a ginormous problem, but not one she could ever admit to anyone.

Chapter Fourteen

On Sunday afternoon, Dylan had to circle Redbud Street looking for a parking spot. Evidently, all the active adults living at Bayview Vistas were hosting Easter dinners for their loved ones. There wasn't a vacant visitor's spot to be found.

Having Easter dinner at his soon-to-be step-grandmother's wasn't high on Dylan's agenda because it would require him to be on his best behavior. And he wasn't interested in being a good boy.

For one thing, he was ticked off at Dad. He'd intervened again, this time with Coreen Martel, one of his geriatric patients. Coreen was in her late eighties and suffering congestive heart failure. She needed to be in a nursing home, getting hospice care. But she was sharp of mind and resistant to the idea of leaving the home she'd lived in most of her life. She was getting home care a few days a week, but Dylan didn't think it was enough.

But Dad disagreed. He thought she was fine being at home because that's where she wanted to be. They'd had a big blowup about it yesterday.

And then there was the engagement party. Dylan had no idea how Brenda would react when she found out that Dad had booked Grace Church without consulting with anyone. He expected a nuclear explosion, and the fallout was going to be bad.

Epic even.

Which would certainly advance his plan to break up Dad and Brenda. But would it break the promise he'd made to Ella not to use the party planning as a means for breaking them up?

For some reason, he wanted to keep that promise. And he also wanted to protect Ella. He didn't want Brenda blaming her for what was going to happen. And he didn't want Brenda to blame Dad either, which made no sense.

So he'd been nominated to play the heavy in this family drama.

With a resigned sigh, he left the car in the spot he finally found two blocks away and made his way up to Nancy's condo. Brenda answered the doorbell, wearing a go-to-church dress in a bright flowered print and a strand of pearls around her neck.

"Happy Easter," he said, trying to invest his voice with holiday joy. But his greeting bounced off Brenda like bullets off Superman.

She stood aside and let him enter the long hallway into the main living area. Nancy had settled into her new home. The boxes were gone, pictures were hung on the walls, and family photos of people Dylan didn't know graced the end tables on either side of her living room sofa.

He tried not to resent the fact that Dad had ditched the office to hang these pictures and put up these shelves. He tried not to stare at the photographs of strangers, but all those smiling faces seemed to be telling him that he didn't belong here.

"Hey," Ella said from behind. He turned and froze.

She was standing in the galley kitchen putting deviled eggs onto a cut-glass dish. Like her mother, she wore a dress with a flowered print, but unlike Brenda's, it came down below her knees in a wide, loose skirt with an opening up the front that exposed her long legs. Like everything she wore, the dress was a little bit big for her slender frame, and the V of the neck drooped down on one side, exposing a hint of lacy bra underneath.

The spit dried up in his mouth. With her beautiful messy hair piled up on top of her head, she looked as if she'd just come out of someone's bedroom. The memory of her slightly inebriated kiss ran through his mind, and he had a sudden, overpowering urge to taste her again.

What was wrong with him?

He turned his back without speaking to her and headed off toward the living room, where Dad was standing by the fireplace drinking something that might be scotch or bourbon. "Can I have one of those, please?" he asked.

Dad happily poured him a few fingers of Maker's Mark into a glass of ice and pressed the drink into his hand. It might be called Tennessee sipping whiskey, but Dylan took a bracing swallow of the stuff before sitting down in one of the side chairs and trying without much success to ignore Ella.

That skirt swirled around her legs every time she brought something to the table. Her voice had a musical ring to it that made his brain cells hum along. Her laugh...

Oh boy. He was in trouble. He squared his shoulders and focused like a laser on the small talk.

Dad was giving a blow-by-blow description of the sailboat races that had taken place on Saturday. Brenda and her mother were talking about yarn, in a conversation that was filled with so much jargon it numbed his mind. Ella said almost nothing, and weirdly, she was the only one he wanted to talk to.

Dylan was on his second bourbon by the time they sat down to a traditional Easter dinner, complete with a relish tray and deviled eggs, a glazed ham, scalloped potatoes, asparagus, fresh-baked rolls, and a German chocolate cake that Nancy had made from scratch.

It had been years since he and Dad had celebrated Easter with a home-cooked meal like this. Usually, they headed off for brunch at the yacht club after church and called it a day. Thinking back over his childhood, Dylan couldn't even remember having a meal like this when Mom had been alive. But then again, his memories of Mom were sketchy even though he'd been ten when she'd passed away.

As dinner progressed, Dylan grew more on edge. Brenda and Ella talked about various classical violin pieces that might be appropriate for Ashley Scott's Saturday tea service. Dad weighed in because he was a classical music aficionado. Nancy made sure everyone had seconds and then brought out the German chocolate cake.

But no one said one word about the elephant in the room—the planning for the famous engagement party. What were they waiting for? Christmas?

Suddenly the whole thing seemed like such a sham. Or maybe a setup. Had innocent-looking Ella arranged this so he'd be the bad guy?

Maybe she had. But someone had to do the dirty work.

"So," Dylan said, casting his glance around the table and his soon-to-be family, "Ella and I have been busting our humps searching for a place to have your engagement party. We've checked out Cibo Dell'anima and a bunch of smaller places around town, as well as a couple of spots in Georgetown. None of them are going to work. So earlier this week we took a tour of Grace Church, and we've booked it for April sixteenth. I think the next item on the agenda is to talk about catering. We were thinking about Annie Robinson. So—"

"You booked Grace Church? For April sixteenth? Oh my goodness, that's only two weeks away," Brenda said, pressing her hand to her sternum in a dramatic way, as if this news had given her palpitations. Which, now that he thought about it, it probably had.

"I'm sorry about the date. It was the only day available, and since we've jettisoned the yacht club..." Dylan gave a little shrug, then concentrated on the cake in front of him. He popped a piece into his mouth and savored Nancy Jacobs's cooking while he waited for Dad to admit that he'd booked the church.

But before that happened, Ella blurted, "Dylan, this is not what we agreed to. We were going to run this idea by Mom and Jim before we settled on it. You promised me that you wouldn't use the engagement party to—"

"Why do you have to be so disagreeable all the time?" Brenda interrupted. "I'm starting to think you really do want to sabotage this party. Of course I can't have the party at Grace Church."

"Why not?" Dad finally weighed in. Coward.

"Because she'll be the subject of gossip all over this town, Jim. Come on, don't you know that?" Nancy said, then turned toward Dylan. "And you need to learn that, young man. Why, just the other day, Donna Cuthbert was all over me, wanting to know if Brenda was going to abandon Heavenly Rest and become the director of the choir at Grace Church. Shame on you, Dylan. You've been living here for a while." Nancy turned toward Ella. "And I know you're new here, but your mother is not going to abandon the Episcopalians."

"Oh, for goodness' sake," Ella said, staring daggers at Dad, who was contemplating his uneaten slice of German chocolate cake. "This isn't Dylan's fault. The minister told us on Wednesday that Jim booked the church a week ago. He suggested that Mom and I should both leave Heavenly Rest." She glanced at her grandmother. "Sorry Granny, he didn't mention your name, but maybe that's a good thing. Anyway"—she turned her gaze on Mom—"he's clearly trying to get you as the new choir director over there."

Brenda's mouth dropped open right before she turned on Dad, who was still looking down at his cake with the guiltiest of expressions. "You let Reverend Pasidena think I might consider directing the Grace Church choir? How could you do such a thing, Jim?"

"It was a trade-off. I couldn't confirm the room otherwise."

"Oh my god." Brenda stood up, her face white as a sheet. She didn't look well, but then she'd just had a shock. Dad was losing it. Maybe he needed a physical or a mental acuity test or something. Dylan was suddenly more concerned about his father than he'd been before. What in the world had Dad been thinking?

"Momma, I'm going now," Brenda said in a tight-lipped voice, right before she turned and rushed for the door, stopping at the coat tree in the hall to grab her purse.

Dad mumbled, "Excuse me," and rushed after her.

*　*　*

"That went well," Granny said in a louder-than-normal voice as she collapsed back into her chair, casting quick glances at Dylan and Ella.

Ella stared back at her grandmother because she didn't want to set eyes on Dylan. She was furious with him for the way he'd raised the Grace Church situation. Hadn't they agreed to run the idea by Mom and ask her opinion? And she'd never intended to let Mom know that Jim had acted unilaterally. But once Dylan spilled the beans, she'd had no other choice.

"What is wrong with you?" she finally asked, turning toward him with her best angry stare. "We had a plan, and you—"

"Don't blame Dylan, sugar," Granny interrupted.

Ella turned toward Granny so fast it almost gave her whiplash.

"Are you taking his side? He just blew up Easter dinner by not following the plan."

"I'm not taking anyone's side," Granny said in that tiny voice of hers. "But I know we couldn't have gone on much longer talking about the sailing regatta or violin pieces the way we were." She gave Dylan a hard look. "I don't know as I would have done it your way, son, but you certainly did move us on to more important topics of conversation. And good for you trying to take the blame for your father's misstep. I admire that."

Ella stared at her grandmother. "Granny, Mom just stormed off in a huff. How is that—"

"She needed to storm off. She's been under a lot of pressure lately. If you want my advice, y'all should give up trying to host a big party and do something informal on the beach the way we talked about the other day."

Granny tossed her napkin onto the table. "I've got a blazing headache. I think I'm going to lie down for a bit." She turned and headed into her bedroom, closing the door behind her.

"How could you ruin Easter?" Ella said, getting up from her place and picking up her dishes. She moved into the kitchen, intent on washing up before she left. No way she was leaving this mess for Granny to clean.

She turned on the faucet and began rinsing the dishes before loading the dishwasher. She didn't expect Doctor Dishonorable to hang around. In fact, she wanted him to—

Not be clearing the dishes from the table and bringing them into the kitchen, as if he intended to help. That was not something she wanted him to be doing. She wanted him to leave.

But instead, he took off his jacket and rolled up his shirt-sleeves, exposing the rope-like muscles of his forearms, which were attractive and made her insides melt a little. He kept making trips back and forth to the table, as if he knew how to help. What a concept. Had Cody washed a dish ever?

No.

Damn.

She put her head down and concentrated on loading dishes. There were more dishes than space in the washer. So she started a cycle and then filled the sink with warm water and dish liquid. In the meantime, Dylan made himself busy wrapping leftovers.

And when she'd rinsed the soapy water from the first pot, he materialized at her side with a clean dishcloth and started drying. She became uncomfortably aware of his body heat. The man was like a walking furnace.

"Missed a spot," he muttered, way too close to her ear as he handed back one of the casserole pots.

"Uh, thanks," she said, as a medley of emotions settled over her—annoyance and attraction and remorse and guilt and a bunch of other overwhelming feelings. Her eyes watered up under the assault. And through the haze of confusion, one thing rang true. Having him help was…nice. Pain-in-the-butt Dylan was nice.

Maybe he hadn't blown up Easter. Maybe he'd just been covering for his father, which he didn't have to do. She'd been the one who'd blown up Easter by telling the truth.

Another tear escaped and rolled down her cheek.

Dylan noticed the waterworks. "I'm sorry," he said in a contrite tone.

"For what? I'm sorry. I'm the one who blew things up."

"Doing what? Telling the truth about my father's dumbass move?"

She'd refused his apology once when all he'd done was speak the truth. She stopped washing dishes and turned toward him. He was so much taller than she was, and they stood so close together she could count his amazing eyelashes. No man should have lashes like that. It was unfair.

"Sometimes the truth can hurt people," she said.

"I know."

"So, really, I should have figured out what you were trying to do. You know? Sparing Mom the truth about what Jim did."

"Or maybe your mother needed to hear the truth."

"Why? So she could fight with your Dad?"

He shrugged. "I didn't plan it that way, Ella."

"And now you think you are so smart. You think she's going to get all up in your father's face and blame him for a bunch of things. You think she's that kind of person, but you know what? You're wrong. She doesn't blame people for things. She simply has incredibly high standards. Sometimes they are so hard to meet."

"So you've said before, and I heard the conversation at the table about those violin pieces. Your mother kept warning you away from the ones she considered difficult."

Ella shrugged and turned back to the last casserole dish, but he gently took her by the upper arm and pulled her back toward him. His fingers were warm against her bare skin and gentle despite the force.

"We don't need to blame anyone but Dad for today's debacle, okay? And I was only trying to get your mother to accept Grace Church as a locale for the party because finding a venue has taken over my life. Why don't we give ourselves a little break in the blame department?"

She met his gaze. "Okay, but we still need to find a place for the party."

"One that will meet your mother's standards?"

"You know, we should listen to Granny. She's wise. Let's have the party on the beach. I know for a fact that Mom likes that idea."

"It might rain."

"Let's get a tent."

She waited for Dylan to argue with her, but he kept his mouth shut.

"So you're okay with this idea?"

"I don't know. I guess we don't get hurricanes in April."

She snorted.

"What beach were you thinking?" he asked.

"Paradise Beach, right in front of Cloud Nine. It's lovely. We could do it at sunset."

"Prime thunderstorm time."

"Are you always so negative? Sunset is romantic."

He shrugged again. "I don't know."

"I tell you what, why don't I pack a picnic and we can check it out tomorrow evening at sunset."

* * *

Brenda reached her car, parked in one of the condo's guest spots, just as Jim rounded the corner in a lope. "Stop," he called.

Ignoring him, she yanked open the car door, got inside, and locked herself in. Or maybe she'd locked Jim out. Either way, her heart was pounding so hard it made her whole body shake.

She expected Jim to bang on the door or yell, but she wouldn't even have cared if he had. Instead of yelling, though, he bent over and stared at her through the passenger's side window. "Please open the door," he said in that voice—the one that wormed its way into her core and made her heart stop doing its tap dance on her sternum. How the hell did he do that? No doubt he was a born healer.

"Brenda, honey, don't sulk."

Well, that was a tiny bit annoying because she wasn't sulking. She was crying and having some sort of panic attack. She turned toward him, tears smearing her vision. "It's my party and I'll sulk if I want to."

"If you're talking about that old Lesley Gore song, I think the title is 'It's My Party and I'll Cry If I Want To,' and it looks like you're crying. Honey, don't cry. Unlock the door. Let me explain."

She brushed the tears from her cheeks. "How could you?"

"Honey, there's an explanation. But you'll have to let me in to get it. Open the door."

She pressed the unlock button, and Jim climbed into the car. "I'm listening."

He cleared his throat. "Well, it's kind of a long story."

"I have nothing else to do."

"Well, it started when Grant Ackerman and I arrived at the church office at the same moment."

"And why were you at the church office?"

"Well, I'll be honest. I was there to see if the room was available. It gets booked up fast because it's the only party room big enough to host a sizable event."

"And you did that because you didn't trust the kids?"

"Well, no. To be honest, Dylan has been trying to sabotage us, and Ella doesn't know the lay of the land. So I thought I'd jump in to have a fail-safe, you know?"

"Okay. So you booked the room."

"Well, not exactly. You see, Grant was there, and he wanted the room for Jim Miller's party. He's retiring from the volunteer fire department. And Mrs. Walsh, the church secretary, wasn't in that day because her mother is ill. And Reverend Pasidena was not above making Grant and me compete for the room."

"Oh my goodness. Really?"

"Yeah. He was trying to get help from the volunteer fire department for some fundraising for the playground equipment, and I might have piped in that I would try to convince you to become the choir director."

"You did not."

"I did. And I'm sorry. But you know, there are worse things in the world. The Grace Church choir is twice the size of the choir at Heavenly Rest. And besides, I didn't commit you to coming over to the Methodists, I just said I'd raise the topic with you."

"I'm furious with you."

"Well, I should have told you about it, but I was hoping the kids would come up with some other plan. But it looks like they're stumped."

"They aren't working very well together."

"So it would seem," he said on a sigh. "But you know, Brenda, you might consider the idea of becoming the choir director at Grace Church."

Her heart started pounding again. Was this that important to him? Until this moment, she hadn't considered that him being a Methodist and her being an Episcopalian would create problems. This was a second marriage for both of them. They weren't going to be bringing any new children into the world.

Thank goodness. They already had too many kids to deal with.

She took a big breath, but her heart wouldn't stop rocking in her chest. "Do you *want* me to direct the choir?"

"No. I'm only saying that it might be more challenging for you."

Ah, yes. Because she was a perfectionist—the very thing Rev. St. Pierre had been suggesting that she give up to become her best self.

She smiled. "No. I'm happy where I am. I gave the people at Heavenly Rest my word. I started that choir, and it might be small and amateurish. And those people know nothing about reading music. But we make a joyful noise every Sunday. And the congregation is so happy about it. I can't walk away from that."

"Okay, if you're sure."

He didn't sound sure.

"I'm sure. But the thing is, are you sure? Is this about me worshipping at one church and you at another? Because if it is, then I need to make something clear. I love you. I want to be with you. But if you think I'm leaving Heavenly Rest, where my momma has worshipped her entire life, then you need to think again."

He chuckled. "No, it's not about that. I honestly thought you'd jump at the chance to take over the choir at Grace Church."

She could even understand why. "No. I'm happy where I am."

"Good. Because I'm not. Next Sunday, I'm coming to church with you. I want to hear this extraordinary choir."

"Jim, you don't have to—"

"No, I think I do. I think I need to send a message to everyone in this town that my fiancée has made up her mind."

"I love you, Jim."

"I love you more."

"Oh, wait . . ." Her heart refused to stop pounding.

"What?"

"What about Dylan?" she asked. "You can't abandon him. He's been going to Grace Church all his life."

"Uh, well, maybe. I'll talk to him."

"No. We need to keep things the way they are, okay?"

"Honey, are you sure that's wise?"

No, she wasn't. But taking this stand seemed necessary. If Jim changed churches, she could almost hear what the Methodists would say about her. And even worse, every instinct told her that Dylan would be hurt.

Creating a new family where there hadn't been one before was turning into a difficult problem.

Chapter Fifteen ——————————

When the last dish was dried and put away, Ella knocked on Granny's door to check up on her. She'd gotten into her pajamas and was settled down into her bed reading a book.

"We cleaned up the kitchen."

Granny looked up from the page. "Together?"

Ella nodded and tried not to blush. "He's surprisingly helpful in unexpected ways."

Granny's lips twitched in a tiny smile. "I'm sure he is. His father probably trained him well. Jim is handy to have around the house." She gestured at her new curtains and blinds. "It would have cost me a fortune to hire a handyman to install those."

"Yeah, I think Jim is terrific."

Granny nodded.

"Um, about the party. Dylan and I were talking while we did the dishes, and I'm going to try to convince him that a beach party is the way to go."

"Good for you."

"I'm going to pack a picnic and show him how beautiful the beach is at sunset."

"Oh, really?" Granny looked over the rims of her glasses. Her stare was surprisingly acute.

Ella blushed. "Yeah, I know. I'm not exactly a cook, but..."

"You're planning to cook the food for this picnic?" Granny's focus sharpened further.

"Well, yeah. I mean, I have the use of Ashley's kitchen. Why not?"

"Oh, well, that's true. But you know, Ella, if you want to convince Dylan that this is a good idea, the food is going to be important."

She nodded. "I know. I've been surfing wedding sites on the internet, and I saw this idea on Martha Stewart of a fried chicken and champagne party. And it seemed so...I don't know, Southern or something. I'm not a Southerner, but...what do you think?"

"I think you need my fried chicken recipe. I'll email it to you tomorrow morning."

"Granny, your fried chicken is the best."

Granny beamed a smile. "I know. It's the secret ingredient. And for Brenda's sake, I will share this recipe with you. But you have to promise never to tell Ashley Scott about it."

"I promise."

Granny settled back on the pillows and adjusted her glasses. "Sugar, is Dylan driving you home? It's late."

Ella nodded. "He insisted."

"Of course he did." Granny smiled again. "Turn the alarm on when you leave. And call me if you have any questions about the recipe."

Five minutes later, Ella found herself ensconced in the soft leather seat of Dylan's fully loaded Honda Accord—the quintessential millennial-mobile. Boy, this was a far cry from Cody's fifteen-year-old pickup truck. She didn't want to compare Cody to Dylan, but she found herself doing it anyway.

Cody was attractive in that dangerous, bad-boy way. He was also adept at delivering lines that turned females into mush, and he was pretty damn hot in bed. He'd lured Ella away from home with his sweet-talking ways and extracted endless second chances from her despite his peccadilloes. Until tonight, she'd never met a man who was better at apologizing.

But maybe Cody had met his match, although Dylan's approach was inventive. He hadn't said much more than "I'm sorry." He hadn't made big promises he couldn't keep. He'd just whipped out a dish towel and helped her dry the casserole dishes.

His helpfulness had been novel and unique. It made her burn in an unholy way. She sank down in the luxurious leather and forced herself not to look at his hands on the steering wheel. Like his father, he had incredibly long fingers.

Ooops. She was staring at them, idly wondering how they might feel against her skin. She pulled her gaze away, focusing instead on her fingers intertwined in her lap. The silence became oppressive as raw desire raged through her.

Was she curious about him as a lover because he was forbidden?

Maybe.

For thirteen years, she'd remained loyal and faithful to a man who was unworthy of it. She'd been hit on by all sorts of drunks in countless bars and county fairs and musical venues over the years. Some of those guys had even been attractive. She might even have flirted back a few times when Cody wasn't paying attention to her.

But she'd never been unfaithful.

She'd never had the nerve. She might be thirty years old, but she'd only ever been with one guy. Unfortunately, that man was still running around her head, messing with her thinking. She needed to branch out. Excise Cody from her brain. She'd already kicked him out of her heart.

But Dylan? He was forbidden. Was that why he seemed so...safe?

Dylan pulled the car into the parking lot at Howland House and turned off the engine. Whoa, why'd he do that? She should get out of the car now. She should run. She should be a good girl and try to meet Mom's expectations.

She met his gaze, instead. He looked all buttoned up, and she wanted to undo him. She wanted...

A lot.

"So," she said, swallowing back her desire, "Granny has promised to give me her fried chicken recipe. So you're in for a treat tomorrow night."

"Oh? That good, huh?" His deep blue eyes seemed to capture the light from Howland House's carriage lamps.

"Yup. Wait till you taste it." She reached for the door handle, but he grabbed her right forearm before she could get to it. His touch was like fire, branding her skin, melting her all the way to her core.

She didn't fight him when he pulled her closer. "It's not fried chicken I want to taste, Ella." His words were low and deep.

"Oh?"

He shook his head. "I'm going to be honest."

"I have a feeling you always are," she muttered.

"I keep thinking about that kiss. On the boardwalk."

"Oh, yeah. Uh..." She hesitated. Should she tell him the truth? Absolutely. They had been truthful from the start, hadn't they? "I keep thinking about it too."

He responded to this by leaning over the console, his mouth coming down on hers, hard and swift and hot and delicious. No sweet talk. Heck, there wasn't one thing sweet about him.

He tasted like the paprika she'd sprinkled over the deviled eggs tempered by the bourbon he'd been drinking. She opened her senses to it, leaning into the console and combing her hand through his too-short curls.

They were soft and silky. So strange and different.

Wow, his kiss was different too. Commanding but soft, gentle but firm, and erotic as hell. And then his hand worked its way under the V of her neckline to capture her breast. The touch was so exquisite she groaned out loud, throwing her head back. He followed the touch with a string of kisses, like red-hot pearls down her throat to the nape of her neck.

Shivers and fire ran through her body. "I want you," she said, surprising herself.

He lifted his head, his hair tousled and falling over his forehead, his lips kiss-swollen. He would stop her, right? He was a good boy. He wore bow ties. But instead of talking some sense into her, he said, "We could go back to my place. I'm living alone these days."

She stared at him, and he didn't press the point. He didn't try to talk her out of it either. He simply waited for her to decide. Having the power of choosing was new and strange and seductive.

"I'm not looking for a forever kind of thing," she found herself saying. "And, you know, this is a huge complication."

"I know. And I'm not looking for anything serious either. Maybe we just need to, you know, get this out of our systems."

And then what? But she didn't say those words out loud. If this encounter was a friendly sort of thing, then it didn't matter, right? Her inner voice sounded suspiciously like Cody. Was she sweet-talking herself into this?

Yeah, probably. But on the other hand, maybe she needed to stop worrying for five seconds and go after what she wanted for once.

"Okay," she said. She could hardly believe the word when it left her mouth.

And so she went home with Doctor Dreamy. Home to the place he'd lived all his life. Home to the room he'd slept in as a kid because he hadn't yet moved into the master bedroom. Thank goodness the room didn't still have a twin bed or posters of superheroes on the wall. His walls were empty and looked freshly painted. But the room had no adjoining bath, and the decor was plain vanilla, with navy curtains and a matching navy bedspread and a bookshelf crammed with books on sailing and fly-fishing.

She took one look at the room and laughed out loud.

"What?" he said.

"You don't do much entertaining, do you?"

He turned around and pinned her against the doorway. "I've been living with my father for the last year."

"Living with *you* didn't stop *him*," she said, right before his mouth landed on hers. After that, all talking ceased. Dylan proved surprisingly adept for a guy living in his childhood bedroom. He'd also perfected the one-handed unbuttoning technique. He made surprisingly short work of the buttons up the front of her dress.

"Did you learn that trick in med school?" she asked.

He didn't answer. And she didn't press. He was not much of a talker when he got busy. So she got busy herself, undoing his bow tie and undoing the buttons down his shirt. She needed both hands though.

But when she had the garments completely undone and untucked, he finished the job, shucking out of the shirt and then making quick work of his pants.

* * *

Ella didn't want to compare, but how could she not? She'd always regarded Cody as pretty good, but Dylan was so much better, in spite of his plain vanilla room and his navy blue suits. Not to mention the bow ties.

Who wore bow ties these days?

And even in bed, he was a bow tie kind of guy. His approach wasn't wild or crazy or even terribly inventive. But oh, he was slow and patient and had an amazing working knowledge of female anatomy.

Yeah, he was an incredible lover. And besides, who said vanilla was boring? She was willing to bet that a Google search on ice cream flavors would prove that vanilla topped the list of favorite flavors. Vanilla was versatile. You could put whipped cream and cherries on top. You could drizzle chocolate or caramel on it. You could slice up a banana and go to town. Vanilla might be plain, but it was spicy if you got the premium stuff with the little bits of vanilla bean in the cream.

Dylan was like that flavor.

And she didn't want to leave his bed. Snuggling up to him was really nice, but ultimately unwise since this was only a fling. And, damn, he was going to become her stepsibling.

Merely saying the word "sibling" had a certain ick factor even if she wanted another gigantic helping of vanilla, please. And especially because he was so warm and cuddly and the air-conditioning in his house had been turned to subzero. She could get used to warm and cuddly. Cody always had cold feet.

The unwanted comparison crept into her brain like a little blinking caution light. She'd repeated history, hadn't she?

She'd gone off with some guy, knowing it would make her mother go ballistic. Crap. Mom would murder her if she ever found out.

The digital clock on Dylan's bedside table said it was after three in the morning. In a couple of hours, she'd need to be up, getting ready for breakfast service at the inn.

The walk back to the inn would take twenty minutes. She should go.

She slipped from the covers, the cold air in the room raising acres of gooseflesh as she scooped up her discarded clothing and tiptoed down the hall to the guest bathroom, where she dressed and tried unsuccessfully to straighten her tangled hair. When she was semi-presentable, she inched the door open, only to find Dylan standing in the hallway wearing a white T-shirt and a pair of gray sweatpants with holes in both knees.

Dammit. She hadn't wanted to wake him up. She'd thought he was sound asleep, judging by the snores. Also, the holey sweats were a revelation that she liked. Too much.

But now she'd have to talk to him. She wasn't sure exactly what to say. So she started with an apology. "I'm sorry. I didn't mean to—"

"You were going to walk back to the inn by yourself." It wasn't a question. His blue stare had a probing intensity.

"I need to get back. I have to get up at oh-dark-thirty for the breakfast service. And I'm sure Ashley has noticed that I'm missing. That can't be good."

He blinked. "She keeps an eye on you?"

* * *

Dylan crossed his arms over his chest, trying not to forcibly pull Ella back into his arms. When he'd awakened a moment ago and found Ella gone, he'd been ticked off.

What? Had she hated it? Because he was pretty sure that the sex had been good. More than good.

But he hadn't considered the fact that Ashley Scott might be keeping an eye out for Ella or worried that she hadn't come back to the inn this evening.

"So you think Ashley will notice?"

"Of course she will. So I'll just let myself out and—"

"I'll take you home."

"You know, it's not necessary."

The hell it wasn't. He was surprised by her attitude and yet not surprised at all. She'd been clear from the start that this wasn't anything serious. Merely lust or something. A fling to get the attraction out of their systems.

Ha. That was a joke. Or maybe the joke was on him. Maybe she was simply horny tonight, and he'd been handy. Wasn't that the way musicians lived? Moving from place to place and lover to lover.

"Well, I'm not letting you walk home in the dark," he said. Maybe she was used to one-night stands, but he'd been raised a little differently. He wasn't going to check his manners at the door. Even if the idea of having a relationship with Brenda's daughter was . . .

Impossible. It almost didn't matter if Dad and Brenda got married. Ella was the one woman he should never have touched.

Damn. She was right. He needed to back off fast. Get her home and hope that Ashley Scott didn't notice and blab her mouth all over town.

"I'm taking you back to the inn. No arguments." He turned and headed off toward the kitchen, and she followed him into the garage.

"Is that Jim's Harley?" she asked as he opened the garage bay. His 1995 Harley-Davidson occupied the third bay of the gigantic garage. Dylan had purchased the bike right after Lauren had ditched him. He'd been restoring it for the better part of a year, working through his pain by rebuilding the bike piece by piece.

He turned toward Ella. "No, it's mine."

Her anime eyes widened. "Really?"

She obviously thought he was boring or dull or something. He considered the possibility of taking her home on the bike. But that would be stupid. It would make too much noise, and besides, she needed proper riding attire, not that slip of a dress. He'd seen the damage pavement could do to unprotected skin, and it wasn't pretty. If you wanted to ride a motorcycle, you needed to do it responsibly.

"Yeah, it's mine," he said. "But we're taking the car." His words may have come out a little hard. He was angry, but he couldn't decide if he was angry at himself, or her, or Ashley Scott, or the situation, or maybe all of it.

They didn't say a word during the five-minute drive to Howland House. But when they got to the driveway, he doused the lights and set the brake. "I don't have any regrets," he said, turning toward her.

"No regrets here either. But..." She paused, and he braced himself for whatever hard thing she was about to say.

When the silence stretched out for several long heartbeats, he asked, "But what?"

"I don't think we should do it again."

She was right, of course. But he wanted to do it again. Hell, he'd hoped to do it again before dawn. "What about our plans for this evening?" he asked.

"What plans...Oh, you mean the picnic?"

"Yeah."

"There's no reason to cancel that. I mean, you wanted to check out the beach, right? Or do you want to concede the point and agree to a beach party?"

He squeezed the steering wheel. He should probably concede the point, but he didn't want to. "I'll pick you up at six."

Chapter Sixteen

What had Ella been thinking?

She'd gone to bed with Dylan, and now she was foolishly trying to prove something to him with this damn picnic. She should have picked up the phone and called Annie Robinson the moment she read Granny's fried chicken recipe and realized that she didn't have the first clue how to actually fry a chicken.

She should have gotten this damn picnic catered.

But no. Some stupid part of her female brain wanted to cook for Dylan, when she knew good and well that whatever had happened last night was over. Done. Never going to happen again.

So here she stood in Ashley's kitchen, feeling a little sleepy, working up the courage to fry the chicken she'd bought at Miller's Market but also boiling potatoes for homemade potato salad while getting ready to chop cabbage into slaw.

She was on the brink of making a total hash out of it when Jackie came sailing through the front door wearing his school uniform, which consisted of navy-blue pants and a white polo shirt with a stain on the front that might have come from ketchup. He hopped up onto one of the kitchen stools, planted his face in his hands, and asked, "Whatcha doing?"

She needed the kid like she needed a hole in the head. "Making coleslaw."

"Why?"

"I'm going on a picnic tonight."

The kid hopped down from his stool and headed to the gigantic Sub-Zero refrigerator, where he pulled out a can of diet Coke. Then he strolled over to the stove. "Your pot's about to boil over."

"Oh, yikes." Ella turned and reduced the heat on the potatoes.

"I think they're done," Jackie said. "Maybe overdone."

She turned the heat off. The potatoes did look a bit over-boiled, which would have been great if she was making mashed potatoes. Well, better overdone than underdone.

She drained the potatoes into a colander and went back to chopping cabbage.

"The captain likes your music," Jackie said, returning to the stool, where he eyed her every move like a hawk. The kid had probably watched his mother for years, but when Ashley entered her kitchen, she was like a captain of a great ocean liner, totally confident and in charge. Ella was neither of those things.

"I'm glad the captain likes my music," she said to the kid, while she measured out mayo and mustard.

"So when are you going to go out to the tree and play the violin for him again?"

She looked up at the kid. "The captain could come in on Saturdays if he wants to hear me play."

"I don't think he can leave the tree..." Jackie paused. "Well, not unless it's super important. He was able to go to the library once, but that was important to him. Music, maybe not. He says you should play more jigs and reels and less of that sad stuff. He doesn't like sad stuff."

"And everyone's a critic," she muttered as she poured some vinegar into the coleslaw dressing.

"Jackie?" Ashley's voice came from up the back stairway.

The kid turned on his stool. "Hi, Mom," he said in a perfectly angelic voice.

Ashley entered the kitchen and gave him a motherly look. "Stop bothering Ella. It looks as if she's busy right now."

"Okay." He slipped from the stool, picked up his book bag and soda can, and headed for the stairs, but before he got to the first step, he turned. "You should come out to the tree and play some jigs and reels. It would cheer him up." Then he turned and raced up the stairs, ignoring his mother's frown.

Ashley turned around. "I'm sorry he was bothering you."

"He wasn't," Ella said, eyeing the slightly mushy potatoes. "I think I was managing to screw this up well before he arrived."

"What's the occasion?"

Ella's face flamed hot. Ashley had already given Ella one serious woman-to-woman talk about Dylan Killough. Had she heard her come in at three o'clock this morning? Had she seen Dylan's car in the drive? And now here she was making a picnic for him. It wouldn't take a genius to connect the dots. But she couldn't flat-out lie about things. She just had to spin the truth the way they did in Washington these days.

"Well, you know Mom has asked Dylan and me to plan an engagement party for her and Jim, so I'm trying to prove that a picnic on the beach would be perfect. Dylan is skeptical. And I have this feeling that I'm not going to win him over to my point of view when he sees this mess. Granny told me the way to convince him was with excellent food. This is going to be an epic fail." She sighed. Maybe by focusing on her less-than-competent kitchen skills, she could distract Ashley from this truth.

"So all this is for Dylan, huh?" Ashley asked, dashing any hope Ella had of fooling her.

"Oh, absolutely," she said. Maybe if Ella admitted it, Ashley would buy her line about convincing Dylan with food. "He's so skeptical about a beach party, and I had this idea about a fried chicken and champagne reception that I got from Martha Stewart's webpage."

"Fried chicken and champagne?"

Ella nodded.

"Need help?" Ashley asked, glancing at the soggy potatoes.

"Oh, that's not necessary. I can—"

"It's no trouble. And besides, this is for your mom, right?"

Ella let go of a little breath. Had she bought the line? Maybe. "Right." Ella nodded vigorously because it *was* for her mother. Not Dylan. At all.

"So, have you ever fried chicken before?"

"Uh, no, but I've got Granny's recipe and—" Oh crap. Had she just told Ashley Scott that she had her grandmother's fried chicken recipe?

This transgression was far worse than sleeping with Dylan. And the avarice in Ashley's eyes confirmed it.

"Um, well, uh…damn. I wasn't supposed to tell you that. Granny is sure her fried chicken will convince Dylan that a beach party is the way to go."

"Okay, here's the deal. I'll help you fry this chicken, and then I'll share my hummingbird cake recipe with Nancy. Don't you fret about it. We'll work it out."

"I don't know…I'm starting to think I should have called Annie Robinson to cater this picnic."

"Maybe you should have, but since you didn't, why don't we get busy?"

"Thanks. You've been so incredibly kind to me."

"Nonsense. Kindness has nothing to do with it. I'm getting

your grandmother's chicken recipe. Honey, you have no idea how valuable that is."

"Yeah. I have a feeling I'm never going to hear the end of this."

* * *

Dylan arrived at Howland House at six on the dot to find Ella waiting for him. Once again, she showed up in a shapeless India-print dress with her damp hair piled up on top of her head in its usual messy bun. She'd obviously just stepped out of the bath, and the scent of sandalwood rose from her skin, making him a tiny bit dizzy.

He wanted to scoop her into his arms, bury his nose in the nape of her neck, and drink in her sandalwood scent. And after that, he wanted to carry her upstairs and have his way with her, after he'd taken all the pins out of her hair.

Yeah. He had fallen into lust for his soon-to-be stepsister. Tonight was going to be agonizing.

"Can you help me carry the cooler and the hamper?" she asked, with a smile that threatened to melt his bones, except for the operative one.

"Sure," he said, picking up the cooler and the hamper and following her like a little puppy right out the door. The breeze stirred the edges of her skirt giving a glimpse of leg, while the early-evening sun through the gauzy fabric created a silhouette of her slim body that turned his mouth into the Sahara. She had this lovely way of walking, with a sexy little sway to her hips.

Dammit, he wished he hadn't noticed.

He stowed the picnic hamper and cooler in the trunk, and they set off for Paradise Beach, which was on the other side of the island. They didn't say more than three words during the drive, but the tension in the car was thicker than overcooked oatmeal. When he pulled into Cloud Nine's driveway, he was ready to concede the whole beach party point and take her right back to Howland House.

Coming out here was a bad idea. Who could fight her beauty or the blended scents of sandalwood and fried chicken? He took one look at the beach and decided she had a strong case for the beach party idea, or any other idea she might have for the evening.

The night was perfect, with a gentle sea breeze tempering the constant humidity. As they walked out onto the sand, the sky was just turning a deeper blue, and the calm ocean sparkled as if someone had scattered diamonds on its surface.

She spread an old quilt in shades of faded green and pink over the sand, and he anchored the corners with the cooler and picnic basket.

Yup, this was a perfect spot for making out. Only he wasn't here to make out with her. He saw multiple cold showers in his immediate future.

He stopped to shuck off his boat shoes before stepping onto the blanket but took another moment to glance at her. Her hair was starting to dry, and the breeze sent tendrils into her eyes and around her beautifully shaped ears.

He settled on the blanket, and she turned those big, sad anime eyes on him, inspecting him. Her mouth softened a little. "I don't think I've ever seen you wearing a shirt with a collar with the top button undone."

Except for that time on the boardwalk when she'd unbuttoned it herself or last night when she'd seen him without any shirt. But he decided not to mention that.

She bent over, the loose dress sliding down one shoulder. Oh man.

She opened the cooler and withdrew a bottle of Magic Hat #9. "Thirsty?"

Yes, he was thirsty. But not for a beer. Instead of admitting the truth, he asked, "How did you know I liked Magic Hat?"

"I know a guy," she said, dropping to the blanket and hastily readjusting her dress. He was so disappointed. If he couldn't touch her, looking at her was still good.

"So, what's for dinner?" Maybe the food would distract his one-track mind.

"Fried chicken, coleslaw, and potato salad. I made it myself."

"Oh?"

She gave him a glance that he couldn't quite read. Was she annoyed? Amused? What?

"I did. But the recipes all belong to Granny, and Ashley Scott may have given me some tips on how to keep the oil hot when frying chicken."

"You know," he said, taking a swig of his ale, "any other woman wouldn't have felt the need to admit that she had help."

"Oh, so you're an expert on women, then?" She reached into the hamper and pulled out a couple of red-checked napkins. Man, she'd gone all out, hadn't she?

Why? Did she want to win the argument about party venues, or was it about something else? He so wanted it to be about something else. Although that would complicate everything.

She handed him the napkin. "So I'm taking your silence to mean that you are an expert on women."

He snorted. "I've been around the block a few times. How about you?"

She didn't answer his question. Instead, she reached into the hamper and pulled out several Tupperware containers, a couple of paper plates that had been tucked into wicker holders, and real silverware.

When her silence had stretched out for an eternity, he said, "I guess, being a musician, you have vast experience with the male gender."

"Why would musicians have more experience?" She gave

him a frown that underscored the resemblance between mother and daughter.

"I don't know. You were on the road all those years."

"I was on the road with Cody all those years."

Wait, what was she saying? He straightened, staring at her, not daring to ask the obvious question. Had she only been with Cody until...?

Damn.

Did that make him special or just the guy she'd decided to experiment with? Either way, he felt gut punched. He was grateful when Ella started popping the lids on the food. Maybe he could stuff his face and avoid inserting his foot into his mouth a second time.

And besides, food was a great way to sublimate his desire. So he helped himself to a couple of chicken legs and some sides. His first bite of the chicken was revelatory. He'd never eaten fried chicken that was as crispy or as delicious or as golden brown as that drumstick.

"This is good," he said with his mouth half full.

She grinned, clearly pleased with herself. "So, what do you think about Paradise Beach now? I want you to imagine a pretty tent with some informal flowers and plenty of fried chicken legs and champagne for the guests."

"So, are you planning to fry up the chicken yourself? For one hundred people?"

"Well, no. We'll obviously have to find a caterer."

"Too bad, because this chicken is really good."

She blushed again, as if this smallest of compliments was something new for her. "Thank you," she said in a tiny voice that the breeze blew away. She looked out at the ocean. She was so beautiful.

"So," she said, barely above the sound of the surf, "are you willing to have the party here?"

"You're acting like it's my decision."

She turned toward him then, her eyes big, expressive, and maybe a little sad. "It is your decision. I mean, I like the idea, but you're the one who needs convincing."

He put his empty plate aside and inched closer to her. "I guess it's okay. If it doesn't rain."

"It won't rain." Her words were barely above a whisper, and the sea breeze carried them off.

If only he could be so sure. Maybe he needed to take a chance on the weather. Maybe he needed to take a chance on her.

What would happen if he asked her another personal question? Would she pull the conversation back to party planning? If she was any other woman on the face of the planet, he might have asked her about her childhood, or probed to discover her favorite color, or asked any of a million other little questions.

His original plan had been to probe her for all of Brenda's secrets. He still wanted to know the secrets. But not for any nefarious plan. Now he simply wanted to know the answers. Just because.

But Ella wasn't any other woman on the face of the planet. She was Brenda's daughter. And it seared him to think that one day he would probably know all her secrets, but she would forever be the one just beyond his reach.

* * *

Ella tried not to look at Dylan. She studied the surf, and the darkening sky, and the colors of the sunset. But every once in a while, she glanced at him. The sea breeze lifted his curly hair, blowing it over his forehead and making him look decidedly Byronic.

She wanted him to say yes to the beach party, but more than that, she wanted him to talk about himself. He never did that.

Why? Was it because there was nothing to share, or did he keep all those things close? Was he shy? She had a feeling he was shy. And reserved. She liked that about him.

She suddenly wanted to know what it had been like growing up without a mother. She wanted to compare notes because she'd never known her father as a child.

But she kept her mouth shut. Letting him into her heart would be a huge mistake. She needed to set aside this crazy attraction and move on with her life. Besides, she was terrified that falling for Dylan would bring nothing but misery to her mother.

The silence grew, becoming a living thing that threatened to strangle her. She sat there fighting for breath, when suddenly he said "ow" in a loud and annoyed tone.

He leaned forward, inspecting his bare ankle. "Damn," he said, getting to his feet as if he'd been scalded by a cattle prod. He turned in her direction. "Get up, before you're eaten alive."

"What?"

"No-see-ums. They're everywhere. We've probably already been bitten. We just don't know it yet." He started packing up the food without explanation, snapping lids on containers and throwing stuff into the picnic basket and cooler. "That does it. We can't have the party here. We'll get chewed up and spit out."

What the hell was he talking about? She hadn't been bitten. There was no bug problem at Paradise Beach. She'd enjoyed the sunset out here many times over the last couple of months. "What, are you afraid of a few bugs?"

He stopped throwing things into the picnic hamper and stared at her, evidently just now realizing that she'd done nothing to help him. "You probably have bites all over you. Sometimes it takes a while to feel the sting. Wait until tomorrow. You'll be covered in welts. Come on, help me with this quilt."

She got up. "I get it. I know we made a mistake last night,

but you don't have to resort to a trick in order to push me away." She turned her back on him and strode up the beach toward Mom's house. If the damn man had to resort to a gambit like this to end the evening... Well, he could go ahead and fold the quilt and carry the cooler and basket all on his own; he was certainly strong enough for the job.

He caught up to her as she reached the deck attached to her mother's home. The sky had turned a fabulous shade of magenta as the sun sank over the island. It might have been a perfect moment for romance or something.

Was that it? Was he afraid of romance?

Was she?

She whirled around, ready to broach the untouchable subject, when she saw the red bumps swelling across the patch of chest that his unbuttoned golf shirt exposed.

He scratched absently. "I'm being eaten for supper."

Her gaze dropped to his exposed feet, and sure enough little red welts encircled both of his ankles.

"Oh my god. You *are* being eaten." She gave her exposed arms and legs a quick exam. No sign of bites. "I guess they like the way you taste?" The words made her blush, but she continued. "You do taste good, you know."

He ignored the flirtatious remark and strode past her, opening the unlocked sliding door that led to Mom's living room. "I need to take a shower. Now. Which way is the bathroom?"

She pointed.

He ran, and a moment later, the sound of water running in the bathroom reached her ears. A little part of her wanted to tiptoe into the bathroom with him. But she couldn't do a thing like that. Not in Mom's house. Even if Mom and Jim had gone out for dinner and probably wouldn't be home for a while yet.

She jettisoned her evil thoughts and went in search of some calamine lotion or hydrocortisone cream, but she couldn't find any in the linen closet. The best she could manage was a big container of aloe gel.

She returned to the living room, aloe in hand, just as Dylan came out of the hall bathroom with Mom's fuchsia and yellow beach towel around his middle, the words HELLO SUNSHINE strategically centered on his butt.

She tried mightily but she couldn't keep the laugh from bubbling up out of her. He looked more delicious than Granny's fried chicken. Last night, the lights had been turned down low, and she hadn't gotten a good look at his chest. Now it made the spit dry in her mouth.

But the welts along his neck, which continued in a line down toward his left armpit, brought out her inner Florence Nightingale. "Oh my. You've been eaten."

"You should go shower too. Now. Just to be on the safe side. And don't put your clothes back on." He said this like a doctor issuing orders, not a lover giving her a direction. It was kind of disappointing.

"I'm fine," she said. Her chance to get naked with him had come and gone. She wasn't going to shower alone. Besides, she didn't have any bites that she could see or feel.

"I've got aloe." She held up the bottle of green goo. "It should tide you over until you get some hydrocortisone."

He snatched the bottle, a grumpy frown on his face as he went to work smearing the gel on his chest and ankles, giving her an exceptionally entertaining show that made the palms of her hands itch.

So when he turned around and said, "Do I have bites on my back? I'm itchy down my back," she stepped closer to him and investigated. He did have bites all down his back, across the bumps in his spine, and over one hip.

"Oh my word, it's like one of those chiggers got stuck in your shirt and went on a march over your skin."

"And all because I unbuttoned my top button," he said in a somewhat savage tone.

"Hand me the gel," she directed.

He handed it over, and she pumped out a generous dollop that cooled her palm. She rubbed the gel into the welts along his warm back, her fingers tingling, not from the aloe but from system overload. His back was just as sexy as his front.

She put heart and soul and libido into rubbing the gel into his skin. And she might have worked harder than was absolutely necessary because touching him was such a turn-on.

But when she let go of a small, inarticulate sound, he turned. His eyes dark, wide, and unreadable as he began to lean in. She braced herself, ready to receive the kiss that was coming, her heart thumping in anticipation.

But right before he made his move, the sliding-glass door opened, and Mom and Jim walked into the house.

Dylan jumped back as if someone had goosed him.

Mom gasped.

Jim said, "What the hell?"

Ella turned, and without so much as a blush said, "The chiggers came to our picnic. I think we need to find another spot for the party."

"Oh, thank goodness," Mom said, pressing her hand to her chest.

Jim gave her a weird look, then strode over to Dylan, who had the presence of mind to say, "I took a shower."

"Right. Good move," Jim said. "You need more than aloe on those bites." He turned on his heel and found the hydrocortisone cream in the linen closet, which someone (probably Jim) had moved to the upper shelf, where Ella hadn't seen it.

She stepped back and let Jim take over the doctoring, while Mom gave her a strange, assessing look out of a suddenly pale face.

Chapter Seventeen

Dad lent Dylan a pair of sweatpants and a T-shirt for the drive back to town and seemed perfectly happy to accept the explanation that Ella was rubbing aloe onto his back when they were caught.

Dylan never thought he'd regard a hundred chigger bites as a silver lining, but the welts were there as evidence that nothing untoward, or even salacious, had happened.

Good thing Ella hadn't followed his orders and taken a shower. Otherwise she might have been caught naked too. And that might have been a lot harder to explain, since she seemed to have escaped the no-see-ums.

Now she sat in the passenger's seat as he guided the Honda along the beach road that would eventually connect with Harbor Drive. She hadn't said a word in five minutes, and the tension between them had grown as thick as the humid night outside.

"We're okay," he finally said, hoping to put her at ease. "I have a hundred bug bites to prove it."

She let out a little puff of air. "I'm so sorry. Are you really itchy?"

"Yes." He fought the urge to scratch his chest, but if he was going to be completely honest, his itches weren't limited to the bug bites. He had a powerful itch for Ella McMillan. And she had almost scratched it right before their parents had caught them in the act.

Was this itch wrong? He thought about it as he gripped the steering wheel in an attempt to keep his hands away from the bites throbbing all over his torso.

No. He could honestly say that having a little crush on Ella McMillan wasn't wrong at all even if she was his father's fiancée's daughter. They weren't siblings. Not really.

But pursuing this would undoubtedly become awkward for everyone.

"I'm sorry you got bitten," she said in a tiny voice that reminded him of her grandmother.

"It's not your fault. Why do you do that all the time? Apologize for things beyond your control."

She didn't answer for a long time. He didn't expect her to. But he wanted to stop the car, take her by the shoulders, give her a good shake, and then kiss the daylights out of her. That might not be the right approach though.

Damned if he knew what the right approach might be.

"You know," she finally said a few moments later, "I think I just got in the habit of saying I'm sorry."

"Why? Because your mother was so difficult?"

She settled back into her seat with a short laugh. "You have the wrong idea about Mom. I never really apologized to her. I went out of my way to make her feel crappy. I was horrible to her when I was a teenager. We had some serious control issues. No, I didn't apologize to Mom, or even tiptoe around her the way you think I did. I resented the hell out of her and let her know at every turn just how much. And you know what? She kept coming back. Loving me in spite of my terrible behavior."

"Oh." A weird emotion seized him. She may not have apologized to her mother as a teenager, but she was sure doing it now. All the time.

"I got in the habit when I was living with Cody," she said after a moment.

"Oh?" He wanted to press, but he knew better than to start asking detailed questions about her ex. She would resent it the same way he would resent questions about Lauren.

"Cody made me feel responsible for his moods," she said, "and I took the easy way out. I got tired of arguing with him. It was such a waste of time.

"So okay, I'm not responsible for your bug bites, but I do feel sorry for you." Her voice warmed. "You must be a lot sweeter than I am, because I don't have a single bite anywhere. That seems a bit unfair."

"Actually, the bugs aren't attracted to sweetness. It's because of the amount of carbon dioxide and heat my skin gives off. More heat, more bug bites."

She turned in her seat, just as he turned onto Harbor Drive. In a moment he'd have to choose whether to turn left toward Howland House or right toward home. He wanted to take her home. He wanted to finish the kiss.

"You do give off a lot of heat," she said, her voice an invitation.

"I want to take you home," he said.

She exhaled sharply. "And I wouldn't mind going home with you, but surely you can see how that would be a huge mistake."

"No, actually, I don't."

"We'd have to hide what we're doing. My god, we were

almost caught tonight. I can't even imagine the crap storm that would happen if Mom and Jim found out we were sleeping together."

"Why would there be a crap storm?"

"Uh, well, because there would be."

"I'm not so sure. I mean, they want us to be friends."

"Friends, not lovers."

"I don't see the problem." He came to the stoplight where he'd have to decide—right or left.

"What if they break up?" she asked.

"Then there's no problem at all."

"Oh my god. You are such a guy. Of course there would be problems. Emotions all over the place. And we'd never be able to get together as a family. I mean, what about Christmas and Easter?"

"Like Easter was so great this year."

"You know what I'm talking about. And what if we—" She abruptly stopped speaking.

"What if we what?"

"Never mind. Us being together is a terrible idea, Dylan. We need to cool it."

"Do you think we can?" he asked, just as the light turned green.

The car behind him honked. He ignored it as he stared into her big, expressive eyes.

"I don't know. But we need to. We can't rock the boat."

"Rocking the boat is exactly what I want to do."

The driver in the car behind them laid on the horn.

"Dylan, please."

He gave up and turned left toward the inn.

When he reached the parking lot, he killed the engine and helped her carry the cooler and the picnic hamper into the kitchen. Once he'd left it on the countertop, she walked him back to the front door. A group of B&B guests were hanging out in the library, so he couldn't grab her by the shoulders and kiss her the way he wanted.

Ironically, though, he still had a reason to spend time with her. He gave her a smile. "So, I guess we're back to the drawing board on the engagement party, huh?"

She met his stare. He wasn't stupid. He saw the desire in those big eyes of hers. When she'd spread that aloe gel on his back, it had turned them both on. One bucket of cold water—in the form of parents with bad timing—was not sufficient to end this thing.

He would live to fight another day.

"Yeah, but I'm completely out of ideas. You tell me. What's the most romantic place in town, and do they have a party room?"

He stood there slightly thunderstruck. "Jude St. Pierre's schooner."

"What?"

"It's the most romantic place in town. Everyone pops the question during his sunset cruises. But I don't think we could have a party with a hundred guests there."

"Good. Because a hundred guests has always been ridiculous. Tell me more about this boat."

She leaned into the doorframe, giving him a momentary reprieve. So he gave her the whole rundown on *Synchronicity Too*, the new schooner Jude had purchased last year. "Dad and Brenda cruised on the boat during the Festival of Lights last Christmas. Now that I think about it, that was sort of their first date."

She rolled her adorable eyes. "Now you tell me this. We need to check this boat out."

"Okay. I'll call you tomorrow."

He should probably go, but he didn't want to, and the guests in the library showed no interest in leaving. Dammit, he was not leaving without some small token of his affection.

So he leaned in and gave her a kiss on the cheek that hardly satisfied. When he pulled away, she stood there, wide eyed and breathing hard. He'd much prefer to take her home, but leaving her like that wasn't a bad second option.

*   *   *

"Brenda said Dylan was wearing her favorite beach towel and not another stitch of clothing when they walked into the living room," Nancy Jacobs said, looking up from her plate of blackberry jam cake. As always, her voice was pitched low and quiet, which was probably a good thing, seeing as Ella was upstairs giving Jackie tin whistle lessons.

Which Ashley devoutly wished the young woman hadn't chosen to do. Her son had been practicing the dang thing since he got home from school, trying to play the "Sailor's Hornpipe" but missing every other note. Jackie had informed Ashley that he wanted to learn the whistle so he could entertain pirate ghosts all on his own.

Maybe the boy would make so much noise—and Nancy would speak so quietly—that Ella wouldn't discover that she'd become topic number one among the Piece Makers.

"You don't say," Donna Cuthbert said, placing her empty plate on the kitchen counter and helping herself to a second slice of cake.

"But Jim said the boy had chigger bites all over him. Ella didn't have a one."

"That's odd. You don't think she set him up, do you?" Karen asked.

"Ella wouldn't do something like that. She was putting lotion on his back when Jim and Brenda walked into the room."

"That sounds very suspicious," Patsy said.

"Why? He had bites all over his back," Nancy countered.

"Nancy. Those kids aren't... you know."

Nancy blinked behind her glasses as Patsy turned toward Ashley. "Are they?"

Now, that was a loaded question. On the face of it, Ashley could argue that this was a classic case of bugs ruining a picnic. On the other hand, she had eyes, and she'd seen Dylan watch Ella play. And she had ears, and she heard the way Ella said Dylan's name.

If she was a gossip like Donna, she could probably turn this episode into something hot and racy. But she wasn't a gossip, so she shook her head. "As far as I know, it was a picnic. Ella wanted to convince Dylan that an engagement party on the beach would be nice. I helped her fry some chicken, if that matters."

"Did my granddaughter share my secret recipe with you?" Nancy asked in a hard voice.

"Now, Nancy, I was going to talk to you about that." She glanced around at the rest of the Piece Makers. "In private. She did share your recipe because she had no clue how to fry a drumstick. And I promised her that I'd reciprocate by giving you my hummingbird cake recipe."

Nancy folded her arms over her chest. "That's mighty nice of you, Ashley, but I need you to promise never to divulge the secret ingredient in my fried chicken recipe."

"I swear on my grandmother's grave, Nancy."

"All right, then."

"I don't know," Patsy said. "Him being naked troubles me."

"He says he took a shower," Nancy said.

"Good thinking," Karen commented. "Those no-see-ums are sneaky."

"So there's nothing going on between them?"

"No," Ashley said. It wasn't exactly a lie. She didn't know for certain that love was blooming in the most unlikely of places. She did know two things: first, Ella had come in early on Monday morning, and second, Dylan had given Ella a kiss at the door on Monday evening. On the surface, that kiss might have looked like a simple peck on the cheek, but their body language said otherwise.

"Well, just in case there is something going on, I think you should have a word with her," Patsy said in the dictatorial tone that had worn thin over the last few years. "And, ladies, we *all* have to help Nancy out. We can't let Dylan and Ella ruin Jim and Brenda's relationship. Donna, you Methodists have been trying to find Doctor Jim a new wife for years. And we Episcopalians are thrilled that he found Brenda and transformed her. Without Jim insisting on her directing the Christmas Chorale last year, I don't think Brenda would ever have started a choir at Heavenly Rest. We need to make sure Ella and Doctor D behave themselves."

She turned toward Ashley with a raised eyebrow when she got to the last sentence, as if it was Ashley's job to keep Ella in line.

Ashley pretended she didn't understand. "Excuse me, Patsy, but how has Ella not behaved herself? She packed a picnic. It wasn't her fault that Doctor D ran into a nest of chiggers."

"You know what we mean, Ashley. Ella is a musician who's used to who knows what kind of life living on the road. I don't think any of us expect her to stay here permanently or to ever settle down and get married. So we don't want her playing with Dylan's emotions."

"I don't think Ella's playing with anyone's emotions, Patsy," Ashley said. She didn't say that the situation might be the reverse. Besides, what else could she do? Ashley had already given Ella a couple of friendly warnings about getting too close to Dylan. But if Ella and Doctor D were falling in love, well . . .

She wasn't going to stand in the way of that even if it

rocked a few boats. She'd lost her own true love almost six years ago in Afghanistan. She knew the deep, abiding loneliness of being left behind. She wouldn't wish that on anyone. But arguing with Patsy was futile, so she nodded and said, "Okay, I'll talk to her."

"Good. Now, what's this I hear about Reverend St. Pierre eating his breakfast at Bread, Butter, and Beans the last few days?"

Ashley went cold. She had no explanations for the sudden chill in her relationship with the minister who lived across the street. She still made oatmeal for him, but he evidently didn't want it anymore. She didn't know why, and she couldn't confess her fears to the Piece Makers because Micah's sudden coolness had started with their argument over the scratch-made cakes she baked for the quilting group every week.

Why did she suddenly feel cornered? And why did she let these women make her feel that way?

"Reverend St. Pierre is free to have breakfast wherever he wants." She met Patsy's accusatory stare.

"Oh, darlin', don't be so defensive. I wasn't casting aspersions on your cooking. I'm just curious as to whether anyone knows why he's been spotted at the coffee shop every morning since Palm Sunday," Patsy said.

"Why do you care? He can eat where he wants to," Sandra said.

"But why would he want to?" Karen asked in a querulous voice. "Ashley's biscuits are better than Brooklyn's scones any day."

"Micah usually eats oatmeal," Ashley supplied, then regretted sharing that information.

"Well, he's not eating oatmeal now," Patsy said. "I wish I knew why."

"Because, dear friends, Brooklyn Huddleston owns Bread, Butter, and Beans," Donna said with a twinkle in her eye and a slightly smug grin.

Everyone looked in Donna's direction, while a strange sensation worked its way through Ashley. What the heck? Was Micah interested in Brooklyn? And here she'd been wondering for days and days whether it had been something she'd said or done that had driven him away. Good grief, how could she have missed this?

"Oh my goodness," Patsy said. "He's courting Brooklyn?"

"Well, she's about his age, and she's available. And they smile a lot at each other. I was over there just yesterday. He was flirting with her."

"Oh, no. We can't have that. She's a Methodist," Patsy said. "Ashley, we need to put a stop to this right now."

Chapter Eighteen

Dylan called on Wednesday morning during the inn's breakfast service and left a message on Ella's voice mail. "I've made a reservation for tonight's sunset champagne cruise on *Synchronicity Too*," he'd said. "I'll pick you up precisely at five o'clock, and please dress appropriately."

What the hell did that mean? And she was kind of disappointed that he'd called when she'd been at work. Because she wouldn't have minded talking to him.

Which was the problem right there. A girl could fall in love with Dylan Killough, and what a disaster that would be, because he'd made it pretty clear that whatever was going on between them was nothing more than a summer fling.

And she didn't blame him for thinking that way. She'd told him that was all she wanted. But then again, sleeping with Dylan had been mind-altering. More important, there had been that moment at Granny's when he'd leaned in and told her that she'd missed a spot on that casserole dish.

Yeah. That had been sexy as hell. No, not merely sexy. It had been endearing. It had been the sort of thing that wormed its way into a woman's heart.

So yeah. She liked him. More than was wise. More than she could ever admit.

And he didn't understand. He thought they could sneak around, have a fun time, and it would all be okay in the end. But that wasn't possible. There would be heartbreak if she let herself fall all the way. And that would ruin everything for Mom and Jim.

She couldn't do it.

She needed to discourage him. She needed to discourage herself. And that little tag at the end of his message was a good place to start. Did he think she dressed inappropriately?

Her mind flashed hot on the memory of his long fingers deftly working the buttons of the dress she'd worn on Easter Sunday. It hadn't been an overtly sexy dress, but he certainly hadn't had a lot of trouble getting her out of it.

She opened her closet door and considered a wardrobe filled with dresses exactly like the one she'd worn on Easter. Maybe she needed something more like a chastity belt.

Or maybe he was sending a signal that he was ready for more fun times between the sheets.

What did *appropriately* mean, exactly? She stared at her paltry collection of dresses and decided she had nothing "appropriate" to wear tonight. What she needed was something that would discourage him. Like a high-necked, long-sleeved, ugly thing that maybe a grandmother—not Granny, of course—might wear to a funeral.

A shopping trip was required, but she had no car, no time, and, really, no clue. So she flopped down on the bed and called Granny. "Dylan and I are going on the champagne sunset cruise tonight."

"What?" Granny sounded concerned.

"Yeah. We're checking it out as a party venue."

"Oh. That's a novel idea. You know Brenda and Jim's first date was on *Synchronicity Too*."

"So I heard."

"But that boat isn't nearly big enough."

"That's good, right? We can pare down the list."

"I guess. I think Brenda might like the idea."

"I hope so, because I've run out of ideas. But, Granny, I have a problem."

"Oh dear." Granny sounded even more concerned.

"It's not that big of a problem, Granny."

"Oh, good. What is it, sugar?"

"Dylan left a message on my voice mail. He told me to dress appropriately for this thing tonight. Any idea what that means?"

"Uh...no. Not really. I haven't ever been on the sunset cruise. I'm afraid I'm too old for that sort of thing."

"You are not. But anyway, I just looked at my closet and you know I've got nothing that Doctor D is going to think is appropriate."

"Sugar, you should not spend one minute of your time trying to please that man. Just be yourself. Wear what you wore to Easter dinner. That was a very pretty dress on you."

"I can't wear that one. It's...at the cleaners." She prayed that Granny didn't have a BS detector.

There was a long silence on the other end of the phone. "Well..." Granny's voice had a funny ring to it when she finally spoke again. "If you're asking me where you should go for a wardrobe update, I'd suggest Daffy Down Dilly. Kerri will fix you up with the perfect outfit for a champagne cruise."

"Thanks. That's exactly what I needed."

"Sugar?"

"What, Granny?"

"Be careful, okay?"

Ella paused. Had she said too much? Had her grandmother figured out that she had a crush on Doctor D? Oh, good grief. She should never have consulted with her. She reached for the first, lame thing that came to her mind. "Of course I will be. I bet they have life jackets on the cruise. Don't you worry. I'll be fine."

"Uh-huh."

"Love you." She disconnected the line before Granny said another word.

Thirty minutes later, she walked into Daffy Down Dilly and found the collection of sundresses in the corner. Unfortunately, most of these dresses were not funereal. They were adorable and completely inappropriate because they showed way too much shoulder and cleavage.

She pawed through the rack, jettisoning one cute dress after another, until she finally found a boring navy dress with white polka dots, a crew neck, and short sleeves that probably wouldn't have worked for a funeral. But Ella could see some DAR-type wearing it to a baptism.

Ella left the store an hour later with the conservative garment and a pair of boring navy ballet flats. She couldn't wear her Doc Martens with this dress. That would just be weird. With her boho dresses, the Docs made a statement.

So she felt completely out of her element when she stepped through the doors to meet Dylan. She hated the way she looked in this dress, and she hoped he hated it too. But she was still insanely happy to see him, at the same time she dreaded the moment of first contact.

Would it be awkward? Or hotter than she could bear? It could go either way. She was hoping the dress, which was uncomfortable as hell, would throw cold water on the whole affair.

Dylan was looking down at his phone, checking messages

as she approached the car in the circular drive. That was a bit of a disappointment, really. She'd kind of wanted him to be anticipating her arrival.

When he finally did look at her, his gaze was cool and unreadable. But what should she have expected? She'd told him to cool it. He was following instructions.

And he didn't seem to be having any trouble with his emotions either. In fact, he seemed like his normal self, wearing his usual uniform: navy jacket, white button-down, and a bow tie. He was living large today; his noose was made of yellow and blue silk.

He continued to coolly assess her as she slipped into the passenger's seat. "You should probably bring a sweater," he said.

That was the absolute last thing she'd expected him to say. A little part of her wanted him to ask her why she was wearing this dress from hell. An even larger part of her wanted him to grab her by the shoulders and kiss her senseless. Which would have been stupid because she'd asked him not to do anything like that.

"I don't have a sweater," she said truthfully.

"A jacket?"

"I'm fine," she said, tearing her gaze away from him and reaching for the seat belt. The top of the dress cut her armpits as she moved, as if the sleeve openings were just a tad too small. Thank goodness she would never have to fiddle in this straitjacket.

"Suit yourself," he said.

She settled back for the ride to the marina, watching his long fingers on the steering wheel, having flashback memories that really needed to be excised. She forced herself to look away, and the silence in the car became charged and uncomfortable.

Synchronicity Too was berthed at the end of the marina's long pier because of its sheer size. So the walk down the pier seemed interminable, especially since they weren't talking or touching.

She ought to be grateful that Dylan had taken her seriously and not shown up ready to play games or engage in verbal banter. But now, suddenly, she realized that she liked the games. Sparring with him was fun.

They stepped up a gangplank to reach the yacht, which was huge—at least a hundred feet long, with several masts and a dozen portholes marching down its sides. The sun gleamed off the boat's brass work and the high shine of the wooden decks.

"Oh my goodness, it's beautiful. And romantic. Dylan, why didn't you think of this from the start?"

"Yeah, it's pretty, but it's not perfect for a party. What if the weather's crappy? The party would have to be postponed. And we still have to convince Dad and Brenda to cut back the guest list. We can only invite a max of forty. I checked with Jude about that."

Boy, he was in a sour mood. "Stop trying to rain on the parade," she said, her voice brittle.

She turned away from him and took three steps up the ramp, but the damn skirt was narrow, and the shoes were a tiny bit too big. She slipped on the aluminum decking and might have taken a serious tumble if Dylan hadn't been Johnny-on-the-Spot, catching her before she face-planted. The slide of his warm palms against her upper arms made her insides reach critical mass.

When his hands lingered, she almost melted down. She needed to get away from him. Even in a sour mood, he was disrupting her thought patterns.

"I'm fine," she said, pulling away. If only she could walk in this dress. She gave the skirt a little tug because it had ridden up, but that didn't make walking any easier.

The moment she stepped onto the boat, a member of the

yacht's crew, all of whom wore pristine white uniforms, handed her a flute of champagne and directed her aft.

She took a gulp of wine and then remembered the disastrous night at Cibo Dell'anima, when she'd had too much to drink and kissed Dylan in public. She needed to limit herself to this one glass. "Sip, don't gulp" was the message of the day.

She moved toward the back of the boat, trying to outpace Dylan. "This is really beautiful," she said, trying to fill the awkward silence. "I didn't think they made boats with all this wood anymore."

"They don't. *Synchronicity Too* was originally built in 1930. The decking is all mahogany."

She glanced up at him. "You seem to know a lot about it."

"It's been the talk of the yacht club since Jude bought it last year and completely refitted it."

His mention of the yacht club irritated her, but maybe that was a good thing. She needed to be irritated; otherwise she might lose her mind and jump his bones . . . again.

She took another generous sip of champagne. "So I gather you spend a lot of time at the yacht club, huh?" Talking about his membership in the club seemed like a good way to remind her that they were not made for each other.

His gaze slid away. "I learned how to sail as a kid. And I guess it's one of my hobbies. I have a small laser sailboat I take out when I get a chance."

Of course he'd learned to sail as a kid. It was like a big red warning sign that they came from different places. She'd grown up in land-locked Muncie, miles away from Lake Erie and Lake Michigan. He grown up on a sea island, surrounded by bay and ocean.

"Well, I didn't learn to sail as a kid," she said, leaning back to inspect the mast. "We've got lots of wind in Muncie, but no sailing."

He chuckled. "Mom wanted me to learn. I was not quite ten when she signed me up for sailing camp. I remember her watching me from the dock."

This was the first time he'd ever talked about his mother. It seemed like a confidence or something. Not the sort of thing someone who was looking for a tumble would share.

"Was she always giving you pointers from the sidelines?" she asked.

"No."

His one-word answer seemed like an emotional retreat. Which was a good thing, right?

But it annoyed her. So she turned to face him and pressed the point. "Tell me about your mom."

* * *

Oh great. The last thing he wanted to do was talk about his mother. How the hell had he even fallen into this conversational black hole? He hated talking about his mother, and today especially, he had no heart for it.

So he ignored her question, took a sip of his champagne, and tried not to let today's news about Coreen Martel ruin this moment.

Ella had worn a dress that reminded him of Lauren. And that was annoying too. He didn't want Lauren.

He wanted Ella. In fact, he wanted to convince her to come home with him after this cruise was finished because she might be the antidote to the poison running through his veins right at the moment.

Earlier today, Grant Ackerman, one of the volunteers with the Magnolia Harbor fire department, had called the office to let them know that Coreen Martel had been found dead in her bathroom, evidently the victim of a fall. She'd died utterly alone.

He'd lost patients before. And Coreen was suffering from end-stage heart failure, so her days had been numbered, but the manner of her death had left him feeling a deep melancholy he couldn't shake.

He glanced at Ella. It might be nice if she would hug him, but he couldn't ask for a hug. Not here on the boat with a crowd surrounding them.

"I take it from your silence that your mother is a forbidden topic," she said, pulling him back into the conversation.

"Uh, no. It's just that..."

"You never talk about her. Is that because you're trying not to compare her to my mother? I'm sure your mother was a paragon."

He actually managed a smile. What was it about Ella? She amused him sometimes. "I'm sure she was, but I was only ten when she died. I don't remember her that well. And you know, she was sick for a long time before she passed away."

"It was cancer, right?"

He nodded. "She'd lost her hair that summer when I started sailing camp."

"I'm so sorry. I..."

"It's okay. She loved sailing even more than Dad does. But I guess..." His voice faded out.

"She wanted you to learn to love sailing before she died. She wanted to live long enough to see you sailing by yourself." What the hell. Could Ella could read his thoughts or something?

"I guess. I didn't really understand at the time. All I knew was that I was younger than all the other kids at camp. And I felt like a loser."

"You? Really?"

He leaned back onto the boat's railing. "You know what they do on the first day of sailing camp?"

"Do I look like a sailor?"

"They make you capsize your boat. And then you have to get it upright and bail it out. Over and over again."

"I guess that makes sense. But it doesn't sound like much fun."

He nodded. "The thing is, I was a year younger than everyone else because Mom had guilted the sailing school into making an exception for me. And since she was terminally ill and a member of the board, they broke the rules. So all the other kids got to practice capsizing their boats with seven-foot-long dinghies, but they gave me this tiny four-foot sailboat because I wasn't big enough to capsize the bigger ones. I got teased. I hated it."

"Did you get the boat upright?"

"Yeah, but—"

"Then don't complain. I mean, they were just helping you succeed. When I was six, I had a tiny violin. I couldn't play a full-sized fiddle, so . . ."

He shook his head. "Brenda started you at six?"

"Yes, and your mother started you sailing at ten."

"Yeah, but—"

"And you still enjoy sailing. You're a member of the club, right?"

He nodded. "I like fly-fishing more," he said. "But it is true that there are times when . . ." His voice trailed off as his throat got tight. He didn't like talking about Mom, especially in emotional times like the present. How had he even started this conversation?

No, wait, he hadn't really started it. Ella had.

"When what?" she coaxed.

He dragged in a breath of air filled with the scent of the bay. Funny how he rarely shared any of this. Lauren had never even asked about his mother. She'd accepted that Mom had died when he was young, and therefore Mom was a part of his past. Lauren had never much cared about his past because she'd been too busy planning his future. But the past mattered, didn't it?

It mattered a lot.

He closed his eyes and actively remembered that summer before Mom died. She'd sit out on the yacht club deck wearing a knitted hat over her bald head, even in the heat of the summer. She'd wave at him every time he looked in her direction, as if watching him sail in that puny little dinghy had made her day.

God, he wished he'd pleased her. He wished he'd done better. But that summer he'd been too little. Nothing about sailing had come easily. And Mom had never said a word about his failures.

But what if he'd been good? Would Mom have given him pointers? Would he have taken the advice or seen it as criticism?

He didn't know.

"What's going through your head, Dylan?" Ella asked.

"Nothing," he said, anxious to shut down the conversation. It seemed wrong to compare his mother to Brenda. Except he'd been doing it for weeks, hadn't he?

"I should never have tried to compare Mom to your mother," he said. "That wasn't fair."

"True, but probably inevitable. Since you're human. You are human, aren't you?"

"I'm trying."

"Good." She turned away, staring out over the bay.

"And what are *you* thinking?" he asked, employing the question as a cheap trick in order to keep his thoughts private.

"To be brutally honest, I was thinking about my father."

"What?"

She blew out a sigh and glanced at Dylan out of the corner of her eye. "I was thinking that we both have an absent parent."

"Yeah. But your father is still alive, isn't he?"

She shook her head. "No. He died right before Christmas. I looked him up a few years ago. We had a relationship for a little while."

"I'm so sorry, Ella. Was that this past December?"

She nodded.

"Right before you came home?"

"Dylan, Magnolia Harbor isn't my home. It's yours. It's Mom's. I grew up in Indiana, but I don't have any family or real connection there. For a long while, I wanted Cody to settle down on this piece of land near El Paso. But that didn't happen either. I'm starting to think I'm the proverbial rolling stone."

He studied her as *Synchronicity Too*'s engines fired to life, and the crew went to work on the mooring lines. It seemed important, suddenly, to remember that Ella was only visiting Magnolia Harbor and would leave one day. She needed to go someplace where she could play her violin and make a living at it.

So they were having a summertime fling. And maybe it wasn't worth it in the end. He'd like to believe they'd end up friends, especially if she came visiting on holidays or in the summer.

The thought deepened his depression, just as the yacht slipped away from its berth and headed through the channel markers. The crew got busy raising the gaff-rigged mainsail, so the yacht was moving under wind alone by the time they reached the channel.

"Oh my goodness. It's amazing," Ella said in a bright, happy voice, bending backward to look at the wind-filled sails. The yacht shot forward, heeling a tiny bit to leeward, and Ella stumbled as the deck shifted beneath their feet.

Dylan caught her by the shoulders for the second time that evening, the heat of her body flowing through his palms and into his core. Desire almost blew him over. But his hunger for this woman was tempered by something else much stronger.

He wanted to keep her safe right here beside him. But she was more like Lauren than he'd thought, the dress notwithstanding. Neither Lauren nor Ella would ever be happy living here in Magnolia Harbor.

Chapter Nineteen————

The cruise had been lovely, the bay had been calm, and the sunset had been gorgeous, lighting up the sky in shades of yellow, pink, and magenta. But Dylan's melancholy seemed to hang over it. What was wrong with him?

As the schooner turned back toward the harbor with the day turning toward twilight, a deep exhaustion seeped through Ella. She wanted to ask him what was wrong, but even a simple question like that seemed dangerous, especially after the conversation they'd had about his mother and her father. They needed to keep it light between them.

So when Jude St. Pierre handed the ship's wheel over to one of his crew and strolled over to where Dylan and Ella stood, she was thankful for the interruption.

"If y'all would like to take a tour below decks, feel free. I left a couple of brochures on the table in the salon about evening party rentals and catering details. You better jump quick though because I only have a couple of evening sailings available. Charter sailings can be booked any Tuesday or

Wednesday evening." He shook their hands and then strolled away to chat with other passengers, like any good ship's captain.

"Come on," Dylan said. "I've seen the salon, but you should take a look. If you think the decks are beautiful, wait until you see the woodwork down there." Dylan snagged her hand and pulled her toward the ship's ladder.

Damn. Holding his hand was nice, even though the touch of his skin against hers made fireflies spark to life in her middle. That simple touch, and her deep reaction to it, was a warning she chose not to heed. She probably shouldn't have held his hand in public, but she didn't let go until she had to climb down the steep steps to the salon.

The space was paneled in gleaming mahogany with porthole windows and skylights that provided views of the rigging and the dusky blue of the twilight sky beyond. The salon wasn't cavernous like Grace Church, or ordinary like Cibo Dell'anima. Decorated in beautiful shades of blues and greens, it had an intimate feel. It wouldn't hold many guests, though.

"I love it," she said, turning to inspect the comfortable furniture, all of which was built into the bulkheads. She had a Goldilocks moment. After all the searching, she'd finally found the right place.

"We should book it for the first available Wednesday. We can't have a party on Tuesday because of the Piece Maker meetings. I have discovered that *nothing* stands in the way of those."

"And what if it rains or storms?" Dylan asked, repeating his concerns like some oracle of doom.

She turned on him. "What is wrong with you? You've been Doctor Depressed all night. Was it me asking questions about your mother that put you into this mood?" Or was it her dress? She didn't dare ask that because the dress had been a mistake. The arms were so tight they were cutting off circulation to her hands. She turned away from him and headed down a narrow hallway right off the salon.

"I'm sorry. I've been distracted," he said, following her.

"By what?" she asked over her shoulder. This was too dangerous a question to ask when looking him right in the eye.

"One of my patients died today."

"Oh. Gee. I'm so sorry. I'm an idiot." She turned, leaning against a bulkhead. "Was it sudden?"

"No, not really."

"Do you want to talk about it?"

He reached out and took her hand, interlacing his fingers with hers. Oh, his touch made her long for things she could never have. He shook his head. "She was an old lady," he said. "Alone in the world. Her husband had died. She didn't have kids. Not even any friends left. They'd all died and left her alone. She was suffering from heart failure, and the meds were starting to lose their efficacy. I thought she should go into a nursing home, and Dad was opposed to that."

His voice got hard at the end. "If Dad had listened to me, she'd be alive today."

She squeezed his hand. "But would she be happy about that?"

He met her gaze. "She'd be alive. Dead is dead."

Spoken like a doctor who spent his life battling for life. She had to love him for caring so much, but if she were in the same situation, she'd be ready to meet her Maker.

She rocked up on tiptoes and gave him a kiss on the cheek. Then she pulled away from him, putting space between them.

"Where are you going?" Dylan asked, following her down the hall.

She opened one of the hallway doors, which led to a cabin with a small bedroom. "I'm checking out...the bedrooms," she said, and then regretted the way that sentence sounded, so she continued down the hall, opening doors until she found a large stateroom at the end of the hallway. A queen-sized bed sat in the middle of the room on a platform of highly polished wood with drawers underneath. The bulkheads were paneled like the library at Howland House, with decorative inlays and millwork. Tongue and groove planking, painted a creamy white, covered the low, curved ceiling, and two porthole windows provided a view.

"Wow," she said, leaning into the doorway. "I wonder how much it would cost to charter this boat and sail to the Caribbean."

"More than either of us can afford," Dylan said from behind her, his breath feathering against the nape of her neck. "It would be fun sailing away with you. If we went alone, we wouldn't have to skulk around like sneaks."

Time hung suspended as her mind spun off on a wild and crazy tangent in which neither Jim nor Mom existed. What would it feel like to be utterly free to simply let this thing—fling or relationship—unfold in its own time?

If she was free right now, she'd step across this threshold. She'd pull him into the room with her and give him the comfort he so desperately needed tonight.

Just then, his mouth touched the skin right below her earlobe, his lips hot against her skin. The kiss was like a spark dropped onto dry kindling. Her body burst into a rush of heat and fire.

She turned to face him. He took her by the shoulders and backed her up through the doorway as his mouth came down hard and hungry on her lips.

He closed the door. She pressed herself against him. He was sturdy and male and utterly delicious. He linked a string of kisses down her neck like fiery pearls.

In every spot where he touched her, she came to life, hungry and needy. She groaned out loud, and he turned the tables, pressing her up against the door, his body a welcome weight against her.

When he managed, with some serious effort, to tug the hem of her tight skirt up over her hip, she pressed into him and kissed his ear, her fingers roaming through the curly texture of his hair.

She was about to suggest a tumble into the beautiful bed when Jude St. Pierre's voice pierced the fog of her desire. "Dylan? Are you down here? One of the guests just fell and gashed her head."

Dylan stopped, pulling away from her, his eyes dark and hungry. "We're not finished," he said, then turned around, deftly straightening his bow tie as he opened the door and headed down the hallway.

"I'm here," he said in a loud voice. "Ella wanted to see the staterooms."

* * *

Dylan didn't know whether to be annoyed about the young woman who had tripped and fallen or relieved that the accident had prevented him from getting caught with his pants down...literally.

As it turned out, the passenger's scalp wound was superficial, and there were no signs of a concussion. So he doctored her with the medical kit on board and suggested that she contact her GP in the morning if she had any further symptoms.

He got a round of applause for this minor medical non-miracle. It seemed kind of stupid to be applauded for applying a Band-Aid to someone's forehead when Coreen Martel had needed so much more from him. Why was the woman's demise weighing so heavily on him?

He didn't know. In medical school, they had taught him to remain detached, and he'd thought he'd managed that. Except that Dad was always telling him to care more. Because Dad cared. Dad had cared enough to let Coreen stay at home and be independent even though, strictly speaking, that hadn't been the best medical advice.

There was more to being a country doctor than what they'd taught him in med school. And he was only starting to learn the truth.

The yacht made it back to dock without further mishap, and Dylan found himself below decks discussing its availability for the engagement party. He allowed himself to be distracted from his sadness and the tug of longing he felt every time Ella turned her big eyes in his direction.

He wanted to take her home because he didn't want to be alone tonight in the big house he'd once shared with Dad. In fact, the loneliness of his future life weighed on him. He didn't want to end up like Coreen.

He pushed the negative thoughts from his head as they discussed possible sailing dates with Jude St. Pierre. They didn't have many choices, and they'd still be up a creek if the weather didn't cooperate. But they booked the yacht for April twenty-second. Just two weeks away.

"So…" Ella said in a bright, happy voice as they left the yacht and headed down the long pier to the parking lot. "We need to check out caterers right away. We might have trouble booking one."

"I'll call around and make some appointments," he muttered. Talking about catering was the last thing on his mind. What he wanted was to finish the kiss they'd started in the stateroom. But maybe that was a bad idea. Maybe he should disengage.

After all, their parents were getting married. With the yacht booked for the party, the reality settled in. Dad was never coming back to the house. Ella was just a momentary lapse of judgment. His future seemed to open up in front of him like a big, dark, lonely thing.

"We should have a chocolate fountain," she said. "You know, with strawberries. Mom loves chocolate-covered strawberries."

She was oblivious to his pain, and her excitement about the party left him sour. "A chocolate fountain on a yacht? Are you crazy?" he said.

She turned as they walked down the pier. "Oh my god. You are such a stick in the mud sometimes. You know that?"

"Do you want to come back to my place?" he asked abruptly. He didn't want to talk about catering and chocolate fountains or champagne or any of that. He just wanted to finish the kiss. He just wanted company tonight.

She stopped dead in her tracks and hugged herself against the freshening breeze, which had turned chilly now that the sun had set. Was she cold or uncertain? He couldn't quite tell, so he took off his jacket and draped it around her shoulders. "I told you to dress appropriately," he said gently, resting his hands on her tiny shoulders.

"What?"

"In my message. Didn't I?"

She threw back her head and laughed. He had no idea what was so funny, but suddenly he was laughing too. Not just a little chuckle or a giggle, but a big, fat belly laugh that had tears streaming from his eyes. The laugh eased something that had seized up in him this morning when the fire department had delivered the news about Coreen Martel.

When he finally caught his breath, he managed to ask, "What's so funny?"

"I thought you wanted me to dress appropriately."

"Well, I did. I looked at the weather forecast and…" His voice faded out, stilled by the look on her face. Her beautiful mouth had tipped up in a winning smile, and her big eyes danced with merriment.

"Right. And since you didn't say one word about the weather,

I interpreted your request to mean that you wanted me to, you know, dress conservative and boring. I thought either you were embarrassed by me or maybe you wanted me to wear something that wasn't sexy." She reached up and pulled the end of his bow tie, untying the knot.

"Really? That's what you thought? Damn, Ella. I'm not sure I could stop wanting you even if you dressed in a gunnysack. And I do hate the dress."

"Even though it's got polka dots? We would have matched if you'd worn your navy tie."

"You are not a polka dot kind of person, and I'm okay with that. I like you the way you are."

She blinked. "Really? I didn't think so at first."

"Well, okay. I need to apologize for judging you when I first met you. I was wrong about it all." He stepped a little closer. "What I want," he said in a near whisper, "is to get you out of that dress."

"I'm trying so hard to be good," she whispered.

"I know. I am too. But I still want you to come home with me." He cupped her head and kissed her. She tasted like spring flowers or something growing from deep, dark earth. Elemental. Perfect. He didn't want it to end, so it lasted for a long time until someone said, "Y'all need to get a room."

They jumped back as a sixty-something tourist in a loud Hawaiian shirt passed them on the way to one of the houseboats docked up the pier.

"Oh my god," she gasped. "We need to be more careful."

"He was a tourist. But you know, we might as well hang for a sheep as a lamb."

She snorted. "Where do you come up with these sayings?"

"Dad mostly. Which is weird because he's not originally from the South, but you'd never know it. I think he collects them from his older patients. Come home with me, Ella."

Chapter Twenty——————

Louella Pender, the owner of A Stitch in Time, could be a difficult boss at times, but on Thursday, she surprised Brenda by agreeing to let her take a longer-than-usual lunch break. So today, instead of eating a bag lunch out on the boardwalk, Brenda strolled down to Rafferty's deck, where Ella was waiting for her underneath one of the restaurant's brightly striped umbrellas.

"Hey," Brenda said, sprinting up the stairs to the deck and giving her daughter a kiss. Oh, what a beautiful day it was. The sun was shining, Jim had revamped her outlook on life, and Ella had returned to the family fold, at least for the moment. The day was so perfect that a multitude of mid-week sailors had skipped work. Sails dotted the bay in all directions.

"So," Ella said once Brenda had seated herself, "I have good news and bad news."

Her ebullient mood fell right into a pit. Brenda closed her eyes and braced for the inevitable. She fully expected Ella to tell her she was going back to touring with Urban Armadillo. "Okay, I'm ready. Lay it on me."

Ella laughed. "Mom, it's not that bad."

Brenda opened her eyes. "I don't care. I don't want any bad news."

"Okay, I'll start with the good news. We've booked *Synchronicity Too* for the party."

"What? Is it big enough for a hundred guests?"

"Right, that's part of the bad news. We're limited to no more than forty. And the only date we could get was April twenty-second."

"That's two weeks from now."

"I know. And I checked with Annie Robinson and she's already booked for that night, so we have to find another caterer. But what do you think about the boat? I think it's perfect. And Granny told me that you and Jim had your first date on that yacht, so it's romantic."

So the bad news had nothing to do with Ella leaving, thank goodness. Brenda's smile came easy then. "Yes, Jim and I had a first date, of sorts. He pressured me into joining him on the yacht for the Festival of Lights boat parade at Christmastime. To this day, Jim insists that he cured me of my Christmas-itis on that cruise."

"Christmas-itis?"

"Don't ask. Jim turns into Santa's clone at Christmastime, as you well know. He didn't think I was sufficiently joyful, and he set about to correct that."

"Good for him. So you have nice memories of the boat?"

"Well, if you must know, Jim kissed me for the first time during the Christmas cruise. Jim and I were checking out the stateroom, and Jude had put some mistletoe on the door of the captain's quarters. Jim caught me unawares."

"You mean that big stateroom at the end of the hall?" Ella asked.

Brenda nodded. "Yup. That one. I have to say the kiss was more than a peck on the cheek."

"Mom, TMI," Ella said, her face going bright red.

Brenda studied her daughter's blush. Ella usually wasn't that squeamish about sex talk. What was up with her?

Just then, the waitress came by, and they both ordered shrimp Caesar salads and unsweetened iced tea, which was a good indication that both of them had spent much of their lives living north of the Mason-Dixon Line.

"So, there is one other thing," Ella said once the waitress left.

Brenda's heart rocked in her chest. "What?" she asked a little too quickly.

"Well, I was wondering if you wanted to work on something to play for the guests."

Brenda straightened in her chair. Who was this child? In the months since she'd been home, Ella hadn't once suggested that they play a duet. But suddenly the clouds she'd imagined on this beautiful day evaporated into nothing.

"What did you have in mind?" she asked, trying not to sound too enthusiastic.

"I was thinking about Mozart's 'Duo for Two Violins.' The allegro number 5. We used to play that a long time ago."

The familiar pressure in Brenda's chest eased, and she floated entirely free of her worries. Once, before Ella turned fifteen, they had bonded over the notes on the page. But she'd pushed too hard and driven Ella away. This was her time to get her daughter back.

"I think it would be fun to play a duet," she said. The words were an understatement.

"Great. We'll have to get together a few times to practice." Ella watched the sails in the harbor for a long moment, her gaze sorrowful or something.

A frisson of worry replaced the floaty feeling. "What's the matter, honey? Something bothering you?"

Ella shook her head, maybe a little too quickly. "No, I'm fine. Really."

"Are you sure you've told me everything?" Brenda asked.

Ella gave her a long stare, hesitating as if she wanted to say something toxic. But the look faded quickly. "We're screwed if it rains on the day of the party," she said with a little smile.

"Do we have a rain-check plan?"

She shook her head. "No. Jude said we could still have the party on the boat, but it would have to be below decks and the boat won't leave the pier. So I think we should alert the altar guild. All those church ladies need to put your engagement party date on their prayer list."

Brenda laughed in spite of her worries. "I'll make sure your grandmother knows."

"That's all it'll take, I'm sure."

Brenda couldn't shake the feeling that the rain plan wasn't the reason her daughter seemed tired and distracted this afternoon. She took a wild guess at the problem. "So, is Dylan okay with this plan? He seems so—"

"What?" Ella almost jumped down her throat.

Aha! Eureka. The problem was Dylan. Brenda was not surprised.

She leaned forward and patted Ella's hand where it rested on the table. "I'm sorry you've had to put up with him. I think it was a huge mistake for me to suggest that you and he plan this party together. I thought... Well, it's not important."

"He's not so bad," Ella said without making eye contact.

The waitress interrupted the conversation, delivering their salads. Brenda used the break to collect her thoughts. She needed to make Ella understand that she would always come first, no matter what.

When the waitress left, Brenda captured her daughter's gaze. "Honey, I want to say something important to you. Something I think you need to hear." Brenda paused and was encouraged when Ella didn't roll her eyes or look away.

"You know how much I want us all to become one big, happy family, but you know what? That doesn't mean you have to let Dylan run roughshod over you. I'd rather you just be yourself, okay? And let's face it, Dylan is not his father. He's not easy to like."

"You think?"

What was it in Ella's tone? Not the usual sarcasm. Something was off.

"I want to apologize," Brenda continued. "I've been guilty of pushing you in directions you never wanted to go. And I'm starting to feel as if my desire to see us all become one happy family is another example. So I'm going to stop now, okay? If you don't want to spend time with Dylan, that's fine. I don't ever want Dylan to be a reason you can't call Magnolia Harbor your home."

* * *

Wow. There was so much to unpack in what Mom had just said.

First, was the basic question of home. Was Magnolia Harbor Ella's home? Hardly. Mom had grown up here, and so had Granny. Dylan too. She'd visited as a child, and she was merely visiting now, when you got right down to it.

There would always be a room at Cloud Nine with her name on it, but Mom's beach house wasn't home either. She didn't have a place of her own. Not now. Not ever, really.

And then there was Dylan. Oh, the irony. Dylan might be a reason to come visiting. He might be a reason to stay put. But she didn't know for certain either way. And she couldn't even talk to Mom about her confusion.

It was far too early to know where this thing was going, but she could see herself falling hard for Doctor Delicious. Would that be good for Mom and Jim? She didn't know the answer to that either.

And what happened if Mom and Jim didn't work out? Maybe that was asking for trouble, but she couldn't help it. If Mom and Jim broke up, while she and Dylan got together, there would be misery for everyone.

She wasn't stupid about Dylan either. What if he broke her heart? She'd have to move away, and that would hurt Mom.

The cause and effect rippled across her brain like waves on a still pond. This was complicated and fraught. A wise woman would stop now. But she knew damn well that if Dylan called her tonight, she'd gladly go spend time with him.

She needed to change the subject, so she drew Mom into a conversation about the Mozart piece and party details while her guilty conscience twinged.

An hour later, they headed toward the restaurant's front entrance linked arm in arm, as if they'd always known harmony in their lives. But all of that came to an abrupt end when Mom stopped in her tracks and said, "Oh no," in a voice more like a gasp than a whisper.

"What? Are you okay?" Ella turned to face her mother, suddenly concerned.

"I'm fine. But maybe you aren't going to be when you turn around."

Ella turned and scanned her surroundings, doing the classic double take when her gaze fixed on the poster in the restaurant's vestibule. An expletive escaped her mouth, and Mom didn't even seem to notice.

The flyer listed the bands that had been booked to play Rafferty's patio during the month of April. Urban Armadillo was listed as the patio entertainment for Saturday, May 1—a week after the engagement party.

A buzz of unexpected fury jangled in the back of Ella's mind. For thirteen years, Cody had resisted touring the band anywhere east of the Mississippi. Now, suddenly, he'd changed his mind? This booking was not serendipity. Cody was coming for her.

"Maybe it's not the same band," Mom said.

Ella rolled her eyes in Mom's direction. "You don't believe that for a New York minute. What other band would be dumb enough to pick a name like that?"

"You'll stay away from him, won't you?" The pleading tone in Mom's voice was almost heartbreaking.

"Mom, I promise that I won't seek him out. But we both know why he's brought Urban Armadillo here. He thinks he can sweet-talk me into joining him on the road."

"Can he?"

"No. I don't want to go back to Urban Armadillo."

"But what about Cody?"

"Him either. I mean it, Mom. Relax. Cody is not a problem." But Dylan might be. And she would have to find a band sooner or later because she couldn't continue working part time at Howland House. Especially now. Last night, she'd all but spent the night with Dylan. She'd nearly been late to work. That couldn't go on without Ashley noticing something.

She felt as if she were walking on a tightrope with a big arc light blinding her. The future was impossible to see, and any misstep would end with her falling hard.

They walked back to the yarn shop together, where Mom gave her a quick kiss on the cheek. "I'll call Granny, and we'll schedule a time to get some invitations addressed and in the mail. We can practice the Mozart at the same time."

"Okay. Dylan and I are supposed to check out catering companies over the next few days. You want to join us?"

Mom shook her head. "No. I think Dylan and I would probably disagree. Thank you for running interference with him. Are you sure you're okay doing this?"

"I'm fine. I just don't want to choose—"

"Surprise me, okay?"

"Right. But I promise that if it's possible, we're going to have a chocolate fountain."

Mom laughed as she headed into the yarn shop, which made Ella feel good about herself. She didn't want to blow Mom's trust in her. Not only with the catering, but with the whole Dylan thing.

She headed up the street to the inn, a gnawing restlessness settling over her. She didn't have anything to do this afternoon except obsess about the men in her life. Cody, who might show up unannounced at her front door, and Dylan, who'd made her body sing last night with the sweetest kind of music.

At moments like this, it was best to take out her violin and practice until she could clear her mind. Remembering Jackie's request (or was it the ghost's?), she took her violin out to the lawn and sat in the shade of the old oak tree and practiced a somewhat simplified version of the second movement of "Borodin's String Quartet no. 2."

She couldn't do the piece justice. It required four voices. But it suited her mood. The movement, sometimes called "This Is My Beloved" because it had been turned into a song in the musical *Kismet*, was hopelessly romantic. In any event, Ashley's guests would probably recognize this classical piece because of the musical, and she wanted to perfect it before next Saturday's tea.

She'd been working on the arrangement for about an hour when Jackie came racing across the lawn, his penny whistle clutched in his fist. She had to hand it to the kid; he'd been practicing like a champ. And even though all that practicing was driving his mother nuts, it had also improved his whistling skills.

Ella had already told Ashley that she should explore music lessons for the boy because Jackie, like so many children first exposed to music, had developed a burning desire to learn. It was a little ironic for Ella to suggest this, given the way Mom had pushed her into music. But music had always been a part of her, despite Mom's ambitions.

In fact, music had always been the one thing she could depend on. It could lift her up when she was down. It could fill her world. It could carry her away. It could calm her down. Music had never demanded anything she wasn't willing to give to it. Nor had it ever abandoned her or disappointed her.

"Hey," the kid said, rushing up to where she sat in a folding chair she'd purloined from the stash Ashley used for weddings. "I heard you practicing. You wanna hear the 'Sailor's Hornpipe'?"

"Sure."

Jackie put the whistle to his lips and slowly played the first musical theme of the famous sailor's song without a single mistake, which was impressive because the song required him to use more than one octave—a difficult thing on a penny whistle. Ella clapped. "Well done, Jackie."

"There's more to the song though," he said. "I listened to it on YouTube. And I tried to play faster, but the whistle squeaks, especially on that one really high note."

"It's okay. You'll get faster the more you practice."

"Will you teach me the rest of it?"

"Sure." She spent the next hour teaching the second theme to the boy. He had a remarkable memory and a good ear, which made learning the song fun. He hadn't yet been exposed to the drudgery of having to learn musical notation. That would come later.

"You want to play it together?" she asked.

"Only if you go real slow."

The kid amused her. He was such a sweet boy. "I promise. But if you make a mistake, don't stop. That's the trick of performing.

Musicians make mistakes all the time." She only wished some-one had told her that when she was eight or nine.

She tucked the violin under her chin, and they played the first and second variations all the way through. When they got near the end, she said, "Keep going." The kid went back to the first theme and played it again. They played like that over and over again, Ella gradually increasing the speed. In the last round, she started playing harmony to his whistle, and the hornpipe came to life along with a little light in Jackie's eyes.

When they finished, a couple of the inn's guests who had been sitting out on the lawn turned and applauded Jackie. He took a sweeping bow. The kid was a natural-born performer.

"That was fun," he said. He looked off into the distance for a moment, his gaze focused on something Ella couldn't see. "The captain says I could play whistle on his ship anytime."

The boy's gaze returned to Ella.

"The ghost was talking to you?" she asked. She'd felt nothing—no cold air, no shiver down her back, not one para-normal experience. Ella had to admit that Jackie's odd fixation on the inn's imaginary ghost was unsettling.

"Yeah. He hangs around the tree most of the time. He's pretty lonely and sad," Jackie said.

"Really?"

"Well, yeah. Think about it. He died trying to come back to Rose. He was in a hurry and ignored the hurricane that sank his ship. He's responsible for all those pirates drowning in the inlet. And then the one survivor, Henri St. Pierre, fell in love with his girlfriend. That had to suck."

"Wait...his first mate fell in love with Rose?"

"Yeah. Kind of a shocker. They had a baby together."

"No. How do you know that?"

"We found Rose's diary last year, and some stuff buried in the backyard."

"Oh. Wow. Wait, does that mean all the Howlands and St. Pierres can trace their ancestry back to Rose?"

He nodded. "Yeah, Mom and Reverend St. Pierre are like seventeenth cousins or something. It was all hundreds of years ago."

"So at least Rose had a happy ending, then?"

"I'm afraid not," the kid said on a long sigh. "You know, Henri was black, and Rose was white, and it was 1716 or something like that."

Oh wow. The tale was like one of those tragic Irish ballads. But really the captain's misery, if indeed there was a captain, was entirely self-made.

"Well, now that I know the story, I'm not exactly sorry for the captain. He deserves his misery," she said.

"You think?"

"Yeah. The guy should have married Rose instead of running off to gain a fortune by robbing people on the high seas."

"But—"

"I mean it, Jackie. Captain Teal wasn't a hero. He fell in love with Rose, and then he left her to raise a kid on her own." Ella left out the part where the famous pirate talked Rose out of her virtue, although Jackie seemed to understand all the sordid details of the story. Nevertheless, some of her irritation at Cody Callaghan managed to infect her tone. Cody had never walked out on her, exactly, although he'd been unfaithful more times than she could count. And now he was coming to her like the famous Captain William Teal, only he was sailing across the country in his land yacht.

What was he going to do when he got here? Sweep her off her feet? Hand her some line? Or try to rehire her as his fiddler? Two of the three options were possible.

But she was like Rose Howland now. Someone else had come along to sweep her off her feet. Only problem was, he might not be exactly suitable.

* * *

Dylan showed up for work on Thursday bleary eyed. He'd gotten what he wanted last night because Ella had stayed until almost dawn. He'd driven her back to the inn at 5:00 a.m. so she would be ready for breakfast service.

Heaven help them if Ashley Scott figured out what was going on and blabbed her mouth. On the other hand, maybe it would be better to get in front of the crap storm by telling the truth. Dylan hated sneaking around.

The day was exceptionally busy for him, with office hours at the free clinic, which was always slightly overwhelmed with too many patients.

As he made it through the day, Ella was always on his mind. There, just below the surface. But Dylan was a realist. Ella would never settle here in Magnolia Harbor. She wasn't the kind who settled down. She was a lot like the fireflies he used to catch on a summer evening in the backyard. Incandescent, but free. He could hold that light for an hour or so, but he'd learned quickly as a child that no one can trap a firefly forever. If he pinned her down, she'd lose her glow.

As much as he wanted to shout to the world that he was falling in love, he couldn't do it. Not just because of who Ella was, but because he and Ella weren't a forever thing. Three nights between the sheets did not a relationship make.

So he pushed the entire situation out of his mind as best he could and spent a crazy day at the clinic that kept him busy until five when he finally retreated to his office to review emails.

The emails were routine, requiring not much in the way of responses until he got to the one from the endocrinologist in Georgetown. The doc was following up with a copy of Ginny Whittle's test results.

He stared at the report for a full minute as it dawned on him that he'd been right. Ginny's symptoms were not all in her head. She had diabetes insipidus.

Dad had been wrong about Mrs. Whittle.

The idea of Dad making mistakes sent cold prickling across his skin. What if this was a pattern? What if Dad was losing it?

Should he keep these lab results from his father?

No. He was overreacting. He printed the email and test results and headed down the hall to Dad's office with the intention of leaving the printout on his desk.

But Dad was at work still.

"Hey, you got a minute?" he asked.

"Sure." Dad gestured toward his side chair.

"I got back Ginny Whittle's results," Dylan said, settling into the chair.

Dad looked up from his tablet out of a pair of tired eyes. Whoa. What was up with that? He looked bone weary.

"Are you okay?" Dylan asked.

Dad leaned back in his ancient office chair, the springs squealing as he rubbed his eyes. "I'm fine. Why?"

"You don't look fine. When was the last time you had a physical?"

Dad chuckled. "Six months ago. I'm fine. I just stayed up too late last night binge-watching *Breaking Bad*."

"We watched that together years ago."

"I know, but Brenda had never seen it. She hasn't had a television in ages. Now that we have cable at Cloud Nine, I'm helping her catch up on popular culture." He cocked his head. "You look a little tired yourself."

"I'm fine," he shot back, waving the printed email. "I have news." He slid the paper across his father's desk. "Turns out Ginny Whittle has diabetes insipidus. It's not all in her head."

Dad picked up the email and read, his eyebrows arching.

"So you sent her to an endocrinologist despite my views on the matter?"

Dylan looked down, unable to meet his father's eyes. He wasn't ashamed of sending Ginny off to the specialist, but he was uneasy about Dad's reaction. Dad had been a little bit unreliable the last few months.

"I'm not angry," Dad said into his silence.

Dylan looked up. "I know. And I'm not trying to win a point. I just thought you should know."

"I didn't think you were here to crow, son. Thanks for letting me know. The good news is that Ginny's condition is treatable. She should have a great quality of life. I'm proud of you."

"And I'm worried about you." There, he'd said the words out loud.

Dad's lips twitched. "Because we argued about this?"

"Among other things. We've disagreed about a lot of stuff recently. Not just Mrs. Whittle, but Mrs. Martel as well."

"Well, I hope we argue about cases more frequently. I'm not perfect, and one of the best things about having you back home is that you're going to make me a better doc."

That stunned him. How many mistakes had Dad made over the years?

"Don't look so shocked," Dad said. "We're all human. And having two doctors to collaborate is a good thing for our patients. Along those lines, I think we need to get on the ball and hire that nurse practitioner. Maybe while I'm on my honeymoon, you could take the lead on that."

"You want me to handle a staffing issue?" What the hell? Was Dad worried about being able to manage the practice? Was there something wrong with him?

"You can shut your mouth before you swallow a fly," Dad said, his blue eyes as bright and as sharp as ever. "I'm not losing my mind. I just want to back off a little. I've been busting my butt for years building this practice and keeping the free clinic going, and I'd like to take some time to enjoy life a little before it's my time."

"You're only fifty-one. Good grief, stop talking like you're going to die tomorrow." Dylan's voice rose with his concern.

Dad cocked his head. "I don't intend to die tomorrow. But I do intend to retire someday. Maybe sooner rather than later now that you're here and are proving yourself with every passing day. I've earned the chance to kick back and enjoy."

"With Brenda."

"Of course."

Dylan stood up, his emotions suddenly adrift in a raging sea. "I need to get going."

"You have a hot date tonight?" Dad asked.

He whirled around. "No." It was a lie. When he'd left Ella this morning, they'd known they would find a way to hook up later.

"Oh. Too bad. You need to find yourself a nice wife and settle down."

"Dad. Come on."

"What? You're almost thirty-two. Time's a-wasting. Besides, you might come on in. The water's nice."

He sighed and rolled his eyes. "You're ridiculous. I'm going now."

He turned, but Dad called to his back, just as he reached the door.

"Dylan. Come on. I know you and Brenda haven't warmed up to each other much. But I have every confidence that one day we'll look back on this time and laugh about it. Brenda's very stressed right at the moment. You know, about the wedding and Ella and all that. It would be nice if you gave her a chance."

He turned to face his father. "She's stressed about Ella?"

"Of course she is. Even more today than she was yesterday, I'm afraid."

"Why?"

"Well, you know she lost meaningful contact with Ella for more than a decade when Ella ran off to perform with a country music band. Brenda has been worried since last December that Ella is going to find another band and leave again. She isn't living up to her best potential here in Magnolia Harbor.

"And then I just heard this afternoon that her ex-boyfriend is going to be here on tour in early May."

"Ella's ex is coming to town?"

"Yeah. And Brenda is terrified that he's going to convince Ella to go on the road with him. And she's sure that, if that happens, she'll lose contact with her again for years. That would break Brenda's heart, Dylan. God, I can't imagine being out of touch with you for more than a day or so. So I'm asking you to be nice to Ella. Please. Don't become the reason she decides to move away. Understand?"

"Yeah, I do," he said.

Chapter Twenty-One

The Harley rumbled with a satisfying, deep-throated growl as Dylan rode it up the long hill to Howland House. The roar of the bike was like a soundtrack to his emotions. Another day of sneaking around, which was kind of thrilling. And yet fraught with so many risks.

Was it the danger that had him coming back night after night? Or was it Ella, messing with his brain? Dylan didn't know, but it hardly mattered.

All day on Friday, he'd been anticipating this evening's tasting at A Night to Remember, the caterer that Jude St. Pierre had recommended. He was waiting to see what Ella thought about her ride this evening.

He was hoping the caterer's name was prophetic. He planned a night to remember. Like their date on the mainland had been last night. And the night before. Funny how he was dragging around from lack of sleep during the day, but when quitting time rolled around, he was ready and raring to go again.

He killed the bike's engine and set the kickstand. He was

about to go knock on the door when Ella came strolling out wearing a pair of blue jeans and a tight-fitting T-shirt with the words NEVER UNDERESTIMATE A GIRL WITH A FIDDLE across her breasts. She wore her Doc Martens and carried a jean jacket over her arm. Like always, her red hair was piled on top of her head in a messy bun, tendrils escaping to fall around her ears, neck, and eyes.

He'd been explicit about how he wanted her to dress tonight because they were riding the bike. She'd complied with his request that she wear long pants and a jacket for safety reasons.

She strode up to him, taking in his riding leathers and the Harley as if she might be seeing him in an entirely new light. "So you're going to take me for a ride?"

"I am," he said, grinning. Really, when you boiled life down to the essentials, nothing could beat a Harley and a red-headed girl.

He reached behind him and unhooked the second riding helmet. "This is for you. Have you ever ridden on a motorcycle?"

She gave him that sultry smile and shook her head. "I probably shouldn't admit that out loud. I mean, I was a member of an outlaw country music band for years. We regularly played at biker bars."

"Really?"

"Yeah. But honestly, you don't look like a common, run-of-the-mill biker. You don't have a beer belly and a beard down to there." Her smile widened. "But you know, that's a stereotype."

"Good for me. So. We need to get going. We have an appointment at six."

She mounted the bike, her warm body snuggling up against him. His riding leathers were designed to protect his skin from pavement burn, but right now he wished he was riding naked.

Boy, that would turn some heads on Harbor Drive, wouldn't it?

"How do I stay on this thing?" she asked.

"There are handles, but if you want, you can hold on to me."

"And where is this caterer?"

"On Harbor Drive. Down on the East End."

"Are we tempting the fates by riding right through the middle of town?" she asked.

"Uh, well. No. Maybe. But you can hold on to the handles if you want."

She didn't. Instead, she wrapped both arms around his middle and snuggled even tighter against his back. It was perfect. He wished they were taking a long drive up the coast to find a deserted beach. Although making love in the sand wasn't all that much fun, really.

He fired up the bike and looked over his shoulder. "Lean through the turns like you would if you were on a bicycle."

"Right," she said in a breathless tone, her hands a little restless where they gripped his chest.

He took off at a moderate speed. He'd intended to give her a different kind of thrill this evening, but unfortunately, an accident snarled downtown traffic, and they inched along. Some idiotic tourist hadn't been paying attention and made a turn into oncoming traffic at the intersection of Harbor Drive and Magnolia Boulevard. No one was hurt, thank goodness, but every few feet he had to stop and put his foot on the pavement.

That didn't mean he wasn't having a few thrills though. Ella had developed a death wish or something. Or maybe she had gotten tired of hanging on tight when they were going slower than a pedal bike. She quit clutching his chest, and her hands strayed down to his inner thigh. His riding leathers suddenly felt hotter than normal.

"So," he said half turning, unable to see her because of the helmet. "Are you trying to get caught with your hands in the cookie jar?"

She moved her hand back to his chest. "Uh, well, um. Sorry. I guess my mind started wandering."

"I wasn't complaining," he said.

"No?"

She moved her hand down slowly across his abs on its way back to other places when, out of nowhere, they were hailed.

"Ella, is that you?"

She straightened as if she'd been hit with a taser. Her sudden move, withdrawing her hands from his body, upset their balance. Good thing they were going only two miles an hour. Dylan was able to stop the bike and rest his foot on the ground before they toppled.

"Granny?" she said in a strangled tone that carried even through the muffling helmet.

Dylan glanced toward the sidewalk in front of A Stitch in Time. Sure enough, there stood Ella's grandmother, shading her eyes against the late-afternoon sunlight. "My word, Dylan, I had no idea you had a motorcycle," she said in a voice that was surprisingly loud for Nancy Jacobs.

In fact, several other people turned and glanced their way, including Milo Parker, one of Dylan's patients, who was walking down the street carrying a bag from Annie's Kitchen—precisely the kind of eatery the man should have been avoiding. Milo grinned at him sheepishly.

"Isn't it fun?" Ella said to her grandmother.

"Well, that's debatable. Where are y'all off to?"

"A Night to Remember," Ella hollered.

"What?" Nancy's mouth almost fell open just as the traffic moved forward several feet, taking them farther down Harbor Drive.

"It's a catering place, Granny," Ella yelled, but Nancy didn't hear her. The woman cupped her hand around her ear and frowned at them. There was a certain resemblance between that frown and the one Ella referred to as her mother's frown-of-death.

Before Ella could explain the caterer's name again, Ethan Cuthbert, a deputy with the Magnolia Harbor Police Force, who was on the scene directing traffic, waved them forward past the smashed-up Chevy in the middle of the road.

"Hey, Dylan," the deputy called, "y'all out for a little evening ride?" Ethan squinted. "Is that you, Ella?"

"Yes, it's me. And no, we're off to A Night to Remember."

Ethan's mouth dropped.

"Hang on, Ella," Dylan shouted, right before he hit the gas. Her arms came around his middle again as they shot forward past the accident.

"I hope you do have a night to remember," Ethan hollered after them.

Five minutes later, they arrived at the caterer and divested themselves of their helmets. They stared at each other for a long, serious moment. People were going to gossip about them. Of course, they could explain the confusion, given the name of the caterer.

So maybe that explained why they both cracked up laughing so hard that tears fell from their eyes.

"You know," she finally said as they walked toward the caterer's office, "my grandmother is going to grill me about what she thinks she just heard. Which was innocent enough, but not really."

He stopped at the caterer's door. "We could always tell the truth."

"And what is the truth?" she asked, her face sobering.

Good question. Was this a fling that would be over in a week or two when she got ready to move on? Or was it something more?

Or maybe it didn't matter what *it* was.

* * *

After church on Sunday, Ella rode back to Granny's house with Mom. She'd brought her fiddle with her because they intended to practice the Mozart duet and get the engagement party invitations addressed.

The mailed invitations were unnecessary since Dylan had set up an Evite and had already gotten half a dozen RSVPs online.

But Mom didn't trust the internet, or Dylan for that matter. So to keep the peace, Ella had borrowed her mother's car yesterday and gotten cards with matching envelopes printed up at one of those quick-print places in Georgetown. Granny had volunteered to address envelopes because her handwriting was so much better than Brenda's or Ella's. And since they'd cut the invite list down to forty guests, it wasn't a big deal.

Ella was just a tiny bit nervous about rehearsals with Mom. Many years ago, they had played this piece together. She'd been fifteen, and it had been a difficult piece for her then. She was a better violinist now. But she was still rusty when it came to reading notes on a page. For years she'd been playing fiddle by ear or making up arrangements on the fly. That was the beauty of fiddling with a band.

Today she'd have to be perfect. So she'd been spending a lot of time out by the tree practicing this piece. She had no idea if the questionable ghost liked Mozart as much as her jigs and reels. At least the ghost kept his critiques to himself. Mom was unlikely to do that.

They set up their music stands in the condo's living room while Granny settled at her kitchen island with the cards and envelopes. The Mozart piece was a fast-paced allegro with lots of arpeggios. The lead melodic line jumped from one violin to the other and back again. And if ever there was a "fun" piece of classical music, this was it.

"I'll take first violin," Ella said, because she'd been practicing that part. Years ago, she'd played second fiddle, but not today. Of course, the second violin part wasn't any easier, but Mom had always played first violin.

Ella braced for an argument, but Mom only nodded and re-arranged her music. They started playing on Ella's count. She set a quick tempo because that's how she'd practiced it. The duet was typical chamber music, full of fast notes, and didn't require a lot of emotion to play. Speed was the thing. Which made baroque music more like jigs and a reels than the Borodin she'd been messing around with.

They played it with few mistakes, although Ella had the upper hand because she'd practiced the first violin part and Mom was probably sight-reading the second violin. So kudos to Mom for her music-reading chops.

But when the four-minute piece came to an end, Mom was seriously out of breath. "Well," she said, "you just gave my fingers a workout." She grinned.

"I'm sorry. That was kind of unfair because I've been practicing."

"I know. You never did have any faith in your sight-reading. Shall we play it again? This time we can switch parts. And I haven't been practicing." Was that a passive-aggressive dig or a challenge?

Ella wiped a little perspiration from her fingertips. "Okay," she said. *Game on.*

They played it a second time, but since the second violin part wasn't all that dissimilar to the first violin, Ella was able to keep up even though she was sight-reading the music. And, of course, Mom set a much slower pace the second time through. Neither of them played it error-free, so there was that.

"You played that slower. Were you trying to give me a break?" she asked.

"No. I was giving myself a break. Honey, I can't play as fast as you do."

"What?"

She smiled. "You've become a much better violinist than you were at fifteen."

"Guess that means there is some value in country music after all," Granny said from her post in the kitchen.

"I guess so, Momma. Shall we do it again? You play first violin," Mom said.

They practiced for an hour and a half, and by the time they were finished, the piece was almost performance ready. Even more important, they hadn't had a single argument, and the music did nothing but make Mom smile. Ella realized that Mom had been stressing out about a lot of things recently. So this duet had been a really good idea.

They put away their violins and joined Granny at the kitchen island. "How's it going?" Ella asked.

"Almost done." Granny dropped her pen and flexed her fingers. "Y'all were great."

"Thanks," Mom said. "But now my aging bladder is calling. I'll be right back."

Mom headed off to the powder room, and Granny leaned forward and spoke in a voice even quieter than usual. "You want to explain the other day?"

Ella got up and headed toward the fridge as her adrenaline spiked. She'd been waiting for Granny to ask this question. All morning at church, and even before that. She'd expected a phone call.

But evidently, Granny wanted to have this conversation face-to-face and privately.

"There's nothing to explain."

"I know my hearing isn't what it used to be, but I distinctly heard you say that you and Dylan were off for a night to remember. Sugar, I've been concerned ever since that night Jim and Brenda caught Dylan wrapped up in that beach towel. You and Dylan aren't... you know... ?"

"No," she said with her back turned as she pulled the iced tea jug from the fridge.

"Y'all looked chummy the other evening."

"Granny, have you ever ridden on a motorcycle?" Ella reached for three glasses.

"No, can't say as I have."

"Well, there aren't that many places to hang on."

"Y'all were barely moving at the time, sugar."

"Well, we were stopping and going, you know. Kind of jerky motion. And to be honest, I was terrified. And as for what I said, you've got that all wrong. A Night to Remember is a catering place on the East Side."

She turned and met her grandmother's probing stare just as Mom came down the hall from the bathroom. "What's this I hear about catering?"

"We booked a place called A Night to Remember. Jude St. Pierre recommended them. And I found out that it's perfectly okay for us to have a chocolate fountain."

"Oh, fun," Mom said with a gigantic grin, while Granny kept staring at Ella as if she'd just told an enormous fib.

Which she had. Not about the chocolate fountain, but about every other thing related to her ride on Dylan's Harley through the middle of town.

Chapter Twenty-Two————

The ten days leading up the Dad's engagement party passed in a blur for Dylan. He was insanely busy at work, scheduling interviews with potential nurse practitioners, covering for Dad at the free clinic, and finding moments, when no one was looking, to spend time with Ella.

Outwardly, they were working on the engagement party, but really, they had delegated most of the work to An Evening to Remember. Ella kept track of the phone RSVP list, and Dylan kept track of the online RSVPs. And they'd booked a photographer.

Other than that, they spent many an evening chilling with Netflix over at his place. He'd gotten used to getting up with the chickens in order to have her back to Howland House in time for the morning breakfast service. This had, of course, required her to leave a few things at his place. Suddenly his shower had collected a bottle of girlie shampoo, and his sink had an extra toothbrush.

He welcomed these things. Somehow she filled up the empty

places Dad had left when he'd moved out. He was even starting to think about painting the master bedroom and maybe buying some new furniture for that room. He didn't think he'd like the idea of entertaining Ella on the bed his parents had once shared.

In fact, if he could find a few minutes of spare time, he might invite her out for a shopping trip to the mainland. Or maybe they could just cuddle on the couch and peruse the options on Wayfair.com.

But he never quite found the courage to suggest either of those things because he was afraid that if he said it out loud, she'd turn away and stride right out the door. Ella didn't seem to know what she wanted in life. And far be it from him to pressure her into settling for something.

Besides, he didn't want to be the guy she settled for. So instead, he was eyes wide open, sure that he was the rebound guy. And in fairness, maybe she was the rebound girl. The one who was so obviously different from Lauren that she would help him excise the unhappy memories.

The day of the party dawned like every other day, with him up early to drop Ella off and then off to shower and shave and show up at work. It might be Dad's engagement party, but someone had to see patients, because Dad was taking a personal day.

At least it looked as if the weather was going to cooperate. The forecast was for a high in the low eighties with relatively low humidity. Perfect, in fact.

Which was a good thing because everything else about the day turned sour the moment he stopped at the dry cleaners to pick up his gray suit only to discover that they'd put a hole in the jacket. Unfortunately, that was his only tropical-weight suit. So he'd have to wear his blue blazer and khakis to the party. Which seemed wrong. He wore the blue blazer and khakis most days. He ought to dress up for his father's party, right?

And then his workday unraveled fifteen minutes after his second cup of coffee, when Milo Parker came in complaining of chest pains. A quick EKG suggested something serious—no surprise considering Milo's out-of-control diabetes and the fact that he ate at Annie's Kitchen at least two times a week.

But what could Dylan do? He had to call the ambulance service and dispatch Dad's longtime patient to the hospital on the mainland. After that, he was so far behind he couldn't catch up, especially when a second emergency arrived in the form of a tourist who'd cut her foot on something wading in the ocean. She needed sutures and a tetanus shot. And she put him almost an hour behind. In the end, he had to have Lessie, his office manager, call a couple of patients and reschedule them.

And even so, he missed lunch and was a good half hour late getting to the pier where *Synchronicity Too* was docked. He was sweating a little under his jacket by the time he'd sprinted down the pier and stepped onto the yacht's gleaming deck. Dad was standing there checking his watch, which was bad. But on the good side, Dad was dressed in his own blue blazer and khakis.

"Hey," he said, giving Dad a quick man-hug. "Sorry I'm late. I had intended to be here an hour ago to help with last-minute details, but Mr. Parker came in with angina. I sent him off to the mainland, and he was admitted to the hospital. They're going to do a cardiac cath tomorrow morning. But after he showed up, it was a zoo."

"I should have been down at the office," Dad said.

"No, it's fine. We had to reschedule some patients. But we'll catch up tomorrow."

"Look," Dad said under his breath. "Brenda is a little stressed that you're late."

"But I got here before any guests arrived." The last thing Dylan needed right now was Brenda getting on his case for nothing.

"I know. But she feels as if you left Ella to handle everything."

"The caterers handled everything."

"Just lie low, okay? You're in the doghouse with her right at the moment. I would advise you to avoid her as much as possible."

"You think that's wise?"

"Yeah. Just don't say anything to her. She's in bridezilla mode."

"That bad?"

Dad chuckled. "Well, not really *that* bad. But stressed, you know. She wants everything to be perfect."

"There's no such thing." Dylan quoted his father.

"I know. I've even told her that a time or two. But forewarned is forearmed. And not to change the subject, but how are you doing on hiring that nurse practitioner?"

"I'm working on it. I've been interviewing all week. There are a lot of candidates to choose from. It's not an easy decision."

"Good. We might want to consider adding another doc."

"Dad, are you okay?" His father looked tired. Not at all the look of a man who was about to marry the woman of his dreams. Was he sick? Was that what this was about? Was he pushing Dylan to take over because he needed to make sure the practice was in good shape?

A raft of worries assailed Dylan as he looked into his father's eyes. There seemed to be more fine lines around them than there had been a few months ago.

"I'm fine," Dad said. "I'm just tired of trying to manage the free clinic, the practice, and a full life is all. A nurse practitioner could handle a lot of the load at the free clinic, and another doc would help you. You need to have a life too, you know."

"I have a life," he said.

"No, you don't. When was the last time you went fishing or sailing? I can see that you've been spending your time at the office or working on this party. That's not exactly a life. And I'm thinking it's my fault."

"I'm happy with my life." Especially the last couple of weeks, but he could hardly tell his father that he was falling in love with his fiancée's daughter.

"You need to move into the master bedroom and redecorate."

Dad's words almost made his head explode. Did he know what was going on? Or maybe Dad was simply worried that Dylan was feeling lonely in the big house all by himself. Which was true, except for when Ella was there.

"I'm fine," Dylan said in a tone that might have conveyed just the opposite.

"You should find a nice girl, Dylan." Dad gave him a wink, his blue eyes catching the bright sunshine.

This was the second time Dad had suggested this. What was it, guilt for moving out? Or had Dad become like all the other engaged people in the world who thought everyone should join them in the bliss of holy matrimony? "So, what kind of girl do you think I should find?" he asked, just for fun.

"A pretty one...with brains." Dad gave him a swift elbow to the ribs, the way he used to do when he was teasing. God, it had been a long time since he'd seen that twinkle in Dad's eyes.

But Dylan didn't have a chance to laugh out loud because Ella came up the ship's ladder and strolled in their direction, and damned if she didn't look exactly like the kind of girl Dad had so recently described. Instead of laughing, a gigantic hole formed in his chest. He'd found the girl. But he didn't think the relationship would work out.

As if to punctuate the point, Brenda followed Ella up the ladder. They were dressed almost like twins in free-flowing flowered dresses. Brenda's was dark blue. Ella's was forest green—a color that made her fiery hair seem all the redder. She had it piled on top of her head in a somewhat neater bun than usual, but the sea breeze had already started to tug at the hairpins, leaving wisps to fall down her neck and cheeks.

He wanted to nibble those cheeks and kiss that neck. His fingers itched to take all those hairpins out, and his brain stalled on a searing memory of her kneeling above him in his bed, her hair falling down over her shoulders all the way to his chest. His mouth went dry.

"I need a drink," he muttered, when what he really wanted was to take her in his arms and give her a big hello kiss. But he couldn't do that, and besides, Dad had told him to keep his distance from Brenda. So he had a good excuse to become scarce.

* * *

Ella watched her mom's back stiffen the moment Dylan walked away without a word of greeting. His casual dismissal had hurt Mom. And who could blame her?

Mom was out of line blaming Dylan for being late, even though Ella was perfectly capable of dealing with the caterer and Jude St. Pierre's people. And Dylan's receptionist had called a couple of hours ago to tell them that Dylan's day had spun out of control.

But Dylan was still out of line for walking right past Mom without even saying hello. Why had he done that? Was he reneging on his deal? Was he still trying to break Mom and Jim up? Ella didn't think so. But she wasn't happy with him walking past Mom like that. And she hated the fact that she was the one who had to run interference between the two of them. Would that become a habit?

"I need to go check on the bar setup," she said to Mom, providing an excuse to break away. "I'll be back before guests start arriving."

Mom nodded. "Thank you, honey. You've outdone yourself. Everything is perfect."

Wow. In her lifetime, Mom had never said anything like that to her, ever. She gave Mom a big hug. "Thanks, Mom. Now stop worrying. Jim loves you. And I love you. And Granny loves you. We're going to have a wonderful time tonight." She let go. "I'll be right back, okay?"

She turned away and headed down the ship's ladder into the salon, where she found Dylan accepting a drink from the bartender.

"Hey, get it together, okay?" she said in a low voice. "You just hurt Mom's feelings."

He studied her over the rim of his glass. The amber flecks in his eyes were the same color as his drink. "What? How? Dad told me to give her a wide berth, and that's what I did."

"Oh, for goodness' sake." Ella rolled her eyes. "Did he tell you that? I can't believe it. Don't listen to him, okay? She's been all worried that you were going to be late."

He blew out a long breath. "I'm sorry. Without Dad at the office, things got crazy. I was fully intending to be here to help you deal with the caterers and stuff, but I had a very sick patient that put me behind."

Oh no. Now that she was standing in front of him, Dylan looked exhausted. Too many late nights, too much work at the clinic. He deserved a break.

"I was fully capable of dealing with the caterers on my own. What happened? Did you have another patient pass away?" she asked.

He shook his head. "No. But I had to send one to the emergency room. And my day was a zoo after that."

"Is your patient going to be okay?"

He shrugged. "He was admitted with angina. My guess is that he's going to need coronary bypass surgery."

"I'm sorry."

He took a gulp of his drink. "It's okay. He's been heading in that direction for a long time. Dad and I tell him to change his lifestyle, and he ignores us."

"Frustrating."

He nodded.

"But you should still go upstairs and give Mom a hug."

"I will go upstairs and be civil. I promise. Although giving your mother a hug would probably blow her mind."

"Yeah, probably. But the guests will be here any minute, and we need to be upstairs to greet them."

"Yeah," he said, rubbing his eyes. He seemed so weary right at that moment that Ella threw caution to the wind and threw her arms around his shoulders and hugged him. She'd intended the hug to be sisterly but it morphed into something a whole lot more erotic when he pressed his body against hers.

They stayed that way for too long and didn't break apart until they heard someone coming down the ship's ladder. Ella's face went hot as she turned to find Ashley Scott standing at the base of the ladder giving them both a sober look.

"Y'all should be upstairs with your parents greeting the guests," she said, then headed for the bar.

Behind her, Jackie, Ashley's plus-one for the evening, came rushing down the ladder. "Isn't this cool?" he asked.

"Yeah, it is," Ella said.

"Oh, wow, chocolate." The kid's eyes grew wide as he spied the chocolate fountain in the corner of the salon.

"Help yourself," Ella said as she turned away from the Scotts and headed up the ladder with Dylan close on her heels. With each step, she started constructing the lie she'd need to cover for what Ashley had seen. It would start with Dylan's hospitalized patient, which was probably seriously bad karma. But what else could she say if she was confronted?

She couldn't tell the truth. Not tonight of all nights.

* * *

Brenda breathed deeply and told her heart to quit bouncing around her chest. She was supposed to enjoy this event, but things had gotten off to a rocky start. As near as Brenda could see, Ella was doing all the work, and Dylan was along for the ride, probably taking notes and waiting until the right moment to try to create a scene.

And what better place than at this party?

She pasted a reception-line smile on her face. Ashley Scott and her son, Jackie, had been the first to arrive. They hadn't seemed to notice Ella and Dylan's absence. So maybe it would be all right. A few more guests came over the gangplank before Ella finally materialized at her elbow, checking names off the RSVP list. Dylan followed her and took up a spot next to his father.

Momma was playing hostess down at the front of the boat, where the ship's crew was handing out glasses of champagne. Finally, everyone was in place, and for this moment, it looked as if they were one happy family. It was a sham, of course, and Brenda hoped to God they avoided the drama that had blown up Easter Sunday. But just as she started to relax and actually enjoy herself, Jim stiffened noticeably.

The next guest in the informal receiving line was Preston Everly, a former member of the town council and Magnolia Harbor's newly elected state representative. He'd won a land-slide victory in a special election last fall to fill the seat recently vacated by Caleb Tate, who had resigned under a scandalous cloud involving several shady real estate transactions. Rep. Everly was squeaky clean, had run on a reform platform, and was a longtime member of the Magnolia Harbor Yacht Club.

Brenda had wanted his name dropped from the list, but Ella had told her that Dylan insisted. Evidently, they went way back or something. In the end, Ella had negotiated several names with Dylan, including Rep. Everly's, and had managed to get Jackie Scott added as a concession for allowing this politician's name to remain on the list. Ella had become fond of the little boy and hadn't wanted him to miss out on a cruise.

So that's what they'd done. But now Brenda wondered if Dylan had put a fast one over on them. If Preston and Jim went way back, why was Jim suddenly so tense? A deep unease welled up in her, and her heart went on another familiar gallop around her chest.

The woman on Rep. Everly's arm—his wife, Brenda presumed—was the kind of fifty-something woman every female aspired to become. Blond, slim, with chiseled features, and wearing a gorgeous sundress with a pink flower border. Her shoes and bag were probably from some designer, although Brenda never paid any attention to brand names. Expensive-looking diamond rings on her fingers sparkled in the afternoon light as she gripped her husband's arm.

"Congratulations, man," Preston said, giving Jim a practiced slap on the back. Boy, the guy had the classic politician's smile. Were those teeth his own, or had he gotten a full set of implants? They were dazzling.

He turned toward his wife. "I think you know Tammy."

"Hello, James," the woman said in a low, husky voice, then turned toward Dylan. "And this is Dylan. The last time I saw you, you were what...?"

"Fifteen," Dylan said in a curt voice that telegraphed to the world just how much he didn't want to be there. Could Jim's son be any more unpleasant if he tried? Not really.

"Meet Brenda." Jim touched her back and gave her a gentle push forward. When had she taken a step back? She didn't remember. But she fought against the ridiculous urge to run away from Rep. Everly's wife.

"Hello, Mrs. Everly," she said.

The blonde threw back her head and laughed. "Oh no, Preston and I aren't married. We're old friends. I'm his plus-one for the evening. Jim and Preston and I go way back to our younger days sailing at the yacht club. I was Julianne's best friend. We went to Duke together. I was there when she fell for Jim all those years ago."

Tammy studied Brenda out of a pair of sharp brown eyes and seemed to be totaling things up in her head: the extra fifteen pounds Brenda hadn't been able to lose for years, the plain gold studs in her ears, the simple chain around her neck. She probably even noticed the lack of an engagement ring she'd refused to let Jim buy her. God only knew what the woman thought about her dress, which Ella had found online for less than fifty dollars.

So this woman had been Julianne's best friend? It seemed so unlikely after the things Jim had told her about his late wife. Julianne had sounded like a down-to-earth sort of person, much like her younger sister, Brooklyn Huddleston. Brenda had a hard time squaring what she'd heard about Julianne Huddleston with the bejeweled woman standing in front of her.

Unless Tammy had come to ruin the party.

"Dammit," Jim murmured when the woman finally moved on. "Why didn't you tell me Tammy Hansen was on the list?" he said, turning toward Dylan, his obvious annoyance confirming Brenda's worst suspicions.

"I didn't know," Dylan said, looking toward Ella. "Was she on the list?"

"Um," Ella said. "She wasn't on the invited guest list. But Representative Everly RSVP'd yesterday by email and her name was on his email. So, um, no one snuck her in, if that's what you're asking."

Wait, had Ella just come to Dylan's defense? Evidently, Jim's son had thoroughly snookered her daughter. But then Ella had a gullible streak a mile wide; otherwise she would never have believed the BS Cody had handed her over the years.

Jim stared down Brenda's daughter. "Are you sure?"

"Of course she's sure," Dylan said.

Jim scowled at his son.

"Come on, guys," Ella said on a long breath. "The guest list is no longer a subject for debate or name trading. Who is Tammy Hansen anyway?"

"You didn't hear?" Brenda said. "She's Julianne's best friend."

"Oh. Yikes. I didn't know. But, even if I did, it's not like we could have..." Her voice faded out.

"It's worse than that," Jim said in a hard voice. "She's the woman I almost married when Dylan was fifteen."

Brenda's heart went on another breath-stealing romp through her chest. Why the hell hadn't Jim ever said one word about almost being engaged to someone else?

Jim took her by the shoulders. "Are you okay?"

She nodded, not knowing what to say to him. Until this moment, she'd never mistrusted him. What other secrets had he kept from her?

"It's not what you think. I'll tell you all about it later, but we still have a few guests to greet, okay?"

She wanted to believe Jim, but she'd lost a little faith in him. Maybe he hadn't lied to her exactly. But he'd certainly kept the truth from her, and that didn't seem like a good place to start a marriage.

Chapter Twenty-Three

$\mathbf{O}$f course Brooklyn Huddleston would be invited to this engagement party. Brooklyn was Dylan's aunt—his late mother's younger sister. Some people might have left Brooklyn off the list, but Jim Killough wasn't that kind of person. Brooklyn would always be his sister-in-law no matter what. Not even a new wife would change that.

And really, Ashley didn't hate Brooklyn, although she was mildly jealous because Micah St. Pierre seemed to prefer Brooklyn's scones to her oatmeal. Although, in truth, Ashley made scones too, but the Rev had always insisted that he preferred oatmeal.

The answer to this confounding problem was quickly answered though, when Micah showed up on Brooklyn's arm, evidently her plus-one for the evening. The turn of events quickly confirmed the worst fears of the Piece Makers. It was one thing for their minister to have his coffee at Bread, Butter, and Beans, Brooklyn's coffee shop, and quite another for him to be squiring her around his younger brother's yacht.

Since all of the Piece Makers had been invited to this party, it wouldn't take long before one or more of them pulled Ashley aside, utterly scandalized by the Rev's behavior. Of course, a few weeks ago, these same ladies had been bemoaning the fact that their minister was unmarried.

Now, just because he'd chosen a Methodist, some of the ladies would go into meltdown.

On the bright side, no one seemed to be overly concerned that Micah, a mixed-race man, had set his heart on Brooklyn, who was white. Maybe things were changing here in Magnolia Falls.

"Can I go listen to the music?" Jackie asked, tugging on her dress and pulling her from her thoughts.

"Okay. But don't get into trouble, and do not hog the chocolate fountain, you hear?"

"Yes, ma'am. I want to listen to Ella play." His blue eyes got a dreamy look to them, and Ashley didn't know whether to laugh or cry. Her little boy had a big crush on Brenda's daughter. Maybe there was hope yet that he'd one day grow out of his obsession with Captain Teal. Of course, the poor child was going to get his heart broken when he discovered that Ella had a secret lover.

Because what she'd seen earlier was not sisterly. Plus, Ella hadn't been sleeping in her room or even using the bathroom at Howland House. She would arrive half an hour before breakfast service, tiptoe up to the third floor, and then come down the stairs as if she'd been up there all night.

But Ashley had seen the silver Honda dropping her off. She hadn't put it all together until she'd seen Dylan's car parked down at the clinic a few days ago. Ella and Dylan were having a fling right under their parents' noses.

And Ashley had decided not to do one thing about it. And if any Piece Maker asked her, she was going to lie like nobody's business and hoped she could carry it off. Because she was a terrible liar.

She got herself a glass of champagne and escaped to the ship's bow for a good view of the sunset. This spot had the advantage of being far, far away from the Piece Makers, who had congregated at the yacht's stern. She sipped the wine and enjoyed her solitude.

Until Patsy Bauman sneaked up on her. "We need to do something about this," she said, not bothering to even explain what "this" was all about. "Do you think she's flirting with him because Brenda refused to direct the Grace Church choir?" Patsy hadn't even bothered to use Brooklyn's name.

And her whole explanation was so Patsy. The woman had a devious mind. She was forever making up stories about the people who stayed at the inn. Ashley had suggested that Patsy get herself a computer and try her hand at writing mysteries.

"Patsy," she said quietly, "I don't think Brooklyn is seeking revenge. I honestly think that Micah and Brooklyn like each other."

The older woman stared at Ashley, mouth slightly ajar. No doubt she was astonished that Ashley had the temerity to contradict her. Or to suggest that their minister would even dream of finding a Methodist attractive.

"But she's—"

"Don't say it, Patsy. Brooklyn is pretty and smart and nice. Micah could do a lot worse."

Patsy blinked. "You don't care?"

Ashley heaved a big sigh. She did care, but for stupid reasons having to do with her oatmeal. And also because she missed him. Jackie missed him too. But he deserved happiness like everyone else, right?

She squared on Patsy. "If Micah has a thing for Brooklyn, it's his business."

"But—"

She put up her hand in a rude gesture. "Stop it. I'm not going to talk to him, okay? I'm not going to be the one you send off to convince him not to date her. Or whatever you have in mind. I'm tired of it. And I do not want to gossip about him. I wish him well. I hope he and Brooklyn find love together."

"What?"

"I do. And I'm sure that, if that happens, Brooklyn will figure out that, as a minister's wife, she'll need to support her husband."

"Oh my god. You've got them married already."

Yeah, she did. But then, wasn't that what Patsy wanted? "You've been fussing for a few years about how he needs a wife. And you're right. A minister should have a wife, and maybe he's finally getting around to it, you know? Brooklyn would be a great addition to our altar guild."

"Really, Ashley, I don't think—"

"And you know what? I've been thinking about a lot of things lately, and it might be nice if we could move the Piece Makers meetings from the inn to your house. I mean, we've just finished a quilt, and this would be a good time to make the change."

There, she'd said it. And it hadn't even been all that hard. And once the words had left her mouth, she felt completely unburdened.

"You want to move our meetings?" The astonished look on Patsy's face defied description.

"Yes, I do. I can't commit to being there every week anymore. My business has taken off. And to be honest, I'd like to let my guests use the solarium. Things change, Patsy. We can't keep them the same as they were when Grandmother was alive. Heck, I'm sure Grandmother isn't pleased that I've turned her house into an inn. But I had to do what I had to do. So this is just the next step."

"The next step in what? Are you leaving our group?"

Was she? No. But she wasn't going to be baking a cake every week. "Of course not. But I think we need to rethink the weekly refreshments."

* * *

Dylan was standing at the bar, sipping another scotch on the rocks, when Dad grabbed him by the upper arm and walked him down the companionway off the main salon.

"You knew Preston was bringing Tammy, didn't you? You probably arranged for that to happen," Dad said in a hoarse whisper.

Whoa. His father was furious. And rightly so, but Dylan was innocent.

"I would never do something like that."

"No? Not even if you were trying to damage my relationship with Brenda?"

Wow. Dad was worried. Otherwise this wrinkle in the plan wouldn't have upset him so badly. He met his father's suddenly somber stare.

"Look, when we were negotiating the guest list, I thought you might like connecting with Preston again. You guys used to go fishing all the time. I had no idea he'd bring Tammy. I thought he had better taste in women."

"Wait. You used to adore Tammy." Dad frowned. He was evidently taking lessons from Brenda.

"Yeah, I did," Dylan said on a long breath. "You did too."

Dad shook his head. "Not really. I mean, I did let her swoop down on us. And you liked her so much, I thought…Well, you missed your mom, and Tammy knew Julianne so well. It was fun to have her around reminiscing, I guess."

"Like I said, you liked her. And I thought I would try to like her too."

"You didn't?"

Dylan shook his head.

Dylan's father nodded. "I'm sorry. I did like her for a short while until I realized she was trying to land me like a big, fat catfish, and she was using you as bait. So I told her to get lost."

"What? But I thought she dumped you. I thought—"

"She gaslighted you, Dylan. She told you a lot of lies about your mom, and I got sick and tired of watching that woman pollute Julianne's memory. I told her never to darken our door again."

"Oh. Wow. Dad, I knew she was BSing me. I went along with her to make you happy. I thought you loved her, and I was so ticked off when she left because I thought you were sad about it."

"I guess I liked having someone around, you know. But I wasn't really sad to see her go."

"Well, for what it's worth, I would never have invited her. What on earth possessed Preston to invite her?" Dylan asked.

"She probably gave him some BS reason, and Preston is so good, he never sees anyone's ulterior motives. He isn't going to last long in politics."

"What are we going to do? I don't trust her."

Dad managed a small smile. "I would have thought that you welcomed this difficulty."

Well, that might have been true a few weeks ago. Now Dylan was worried about his father. "Dad, I gave up trying to wreck your relationship with Brenda. And you can thank Ella for that. But I'm still worried about you. I still have my misgivings about Brenda."

"Unfortunately, those misgivings show all the time. She feels like you're not giving her a chance."

"I'm trying."

"Well, Tammy being here isn't going to help. Look, I need you to keep an eye on that woman. I don't want her to do anything to hurt Brenda's feelings. You understand? And I figure you'll have an easier time of it than I will. Because she liked you."

"She used me."

"Well, that too. But I think she had more trouble leaving you than me. I'm going to keep Brenda as far away from that woman as possible, okay?"

"I got it. I'm on it."

Dad gave his shoulder a squeeze. "I'm counting on you. Now, if I'm not mistaken, the girls are tuning up." He cocked an ear in the direction of the salon.

"Sounds like it."

"You're in for a treat. This duo they've been working on is incredible."

They headed back down the passageway into the salon, where Ella and Brenda had taken up a corner. Dad got up in front of them.

"Hey, everyone, I'm sure some of you know that my bride-to-be is a gifted musician. What you guys don't know is that my soon-to-be daughter is maybe a little better than her mom. They've been working on something special for you. A performance of Wolfgang Mozart's 'Violin Duo Allegro.'"

Dad stepped away from Brenda and Ella, and they began to play at a breakneck pace that blew Dylan's socks off. They were both incredibly good, their fingers flying over the fingerboards of their instruments in a mesmerizing musical dance of dueling violins.

A lump formed in Dylan's throat, not because the music was terribly emotional. But because it dawned on him that he could never keep Ella here with him. One day, sooner or later, she'd be gone. Off to pursue her career in music, Off to play for audiences bigger than this one.

She would leave him sooner or later. She might come home for the holidays. She might visit in the summer. But Magnolia Harbor would never be her home. What was she going to do with her talent in this small tourist town? Find another loud country band? Continue to waste herself waiting on tables?

No. She would leave him and break his heart, and he'd never be able to tell a soul about what he'd lost.

When Brenda and Ella came to the end of the piece, the guests in the salon applauded. Several even shouted "brava." The two violinists bowed and beamed.

Brenda waved for their audience to quiet. "Thank you all so much for coming tonight. Jim and I are so happy to celebrate with our friends and family. Now I'm going to get some champagne and maybe one of those strawberries dipped in chocolate. And Ella has agreed to continue to serenade you. And by the way, y'all, if you like her music, she plays at Ashley Scott's teas most Saturday afternoons. And I'm extremely proud of her." Brenda leaned forward. "And she's the one who did most of the work for this party. I'd say she did a wonderful job."

Everyone clapped again, and Ella stood there blushing to the tips of her auburn hair. Holy crap, Brenda had praised her daughter in front of everyone. Would wonders never cease? Well, Ella deserved it.

And Brenda was being delightful and gracious tonight. And after hearing her play the violin, he could almost understand what Dad saw in her. Dad was, himself, a gifted musician. So maybe they had a lot in common.

He scanned the room as Ella started to play one of the numbers he'd heard at the tea party weeks ago. Tammy was standing in the corner, a sour look on her face as she studied Ella and Brenda. He sidled up to her, determined to do Dad's bidding tonight.

He reached her, blocking her path as Dad escorted Brenda up the ship's ladder to the deck. "So, Tammy, it's been ages," he said.

She gave him a cool smile. "Dylan, I can't believe how much you look like your mom," she said. "How have you been? I missed you."

"Did you really?"

She nodded and then asked, "So, do you like this woman?"

"This woman?"

"Brenda. She seems a bit...dowdy."

Dylan let his gaze drift to Ella, who was playing something bright and lively that sounded like an old Irish jig. Her hair was falling out of its pins as she vigorously bowed the violin. She and her music made his heart sing. In fact, she looked a great deal like her mom right now, and it struck him that neither of them was dowdy.

They weren't like Lauren or Tammy though. They didn't wear designer dresses. They didn't worry about their hair or their makeup much. They were down to earth. Like Aunt Brooklyn, who looked a whole lot like Mom, which made sense since they were sisters.

"Well," Tammy said when he made no response to her cutting remark. "Her daughter is sort of cute in a hippy-dippy way. They certainly can play the violin. I suppose it's a redeeming quality."

Dylan turned, a nasty retort on the tip of his tongue. But right then, the chocolate fountain exploded.

* * *

One minute Ella had been playing "The Streets of Derry," and then suddenly she became the victim of a...chocolate attack?

That wasn't exactly the first thought that went through her head when a clump of congealed brown stuff hit her in the face and splattered over the violin's fingerboard.

She may have screamed. Or at least gasped before she turned toward the chocolate fountain that had been behaving quite normally up until then. Jackie Scott had encamped near it and had been happily feeding himself copious quantities of chocolate-covered strawberries.

But now suddenly the fountain was having a meltdown, turning out big globs of congealed brown goo that looked like...well...She stood there stunned for a moment before someone in the room shouted, "Good god, that looks like poop."

It did. And she was covered in it. She reached for a napkin and furiously began to wipe the stuff from the violin's fingerboard. Thank God it hadn't landed on the violin's body. Almost anything could damage the varnish, and the sound of the instrument was all in the varnish. Dammit. The Holstein violin was her most prized possession. It had cost thousands of dollars, which she'd saved out of her gig money over the years.

People were starting to laugh. She turned to find them pointing at the fountain and her. She looked down. She had brown stuff all over herself. The dress was a total loss, although she hadn't spent all that much money on it, so there was at least a small silver lining to this disaster.

She wanted to slink away from the demented fountain, especially after what Mom had said about her being in charge of everything. She'd get blamed for this disaster. She was certain of it.

She looked across the room. Dylan was standing with that woman. Holy hell, had *she* orchestrated this?

Sudden rage filled her. The woman had been standing across the room talking a mile a minute to Dylan. Had she been waiting for this to happen? She was smirking at Ella like the cat who'd swallowed the canary.

She wanted to scream at the woman for coming in here and messing everything up. But screaming wouldn't fix the violin or her performance or the party, for that matter. She had to remain calm and figure out how to turn the fountain off. But even before that, she needed to get the alcohol wipes and cleaning cloths in her violin case and tend to her fiddle.

She turned away from the crowd, trying to swallow back her anger when, like some miracle, Dylan materialized at her elbow with a stack of napkins. He handed them over to her before turning around and yelling, "Someone find the staff from A Night to Remember and get that thing turned off."

"The violin's a mess," she said, her voice as tiny as Granny's. She was on the verge of tears. She clutched the instrument tighter. "And look at me. I'm not much better."

"You're beautiful." He picked up her left hand and began wiping away the brown goop. He got most of it off her fingers, turned her hand palm up, and found a little glob on the inside of her wrist. Instead of wiping it away with the cloth, he leaned down and gently licked it off with his tongue.

The touch sent shivers through her, making her momentarily forget about the violin's screwed-up fingerboard. A little hum escaped her throat, and she was about to melt into a big, sloppy puddle when Mom showed up looking pissed off.

She snatched her hand away. Had Mom seen him licking her wrist? Oh god, could this night get any worse?

"Oh my god, what have you done?" Mom turned on Dylan, evidently too distressed by the horrific scene of brown goo tumbling out of the fountain's top like a poop machine to have noticed Dylan's tongue on her wrist.

Dylan turned to stare at Mom, his face a study in cool determination. Jim had told him to stay away from Mom, and Ella hoped to hell he remembered that. But just in case he'd forgotten, she stepped between them. "Mom, the fountain isn't Dylan's fault."

"No?" Mom seemed unconvinced.

Just then, Diane from A Night to Remember showed up and turned the fountain off. "I'm so sorry," she said, her cheeks turning pink. "We'll give you a full refund and pay for any damage. This usually only happens when water gets into the fountain. Water and chocolate don't mix, I'm afraid."

"Who would do such a thing?" Mom turned toward Dylan with an unfriendly glare.

"Oh my God," Ella said, "I think I know what happened."

"He did it, didn't he? Or maybe that Tammy woman."

Ella shook her head. "No. I think this was an accident. Jackie's been hanging around the fountain all evening. How much do you want to bet he spilled some of his soda into the fountain? So really, you know, it's my fault for insisting that he be added to the invitation list."

"Are you all right?" Mom asked.

"I'm fine, but the violin's a mess."

Mom eyed the goop clinging to the instrument's fingerboard. "We need to get that cleaned right away before it dries." Ella followed Mom into the big stateroom where she and Dylan had kissed that one time, and where she'd left her violin case. "You go into the bathroom and clean yourself up. I'll take care of the violin," Mom said.

"Please don't blame Dylan for the fountain."

"Okay, but what about that Tammy woman?"

"I don't think Dylan knew about her either. Please. Be nice to him."

Mom blinked and then frowned. "What is this? Have you

had a change of heart? You've come to his defense a couple of times tonight. When near as I can see, he left most of the work to you."

"He didn't, Mom. We did this together. And yes, I've decided that he's okay. And, besides, we're all one big family, right? We should soldier on as if nothing happened, okay?"

"You're a better woman than I am," she said, taking the violin from Ella's hands. "I'd like to turn Dylan over my knee and give him a much-needed spanking."

"Please don't spank him. Even figuratively. Please try to get along with him, okay?" Ella said, then scooted into the tiny bathroom, thinking that spanking Dylan sounded like surprisingly kinky fun.

Oh boy, inappropriate thought alert. But she'd never get it out of her mind now. She was thoroughly wicked.

Or maybe on the brink of falling in love with him.

Chapter Twenty-Four

Brenda's heart fluttered in her chest as she waved goodbye to the last of the guests. The corners of her mouth ached because she'd been fake-smiling since the moment Tammy Hansen set foot on the yacht. That woman was poison.

Thank goodness she had decided not to have a big reception on her wedding day because she didn't need another party where she discovered that Jim had an old flame, or where the Methodists were warring with the Episcopalians, or where little Jackie Scott pulled another prank. Although the child insisted that he'd spilled his drink into the fountain by accident.

As engagement parties went, this one was a disaster from top to bottom, with the only exception that the fountain chose to delay its malfunction so that she and Ella could make it through the five-minute duo without a single wrong note. For those five minutes, Brenda had been utterly happy.

"I think it went pretty well, all things considered," Jim said as the last guests stepped up onto the pier and headed off toward the parking lot. "It was certainly a lovely evening, wasn't it?"

She clamped down on her thoughts, her heart rocking like crazy in her chest. Jim always saw the bright side of things. He was a dewy-eyed optimist who could find the silver lining in every cloud. She loved him for it.

And thank the Lord Jim hadn't tied himself to that Tammy woman. She'd been all over the boat gossiping with the Methodists about Jim's decision to abandon Grace Church. To hear them talk, Brenda was evil incarnate for insisting on that.

When she'd done no such thing.

How had Jim managed to tune out all that nasty party gossip? When every word of it flayed Brenda until her emotions were raw.

Jim was such a good soul. She didn't deserve him. And that worried her most of all. Everyone thought he was marrying beneath him. And maybe he was.

Now that the party was over, her heart should have been calming down, but instead, it was galloping away with her, leaving her winded and worried.

She needed a moment to regroup. To calm down. "I need to go down and get my purse from the—"

Dizziness hit her, and she stumbled sideways, her knees buckling. Then everything went black.

* * *

Dylan floored the Honda and sped over the bridge. The ambulance had a good head start on them because they'd taken Ella's grandmother home first to await word on Brenda's condition. She hadn't gone willingly, but her quilting group friends had met them at the condo and were organizing a prayer session.

A long night in the ER seemed likely, after which Brenda would probably be admitted to the hospital. So prayer seemed like the order of the day.

Ella sat in the passenger's seat, tears falling down her cheeks. "This is my fault," she kept saying. But of course she wasn't to blame. It was *his* fault for the way he'd been behaving for weeks.

"It's going to be okay." He used his bedside voice. "It's going to be fine."

"She's my mother, for goodness' sake. What if I lose her?"

Dylan shut up. He'd lost a mother. He understood her panic. It would be ten times worse to lose a mother suddenly, on the day of an engagement party, than to lose one after a long illness during which you had plenty of time to say goodbye.

Oh hell, it sucked to lose a parent any way.

He gripped the steering wheel until his knuckles turned white. Death was the ultimate enemy.

But Brenda wasn't going to die. She'd lost consciousness, yes. And chances were, she'd had a cardiac episode of some kind. But she'd regained consciousness, and Dad had administered aspirin, and she hadn't gone into cardiac arrest. So chances were good she'd live to see another day. But that didn't change the suckiness of this situation.

He pulled into the hospital's physician's lot, which was much closer than the visitors' lot. Ella bailed out of the car before he'd even set the brake. He grabbed his hospital ID from the glove box and chased after her. She'd taken a wrong turn across the parking lot, and he had to catch her and point her in the direction of the emergency room entrance. Like all hospitals originally built in the 1950s, this one had been added on to wherever space could be found. The result was a hodgepodge of buildings and entrances.

Brenda had already been taken into the ER, but Ella had to stop and speak to the gatekeeper at the intake desk before being allowed to go sit with her. And, as usual, the woman behind the desk wanted all of Brenda's insurance information before Ella could go inside. Evidently, Dad hadn't supplied it, even though he'd come in with the EMTs, no doubt because he'd flashed his hospital ID.

"I have no idea what her health insurance information is," Ella said in a rising voice.

"No need to yell," the woman at the desk said in a condescending voice that ticked Dylan off.

He whipped out his hospital ID card and flashed it at the woman. "She's with me. We'll get the information from the patient and be back." He snagged Ella by the arm and pulled her toward the double doors that led to the ER.

"Is the patient one of yours?" the gatekeeper asked.

"No. She's my stepmom." He used his badge to unlock the doors and stepped into the organized chaos of the emergency room.

"Hallelujah," Ella muttered, "you've finally accepted the inevitable."

"What?"

"You called her your stepmom."

"Oh, yeah, I did."

They hurried down the row of cubicles and finally found Brenda. She was conscious and had a nasal cannula supplying supplemental oxygen. Her dress had been unbuttoned down the front to expose the EKG electrodes the EMTs had placed on her chest. She appeared pale, but her lips were nice and pink. He didn't need to read the pulse oximeter output to know that her blood oxygen was within reasonable levels.

"Where's Dad? Where's the ER doc?" he asked.

"Jim's talking to the doctor," Brenda said, sounding winded, which was concerning. Did she have pulmonary edema? That could be serious. A sign of heart failure. She needed a cardiac ultrasound right away.

"I'll be back," Dylan said, and then hurried to the nurse's

station to check the telemetry data on Brenda's heart and oxygen levels. She was in atrial fibrillation, and her blood pressure was low.

"Who's the attending?" he demanded.

The ER nurse gave him an annoyed look. "Doctor Andrews. And your dad has already gone off to pester him, but a stroke came in five minutes before Ms. McMillan. In the meantime, the doc ordered IV digoxin and fluids as well as a cardiac ultrasound."

In short, Brenda was relatively stable and was getting the appropriate care for a patient presenting with A-fib. He should stand down and go hold Ella's hand, but he couldn't do that in public, and besides, he wanted to make sure Dad was okay.

Dylan backed away and went in search of his father, finding him in a cubicle on the other side of the ER, assisting Dr. Andrews, who suddenly had his hands full with the stroke and a newly arrived patient suffering a compound fracture.

Suddenly, Dylan and his father found themselves stabilizing the fracture patient, who was bleeding pretty badly, while the on-call orthopedic surgeon was summoned. It took half an hour before they got back to Brenda's cubicle, but by that time, she'd been whisked away for the cardiac ultrasound that Dr. Andrews had ordered. Ella was missing too, but Dylan figured she was probably back at reception providing health insurance information.

Dad collapsed onto the single hard chair in Brenda's cubicle and dropped his head into his hands, then scrubbed at his unruly hair for a moment. Finally, he pressed his fingers into his eye sockets as if he was trying to hold back tears.

Dylan's chest constricted. He hated it when people cried. But seeing Dad cry was more than he could bear. It took him back to an ancient memory of that night when he'd found Dad sobbing in the kitchen. It had been a few days after Mom's funeral. The family had finally departed, and Dylan and Dad had been left alone in the house for the first night.

Seeing his father cry like that had rocked Dylan's world. Up until that time, he'd been like every other ten-year-old, absolutely certain that Mom and Dad would always be there. That they would always keep him safe. That they would be available to comfort him and listen to him and take care of him.

But not that night. That night he'd learned that it could all come crashing down. And it had scared him silly. He didn't know how to make Dad feel better that night. And because he was powerless to help his father, he'd run away from it.

He'd gone back to his bedroom and folded himself into a tiny ball and hid under his covers. He'd cried too, but in shame, not grief. He should have done something to comfort his father.

He'd promised himself the next morning that he would never abandon his father again. Dad needed him, so he'd dedicated himself to being good for Dad. He'd learned stupid one-line jokes that he told all the time to make Dad laugh. He went fishing with Dad because it pleased him. And he'd never wanted to be anything other than a doctor because that's what Dad wanted.

He'd given up Lauren so he could come back to Dad. Hell, he'd even tried to like Tammy because Dad seemed to like her.

But now Dad had found someone new. Someone he truly loved. And in a misguided attempt to keep Dad safe and happy, all Dylan had done was make things harder for him. Dylan needed to stop interfering in Dad's love life. Now. And hadn't Ella been telling him this from the get-go? Yes, she had.

"Dad?" he said, his voice cracking with emotion.

"I'm okay." Dad sounded gruff as he brushed an errant tear from his cheek.

That single tear tore Dylan to shreds.

"She's going to be okay," Dylan said.

Dad nodded, his chin trembling. "I hope so. Because I don't

know what I'm going to do if I ever lose her." He looked up at Dylan, his eyes glassy with unshed tears. "I know she's turned everything upside down for you. I know this has been hard, but Brenda is exactly what I needed in my life. Son, I was in such a rut. I had forgotten what it was like to share the simplest things with someone, you know? Like walking on the beach or watching some British murder mystery, trying to figure out whodunit. It's the little things that matter." He wiped another tear from his eye and turned to look at the blank wall.

"I can't lose her," Dad continued a moment later. "I can't go through that again. I love her so much. She makes the sun rise in the morning." Dad sank his face in his hands, and his shoulders shook.

Dylan should go comfort him. At least say something. But he couldn't do it. He was that little boy once again, who needed to run and hide from his father's emotions. He couldn't bear to be in that room. He had to get away.

So he slipped from the cubicle, intent on going outside and getting some air, but Ella intercepted him as she came down the hallway from the reception area carrying her mother's wallet in her hand.

Her big anime eyes were puffy and red. She'd been crying too. That ravaged look on her face froze him. He couldn't move. He could hardly breathe, because right then he understood on a deep, almost cellular level what Dad had just said.

Ella had turned his life upside down, and he was so grateful for it. He loved her music, and her wild red hair, and the way her mouth curled when she was amused. He loved her rhythm at night, and the curve of her hip, and her creamy skin. He loved her. Body, soul, heart, and mind.

He finally broke through the uncertainty that had been holding him back and stepped forward, ready to pull her right into his arms and tell her that he'd fallen in love with her.

But she stopped him, holding out her hand at arm's length. "No!" The word was urgent. "Not here. Not now." She paused, biting her lip. "Not ever, Dylan."

"What?"

"Look, I can't lose Mom. Not now. Not after all these years of...I don't know, misunderstanding...between us. I have a chance to make things right. And I can't do that if I'm sneaking around, lying to her. She doesn't like you much, and I can't put her through that again—falling for some guy she disapproves of. And I want her to be happy. You know? I don't want to mess up her life any more than it's been messed up."

He opened his mouth to argue with her, but he understood what she was saying. Hell, he'd spent a lifetime trying to make his father happy. Why had he ever thought she wouldn't side with her mother?

"I understand." He almost gagged on the words.

She looked away, tears spilling from her eyes. Dammit, he wanted so badly to dry those tears. Why did her tears propel him to action, when he'd always wanted to run from his father's grief? He had no explanation.

"No, I don't think you really do understand."

Her words were like sharp knives aimed at him. He responded in kind. "Okay, you want to explain it to me?"

"Mom deserves a guy like Jim. Hell, if I had to go pick a father from the daddy store, I'd choose Jim. In fact, I wish I could call him Dad the way you do. You are so incredibly lucky. And I want Mom to have that. You know. Because my father wasn't like that at all. My father was an a-hole."

She sniffed back tears and wiped them from her cheeks before she continued. "I told you that I had a relationship with him before he died. What I didn't tell you is that he turned out to be every bit as bad as Mom said he was. When I looked him up, he was still living in Chicago, which is where Mom left him in the dead of night on Christmas Eve when I was only three years old. He'd been in and out of prison a couple of times. I tried to have a relationship with him, you know? Stupid me. I thought I could love him and save him or some idiot thing like that.

"But Mom was right. He wasn't a good person, and he didn't love me. He was perfectly happy to use me for booze and drugs. He drank himself to death. So, you see, I want Jim as my father. And I want Mom to be happy. And that leaves no space for us.

"Besides, there isn't really an *us*, you know? Just two horny people having some fun. Right? And we should stop. Now. And we should get with the program and help Mom and Jim any way we can."

"Yeah. I guess so," he managed to say around the choking mass in his throat.

"And besides, the timing is all wrong. I mean, I've had a lot of fun these last few weeks, but I need to stand on my own two feet for a while."

"Of course you do."

She nodded. "It's going to be awkward for us. But we love our folks, right? We can do this."

He nodded. "Of course we can." If only he actually believed that.

Chapter Twenty-Five————

After two days in the hospital and a battery of tests, Mom was diagnosed with persistent atrial fibrillation. Dr. Wilson, Mom's cardiologist, put her on medications that would regulate her heartbeat. Her blackout at the engagement party had been caused by low blood pressure, created by the irregular heart rhythm. After she was given a complete cardiac workout, the docs were sure she hadn't had a stroke or a heart attack.

So the episode had been a scary warning that Mom needed to destress. Her doc told her to go home, eat healthy foods, get regular exercise, and take up yoga. Mom had taken this prescription seriously. On Thursday, she and Jim bought yoga mats on their way back from the hospital. And on Friday morning, they went out to practice positions on the beach at sunrise.

On Friday night, at a dinner Granny hosted at her condo, they seemed so happy together talking about the beauty of stretching on the beach while the sun came up. It had been a lovely family gathering, but Dylan hadn't been invited.

So Mom hadn't sniped at him. And he hadn't sniped at

Mom. And Ella hadn't had to sit at the table with him, feeling heartbroken.

Still, it was so unfair. Dylan wasn't at fault for the disasters that befell the engagement party. But Mom had made him the scapegoat for some irrational reason. And Jim hadn't stopped her from doing so. But then again, Dylan hadn't hidden his dislike of her mother. So he wasn't entirely blameless either.

Ella had to accept this as the order of things from now on. Mom disliking Dylan. Jim tiptoeing around Mom's unhappiness because of her heart condition. And Ella, heartsore and missing Dylan with every breath she took.

Without the engagement party to plan, she had no reason to call him anymore, and she missed the sound of his voice. And since they'd ended their spring fling, she missed his kisses and his touches and the sound of his breathing at night while she watched him sleep.

If only she could convince her heart (and maybe a few other parts) that she was better off keeping him at a distance. But what else could she do? She couldn't run the battle lines between her mother and Dylan without getting seriously wounded by both of them.

She needed to face the facts about her life. She needed to get on with it, and working part time at Howland House and picking up the occasional wedding gig was never going to get her where she wanted to be.

She was on her own, and if she wanted to buy herself a little house somewhere, she'd have to earn the money the hard way...by going back on the road or heading off to Nashville to try to get a gig as a studio musician, which was incredibly hard to do.

Working musicians had to go on tour. She'd been avoiding this truth for months.

And of course she'd like to be in a relationship with a mature man who appreciated and respected her. But she couldn't rely on a man to get her the home she wanted. She was going to have to do what Mom had done. Earn a bit of money, save it up, and buy a house when she could afford it. But maybe she could make a home base in Nashville or someplace, where she could at least *try* to break into the studios.

So she'd decided. Once the wedding was over, she was buying a bus ticket to Nashville. There was work in Nashville for a good fiddler. That's where she had to go.

She wasn't telling Mom about her plans. Mom wouldn't be all that happy about them. But she had to go. It didn't mean she wouldn't be back for holidays and visits, but she couldn't stay in Magnolia Harbor. For so many reasons. Maybe if she wasn't around, Mom would come to realize that Dylan was a good soul. Maybe Mom would find a son if her daughter got out of the way.

In the meantime, her Saturday-afternoon gig at Howland House had taken on real significance. She needed the money Ashley paid her, as well as the tips she received, to build her nest egg. She had to have enough money for that bus ticket to Tennessee, as well as some money to tide her over until she found a job.

So when Saturday rolled around, she got up, served breakfast, managed the webpage and reservations, and then helped set up for tea. When she started playing fiddle in the library, she had more than the usual number of guests sitting on the chairs listening.

For a short time, the crowd boosted her ego. Maybe she could make it in Nashville. But her confidence didn't last long.

About twenty minutes into her set, Cody Callaghan strolled through Howland House's front door on a pair of badass snakeskin cowboy boots. As usual, he was wearing a black Urban Armadillo T-shirt and sleeveless jean jacket. His uniform was about as predictable as Doctor D's bow tie, and it drew stares from the inn's customers, most of whom had dressed for a summer tea party at a fancy inn.

Dammit. She missed a note. What was the date? She'd been so wrapped up in Mom's illness, she'd forgotten that Urban Armadillo was scheduled to play at Rafferty's right after the engagement party.

Cody still possessed an undeniable alpha-male magnetism despite (or maybe because of) the skull tattoo on his biceps, his scraggly stubble, and long hair. He sauntered into the inn ready for a fight, which he got from Candi, who insisted that he wasn't on the reservation list.

Funny how Candi had allowed Dylan to gate-crash the tea, but she wasn't letting Cody take more than one step into the center hall.

"Git out of my way, little girl," Cody said in his too-loud Texas twang. Ella missed three notes in an easy arpeggio and might have stopped were it not for Jackie Scott. The boy was sitting quietly in the corner watching her, and whenever they played together, she made such a big deal about him not stopping when he made a mistake. So she gritted her teeth and concentrated on the music. Unfortunately, concentrating didn't take her to some higher plane where she and the music became one.

Cody folded his massive arms across his equally impressive chest and stood there until Ashley appeared and miraculously managed to get him to leave. But not before he stepped to the entrance of the library and yelled, "Don't think you can ignore me, Ella. And what the hell kind of music are you playing, anyway?"

She continued bravely, stumbling over the Borodin piece she'd been practicing for days. Her face got chili-pepper hot with shame. Nothing upset her more than making that many mistakes in something she'd practiced.

She wanted to run away or break down and have a great big cry. She wasn't happy. She didn't know how to find her happiness. And Cody seemed to underscore the barrenness of her life.

She might have packed it all in, except for the adoring look in Jackie's eyes. She loved that kid, despite the disaster he'd unleashed at the engagement party. And she sure didn't want to teach him any bad lessons about performing. Sometimes you had to suck it up and go on with the show.

She got to the end of the Borodin, feeling drained. The next song was some sad Irish ballad that was sure to make her weep. She didn't want to go there, so she turned to the boy and said, "Do you have your whistle?"

The kid's eyes grew round as he nodded and pulled the simple flute from his back pocket.

"Then get up here and play the 'Sailor's Hornpipe' with me."

The kid showed no hint of stage fright as he hurried to her corner and stood beside her. She let him set the tempo, and she followed. A few moments later, Ashley rushed to the library door and stood there, beaming love and pride at her little boy. When that happened, Ella was almost glad that Cody had messed with her mind. Playing with Jackie changed the mood in the room.

Soon the guests were clapping along with the music, and Cody's ugly words were forgotten by everyone except Ella, who continued with the music, ending the afternoon with a medley of Strauss waltzes.

She'd finished the show, but she was badly disappointed in the quality of her performance that afternoon. Her mind had been off somewhere else, caught between Cody and Dylan and Mom and her future. So she was utterly astonished when one of the guests, an older man with shiny, bright eyes, handed her a fifty-dollar bill and said, "I liked the way you arranged the Borodin. You played it well, under the circumstances."

"Um. Thanks. It's so much better with four voices though."

"Have you ever played in a string quartet?"

She shook her head. "No. I'm afraid not."

He nodded enigmatically, then headed toward the door. His praise and that huge tip did a lot to improve her mood. So she managed a smile when Ashley came into the library a moment later.

"I had no idea you'd been working so hard with Jackie," the innkeeper said. "Thank you so much for paying attention to him. He was amazing. You were...You *are* amazing."

"He's got musical talent, I think. And it wasn't work. It was fun. And I'm really sorry about Cody. He's such a—"

"That was not your fault. But I'm worried about that guy. Maybe you should think about getting a protective order. If you need help with that, I have friends in the police department."

"He's not abusive. Not really. He's just a jerk. And he's desperate for a fiddler."

Which was true. Maybe Cody's arrival was exactly what she needed.

The big question was whether she could go back on the road with Cody and not be his girlfriend. If that was possible, she could save a lot of time. She could join him on the road after Mom's wedding, earn a few more dollars, then leave Urban Armadillo and head off to Nashville. Of course Cody wouldn't like that plan much.

Which would be a complication. But she could make more money if she toured with him for the rest of the summer. In Nashville, she might have to get some minimum-wage waitressing job while she was trying to break into the studios.

"By the way," Ashley said, pulling her from her thoughts, "you should expect a couple of phone calls. I gave your number to a bride who needs someone to play at her wedding, and also you should know that Norton Treloar, one of the board members of the Myrtle Beach Symphony, was here today. He asked for your contact information."

"What?"

"I might have invited Norton to hear you play," she said with a wink. "He's always looking for violinists."

"But I'm not classically trained, and I completely messed up the Borodin."

"Did you? I didn't notice. And Norton seemed to think you had talent. I think he gave you a tip?"

"That guy? He's a member of the symphony board?" Ella asked, her voice cracking.

Ashley nodded. "Yes. Now, I need to go supervise the high school kids in the kitchen before they break things." She turned with an eye roll and headed down the hall, leaving Ella to her insecurities.

Ashley's words were a comfort, but they didn't dispel the stubborn hollow spot in the middle of Ella's core. Would a spot in the local symphony fill that hole? Was she brave enough or good enough for something like that? In a symphony, you had to play the music exactly the way the composer and the director wanted it played. She could do that, with enough practice. But she'd never be as good as Mom at sight-reading. It had always been her downfall.

Staying here in Magnolia Harbor would make Mom so happy. But could she do it?

She spun out a future scenario. If she stayed, she'd have a father figure in her life for the first time ever. Jim was terrific. She'd kind of fallen in love with him too.

If she stayed, she could spend time with Granny, learning all her secret recipes and maybe even learning how to quilt.

If she stayed, she'd have to pretend to be Dylan's stepsister.

Which was never going to work. Her stubborn imagination kept serving up a vision of a perfect yacht club blonde in a polka-dotted dress who would come along and steal Dylan's heart forever. That phantom woman would be a card-carrying conservative who worshipped at Grace Methodist. She'd have a recipe for killer meat loaf and be perfect in every way. Hell, she'd be so nice that she'd probably ask Ella to play the violin at their wedding.

Ella almost threw up in her mouth at the thought, right before a vicious wave of jealousy hit her. Damn. She'd fallen in love with Dylan. Now what?

* * *

On Saturday night Dylan found himself alone. Funny how he'd never felt alone in Magnolia Harbor before. Dad had always been up for dinner at Rafferty's, and there was always the crowd at the yacht club.

But tonight, after a grueling eight-hour shift at the free clinic, he'd found himself utterly alone in a house with almost no food in the cupboards or refrigerator. He'd called Dad, but he and Brenda were off for dinner and a movie. Ella was untouchable. And he didn't want to spend time at the yacht club.

So he took himself to Rafferty's for one of their surf and turf specials and a beer. And just for a change, he opted to sit on the deck. He could hang out here for a while, listening to the band and watching the bay and feeling sorry for himself.

It was early yet, and the band was still setting up. They looked like a scruffy bunch of misfits. The music would probably be loud and give him a headache.

But at least out here he'd have an excuse to stay for a while, because the last thing he wanted was to go home to that big, empty house. In fact, the more time he stayed in that place by himself, the less he liked it. He was thinking about putting it on the market and finding something smaller.

He hadn't mentioned that to Dad though. Dad might not be happy about him selling the house, even though Dad had moved to Cloud Nine, figuratively and literally.

Besides, his relationship with Dad was strained to the breaking point, and Dylan didn't want to rock any more boats. Dad loved Brenda, so naturally he wanted to protect her. Dylan hadn't really enjoyed dinners at Nancy Jacobs's condo, but it was still annoying to find himself dis-invited on a regular basis, as if he'd become the black sheep of the family. When had that happened?

He told himself it was for the best. He wasn't sure what he might do if he saw Ella again. He kept replaying that moment when she dumped him right in the middle of the emergency room.

He kept wondering if maybe he should have fought for her instead of nodding and letting her walk away. He wondered if maybe he should have told her that he'd fallen in love with her.

Or maybe not. The relationship had been doomed from the start. He settled back and ordered a second beer and watched the dinghies sailing in the harbor. They were holding practice races, and the spinnakers provided sparks of color against the horizon. Behind them, the sun sank over the mainland, casting an orange glow over the evening.

He let go of a sigh. He was like some character in a stupid country song, crying into his beer. He drained the last of it and was about to flag the waitress for his check when he noticed the scruffy band member setting up drums on the small stage at the corner of the deck.

The guy was wearing a black shirt with neon writing across the front, like from a spray can. URBAN ARMADILLO, it said.

Holy crap. Dad had told him a few weeks ago that Ella's old band was going to be coming here. Was her ex trying to win Ella back? Or was it merely a coincidence?

Dylan didn't believe in coincidences.

Worry and jealousy flowed through him like a toxic brew. He flagged the waitress and ordered a Maker's Mark on the rocks in an attempt to numb himself.

Which one of those long-haired, tattooed dudes was Cody? He wanted to go tap on the guy's shoulder and tell him what an a-hole he was, after giving him grief for treating Ella so badly.

The waitress delivered his bourbon, and he took a healthy gulp, just as the band started playing. As expected, they were loud, and the first twinges of a headache beat at his temples. It was debatable whether the pain came from the music or the beer or his long day at work. But he wasn't going to leave. Not yet, anyway.

He sipped his bourbon for the next five minutes and had decided to pack it in for the evening when Ella arrived on the scene, striding across the deck to a reserved table right in front of the band. As usual, she was wearing one of those floaty dresses and her army boots. She looked good enough to eat.

He polished off the rest of his drink and ordered another one. He was going to need a lot more booze to anesthetize himself from the sudden agony of his shattered heart.

Chapter Twenty-Six————

Ella had waited until almost nine o'clock to head out to Rafferty's because Urban Armadillo wouldn't start their set until at least nine. She didn't want to be there while Cody and the guys were setting up. She wanted to arrive once the music had started, so she could have time to settle on what she planned to do.

Was she going to tell Cody to get the hell out of her life forever, or negotiate with him so she could join the band in May and finish out the tour with them? On a strictly platonic basis, of course.

Because she wanted to arrive late, she'd had to pull a few strings. Ashley wasn't wild about her coming down here tonight after Cody's behavior at the tea this afternoon, but she accepted that Ella needed to confront the guy.

So Ashley had called Rafferty's owner, who she knew from the Chamber of Commerce, and ensured that Ella would have a reserved table when she arrived. So she could sit right in front of Cody and mess with his mind.

While deciding whether she wanted to rejoin the band or walk away.

She walked across the deck and slipped into one of the chairs at her table and looked up at Cody as he sang the old Charlie Daniels song "Long Haired Country Boy."

She remembered the first time she'd heard him sing this song. It had been at a dive bar in Muncie, and she'd been all of seventeen, sneaking in to catch the show with a fake ID. She'd fallen for Cody's devil-may-care attitude back then. His laid-back philosophy of life had been so refreshing after Mom's rules and plans for her. Cody offered freedom. From Mom. From responsibility. From the need to play music the way the composer wrote it without making any mistakes.

Yeah, he'd looked like a long-haired country boy then, and he still did, even though thirteen years had passed and he'd put on a good thirty pounds. Someone might mistake him for a country boy, but Ella knew the truth now.

Cody was a phony. He'd grown up in the suburbs of Dallas. He might be a Texan, but he wasn't a country boy. He'd never gone hunting or fishing. He'd never chopped wood. He'd never ridden a horse. He might be a laid-back ne'er-do-well, but he wasn't self-sufficient like the character in the song. No, Cody was needy as hell.

The song was in the key of D, about as simple a chord progression as you could get. The band sounded a little thin tonight, but then she wasn't filling in all the empty spaces with her fiddle. That's what she'd always done. She'd stood up there onstage, always behind Cody, filling in the holes, adding a little musicianship to a band that was long on volume and short on finesse.

Cody gave her a smirk and a smarmy, shopworn wink. She'd seen him wink at women all across the Southwest. He'd winked at her that night in Muncie when she'd first met him.

He'd mistaken her for someone older, and he'd been a little shocked a few weeks later when he discovered she wasn't yet eighteen.

He'd almost made her go back home.

But he'd needed a fiddler, and she had consigned all of "Bach's Violin Concerto No. 1" to memory because that was going to be her audition piece for the music colleges Mom wanted her to attend.

She hadn't wanted to play that kind of music back then. Did she want to now?

Staring up at Cody, she honestly didn't know.

And then the universe threw her a curveball because Dylan sat down at her table right next to her, facing Cody and the boys. He wasn't wearing a bow tie today, probably because he'd taken it off. Otherwise he was dressed in his usual doctor uniform of khakis and oxford cloth button-down shirt. The top button was undone today though.

He looked good enough to kiss, but that wasn't what she needed, even if she wanted to kiss him like never before.

* * *

Dylan stared into her big blue eyes, kind of lost. How had he ended up here at her table? He wasn't sure. Only that the urge to move had overwhelmed him, just about the time he'd polished off his second bourbon and paid his bill.

He'd intended to walk away before she noticed him sitting in the corner. But his feet had carried him here. Maybe because he needed to tell her how he felt. Maybe because he needed to fight for her. Or something.

But he didn't exactly know how to fight for her. Besides, the guy up onstage didn't seem too happy to see him take a seat at Ella's table. Was that the famous Cody?

The guy was a few pounds overweight and a little red in the face. Maybe he had high blood pressure and troublesome triglycerides. Maybe he'd have a heart attack at a young age from hard living. A longneck bottle sat beside him on the stage, as if to prove the point.

Of course he was only wishing for the guy's early demise because he was handsome from a certain angle. In a dissipated, biker-boy way.

Damn. The jealousy flared a little hotter. What would happen if he got up and punched the dude in the mouth? What would happen if he leaned across the table and kissed Ella the way she'd kissed him that night she'd gotten toasted?

Nothing good. There were three other dudes in the band, all of them equally large and thoroughly tattooed. Besides, Declan O'Toole, Rafferty's owner, was a friend.

Declan wouldn't appreciate Dylan starting a brawl out here on the deck. And Dad would be furious too. Who wanted a family doctor who got drunk and took potshots at people?

Clearly he'd lost his mind. He should never have come over to her table.

"Why are you here?" she asked above the music. It was a simple question with no easy answer.

He had no clue what to say in order to change the situation. He wondered if he should tell her that he was like a magnet and she was his true north.

Nope. He wasn't going to say something wimpy like that. That was the alcohol talking.

"Why are *you*?" he asked instead. The answer was obvious, but he wanted to hear it from her own mouth. She was going back to that guy up onstage.

Her shoulders tensed, confirming his worst fears. "I thought I'd come down and say hi, you know?" She looked up at the band and frowned at something, almost as if she didn't like what they were playing. But maybe that was wishful thinking. Maybe she was frowning because her ex was looking down at her with a thunderous expression.

"You know," he said, leaning in, "I hate it when you lie."

Her gaze snapped back. "You've been drinking."

He shrugged. "Yeah. Tough day at the clinic."

"I'm sorry." Her eyes got that deep, concerned look in them that made everything feel better. He remembered the way she'd lifted his spirits the day Coreen Martel died. He could get used to that kind of care and attention, but he wasn't about to admit that. To anyone. Least of all the woman he could never have.

"I'm a big boy," he said. It was a lie. He felt like a child who wanted to be loved but was afraid to ask for attention.

"So, what? Are you planning to go back to Cody?" he asked, somewhat savagely.

Her gaze narrowed, like a laser pointer, aimed at his heart. "I don't know."

"You don't know?" He knew a moment of hope.

"Look. I need to get on with my career, you know? And it's not happening here in Magnolia Harbor. So I'm thinking about rejoining the band, after the wedding."

He glanced up at the band, which was playing some god-awful tune that didn't sound like country music to him. It was too loud, and he couldn't understand the lyrics. But the kids on the deck were digging it, so who was he to judge.

Maybe he was too conservative for her. Maybe this was never going to work out no matter what. But the idea of Ella going off with that red-faced guy with the skull tattoo on his biceps left him cold.

"You could do so much better," he said.

She frowned at him, a parody of her mother's favorite expression. "And now you sound just like my mother."

For once, Dylan could understand exactly how Brenda felt.

If that was the guy Ella had run off with, he wouldn't have approved either. He stood up and then leaned over the table, pressing his palms into the surface and getting right up into her face.

"Yeah, I guess I do sound like her. And since she's not here, let me remind you that Cody was never faithful to you. Maybe he fooled you when you were a little girl in Muncie, Indiana. But you're a full-grown woman now. Don't forget that, Ella. Ever."

* * *

Ella's heart pounded in syncopated rhythm to the band's drums as Dylan strode across the patio and down the steps to the boardwalk. He could have passed as one of the many well-heeled boat owners who called Magnolia Harbor their summer home. But she would never belong here the way he did.

Still, his parting words had warmed her heart in some wonderful, awful way. He thought she was a full-grown woman. The urge to follow him almost set her in motion, but she needed to stay, precisely because she was a full-grown woman.

Old enough and strong enough to make her own decisions. And fix her life.

When the set ended, Cody made a beeline to her table and took the chair Dylan had vacated. "Who's the asshole?" he asked.

She found his language offensive, and she didn't like having that word applied to Dylan.

"He's my brother," she said.

"You have a brother? Since when?"

"His father is marrying my mother. So he's sort of my brother."

Cody laughed in obvious relief right before he leaned in. "Oh, that explains it. I honestly couldn't understand what you saw in a straight arrow like that."

"Right," she said, her mouth suddenly dry.

"Well, I'm glad your standards haven't slipped that low. Look, can't we work this out? You and me, we've been together all this time. We've had a good thing going. And you know how I believe in destiny. I will never forget that night you walked into that bar in Illinois."

She stared at him. Was this the best he could do?

She leaned back, crossing her arms over her chest. "We met in Muncie, Indiana, Cody, not Illinois. And you talked about destiny then too. And you know what? I've seen you hand that line off to countless women over the last thirteen years. You'd think you'd switch it up now and then."

"Come on, babe, those groupies never did mean nothing. You know I love you."

"If you loved me, you wouldn't cheat on me. If you loved me, you'd get your butt in gear and fix up the house in El Paso so I didn't have to live in an RV all the time."

"Honey, come on, you know that house in El Paso is falling down."

"I know no such thing. I know you're lazy. And I know that what you love most about me is my fiddle playing."

"That's unfair."

"Is it? Look, I'll cut to the chase. You guys suck without me, and the set list is exactly the same as last year. You haven't written any new songs since I don't know when. Years. But I'm willing to help you out. I'll rejoin the band at the end of the month."

"You can't join us before then?" He sounded desperate. Were they having trouble getting gigs? Probably. They clearly hadn't been rehearsing much.

"No, I can't. My mother's getting married in a few weeks, and I need to stay here until then. And when I rejoin you, it will be only until the end of your tour. I figure you're touring until November?"

He nodded.

"And I sleep in my own room."

"What?"

"You heard me. I'm not coming back as your girlfriend. Not ever. When the tour is over, I'm going to Nashville."

"What you want to do something stupid like that for?"

"It's not stupid. I could get work in Nashville. You're the one who'd struggle. So you can go find yourself another fiddler at the end of the tour."

He blinked a few times, and Ella waited for his arguments and his gaslighting and all the rest of the games he played. She was on the verge of turning blue waiting for him to say something when he finally said, "Okay."

Okay? That was all? His assent was anticlimactic. To say the least.

Chapter Twenty-Seven

On her wedding day Brenda wasn't nearly as excited as she'd hoped to be. She started the morning doing yoga alone on the beach because Jim had spent the night at Dylan's place. It seemed kind of stupid not to sleep together the night before their wedding, but Jim was a sweet traditionalist.

Ella and Momma had picked her up precisely at nine, and they'd spent the morning at the beauty shop getting cut, curled, buffed, waxed, and painted. They all looked fabulous when they arrived back at Momma's place to get dressed for the afternoon's big event.

It should have been the happiest day of her life, but she seemed to have collected her own personal rain cloud. Momma had found out at last Tuesday's Piece Maker's meeting that Ella had given her notice to Ashley. Ella hadn't said one word about that. But Ashley seemed to think Ella was getting ready to leave Magnolia Harbor at the end of the month.

Brenda was terrified that Ella had decided to go back to Cody. The whole world had evidently seen them together at Rafferty's when Urban Armadillo had come through town a couple of weeks ago.

Was Ella planning to sneak away while Brenda and Jim were on their honeymoon? Would her daughter break the news by sending one of those old-time postcards from someplace out in New Mexico? Ella used to do that all the time. For years and years, those postcards had been the extent of their connection.

How could Brenda be on the verge of unhappy tears on this day? She had so much to be thankful for. After all, Momma and Ella were right beside her in the condo's palatial bathroom, repairing the damage the heat and humidity had done to their hairdos on the short ride from the beauty shop back to Momma's place.

"We are a nice-looking family," Momma said. Her words were so kind and reassuring, almost as if Momma knew Brenda needed to hear them. Her mother turned and took the wedding dress out of its garment bag. "And I think this dress is divine. It's like something out of a fairy tale." Momma's eyes watered up as she turned in Brenda's direction. "I've been looking forward to this day for so long."

"Don't cry, Momma," Brenda said, feeling her own tears close to the surface. "If you start, I'm going to bawl, and then all this beautiful makeup that Marian Blake slaved over will be ruined."

Momma nodded and patted her shoulder. "All right, let's get you dressed up." Momma grabbed a tissue from the box and dabbed her eyes, then turned toward Ella. "Come here, sugar. Give me a hug." Momma wrapped her arms around Ella and gave her a hard squeeze that suggested Momma was just as unhappy about Ella's looming departure as Brenda was. Ella hadn't said a word to her grandmother either.

Her silence had to be because she was hiding something unpleasant, like the fact that she was going back to *that man*.

When Momma let Ella go, her daughter's eyes were bright too. She was going away. Brenda could read the truth right there in her face. She had to stop this from happening. She didn't want to lose her daughter again.

"Honey," Brenda said, turning toward her daughter, "I wasn't going to mention this today. But..." She took a deep breath, willing her heart not to race. She wasn't all that successful, but at least it seemed to be beating in a steady rhythm. "I know you've given your notice to Ashley Scott. But when were you going to tell me about it?"

"Mom, please, let's not—"

"Look, I need to talk about this. I just hope you're not going back to Cody Callaghan. I know you don't need my opinion, but I don't think he treated you well. But if you're leaving for some other reason, well, I guess I'd like to know what I've done this time to make you want to leave."

Ella's eyes glistened with tears. "Mom, you haven't done anything."

"Then why are you leaving?"

"I have to go. I need to get my life in order. I need a real job, you know?"

"Oh. So where?"

Ella sniffled, and Momma handed her a tissue. "I'm not going back to Cody, okay? I thought about it for a week or two, you know, when Urban Armadillo was in town for their gig at Rafferty's. But I decided that I'm a full-grown, mature woman, and going back to him was wrong for me. So my plan right now is to see if I can find a gig as a studio musician in Nashville."

"Oh, thank God." Brenda breathed out a sigh.

"And to be honest," Ella continued, "I also had a chance to audition for the Myrtle Beach Symphony. Ashley arranged it. But that was a few weeks ago, and I haven't heard back from them. And well, I didn't want to get your hopes up or..."

"Have me push you in that direction?"

Ella shrugged. "It's not happening. We both know I'm not cut out for that kind of music."

Brenda didn't know any such thing, but she kept her mouth shut and gave Ella a big hug. "I'm sure you'll find work in Nashville. And it's not that far away."

"I'll be home for Christmas. I promise. And I'm sorry I didn't say anything. But I've been so confused about my next steps. First I thought I'd play fiddle for Cody, but then I realized what a mistake that would be. And then the audition happened. And well..." She shrugged. "I guess I ran out of time, and it seemed unfair to Ashley to walk away from her in the middle of the summer when she's so busy. I needed to give her time to find someone. And I need a real job. So Nashville makes the most sense."

"Oh honey, I wish you'd told me. I think Nashville is perfect for you."

"You do?"

"You'll be successful there, I'm certain. And I'm glad we had this talk. Now I don't have to feel as if something terrible is about to happen."

"No, Mom, things are fine," Ella said, but the tremor in her voice contradicted her words. And right then, Brenda understood that she couldn't tie her daughter down. She had to let Ella go.

"Okay, y'all, we need to stop before we all mess up our mascara," Momma said, ushering Ella out of the room. "Brenda, honey, you put on your wedding dress and stop thinking about anything other than getting married. Okay?"

"Yes, ma'am," Brenda said as Momma shut the bathroom door. She slipped into the dress she'd bought in Charleston a few weeks ago, when Ella and Momma had taken her down there and made her spend Jim's money. Constructed of ivory lace with a nipped-in waist and an A-line tulle skirt covered in lace appliqués, it had a retro vibe that Brenda loved.

She opened the door to find Ella looking utterly breathtaking in the coral chiffon dress they'd bought from the same Charleston wedding shop. Ella's dress also had a lace top with a floaty skirt that was just perfect for her. The color brought out the blush in her cheeks and the fire in her hair.

Maybe she had always wanted Ella to play in a symphony, but if her daughter truly wanted to pursue a career in Nashville, Brenda would support her. On the other hand, if Ella was leaving because she felt that she was out of options, that was a whole different matter.

But now was not the time to have a deep family discussion about Ella's future. There would be time after the small reception. So she struck a pose in the bathroom door. "Do you think I look okay?" she asked.

"Oh, Mom. You're beautiful," Ella said. "Here, I've got your hat." She held up the confection of fabric and netting that Momma had talked Brenda into during the shopping trip. Momma was of the view that every bride needed some kind of veil.

"It's a fascinator," Momma said with a giggle.

"Exactly, and when Jim sees it, he will be utterly fascinated." Ella pinned the headpiece to Brenda's fancy hairdo and then adjusted the birdcage veil.

Brenda laughed out loud. "Look at me. I look pretty." She shook her head in astonishment. "I'm so glad y'all talked me into this dress and this silly hat."

"It's nothing, honey. We weren't going to let you get married in sweatpants, which is exactly what you probably would have done without us," Momma said with a big smile.

* * *

The boutonniere Dylan pinned to Dad's lapel had a sprig of deeply fragrant lavender surrounded by some shiny green leaves.

"I hope this doesn't make you sneeze at the wrong moment," he said.

"Have you got the ring?" Dad responded in the tones of a nervous bride groom.

"I've got the ring. I've got the marriage license too. Were you this nervous the first time?" He stepped back and inspected his handiwork. The flowers were cockeyed but not enough to fix.

"Good," Dad said. "Don't sneeze and lose it at the wrong moment."

Dylan gave his father a look. His father returned it.

"So, are we ready?" Dylan asked.

"Yeah, but before we go…"

Oh boy, here it came. Dylan recognized that fatherly tone. They were going to have a father-son conversation. And Dylan preferred to avoid that.

He didn't want to talk about feelings right now. Because they were raw and ugly, and who needed that on a wedding day?

But Dad had other ideas. "Are you okay?" he asked.

"I'm fine. And I'm so happy for you."

Dad gave him a paternal stare. "That's a load of bull."

Dylan shrugged. "What do want me to say? You and Brenda go off to Nancy's for dinner every Friday, and I'm never invited." It seemed like a whiny thing to say on Dad's wedding day, especially since staying away from family gatherings was probably smart. He didn't want to inadvertently expose his deep feelings for Ella. But he still felt isolated and alone. And sad.

"I'm sorry," Dad said.

It didn't help dispel Dylan's gloomy mood. "I don't get it. You know I didn't invite Tammy to the damn engagement party. Why doesn't Brenda believe that?"

"I don't know. Maybe because you treated Ella so badly."

He ground his teeth. That was the trump card Dylan could never play. He hadn't treated Ella badly at all. In fact, she was the one who'd dumped him in the emergency room that night. He'd simply stood there and taken it.

Like a team player.

Okay, he hadn't started out as a team player. So some of this was his own fault. But Brenda didn't give second chances.

Unlike her daughter, who had evidently decided to give that jerk she'd been with all those years another chance. Last Sunday, Donna Cuthbert, the town gossip, told him that Ella had given her notice at the inn and was planning to leave Magnolia Harbor in order to pursue her musical career.

He blew out a breath, trying to extinguish the slow simmer, one part angry and one part pathetic, which burned in his gut.

"Son, I'm sorry but you should never have tried to turn Ella against her mother."

"I never did that."

"No? You bullied her, right at the start, when you told her that Brenda and I wanted her to move out of the beach house."

Well, there was that. "Okay, you have a point."

Dad shook his head and turned away, clearly upset.

"Look, Dad, I don't want you to be unhappy, okay? I'm glad you're getting married. And I know you love Brenda. So it's fine. Maybe in time Brenda will realize that I'm not the bad guy here."

"Maybe she will. But in the meantime, I expect you to be on your best behavior today. Don't screw it up."

"I won't. I promise." So no getting drunk and cornering Ella and grilling her to find out if she was going back to that red-faced redneck. Or worse yet, telling Ella that he couldn't get her out of his mind. Or telling her that he'd fallen in love with her. Nope. That was not allowed.

"You know one thing that would help?" Dad said.

"What?"

"You could find a nice girl and settle down. I bet if you had a couple of kids, Brenda would warm up to you real fast. She loves children. She was a teacher for a long time, you know."

He stared at his father for a moment, letting the irony settle into his bones. "I'll keep that in mind," he said.

* * *

The Killough-McMillan wedding was going to be a small one. Only family and one or two close friends. Maybe fifteen people max. And the wedding guests would be staying after the ceremony for an hour or so for a tea service, which would be limited today to the private party.

A handful of chairs had been set up in the rose garden, along with a small canopy at one end so the guests would have a view of the bay across the lawn and the bride could make her entrance through the arched garden gate. The canopy was decorated with a garland of eucalyptus leaves and blush-colored hydrangeas.

Ashley finished wiring the last of the blossoms to the garland and stepped back to admire her handiwork. The setting, with its view of the bay, always stole her breath. Unfortunately, today was still and quiet and hot as the dickens.

Ashley hated it when the weather refused to cooperate. She loved hosting weddings at Howland House and she wanted them all to be perfect in every way. Weddings brought her joy. And since her B&B wasn't all that large, the weddings here were never big extravaganzas. Like the one scheduled today, they were small, intimate affairs where she got to know the bride and groom.

Since today's bride and groom were locals, she considered them friends. Which was a problem today. She knew a secret that had been weighing heavily on her for quite some time. It had become a millstone around her neck ever since Ella had given her notice.

Ella and Dylan had ended their brief affair. But Ashley couldn't shake the feeling that the couple had backed off because of Brenda's medical problems. That seemed wrong. And it seemed wrong for Ella to be running away.

She'd told everyone that she was leaving to pursue her musical career, but she'd been vague about that. If only Norton Treloar had come through and offered her the open seat in the symphony. But maybe Ella wasn't quite as talented as Ashley thought. She'd had this stupid idea that if Ella got a job thirty minutes away in Myrtle Beach, she would stay, and then the romance between her and Dylan might reignite.

And then everyone would have a happy ending. Ashley loved happy endings these days. She hoped every new bride and groom got to have a long, long life together before death parted them.

She blew out a sigh and turned away from the canopy to go check on the kitchen help, but just then, Rev. St. Pierre came strolling through the garden gate.

He was still having breakfast down the street with Brooklyn, which meant she didn't see him as often these days. Only on Sundays or at museum board meetings. But they'd never again had a conversation like the one they'd had about Adam and Grandmother.

Which was a good thing, probably, because she'd followed his advice, evicting the Piece Makers from the inn, only to discover that she missed baking for them. And she hated going over to Patsy's every Tuesday because she had to find someone to watch the inn and keep an eye on Jackie.

So she'd gotten what she'd wanted. But not really.

Maybe she'd totally misunderstood what he'd been trying to

tell her about moving on in her life. But damned if she was about to knock on his door and ask for further guidance.

"Hey," she said.

He nodded and checked his watch. "I guess I'm a little early."

"You're officiating at this wedding?"

"I am. You were expecting Pastor Pasidena perhaps?"

"I guess not, since Jim's defected."

"Score one for the Episcopalians." His mouth twitched in that almost-smile that was so disarming.

"So…" he said, clasping his arms behind his back. If she didn't know better, she'd swear that the Rev was nervous. Why would he be nervous?

"Well…" She backed up a few paces. "Gotta go check on the—"

"Ashley," he interrupted, "I want to apologize."

"What?"

"You're right. I should never have pressed you about the Piece Makers. I was—"

"But I kicked them out of Howland House."

"You did?"

She nodded. "I haven't baked them a cake in weeks. You haven't noticed the dearth of cars every Tuesday night? We're meeting at Patsy's these days."

He shook his head. "No, I hadn't noticed."

Of course not. "Well, I did what you said I should do."

"I didn't say you should do that."

"No? You sure suggested it. But it's fine. No more obligations." She smiled and decided not to confess her dissatisfaction with the outcome. She had more important things to talk about. And it struck her, like the sun glaring down on her head, that she really missed having coffee with him most mornings.

"You got a minute?" she asked.

He checked his watch. "At least five," he said.

"Walk with me." She turned and walked through the garden's back gate by the cottage and headed down the curving path across the lawn in the direction of the live oak, which Jackie fondly referred to as "the captain's tree."

"What's on your mind?" he asked.

"I know I have a gigantic penance to pay for the mistakes I made last year with Topher. I meddled in his life. I gossiped and messed things up for him. And I promised myself I'd never gossip again."

"Good thinking."

She stopped and turned. "But what if I know something? A secret that needs to be spoken out loud."

"Who's kept this secret? You?"

She shook her head. "No. It's someone else's secret."

"Then you don't get to tell anyone."

"That's what I thought." She looked away toward the bay. The big trees shaded her from the unrelenting sun, and she wondered if maybe she should have set up the wedding here. Too late now. She looked at the Rev out of the corner of her eye. "What if this secret is hurting the person keeping it?"

"There's not much you can do."

"Dammit . . . Ugh, sorry."

"This must be a pretty big secret."

"Micah, I need your special kind of help."

"What?"

"Do you remember that time when you got all up in Jude's face and made him see what an idiot he'd be to let Jenna run away?"

"Yeah, so?"

"And the way you pushed Topher to take a chance on Jessica?"

"I remember that too."

"And I don't know if you had anything to do with Noah and

Lia, but Lia is your friend and you went up to talk to her the night Noah decided not to move away."

"I had nothing to do with that. Honestly. What are you driving at?"

"I need that kind of help. Right now. Today."

"Wait. Are you asking me to be some kind of matchmaker?"

She shook her head. "No. The match is already made. It just needs a little push in the right direction."

"Who are we talking about?"

"Ella and Dylan." Ashley said the names in a hoarse whisper.

And Micah stood there staring at her as if she'd grown another head.

"Are you delusional?" he finally asked. "From the gossip on the street, they hate each other."

"They do not hate each other. They were..."

"What?"

"Well...hanging out. A lot. At night. But they broke it off right after Brenda got sick. I think they're worried about messing things up for their parents. Oh my goodness, this is so complicated."

"Yeah, it is. Ashley, I'm not going to—"

"Forget it. It was a crazy idea."

"How do you know all this?" His tone was almost accusatory.

"Don't worry, I haven't been spying. But Ella lives under my roof, and I'm not blind. There is no question she and Dylan were having a fling. The rest is conjecture on my part. But Jackie says he's heard her crying sometimes at night when he goes to the bathroom."

"Jackie is a spy."

"I know. But in this case, I believe him. He's worried about her. I'm worried about her. She's going away. She says it's to pursue her career, but I don't buy it. I think she's going because she loves Dylan."

"But you don't know that. And you're asking me to do what? Have a talk with her right in the middle of her mother's wedding?"

"Yeah, I know. Crazy. But, Micah, you have a knack for this kind of thing."

He shook his head. "I most certainly do not have a knack for matchmaking or meddling in people's lives. And I don't think revealing this secret to the bride and groom on their wedding day is a good idea. Do you?"

She shook her head. "I guess not. I was just hoping for a miracle, you know?"

"Well, I'm not a miracle worker." He pointed up. "That's the job description of the guy upstairs. So I suggest you pray to Him." Micah shifted his gaze. "Looks like wedding guests are starting to arrive."

Ashley turned, and sure enough, Brooklyn Huddleston, a vision of summertime loveliness in a pink sundress and straw hat, stood by the garden gate waving at Micah. The woman was at least half an hour early for this wedding. But then again, so was Micah.

And he was waving back at her with a gigantic grin on his face.

Chapter Twenty-Eight

Ella took her place on the left side of the canopy and placed her music on the stand. She'd been practicing these selections for weeks now and had them mostly memorized, but the music was a good backup.

The music also provided a safe haven for her to hide behind. She could hold herself together and keep the loneliness and regret from overwhelming her by just focusing on the notes.

As long as she was lost in the music, she wouldn't have to look at Dylan. She could put it off until the ceremony began. Once the processional was finished, she was supposed to put her violin down and join Mom as her maid of honor under the canopy. She wished to hell she didn't have to do that because Dylan was Jim's best man. There would be no way to avoid seeing him.

She'd been avoiding that for weeks now, ever since he'd left her table at Rafferty's that night. Of course, she'd caught a glimpse of him once or twice downtown. And the other night she'd gone to Annie's for dinner and he was there, so she'd turned around and gotten a burger on the boardwalk instead.

She needed to get out of town or she might make a fateful mistake that would send Mom back to the hospital or something. She just needed to get through today, and it would be smooth sailing after that.

She already had her bus ticket to Nashville.

But right now she was standing in the South Carolina sun as she prepared to begin the musical prelude to the marriage ceremony. The weather gods had sent a beautiful, but hot, day. Even the breeze off the bay seemed to be coming from a furnace.

She started with several Strauss waltzes as guests continued to arrive. In the middle of "The Blue Danube," her stomach started to growl.

Damn. She'd grabbed a scone for breakfast this morning right before heading to the beauty shop. But she hadn't eaten any lunch at all. Big mistake. What if her stomach rumbled in the middle of Mom's ceremony?

Well, she couldn't do anything about it now except file it under the heading of Murphy's Law. If her stomach was growling already, it would growl midvow. Hopefully Mom would be so wrapped up in Jim she wouldn't notice.

Damn, it was hot. She was starting to sweat along the fingerboard and chin rest.

She finished the Strauss waltz medley and then launched into Pachelbel's "Canon," which was a head fake for the wedding guests. So many brides walked down the aisle to "Canon," but Mom wasn't one of them. Instead, the piece was the cue for Dylan and Jim to take their places.

Ella didn't look up from the music to see if that had happened. She was busy keeping an eye on the garden gate, waiting for Ashley's cue that Mom was in place.

Ashley's wave came, and Ella ended "Canon" and moved

on to Schubert's "Ave Maria," which was Mom's musical cue. Once the music started, Ella glanced up in time to see Mom come through the garden gate, pause for a moment, and gaze in Jim's direction. She smiled and he returned the smile, his bright eyes adoring even from a distance.

Yeah. They were in love. And Ella was happy for them, even as her own heart was cracking in two.

She put all that emotion into her playing, making the violin soar through the Schubert. She must have found her groove despite the sweat dripping on the chin rest and the hollowness in her gut because Granny's eyes were streaming by the time Mom reached the altar.

Ella ended the piece, put the violin back in its case, and grabbed the tissue she'd left there. She used it to dab the sweat on her chin, but when she straightened up, a rogue wave of dizziness hit her. Damn, this was a terrible time to have low blood sugar.

Or maybe heatstroke.

She breathed in, and the light-headedness ebbed away enough for her to join her mother under the shade cast by the canopy. Unfortunately, it was still three million degrees out here, and in a haze, she let herself glance away from Mom and Jim toward Dylan, who stood just beyond his father.

He was dressed in a gray suit and a blue striped four-in-hand tie. His slightly-too-long hair was doing its Lord Byron thing in the May humidity, the delicious curl falling over his forehead. She flashed on an image of that lock wrapped around her finger. She'd loved playing with his curl on those nights when they'd stayed up until the wee hours talking about nothing and everything all at once.

He was looking the other way, and she feasted on the sight of him until he turned and their gazes locked. Her stomach lurched, and her knees went watery, as if she'd just taken a ride on the

Tower of Terror. She felt weightless for a moment until gravity reexerted its dominion over her body.

If she kept staring at him, she would faint, which would be too girlie for words. Not to mention embarrassing.

Worst of all, Mom would never forgive her. Ever.

She willed herself to look at Mom and Jim. *I'm not going to faint. I'm not going to faint. I'm not going to faint.*

Sheer willpower kept her knees locked and the little curlicues of blackness from edging too far into her field of vision.

"Dearly beloved, we have come together in the presence of God to witness and bless the joining together of this man..." Rev. St. Pierre began the ceremony in the slowest drawl ever. Ella willed him to talk faster.

He seemed immune to her silent pleas. Time slowed to a crawl. She started counting breaths, and her hands started to shake. If they didn't stop soon, she would be unable to play the recessional.

Her stomach growled as the minister said, "Into this holy union, Brenda and James now come to be joined."

Mom didn't appear to have heard the noise, but a glance from the minister suggested that he may have. He appeared to be a little concerned, but he continued. "If any of you can show just cause why they may not lawfully be married, speak now or else forever hold your peace."

The minister paused. Time crawled.

"Excuse me," someone interrupted in a soft voice.

Ella knew that voice. She turned to find Granny standing up in the front row.

"Nancy, do you have an objection?" the minister asked. He didn't sound all that surprised. What the heck was going on? The black dots swam a little further into her field of vision.

"Well, maybe," Granny said.

– "Maybe?"

"I'm concerned is all."

"Momma, what are you doing?" Mom asked, her eyebrows folding down into the frown-of-death. Oh boy. Ella's hands were starting to get cold and clammy.

I will not faint. I will not faint. I will not faint.

"Hush now, Brenda. I'm not concerned about you and Jim. Y'all are in love, and he's a great catch, and I guess there is no legal impediment, but..."

"Okay then, why in the Sam Hill have you objected?" Mom's voice cut through Ella's increasingly fuzzy head like a paring knife.

"Nancy, you can raise legal or moral objections to Brenda and Jim's wedding. Not anything else. So maybe after the ceremony we can—"

"No." Granny shook her head. "We have to talk about this now."

The minister glanced at Ella. No. He wasn't a little concerned. He was a lot concerned. "Um, maybe we should adjourn to the inn and have a conversation."

"Yes, that would be a good idea," Ashley said from her station at the garden gate.

Rev. St. Pierre shot the innkeeper a killing look, and the members of the family who had gathered started to mutter.

"Well, I suppose," Granny said. "But whether I say it here or inside, folks aren't going to like what I have to say. But here it is. Jim and Brenda, if y'all get married, I'm afraid y'all will be destroying the happiness of your children forever."

Ella's knees gave out, and the little swirls that had been dancing in front of her eyes for the last five minutes won the battle of wills. She didn't remember hitting the ground.

* * *

"Quick, Dylan," Rev. St. Pierre said, "we need to get her inside. I think she spent too much time in the sun and hasn't had a thing to eat."

Dylan didn't need the minister to issue any directives. He was at Ella's side before she even fainted, checking her pulse, which was rapid. She looked deathly pale except for two red splotches on her cheeks, but her skin was cold and clammy.

Heat syncope was his immediate diagnosis. She was probably dehydrated, and she'd been standing for a while playing the fiddle in a sunny spot. It was a classic case of not enough blood to her brain.

But while the rational, doctor part of his brain was assessing the medical emergency and knew all the steps to treat the problem, his emotions went on a full-out Tilt-A-Whirl ride.

He scooped her up from the lawn and carried her right through the garden gate, following Ashley, who opened the inn's front door for him. He took Ella to the library and settled her onto the aptly named fainting couch and put the rolled pillow under her feet.

"Do you have Gatorade or maybe a piece of watermelon or something like that? If not, water will do," he said to Ashley, his voice wobbling with the emotions churning in his gut.

Ella moaned and blinked her eyes. She was coming back.

"Ella?"

She groaned again, and Ashley was Johnny-on-the-spot with a bottle of Gatorade and a straw. He couldn't have had a better nurse.

He put the straw to Ella's mouth. "Drink this."

She tried to bat the straw away.

"Dammit, stop fighting me and listen."

Her eyes fluttered open, big and wide and beautiful.

"Drink, dammit," he said in a quieter voice.

She took the straw in her mouth and did as she was told.

But she stared up at him with such a look on her face. He didn't know whether to yell at her or hug her or scream out his frustration.

"Don't you ever do that again, you hear?" His voice got stupid and emotional, and he had to bat away a tear that escaped his eye. His heart was racing too.

"I can't lose you," he whispered, a tourniquet squeezing his chest. "I don't want you to move away or join some stupid band and go back on the road. I want you to stay in one place. I want you to be okay with someone boring and ordinary like me. And I know all the things you said to me that night in the hospital are probably right. But I don't care. I don't care about Dad or your mother. I care about you. And I don't want you to ever faint again from something dumb like heatstroke, you hear?"

But this time, the tears were streaming out of his eyes and dripping off his chin.

"See what I mean, Reverend St. Pierre? This is why I had to stop the wedding," a voice said from behind him.

Oh, great. He'd been professing his love to Ella with an audience. He glanced behind him. The whole family, Rev. St. Pierre, and Ashley Scott were standing there with funny looks on their faces.

Ella spit the straw out. He was pleased to see that she'd drained the bottle of Gatorade dry while he'd professed his undying love. He was such a fool sitting here crying like a sissy. Or maybe like his own father had cried that night in the hospital when he'd thought he'd lost Brenda. Or that night, all those years ago, when Dad had lost Mom forever.

But that's what the tears were for. Because loss and love were simply different sides of the same coin. It had taken Dad forever to find someone new. That's how much he'd loved Mom.

It would take him years to get over Ella. Because she was the girl his father had told him repeatedly that he needed to find. But he'd already found her.

"I want you to love me the same way I love you," he said to Ella, not caring at all what Dad or Brenda thought. He was done trying to please everyone else. The only person who mattered was Ella. "I want you to be mine forever. I want you to stay here in Magnolia Harbor. And I don't give a damn what anyone thinks about the way I feel. Please don't leave me. Please stay here with me. Forever."

* * *

Dylan's amber-flecked blue eyes glistened with tears shed and unshed. Beyond him, Mom was openly weeping, her mascara a mess as tears flowed like a waterfall from her eyes.

Granny wasn't crying. She stood at the end of the couch with her arms across her chest and a gleam in her eyes. *Say yes*, she mouthed.

Ella pushed herself up on the chaise to give Dylan a little more room. She was feeling much better, cooler and clearheaded.

"How are you doing, Mom? You okay?" she asked, and braced for the explosion or the frown-of-death.

But instead Mom said, "I'm fine, sweetie. I think you just got asked an important question that you need to answer."

"Amen to that," Granny muttered in a louder-than-normal voice. For a quiet woman, Granny had certainly used her voice to wreak havoc today. But then, maybe Granny's interruption had been a blessing, because Ella would probably have fainted either way.

She finally gazed at Dylan, who was still waiting patiently. Which, now that she thought about it, was one of the things she loved most about him.

"Why didn't you tell me before this?" she asked. Funny

how Cody had always used the L-word like a weapon against her. It slipped off his tongue whenever he got himself into a tight spot.

But Dylan didn't do that kind of thing. When he said something, he meant it. He'd proved that over and over again. He always told the truth.

"Look," he said into her continuing silence. "If you need to go on the road to make a living, I get it. I don't want to pin you down or own you or whatever. I just want you in my life."

"Oh, bless his heart," Granny said.

"I hate being on tour," Ella managed.

His eyes widened. Had she not told him that before? Maybe not.

"I didn't know that. But you know I heard you were leaving town because of your career."

"I was going to go to Nashville and see if I could start over there."

"Could you start over here?"

"Yes, she can. Absolutely," Ashley said.

Ella stared up at her boss, landlady, and friend. "Uh, well, Ashley, I need to do more than wait on tables."

"I know that. Which is why I was hoping the symphony would ask you to audition."

"They did. But I haven't heard back from them. It's been almost two weeks. And I need to get my life together. So I'm going to Nashville."

Dylan nodded. "That makes perfect sense. You are incredibly talented," he said in a small voice. "And I guess I've always known that this town was probably too small for you."

He visibly swallowed, then looked up at his father. "Dad, I'm really sorry. I know you want to back off on the practice and all. But if Ella is going to Nashville to pursue her career in music, and if she'll have me, then I'm going with her. I love you with all my heart, but you know, ever since Mom died, I've been working overtime to make you happy. It's time to make myself happy. I'm sure I can find a small country practice somewhere outside Nashville."

"What? No." Mom took Jim by the arm. Both of them looked gobsmacked.

"Micah?" Ashley said, lifting her eyebrow in some silent communication. What was up with that?

The preacher turned toward Brenda and Jim and spoke again. "I'll get around to marrying y'all in a minute, but I think Dylan and Ella need a little time, okay?" The minister ushered everyone through the doorway, where Ashley grinned at him like a demented cherub as she closed the pocket doors.

The minister turned toward Ella. "So you love Dylan?" he asked.

Suddenly the library felt like a confessional. Did she love Dylan? Of course she did. She hadn't even let herself think the word for such a long time. But what else could this feeling be?

"Yes," she said, her vision suddenly smearing with tears.

"Good. Dylan, you love Ella?"

"I do," he said. He sounded so strong and sure and in control.

"I see no impediment," the minister said. "Love is a wonderful gift. It's a sin to squander it. So I'm saying that if you want to please the man upstairs, you'll stop sneaking around, pretending you don't care, or living your life for your parents' benefit. They love you. And they will adjust to you loving each other. Trust me on this. It's all going to work out whether you live here or in Nashville or on the Moon."

They stared at the minister. He stared back, then cleared his throat. "So, are we good?"

"Uh, yeah," Dylan said.

"Ella?" Rev. St. Pierre turned his deep brown gaze on her. You could not lie to him.

She nodded. "I'm good."

"You may kiss the girl," he said, giving Dylan a little half smile.

And Dylan did as he was told for once. The kiss he gave Ella melted her down again. It tasted a little like mint chewing gum with overtones of lavender and eucalyptus. And suddenly the sun came out from behind the personal rain cloud she'd been living under. The kiss lasted a long time, and the minister strolled to the front windows and studied the scenery.

When Dylan finally broke the kiss and looked down at her, Ella said, "Yes."

"Yes?"

"Yes, I will stay with you until death do us part. We just need to figure out where. And Dylan, I'm not living in an RV, okay? I want a home. A real home. You know?"

"I do."

Epilogue

Ella carried her suitcase in one hand and her violin in the other as she stepped across the porch and opened the door to the house. She crossed the threshold and drew in a deep breath filled with the faint scent of lavender. What was it about that scent? It calmed her and welcomed her home.

She put her suitcase and fiddle down and then turned around, taking it all in.

This was what she'd always wanted. A house she could call home. And this one was perfect in every way, with a porch, a center hall, a staircase with a turned newel post, and beautiful millwork around the windows. They didn't make houses like this anymore. This one had been standing in this spot for almost a hundred years.

"What the hell, Ella, you didn't wait for me?" Dylan said, stepping up onto the porch. He stopped in front of the door and put down the box he was carrying.

She turned toward him. This house came with a husband who had purchased it with the proceeds from the sale of the house where he'd grown up. He'd given up his childhood home so she could have this house. He'd been enthusiastic about the purchase, especially when he'd discovered the shed out back where he could keep his Harley.

No one, except maybe Mom, had ever given up anything for her before. And she'd never really understood how much Mom had given up. Not until recently.

He stood there, spiking a hand through his unruly curls. He was wearing his hair a little longer these days, to please her. Oh boy, he was perfect in every way, and she loved him with every fiber of her being.

"Was I supposed to wait?" she asked.

"Well, yeah. I was going to carry you across the threshold."

She laughed. "No. I don't need carrying. I'm fully conscious. Besides, you already carried me across a threshold on Mom's wedding day. Actually, now that I think about it, you've metaphorically carried me over numerous thresholds. So, really, I—"

"Get over here," he said with authority.

She was tempted to defy him, but how could she? If he wanted to be a stupid romantic, she wasn't going to stop him. She loved him more because of it.

For thirteen years, she'd hung around a man who didn't care about her except for what she could do for him. And in a few short months, she'd up and married another one who would walk to the ends of the earth for her. A man who was willing to give up everything to follow her to Nashville.

Luckily, that hadn't been necessary.

She strolled through the door, and he captured her, pulling her up into his arms as if she weighed nothing. She rested her head on his strong shoulder and looked deep into his dark blue eyes.

"I've crossed this threshold a zillion times before, you know. I mean, my grandmother used to live here."

"I know. But still. It's our house now. And that's the important thing." And then her husband not only carried her across the threshold but all the way up to the bedroom on the second floor.

She didn't know who exactly to thank for this happy ending.

Was it Bobby Don Ayers, who'd set a price for Granny's house so high that it sat on the market for weeks and weeks, giving Dylan a chance to buy it for her?

Was it the Piece Makers, who'd gotten her the job at the inn, where she'd met Jackie Scott, who'd insisted that she play some jigs and reels for a ghost?

Was it Ashley Scott, who'd heard her playing for the ghost and given her a chance to play for Norton Treloar?

Was it Norton Treloar, who'd gotten her an audition with the Myrtle Beach Symphony, or Sam Rivera, the symphony's director, who'd finally called a day after Mom's wedding to offer her a place as second chair violin?

Or was it Granny, who'd decided to move out of this house, and then, unbelievably, stopped her own daughter's wedding, forcing Ella to confront her problems instead of running away from them again?

Or was it Rev. St. Pierre, who'd simply asked her the basic question about love and made her realize that she'd be a fool to throw away a chance to spend the rest of her life with Dylan?

Or maybe all of them had conspired to give her this happily-ever-after. All these wonderful people who lived in Magnolia Harbor, her new hometown.

About the Author

Hope Ramsay is a *USA Today* bestselling author of heartwarming contemporary romances set below the Mason-Dixon Line. Her children are grown, but she has a couple of fur babies who keep her entertained. Pete the cat, named after the cat in the children's books, thinks he's a dog, and Daisy the dog thinks Pete is her best friend except when he decides her wagging tail is a cat toy. Hope lives in the medium-sized town of Fredericksburg, Virginia, and when she's not writing or walking the dog, she spends her time knitting and noodling around on her collection of guitars.

You can learn more at:
HopeRamsay.com
Twitter @HopeRamsay
Facebook.com/Hope.Ramsay

Want more charming small towns? Fall in love with these Forever contemporary romances!

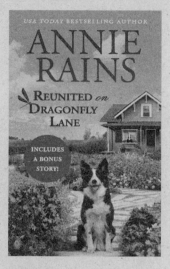

REUNITED ON DRAGONFLY LANE
by Annie Rains

Boutique owner Sophie Daniels certainly wasn't looking to adopt a rambunctious puppy with a broken leg. Yet somehow handsome veterinarian—and her high school sweetheart—Chase Lewis convinced her to take in Comet. But house calls from Chase soon force them to face the past and their unresolved feelings. Can Sophie open up her heart again to see that first love is even better the second time around? Includes the bonus story *A Wedding on Lavender Hill*!

DREAM A LITTLE DREAM
by Melinda Curtis

Darcy Jones Harper is thrilled to have finally shed her reputation as the girl from the wrong side of the tracks. The people of Sunshine Valley have to respect her now that she's the new town judge. But when the guy who broke her heart back in high school shows up in her courtroom, she realizes maybe things haven't changed so much after all...because her pulse still races at the sight of bad-boy bull rider Jason Petrie.

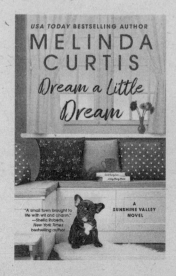

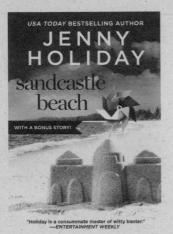

USA TODAY BESTSELLING AUTHOR

JENNY HOLIDAY

sandcastle beach

WITH A BONUS STORY!

"Holiday is a consummate master of witty banter."
—ENTERTAINMENT WEEKLY

SANDCASTLE BEACH
by Jenny Holiday

What Maya Mehta really needs to save her beloved community theater is Matchmaker Bay's new business grant. She's got some serious competition, though: Benjamin Lawson, local bar owner, Jerk Extraordinaire, and Maya's annoyingly hot arch nemesis. Turns out there's a thin line between hate and irresistible desire, and Maya and Law are really good at crossing it. But when things heat up, will they allow their long-standing feud to get in the way of their growing feelings? Includes the bonus story *Once Upon a Bride*, for the first time in print!

A WEDDING ON LILAC LANE
by Hope Ramsay

After returning home from her country music career, Ella McMillan is shocked to find her mother is engaged. Worse, she asks Ella to plan the event with her fiancé's straitlaced son, Dr. Dylan Killough. While Ella wants to create the perfect day, Dylan is determined the two shouldn't get married at all. Somehow amid all their arguing, sparks start flying. And soon everyone in Magnolia Harbor is wondering if Dylan and Ella will be joining their parents in a trip down the aisle.

USA TODAY BESTSELLING AUTHOR

HOPE RAMSAY

A WEDDING *on* LILAC LANE

"Every story by Hope Ramsay will touch a reader's heart."
—BRENDA NOVAK

Connect with us at
Facebook.com/ReadForeverPub

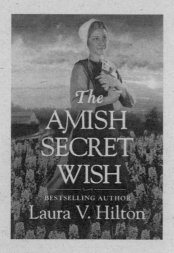

THE AMISH SECRET WISH
by Laura V. Hilton

Waitress Hallie Brunstetter has a secret: She writes a popular column for her local Amish paper under the pen name GHB. When Hallie receives a letter from a reader asking to become her pen pal, Hallie reluctantly agrees. She can't help but be drawn to the compassionate stranger, never expecting him to show up in Hidden Springs looking for GHB...nor for him to be quite so handsome in real life. But after losing her beau in a tragic accident, Hallie can't risk her heart—or her secrets—again.

HER AMISH WEDDING QUILT
by Winnie Griggs

When the man she thought she would wed chooses another woman, Greta Eicher pours her energy into crafting beautiful quilts at her shop and helping widower Noah Stoll care for his adorable young children. But when her feelings for Noah grow into something even deeper, will she be able to convince him to have enough faith to give love another chance?

ONE LUCKY DAY
(2-IN-1 EDITION)
by Jill Shalvis

Have double the fun with these two novels from the bestselling Lucky Harbor series! Can a rebel find a way to keep the peace with a straitlaced sheriff? Or will Chloe Traeger's past keep her from a love that lasts in *Head Over Heels*? When a just-for-fun fling with Ty Garrison, the mysterious new guy in town, becomes something more, will Mallory Quinn quit playing it safe—and play for keeps instead—in *Lucky in Love*?

FOREVER FRIENDS
by Sarah Mackenzie

With her daughter away at college, single mom Renee isn't sure who she is anymore. What she *is* sure of is that she shouldn't be crushing on her new boss, Dr. Dan Hanlon. But when Renee comes to the rescue of her neighbor Sadie, the two unexpectedly hatch a plan to open her dream bakery. As Renee finds friendship with Sadie and summons the courage to explore her attraction to Dr. Dan, is it possible Renee can have the life she's always imagined?